In a rich blend of adventure, fantasy, mystery, science fiction and horror, thirteen fantastic writers offer glimpses into alternate worlds . . .

THE FANTASTIC ADVENTURES OF

ROBIN HOOD

EDITED BY
Martin H. Greenberg

A SIGNET BOOK

SIGNET
Published by the Penguin Group
Penguin Books USA Inc., 375 Hudson Street,
New York, New York 10014, U.S.A.
Penguin Books Ltd, 27 Wrights Lane,
London W8 5TZ, England
Penguin Books Australia Ltd, Ringwood,
Victoria, Australia
Penguin Books Canada Ltd, 2801 John Street,
Markham, Ontario, Canada L3R 1B4
Penguin Books (N.Z.) Ltd, 182–190 Wairau Road,
Auckland 10, New Zealand

Penguin Books Ltd, Registered Offices:
Harmondsworth, Middlesex, England

First published by Signet, an imprint of New American Library,
a division of Penguin Books USA Inc.

First Printing, June, 1991
10 9 8 7 6 5 4 3 2 1

Contents

Mrs. Hood Unloads

by Mike Resnick

Yes, Mrs. Grobnik, it's a new set of tiles. My son the Most Wanted Felon gave them to me. Probably they used to belong to the rabbi's wife.

He just gave them to me last week. He'd been keeping them for me for three months. Two nights a week he can sneak into the castle and annoy the King, but can he come by for dinner with his mother more than once in three months?

You think you've got *tsouris*? Well, God may ignore you from time to time, but He *hates* me.

I don't mean to complain . . . but what did I ever do to deserve such a *schmendrik* for a son? I think they must have switched babies at the hospital, I really do. Twenty-six hours I spent in labor, and for what? You work and you slave, you try to give your son a sense of values, and then even when he stops by he gulps his food and can never stay for dessert because the army is after him.

So at least you can write and tell me how you're doing, Mr. Big Shot, I tell him. And do you know what he says to that? He says he can't write because he's illiterate. Me, I say he's just using that as an excuse.

You break the wall, Mrs. Noodleman. Can I bring anyone some tea?

Well, of course he robs from the rich, Mrs. Grobnik. I mean, what's the sense of robbing from the poor? But why does he have to rob at all? Why couldn't he have been a doctor? But he says no, he's got this calling, that God told him he has to rob from

7

the rich and give to the poor. When I was fourteen, God told me that I was a fairy princess, but you didn't see me going out and kissing any frogs. Anyway, I tell him that maybe he's misinterpreting, that maybe God is telling him to be a banker or a real estate broker, but he says no, his holy mission is to rob the rich and give to the poor. So I ask him why he can't at least charge the ten-percent handling fee, and he gives me that look, the same one I used to smack his *tuchis* for when he was a boy.

Pong! Very good, Mrs. Katz.

No, we're happy to have you here, Mrs. Katz. I just couldn't take any more of that Mrs. Nottingham. She's so hoity-toity and walks around with her nose in the air, and acts like her boy is a lawyer instead of just a policeman. My son the criminal gives away more in a week that her son makes in a year.

You heard *what*, Mrs. Noodleman? You heard him say that he moved to Sherwood Forest because he went off to the Crusades and came back to find out he wasn't the Lord of the Manor? Well, of course he wasn't the Lord of the Manor! Was my late husband, Mr. Hood, God rest his soul, the Lord of the Manor? Are my brothers Nate and Jake the Lords of the Manor? Probably ten thousand boys came home and found they weren't Lords of the Manor—but did *they* go live in the forest and rob their mother's friends?

He was an apprentice blacksmith, that's what he was. He probably made up all this Lord of the Manor stuff to impress that *shikse* Marian.

And while I'm thinking of it, what's all this *Maid* Marian talk? She doesn't look like a maid to *me*.

Not so fast, Mrs. Noodleman. I have a flower, so I get an extra tile.

Anyway, you work and you slave, and what does it get you? Your son runs off to the forest and starts wearing a *yarmulkah* with a feather in it, that's what.

And look who he runs around with—a bunch of merry men! I don't know if I can bear the shame! I just wish I knew what I ever did to make God hate me so much.

Thank you for your kind words, Mrs. Grobnik, but you just can't imagine what it's like. I try to raise him with proper values, and look how it all turns out—he's dating this Marian person, and his closest friend is a priest, Friar someone-or-other.

Oh, it's not? Now his best friend is Little John? Well, I don't want to be the one to gossip, but the stable girl told me what's so little about *him*.

Chow, Mrs. Noodleman. I lost track—whose turn is it now?

So he comes by last Thursday, and he gives me these tiles, and he says he can only stay for five minutes because the Sheriff's men are after him. He gulps his *gefilte* fish down, and I notice he's looking thin, so I ask him if he's getting his greens, and he gives me that look, and he says Ma, of course I'm getting my greens, I live in a forest. So sue me, I say, better I should just sit here in the dark and never even mention that you're too skinny because you never come by for dinner unless the Sheriff's men are watching your hide-in.

Hide-out, hide-in, what's the difference, Mrs. Katz? At least *your* son comes by for dinner every Sunday. The only time I know I'll see *my* son is when I go to the post office, and there's his picture hanging on the wall.

Oy! You're showing four white dragons, Mrs. Noodleman! You see? I *knew* God hated me!

And he says the next time he comes by—if I haven't died of old age and neglect by then—he's going to bring his gang with him. And I say not without a week's notice, and that I'm not letting this Marian person in the house, no matter what, and even if I do, she isn't allowed to use the bathroom. And he just laughs that Mr. Big Shot laugh, ho-ho-ho, like he thinks he can wrap me around his little finger. Well, I'll Mr. Big Shot him right across the mouth if he doesn't learn a little respect for his mother.

Mah Jong!

All right, so God doesn't hate me full-time—once in a while He blinks long enough for me to win a game.

By the way, what do you cook for seventy merry *goys*, anyway?

Robin Hood and the Witch Who Misspelled Sherwood Forest

by Elizabeth Ann Scarborough

We heard the whine of Alen's "dragon" long before we spied the witch, who we naturally mistook for an ordinary damsel, chained to the tree. As the bard of the band, Alen prides himself on the remembering of ancient things and is also something of a knowall, so when I exclaimed in all honesty, "Faith, what can that racket be?" shouting a bit so that my voice was louder than the shrill grinding whine, Alen answered. He had to posture a bit first, as bards all do, cocking his head as if any extra effort was necessary to hear what he could not avoid hearing. Even I could see that he knew not any more than Robin or I did, but Robin merely let a smile play about his mouth, for he's fond of the boy. As he is fond of music. Alen hedged a bit, pretending to consider, and then pronounced, "In truth, I deem it to be a dragon."

Robin is not the lord of Sherwood and the leader of us all because he is the sort of man to jump at shadows or myths to explain that which is beyond his ken. But neither does he fail to respect the talents of any among us, and when one of us expresses what he deems an expert opinion, Robin listens. So now he merely said, very mildly for a man bellowing over such a great din, "Never have there been dragons reported in Sherwood, Alen, nor in Barnsdale and, indeed, no dragons at all from Scarborough to Stamford, lo these

11

many years since Arthur and his good knights slew the lot."

Alen answered him with the gentle kindliness of a true priest to an untaught heathen, "Yet your average dragon was well known to make that precise sound as its armored belly bumped over the rocky soil and it whimpered in protest." He sniffed the air. "And we must carefully progress, for I can smell the heat of the creature now."

I smelled it, too, and without elaborate sniffing. The metallic smell was strong and hot as blood, and cut across the rich autumn air like laughter at a funeral mass. I stepped cautiously forward, my eyes on the ground lest I fall over my own feet. I am larger than most men, and I liked life in Sherwood among Robin's band well enough since I had given him a dunking on the day I first met him. Because of my size, I was more than passing good with my staff, and my bow, as you see, is six feet seven inches worth of seasoned yew. My strength was of more use to me in an outlaw's life than it was when I plied a plow, but I did have a tendency to bang my head on low-hanging branches and sink in places that would hold other men, and I trample or trip on encumbrances they might leap over. Thus it was that I was watching the ground and the last thing I saw before the world went mad was a broad mark lying across the trail—a white line made by sprinkling chalk or lime.

Before I could point this out to Robin, a great noise like the cracking of mountainous knucklebones and the rush of a mighty wind, and also like the rapid slurping of all the waters of the world through a hole no bigger than a man's eye, announced a flash of light so brilliant it dazzled with all colors at once and seemed at once to be white as winter and black as the Sheriff's heart. The earth trembled and fell away as even I was lifted from my feet, whereupon I jumped for the nearest sturdy branch before we were swallowed, forest and all. I admit that I believed Alen in that moment and thought surely the sound was his dragon opening its great maw to devour us. Then I heard the woman's shriek above the echoes of the noise.

"Okay, you muscle-bound chainsaw-wielding tree murderers, it's all up now!" she scolded. "You asked for it! The forest guardian is on his way and you guys are going to be really sorry you ever so much as cut down a Christmas tree."

"Lady, you are nuttier than Rain Forest Crunch," a man's voice cried. I thought these last three words might be some incantation or oath, since I knew of no reason else that they might be so strung together. "Now, I'm warning you. We mean to cut down that tree whether you're still chained to it or not."

Robin tapped me on the wrist then, and pointed silently with his bow. I felt myself grow hot with shame at my clumsiness, for I had almost stumbled upon the people in the glade without seeing them, a potentially fatal mistake for any man of Sherwood.

The damsel was chained to a tree which stood in the place of the massive oak we all climb for a lookout tower. All I saw of her was a lock of her faded red-gold hair, the chain that bound her to a large tree trunk, and the flounce of her skirts, rough-spun and loosely woven wool but bright-colored and spangled like a tinker-woman's. The men facing her were each much larger than any of my companions, though not as large as I am, and each carried what I took at first for swords, though they had serrated edges and broad metal boxes the size of treasure caskets at their hilts. From these swords came the roaring, and that worried me more than the possibility of a dragon. My faith in Alen's dragon had not been of long duration and was shaky at best, but with common swords I am all too familiar and these weapons were far more fearsome than common.

"Don't think you're going to scare us with any of your satanist mumbo-jumbo," cried one of these strange men. His costume was the most extraordinary I had ever seen: his trews made of cloth of indigo with stitching the color of oak leaves in fall, his boots smoothly but heavily made of some brown leather, and his shirt was checked in the colors of roses and ravens, tucked into the trews and fastened with a slender hide belt ornamented with a silvery buckle in the shape of what might have been a cottage, or perhaps it was a wagon, since it had many wheels that looked as large as the miller's on either end. The other men were similarly dressed in colors and soft cloth the like of which I had never seen in all of England—or at least the part of England which I had traveled in my life, specifically the West Riding of Yorkshire. It occurred to me that perhaps, although they did not sound like Scots, they might be; since one's shirt was of a predominantly yellow plaid, while the shirt of the other was likewise plaid but of dark blue and green. On their heads they wore helmets of some yellow metal.

And the woman! I got a closer look at her when Robin signalled me forward. She was young-looking but not, I thought, young, and not particularly pretty; for although her skin was very fair and dusted with freckles, it was webbed with fine lines and covered a face too long for beauty and with that naked lashless, browless look some redheads and towheads have. Furthermore, the red-gold hair, which might have been her glory, was limp and hung without curl or wave to her shoulders. She smiled, her wide mouth spreading over discolored teeth, when she saw Robin, Alen, and me, and leapt up and down on bare dirty feet. Her back rubbed against the tree as she jumped, and her unlikely colored skirts danced. I thought she might be one of the Old People I had heard of at my granny's knee. One of the fey. It is commonly known that, unlike dragons, the faerie are quite real and there are some still about here and there. Robin's luck could not always be attributed to the Virgin, many thought, since she surely would never have approved some of our adventures. That this leaping unlikely creature was a faerie made sense to me. The others seemed to have bound her in iron, which is the sensible thing to do when faced with such creatures.

The woman turned from fawning at Robin to momentarily argue with her tormentors. "I'm not the one who's satanic!" she flung back. "It's you and your saws ripping apart the forest! *That's* why when I read that article about the movie they were making about Robin Hood on location in Sherwood and in the Hoh Rainforest, I got the idea of getting Robin Hood to stop you guys!"

A man of perhaps Robin's age, his beard streaked with red and gray, stepped forward. I understood now that what I had believed to be a sword was, as the woman said, a saw instead. Though this fellow's tool had been silent and motionless, unlike the saws of the other two men, now he pulled a cord and it screeched magically to life. The woman began kicking out as he advanced on her. "No, you don't! Get away from this tree. It's four hundred years old if it's a day, and you'll chop it down over my dead body."

"That," the man growled more with frustration, it seemed to me, than true malice, "can be arranged."

I had been watching the four strangers so intently I never saw Robin nock an arrow until it sped past the speaker, carrying with it the man's yellow helmet. Now the strangers noticed us and stared at us intently, and at Robin in particular—memorizing his features, as I thought, to report the encounter to the Sheriff.

The woman twisted herself against the tree so that she faced us all—she alone seemed unsurprised to see us. "All *right*! It's Robin Hood and his merry men to the rescue! Way to go, Robin! You are Robin, aren't you? Hi, I'm Madonna Warden. I summoned you. Do away with these churls, will you? They're annoying my tree."

"Lady?" Robin inquired politely because she was a woman, and Robin has some inconvenient attitudes about women. We all had mothers, too, after all, but he still risks his liberty and life to disguise himself and visit his mother's grave just to have a pleasant chat.

Between his feelings for her and the irregular streak of piety he has for the Virgin, if not for her bishops and priests, he has developed strong opinions about women and forbids any of us to harm one or to fail to aid one. Not an easy rule to follow when you must leave fine ladies in rare furs and jewels unmolested, knowing what that finery could buy. Nor is such a rule easy to obey if you're a lusty young lad restrained by your banishment as an outlaw from finding your body's comfort in the normal fashion with a sweetheart in a distant village. Nevertheless, Robin claimed that respecting women made for a better class of outlaw, and who were we to argue? In fairness to him, I must say that rule made us more trusted and popular among the common folk, and more than once one of us had been saved when some unmolested woman gave him her Sunday gown as a disguise when the fellow was trapped in town by a posse.

But although Robin's voice held its usual courtesy for the fair sex, it held as well another tone, and that was one of wariness and impatience mixed, which told me that he considered the woman daft.

"My tree. This forest," the woman said. "They want to cut it down and build a golf course for a lot of German businessmen. So I summoned you to help me. God knows the law won't do anything—the governor is part of the conspiracy."

"For the love of mike, sister," said the checkered-shirted man. "If you think you're going to scare us off with some guy dressed up like Peter Pan playing cowboys and Indians, you've got another think coming."

"I'm warning you. I'll have him kill you if you come near this tree," she replied.

"Never mind, boys," said the man in yellow plaid, "there's other trees. Ole, you and Knutson cut down that one over there. We'll just take down the forest around her and leave her there to watch."

The man he had called Ole started his saw again and turned his back on us, facing another tree of great size. The stench and roar of it was enough to allow the Sheriff to sit in his hall at Nottingham and pinpoint our position from that distance by smell and hearing alone. Robin signalled me with his hand, and I let fly. The tip of my arrow sunk deep into the tree, the peacock-feather tickling the man's ear in passing. Usually such a warning was sufficient to delay, if not deter, further activity, but this man grunted, twisted his mouth with annoyance, and turned the whirling saw blade onto the arrow so the pieces produced were no bigger than the smallest nail of Maid Marian's hand. As calm as a frozen pond, the fellow turned his saw again towards the tree.

The woman cried out to Robin, "Stop them!"

Robin put his horn to his lips and blew three times. Usually it took at least a few moments for the men to appear, but now threescore or so of them stepped forward, almost instantly, as if they had been seeking us. What was more unusual, Maid Marian and Alen a Dale's bride and new babe were with them. All of them were talking excitedly and looked to Robin expectantly, as if he held an answer to some question as yet unasked. I thought Marian looked quite pale, and Alen's baby was wailing in its mother's arms.

Will Scarlett and Friar Tuck kept looking behind them and Much the miller's son jumped like a scared squirrel.

The saw in the hand of the man who had cut the arrow stopped whining and the man pulled at the cord in vain. "Out of gas," he said to the others.

"Robin," Will Scarlett said. "So you've found the magicians who made the forest vanish. Make them give it back."

Marian had naturally taken a womanly interest in the wild-haired creature chained to the tree, but her interest shifted suddenly, and she reached out and stroked the tree's bark. Now I noticed that it was as strange as the woman chained to it, the trunk red as a fox with papery curls of bark peeling away from it. The upper branches were knotted like the hands of some arthritic ancient.

"What manner of tree is this?" Robin's lady asked, peeling off a piece of the papery bark. " 'Tis no oak nor yet yew, alder, ash, or willow."

"Grade-A hardwood, ma'am," said the man in the yellow shirt. "Property of T.R. Maete Inc. These logs are scheduled for sale to Germany to build a fancy chalet-style condominium development, and the land is going to become two big golf courses, tennis court, swimming pool, the works. Give a lot of people jobs."

"These *trees*," said Madrona Warden in a voice as severe as that of any prioress, "this *forest*, belongs to the people of the," and here she injected what I again took to be an incantation or oath, "Stayteowashyngtone, to Yewnidedstaytes" and continued in reasonable language, "to the people of the world and to all of the children who come afterward, if people like me can keep people like *them*," she darted a glance sharp as any arrow at the men, "from selling out to the highest bidder and turning the Olympic forest lands into the Olympic great plains."

"Look, lady, we can't all be overeducated underemployed artistes," shot back the man in the yellow shirt wrathfully but, it seemed to me, with reason in his tone if not his words. "There's plenty of parkland left. How many trees do you need to look at before you figure out how to draw one anyway, huh? You people are all alike—go to fancy colleges our taxes pay for, live in towns half-subsidized by the timber industry, and play around at being artsy fartsy while you draw public assistance *we* pay taxes to support. Then you try to take away our jobs to protect some stupid bird or worm or mold or whatever you can think of to keep us from making an honest living."

Robin had been following all of this with an expression of bafflement that mirrored my state of mind, but now he said, "You are woodsmen then, and this lady an artisan?"

"As if you didn't know!" said the man in the red and black checked shirt, but the one in the yellow shirt nodded.

"We're loggers, though people like her have tried to make it so that anyone who admits what he does for a living sounds like some kind of monster. And she's a—"

"Ah hah! Watch it," Madrona Warden said. "Robin Hood is very big on protecting women. That part of the legend *is* true, isn't it?" she asked Marian a little nervously.

Marian gave her a long calculating look and nodded once, slowly. At times I think she wishes Robin's courtesy were less, so that other women did not feel so free to avail themselves of it.

"Sexist as that may be, it's convenient," Madrona Warden said. "He's not going to let you hurt me."

"Wait a minute," said the third man. "I was down at Eatonville last summer when they had their Robin Hood Days Festival, and I found out more about this Robin Hood guy. You ain't done your research, honey. Robin Hood was a friend of foresters—his old man was a forester. If this guy was Robin Hood, he'd be on *our* side."

"Enough of this quarrel!" said Robin Hood, losing his patience with them. He was as baffled as all of us by the diverse strangeness brought on by the *wyrd* woman bound to the tree, although what we experienced at that time was a mere fraction of what we would later come to know. "We will retire to our camp where we may think without distraction from the grumbling of our stomachs. Much, bind them, and Will, cover their eyes lest they betray our hiding places. John, break you the lady's chains."

"No, don't," said Madrona Warden, pulling a key from the layers of bright plumage covering her bosom. "I have a key, and as soon as we are done, I'm chaining myself back up here if you can't make them go away."

She did not appear to believe she would need to do so again, however, for she smiled at me to show she meant no offense at refusing my attentions, and at Robin, Marian, and all of the company, and cast a smug look at her adversaries. The man in the blue shirt pulled the cord to his saw again as Much approached him.

"Nobody's hog-tying this ol' boy," he said. "Not unless they'd like getting sawed in half."

"Knock it off, Knutson," said yellow-shirt, who appeared to be both spokesman and leader. "These boys are armed and there's no sense fightin' 'em when the company lawyers can do it for us. You may have just cooked your own goose with this little escapade, lady," he said to Madrona Warden, who stuck her tongue out at him and flipped her hair in a saucy fashion.

He held out his wrists, and Much tied them lightly while Will bound his eyes with a scarlet printed cloth taken from the back pocket of the man's own indigo trousers.

Then Will stopped suddenly. "Robin, we can't take them back to camp."

"And why is that?"

"Because it's vanished like the Holy Ghost, that's why," said Tuck, turning a little red in the face with exasperation. "That's what we were trying to tell you."

"It hasn't vanished," said Madrona Warden. "I simply brought you forward in time and across the Atlantic to help me. It was a complicated spell, but Gaia knew I was doing it for her and helped me. So did my magic crystal," and she pulled out a glittering shard of gemstone dangling from a chain about her neck, "and my pyramid," and she extracted this from her pocket. "And my authentic Native American medicine bag complete with the feather of a spotted owl, bark from the root of a tree in a dead forest, and the ashes of last year's Sierra Club calendar, and—oh, yeah." She extracted a small box from another pocket and pressed a button and a song with Robin's name in it rasped across the glade before she punched the button again. "Your theme song from the old Disney TV show, overdubbed with a tape I made of the environmental

impact statement for this region presented at the last
council meeting. Oh, yeah, and I'm the seventh
daughter of a seventh daughter born with a caul over
my face and in all my former lives I was a witch,
except for the ones where I was some kind of super-
powerful priestess." She shrugged. "So it was nothing
really. And now you're here to help."

"We'll see about that," Maid Marian said grimly.
"Robin, if you please—"

So off we went through the forest until, within a
few hundred yards, it thinned so that we saw that
beyond lay the bare trunks of fallen trees, and beyond
that smoldering black spots where bonfires of branches
and undergrowth had burned, and beyond that, where
it should have been sheltering at the edge of Sherwood, lay the village of Sayles, naked and exposed.
It was a half-mile distant through the forest from this
point ordinarily, full of deer paths and tall oaks in
which a man might take refuge if the road was traveled, not by fat bishops and rich merchants but the
Sheriff's men. Now a delegation of another sort could
be clearly seen advancing upon us, and though we
stood within the cusp of the forest, we too were clearly
seen, for all our Lincoln green. Robin raised his arm
to signal the salute, but a blast from the horn of one
of the figures below stayed him. The man blew three
blasts spaced in a certain fashion to sound the signal
Robin had given the people of the village to summon
one of us when a friend was in need.

But as we looked upon the scene below, we needed
no signal to recognize the cause of the townsmen's
distress. The village was where it should be and the
road where it should be and the highway where it
should be and all of the other villages where they
should be, their chimney smoke pluming gray against
a bright blue sky. But where Sherwood and Barnsdale
woods should have been lay only stubble-filled, smok-
ing barren lands, so that it seemed a foreign army
might have been through here burning crops and
houses all, except that the burning lay only in spots.

The villages were as undressed as birds before they got their plumage.

Robin turned to Madrona Warden, who stood with her arms crossed and her mouth set in a tight line. "Lady, they call us thieves for taking a few of the King's deer and boars, and cutting the occasional tree. But compared to your plundering, our efforts are shamed as paltry."

The woman hugged herself, as if cold, and said in a fell voice, "I'm not to blame for this. If you want to blame somebody ask these guys and old T.R. Maete and Company."

"What the hell is that little town doing sitting in the middle of company land?" the yellow-shirted man asked.

The one he called Ole answered him, "I don't know, Wally, why don't you report them?"

"Something's wrong with this picture," Madrona Warden said suddenly.

"Yes," said Robin. "That had come to our notice."

But by that time the villagers were approaching. "Will, Alen, take the women back into the forest near where we found these strangers. John, Tuck, come with me."

Madrona Warden shook Alen off, and when Will tried to load her onto his shoulder, used her arcane knowledge so that in a moment he was flying backwards over her hip so that his own rested painfully against the reddish roots of a misshapen tree which had formerly been behind him.

Echoing the foresters, the witch said, "What's that village doing there and who are these people?"

"These are Sayles-folk, mistress," I answered her, since Robin was striding forth with Tuck at his heels. "No doubt come to see what's become of Sherwood and why their tillage lies wasted with stumps and logs and charred places."

"You mean we're in ancient *England*?" she asked.

"By no means. We're in the England of today, and where else would you expect to meet Robin Hood?"

"Oh, wow. Something is wrong. Something is definitely wrong. I wanted you guys to come forward in time and space to the U.S. to help me fend off these lackeys of the timber maggots," she said, nodding toward the foresters. "I didn't mean for *us* to come back *here*."

I left her musing and unprotected, since she appeared to need no protection, and joined Robin and Tuck. The mayor's wife was scolding Robin. "And I'd like you to tell me what we're supposed to say to the Sheriff and the King's men, young man, when they come wanting to know why the King's forest is lying in waste all over our farms with a bloody great brushpile in the middle of the road. Who do you suppose they'll blame for that, eh? This time you've taken your robbing the rich and giving to the poor a wee bit too far, I say."

"That's right," said the miller. "We'll have no need for all this firewood when the Sheriff burns down our houses around our ears, and we'll have no forest to hide in, either."

The baker, a gentle man whose home Robin saved once before, sighed and shook his head saying, "Oh, dear, what can you have been thinking of?"

But one of the foreign foresters, the one called Ole, answered the miller firmly. "You can't use this timber for firewood, mister. It's the property of T.R. Maete Inc. and has already been spoken for by a German developer—same outfit that is going to build a golf course here. So I don't know what this crazy broad here has told you about squatting on company land, but I'm afraid you're going to have to move your little town."

"My good man," the mayor's wife said, "my family has lived in our home since the time of Charlemagne. I have never heard of Lord T. R. Might nor of his companie, but I assure you if it is he behind the destruction of Sherwood Forest, King Edward will send forth his own companie quickly enough to punish his impudence—" she looked him up and down "—and yours."

"Wait, wait. Hold on," Madrona Warden said, and a sickly smile was upon her countenance. "There's just been this big mistake. Whew. Pardon me. I didn't mean to upset you guys. These bozos," she indicated the foresters rudely with her thumb, "don't know what's going on, but I'm beginning to figure it out. See, it's all very simple. This isn't Sherwood Forest, it's the Olympic Forest. I just got the spell a little mixed up. It's no big deal really. I'm this tremendously magical person and I've got plenty of power to spare especially because, like, righteousness and the blessing of the Earth Mother are on my side and all that. But there weren't any spells in old books for handling this kind of problem, so I just sort of made it up, and I overdid it a little and got a couple of words backwards. So instead of bringing Robin Hood forward out of Sherwood Forest and into the Olympic Forest, I brought us back here—forest and all, I'm afraid." She smiled a nervous and ingratiating smile, but Robin frowned at her severely.

"This makes little sense to me," he said. "I want no traffic with your magics. It's plain to see that this forest is not Sherwood. What I want to know is, where *is* Sherwood Forest?"

She waggled her shoulders back and forth and looked studiously at her dirty bare big toe. "Um, I don't know exactly, but I'm sure it's around someplace."

"Wow," the forester called Wally by his companions said in a voice scalding with scorn, "and you talk about what *we* do to the precious effing environment. We're amateurs compared to you, lady."

"Yeah," said Ole, "at least we don't go messing around with countries and time and stuff."

"This is a joke, right?" Knutson asked.

"If we may have your permission, Master Robin, to enter *whatever* that fell forest may be, we shall find an appropriate tree from which to hang yon witch," the miller said. He was always one for getting to the heart of the matter.

"Let us not be in such haste," Robin began.

"Haste nothing. We're far too late, if you ask me," the mayor's wife said. "If only we could have hanged her before she destroyed the forest!"

"*I* didn't destroy it," Madrona Warden said indignantly. "You've got these dudes to thank for the destruction you see here. I tried to prevent them from taking the rest of it. If you all would just chill out for a while, I'm sure I can find a way to get it right this time."

"Good people," Robin said. The sweat was breaking upon his brow slightly and I saw his knuckles whiten as he clenched his bow. Friends turned to foes over lesser matters than this one. "There will be no hangings until I've gotten to the bottom of this. It may be that the witch can undo whatever harm she has done, which she surely cannot do if she is hanged. And these rogues who were with her seem to me to be in some wise to blame, as well. We'll hold court in the greenwood to decide this matter."

That was the Robin I followed and respected! A man who knew what was what. Court inevitably followed a feast, and a feast was what I was more than ready to have. A man of my stature needs nourishment to maintain himself, and a fat haunch of venison would do much to quell the uneasiness fluttering in my gut since first I beheld the strangers. "Now you're talking!" I said.

"John, go fetch the deer you hung in yon tree just before we heard Alen's 'dragon,' " Robin said.

"With all my heart," I agreed, and set out with a good will for the spot.

"Uh—" Madrona Warden stretched out a dirty-nailed hand to stay me.

"What is it, woman?" I asked, barely able to keep from growling with my voice as I was within my stomach.

"Oh, nothing maybe. I mean, nothing. Just, er, don't bother on my account. I never eat anything with a face."

I stalked away from her and ducked through the

unfamiliar trees to where we had first left Sherwood.
The further I went, the more wary I grew, and with
reason. My deer was not to be found, nor the tree
where I hung it, nor the trees surrounding that tree.
The white line was still there, as it was around the
edge of all the strange red trees that had replaced our
oaks and yews. But of Sherwood I saw nothing but
the same sort of stumps, felled trees, and charred circles as those on the other side of the central copse.
An army of armed men led by the Sheriff heading
straight towards me, or a line of trees from which the
corpses of my comrades swung hanging, would have
affected me no more than did the sight of that barren-
ness where the world I knew simply ended.

I sat down abruptly, my rear on the wooded side of
the chalked white line, my feet on the other side.

Even the grass was not the grass I was familiar with.
I am used to hummocks and rocks, not so many ferns,
not so much fearsome space between trees. Where
were the deer tracks, where were the bolt holes that
we used to hide from the Sheriff's men? Where was
the thornbush where I had hid as I watched Sir Richard of the Lee pass before we knew him for a friend?
Where was the stone we marked sometimes to indicate
the direction of the quarry? Where was the stump
against which I had pissed only yesterday? I am unsure
how long I sat there with my butt on that alien grass
and my feet on that even more alien barren ground,
but presently, the copse of standing trees being no
wider and no longer apparently than the field of a
middling poor serf, Robin and the others found me
where I sat.

"No deer, huh?" Madrona Warden asked.

Robin said quietly. "Well then, Will, take Much
and see if you can shoot another, or a boar, or perhaps several hares and pheasants for a stew."

"Try a spotted owl," Knutson suggested, his tone
implying that he was making a bitter jest.

"Anything that was ever in here has been flushed
out long ago by the sound of our voices," I told

Robin. "This whole forest would fit into Wakefield Hall."

Will returned presently and confirmed my fears. No deer, boar, pheasant, hare, squirrel, or so much as an adder could be found among all those trees.

"Damn," said Ole. "I was looking forward to eating, too. I missed my coffee break and my lunch."

"No you haven't," the witch told him. "They're not due for another eight or nine hundred years yet."

Maid Marian stepped forward then until her nose was no more than an inch from Madrona Warden's. "Woman," she said. "I wot not of the quarrel you have with yon knaves, but I'll thank you not to trifle with the appetites of me and mine. Return our greenwood home, *with* its animals intact, and return it before I hear the grumble of my man's stomach or, though he may never harm you, I will make you *long* for angry villagers and a quick noose."

"Hey," Madrona Warden said in return, giving our Marian eye for eye, which is no mean feat, "chill out, sister. I'm sorry you're all missing your dinner, but now you see what this kind of thing can lead to. *These men* cut down this forest and ran off the animals, which is why there's no dinner meat for you. They even cleared the underbrush so there's not even any wild asparagus to stalk. That's why your boyfriend has to help me stop them. If they have their way, *these* trees will be cut down, too, and all of this land will be one big desert."

The man called Wally said, "That's not a fair representation and you know it, Warden. Look, I'm going to go along with this to some extent, okay? This little kangaroo court you've set up."

"You're well-advised," Robin told him in a dangerous voice. "Usually our courts are merry diversions full of jest, but gentle jests made on full stomachs. My mood is less mellow when my belly and those of my men are empty."

"I've still got a full thermos of coffee," Ole said. From a flask round as a tower, he produced a cup and into it poured a steaming brew. He took the first sip, presumably to show us it was not poison, then passed it toward Robin, who courteously passed it to Marian, who passed it by altogether but forced the steaming cup into the hand of the witch, who drank it readily enough.

"What sort of potion is that?" Tuck inquired. "I thought *you* were the witch."

"It's a—uh—restorative," the witch said. "Don't worry, your holiness. It's nonalcoholic. Picks you up. Fills the gap. Try some."

Tuck did, and suffered no ill effects. The cup passed next to Much, who took a sip before climbing the tree to which the witch had chained herself. From the highest branches of this tree he kept our lookout. The rest of us had moved gradually toward the center of the copse, away from the all-too-open ground, and now followed Robin's example and sat with our backs against the trunks. The newcomers were arrayed as if by mutual consent with the woman on one side of Robin and nearest Marian, who would not scruple to restrain the witch as necessary, and the three men on his other side. We all kept our bows close to hand, and our daggers.

"The lady has told me something of her side of things," Robin said to the three woodsmen. "I believe it is your turn to tell your tale. How came you to be molesting her, and why was she chained to the tree, and how came you to cut down this mighty forest and drive off the animals?"

The men consulted among themselves, and then the one called Wally said, "I'm union steward so I guess I'll speak for the others, Hood, if that's okay with everybody. See, this woman is twisting things around to suit herself as usual. This is a real cute little charade you all are making up with the fake town and the fake people and all, but you and I both know there aren't any animals here anymore. There's plenty up in the state park still, of course."

"This *was* a state park," the witch said.

"Your turn is not yet come again, lady," Robin told her, frowning.

"Meanwhile, you folks and the Wicked Witch of the West here can get your groceries at the Super Value, just like the rest of us. Hamburger was good enough for my daddy and it's good enough for me, though I like to go huntin' same as the next man."

"I have not heard of this Super Value of which you speak," Robin told him.

"It's a supermarket, grocery store," Ole said. "Oh, come on, buddy. Even in the old days they had to get groceries somewhere."

"Yeah, you know, like bread, cheese, pickles, Ding Dongs, and Bull Durham?" Knutson put in.

"Bread comes from the bakery, cheese from the goatherd," Maid Marian said. "Pickles a wife may make to preserve what is worth preserving, but what are Ding Dongs and Bull Durham?"

"It's okay, Marian," Madrona Warden said. "They haven't been discovered yet. You wouldn't want to know anyway. Especially about the Bull Durham. Yuck. And neither has the Super Value. Been discovered yet, I mean. Come on you guys, this is the real authentic Robin Hood and his people, and we're really back in England—don't you get it?"

Wally surveyed the scrap of forest and us, his companions, and to me it seemed that he was not as easy in his mind as he had been. "Maybe we are and maybe we aren't," he said. "But we have to get back to work, and I'm afraid we'll have to have company lawyers slap a restraining order on all of you if you don't clear these people away, lady. You understand me?"

She nodded and looked into the cup made by the sag of her skirts. "I understand. Only it's not that easy. I'm telling you the truth. The company won't be invented yet for years. We're on our own except for Robin Hood and his men. They could show us how to live in this forest, only you guys didn't leave enough forest."

"That shows how much you know," Knutson said

suddenly. "It may interest you to learn, Miss Educated Idiot, that you're not the only one who knows about Robin Hood and Sherwood Forest. It so happens *I* visited Sherwood Forest when the wife and I were touring World War II battle sites two years ago. And it was about the size of what we got left here."

"That cannot be," said Much, "for this very afternoon I was myself among the oaks and saw the forest spread all around us."

Alen looked from one of the newcomers to the other to Much and Robin, as if watching a sporting match of some sort. Robin himself looked increasingly puzzled and unhappy and twiddled an arrow between his fingers this way and that, weighing one end against the other.

Madrona Warden huffed herself up like a cat and said to Knutson, "Of course Sherwood is no bigger than this in our time—*you* people stripped Britain of its mighty forests before you started in on the States." She turned to Robin and pled, earnestness filling her narrow face, "I tell you, Robin, you'd be just sick if you could see what they did to Sherwood—"

"Can you not show us?" Alen asked.

"Robin—" Tuck came running, his robes kilted above his knees and his boots slapping the forest floor. "Robin, the Sheriff is less than a mile from here with a large band of men. The village delegation seems set on meeting with them, but whether to deter them or to betray us I cannot tell."

Madrona Warden's head swiveled to Alen initially, then to Tuck and Robin, and now back to Alen, "What did you say?"

"I said, can you not show us Sherwood as you describe it? Now would seem to me an excellent time to bring forth such evidence in your defense, most especially if in doing so you spirit us away from here."

Trust Alen to always go for the most fanciful possible idea! I found myself scoffing at the notion and at him for believing this fey creature's claims, but then I looked about me at the solid evidence of what was and what was not, and concluded that either she was indeed what she claimed or that I was dreaming the entire episode and soon would wake within my shelter against the trunk of the great oak in our campsite.

Robin apparently came to the same conclusion, because he said, "An excellent time indeed. Is there some way in which we may assist you, or shall I have the women and the smallest run for cover in the nearest village save Sayles?"

She looked a little flustered and said, "Well, we could all hold hands and sing 'Sumer Is a Cumin In' and that might help."

"Hold hands? No way!" said Ole. "Hold hands with the damn tree if you want to get cozy, sister."

"I doubt the Sheriff will distinguish which among us are my band and which are newcomers, despite your garb," Robin told him. "If the wise woman bids us hold hands, you will hold hands."

Wally looked for a moment into Robin's eyes and said, "Do it."

"Okay," said Ole, reaching out of his way for Marian's hand with his right and Wally's with his left, while I joined hands with Robin on one side and Alen on the other. Marian began singing in a slightly wavery high voice and others joined in uncertainly as Madrona Warden ducked into the center of the circle.

She held up a black box and touched a lever with her thumb, and music floated out above Marian's voice—a different song altogether than "Sumer Is a Cumin In." This song was accompanied by full band—trumpeters, drummers, and instruments I never heard before nor have ever heard since. Robin Hood's name was repeated over and over, and in the background a voice droned as if reciting the tax rolls. We remained where we stood, however, holding hands like foolish lovers while the weasel-faced woman raised her arms to the sky with the black box in one hand and a crystalline multicolored gem in the shape of a pyramid in the other hand and said, "By Gaia, by Hern, by Hamadryad and Nereid, by Diana and the moon, by oak and ash and thorn, by the holly and the ivy, by thistle and shamrock and heather and broom, take us to the time of Maggie Thatcher, of Princess Di and Fergie." And then she said a lot of other words in some strange language and waved a little leather pouch and a feather around. Still nothing happened. So she raised her arms again and shook them.

Hoofbeats pounded the stripped and charred land around us, and I could all but feel the rough hemp noose scratch my neck.

"It's not working," she moaned. "I can't get us back to our time. You can stop singing now," she told Marian and the others. "I'm sorry. I know I have lots of power and it ought to work but—"

"Well, I never saw anything so pitiful in my life," Ole said, and *he* let forth with a string of colorful curses, many of which were Anglo-Saxon but many of which were Norman or pure Norse, from the sound of them, and as he cursed a wind arose, gaining momentum as his curses increased in volume and complexity.

You could see clear to the edge of the wood by now and the Sheriff's face was quite distinct above his horse's, leading about twenty riders. I could see the whites of his eyes and the yellow of his teeth as his lips parted over them in triumph. I sorely regretted the time we'd sent him riding homeward backward.

"Keep it rolling," Madrona Warden hollered to Ole, raising her skinny scratched arms to the heavens again and screaming more magic words into the wind. "I'm not sure where you're going with this, but something's happening."

As she resumed her incantations and Ole's cursing took on a desperate note, the wind blew up longer and stronger and fiercer than I had ever felt it within Sherwood; a wolf of a wind, a hawk of a wind, unimpeded by the sparse growth of trees remaining. The pressure of it on my ears was such that I put my hands to them to save myself from deafening, and the soil and small stones in the air all but flayed me.

Then the wind was rushing so fast that all around me, faces, bodies, trees and all, was a great blur and the pop and great slurping that I remembered from before occurred once more—this time I didn't hear them, as my ears were still filled with wind's roar, but felt myself and all the others pulled through some small hole, lengthening and stretching and at last popping back into place. When at last the slurping stopped and the wind quieted, the people stopped rushing past my eyes and the trees stopped whipping and merely waved, I saw that they were oaks, well spread, with grass beneath them and benches here and there.

I still held Robin's hand and Alen's, and in the middle of the circle, Madrona Warden finished her chants by saying, "parsley, sage, rosemary and thyme—" and Ole, opening his clenched eyes to see that the countryside had stopped dashing around him, finished his cursing with a heartfelt curse that sounded to me like, "uff da!"

I knew with my first breath that something momentous had happened. On the one hand, the trees suddenly smelled right, as they had not before, though I never could have said at any time before that a forest of oak smells different from a forest of other trees. The rest of what I inhaled was not nearly so heartening nor so wholesome. No charcoal smoke or even peat, but a dizzying collection of fumes so thick I wondered that I could not see them, rammed their way into my nose and chest so that I fell to coughing, as did several of the others. Also, although the woods looked deserted, save ourselves, somewhere in my head new noises hummed and clattered, buzzed and clanged, just out of earshot, felt rather than actually heard. It made me jumpy, the disquieting effect of it more than compensating for the comfort of once more being surrounded by the proper sort of trees.

Marian looked at the trees and bent down, scooping something off the ground. She opened her palm and showed Robin an acorn. He smiled and nodded as if the fact that acorns fell around oak trees was in some way remarkable.

Will Scarlett alone was not bemused by all of the magical goings on, but on his guard as we all should have properly been. Trained hands sent his horn to trained lips, and even though all of us that there were in the band were round about him, he blew three blasts and then, at our startled looks, pointed. Coming toward us through the wide avenues between trees was a party of women dressed as oddly as Madrona the witch, Ole, Wally, and Knutson.

"Oh, will you look at that!" cried a woman who had forgotten to put on her skirt that morning and wore leggings of bright blue-green flowered all over with what appeared to be scarlet roses. "It doesn't say anywhere in the brochure from the Royal Trust that this is a theme park, but lookee there at those people dressed up like Robin Hood and the Lost Boys!"

One of her companions, a woman who was also dressed in leggings, though hers were a red tartan, said in a very un-Scottish voice, "Really, Michelle! Robin Hood had merry men, not lost boys."

"I'll be damned!" said another woman, this one in leggings of black leather and coat to match, with a fetching bodice of opulent red material that allowed a view of her billowing bosoms as she ran towards us. "It's the actors! I heard they were making a movie about Robin Hood. Yoo hoo! Robin! Little John! Can I have your autographs?" she hollered at us.

"Don't be worried, boys, they're harmless," Madrona Warden said. "Just smile and sign things and look like you've got other things on your mind, which you have, and they'll go away."

The one in black leather opened a satchel large as a saddlebag, which I was disappointed to see was not filled with gold, though she wore a quantity of gold chains and gold and gemmed rings and little gold skulls in her ears. Her hair was long and blond and brushed my chest as she dug in the bag and drew forth a slender, featherless stylus and a book. "You must be Little John," she said, fairly ogling me with more boldness than most tavern wenches. "They wouldn't have two guys your size in the movie. I like big men. Are you an unknown? Is this your first break? Sign right here."

The leaves of her book were thin as sheerest silk with small blue lines upon them but contained no document. I wondered why she wished me to sign it and looked to Robin to see what he was doing. He was leaning with one hand against the tree, his face very close to that of the woman in the rose-vined leggings. Marian stood close by on the other side and her face was not wearing one of its pleasanter expressions. "These moving people," he said. "They are like tinkers or gipsies?"

"Oh, no," she said. "We don't believe everything we read. We're sure you're all very nice. I don't believe I've seen your picture in the books, though. Who are you?"

"They call me Robin Hood," he said.

She giggled. "Oooh, you say that very well. I'm sure you're a fine actor."

"These moving people—if they aren't like gipsies, have they wealth?"

"I'm sure the producers and directors do, though unless you folks have a smart agent, you're probably going to have to eke your first Beverly Hills mansion out of this deal, aren't you?"

She shoved her book at Robin and he made his mark with a flourish—though how much one can flourish an X only a monk can know. Taking my cue from this, I did likewise for the vixen before me, who chuckled with quite heartening effect on the red bodice and its contents. "You sure do know how to keep in character, Little John. I bet you're a *great* actor," she said, and from eyelids painted like a sunset she batted at me the longest lashes I have ever seen on woman, man, or beast.

Thus, as you may note, I was enjoying myself exceedingly and was no little sorry when Madrona

Warden clapped her hands as if evoking a magic spell. "That's enough now. There'll be a press conference and more time for autographs later. We have to get back to the set now. Excuse us," she said briskly to the ladies, and they filed away meekly enough.

"Robert, I crave a word with you," said Maid Marian to her mate. She only called him Robert when she meant business.

He turned to her, saying, "Now, now, love, I was but gathering information. We are in a tight spot here and if there are wealthy travelers nearby we must ply our trade, relieve them of their goods, and go deeper into the woods."

Knutson spat. "I hate to tell you this, Bob, but there ain't much more woods to go through."

"Let us repair somewhat deeper into it and we'll see the truth of this," Marian said. She spoke in a low earnest voice to Robin as they led the way into the forest. The spot where Madrona Warden's magic had landed us bore a great ruin of a blasted oak which could have been the lookout tower. Otherwise, of the many large oaks the forest boasted, I recognized not a single one though many appeared to be of exceeding age. Around each of these old trees, however, was an expanse of lawn bereft of all growth but tall grass. The trees which once grew there, I took it, had fallen in ancient times—but perhaps not times so ancient as those from which we came. The nature of the forest more than anything else convinced me that we had come far—sunlight filtered into it, warming the ground, as it had never had a chance to do in the dark and concealing Sherwood of our time. I knew the females we had just met were not from times older than our own, for I have a good enough sense of what came before—and also I know that before our Sherwood was a separate forest, it was part of the larger forest that covered all of England and Scotland. That it was smaller, rather than larger, than in our day told me that time had indeed passed. I did not know how much time, nor how much smaller the forest had shrunk, until, a few moments from walking into it, we began to walk out of it again. Voices raised in the distance and the sound of metal on metal, not the honest sound of swords clanking or even of war machinery, but more complicated and confusing than that, came to us from a distance.

Marian stopped, halting the rest of us before we could go further. Tears stood in her eyes, and that woman never cries about anything. "Robin, I have a riddle for you," she said, and from the way she said it, I took it that she did not deem her riddle more of an amusement, say, than the riddles of the guardian beasts of old who determined from a man's answers whether he was to live or to die.

"Tell it to me, then, love," Robin encouraged her.

"If the strange forest now stands where and when Sherwood stood, and this forest is not, as we see, the same as our Sherwood, where then has our Sherwood home gone and what has become of it?"

"Oh. Ooooh. Oh, *man*. Bummer," said Madrona Warden, looking even more stricken than Marian and sinking to the forest floor in an untidy pile of multicolored skirts.

"Shit. Oh, dear," said Wally, who sounded brighter about it than the women. To Robin he said, "This forest of yours is pretty big, huh? How many acres would you say?"

"I couldn't say, but between Sherwood and Barnsdale they encompass half of the northernmost half of the kingdom," Robin replied.

"Oaks and such, you said?"

"Aye."

"Holee shit. I bet the boss is about to come in his jeans," Wally said.

"Huh?" Knutson grunted.

Robin said, "If the forest we left in our town is not Sherwood, and this wood is not the Sherwood of our time, then do you not deem it likely that our wood now sits, by the curse of this woman, in your land and time?"

"All that virgin old growth forest," Madrona Warden said. "The lumber maggots will cut it all down and sell it!"

"Aye," said Marian, "and if ill befalls Sherwood, it's your fault, woman. My husband may be too chivalrous to chastise you, but I have no such scruples. You had better redress this wrong you've done us and soon."

"You're right," the woman agreed miserably. "It's *not* nice to fool with Mother Nature, but I was doing it to try to help."

"You better get us back to the Peninsula quick, sweetheart," Knutson said, rubbing his hands and grinning. "We got a mess of work—overtime probably, waiting for us, thanks to you."

I frankly felt baffled by all of this moving whole forests back and forth although, admittedly, moving either the scrap of woodland Madrona Warden had left back in our own time or the mere park which called itself Sherwood in her time should scarcely have been a strain for a *competent* magician.

"Therefore," Marian continued, the fire flashing in her eyes, "I suggest that we get back into our circle and you say your little chants again and make your wind and carry us to Sherwood, and Sherwood and us back into our own time. And I suggest that you and these louts you brought with you stay in your own time and place when you're done. We've problems enough of our own with the Sheriff's treachery—we never needed you to deprive us of our home. If so much as one of the King's oaks is freshly notched I'll—"

"She seems to understand, love," Robin said mildly and held out his hands to start the circle joining together.

But try as Madrona Warden did, invoking the ancestors of acorns, all of the deities and supernatural beings of her not inconsiderable acquaintance, she didn't stir so much as a breeze. Ole tried cursing again, since he was very anxious, as he said, to get back to work, but that had no effect this time.

"Sorry," she said finally, grimly. "I could have sworn I had more power than that, but it seems to be all pooped out. My batteries are dead on the tape player so I can't use the music spell with the stuff I have, and you can only just work a spell so many ways. I need stuff from the original Sherwood to take us there. That's the only way I can think of that I could get something going. I use a lot of sympathetic magic—stuff that is symbolic of other stuff, like the spotted owl feather—"

Will Scarlett again was the one who alerted us. The rest of us were all too intent on the dirty-footed witch, who looked as if she was about to weep. I think I was, too, except I didn't want to breathe the noxious air deeply enough to sob. Then Will raised his horn, but Robin caught the gesture and knocked it down. "It's quite all right, Will. We're all here. You can just tell us quietly, you know."

"Over there. Those fellows dressed in Lincoln green. Can it be our mates come looking for us?"

"Naw," said Madrona Warden. "It's just the movie company shooting location shots. They were going to shoot some back in the Hoh Rainforest and the rest up in Vancouver, but they wanted to use some of the real sites first."

"You speak as if you know these people," Robin said.

"Like I told you, I read about them in that article in the *Seattle Times*. The entertainment section had a big piece on movies being shot in the Pacific Northwest and all of the historic forests our forests are supposed to stand in for. These bozos," she jerked her thumb at the woodsmen, "still haven't managed to clear-cut quite all of the Hoh." She laughed suddenly and it had a bitter sound to it. "I guess we should go tell them to hurry. If they beat the chain saws to where our forest used to be, they can use the real

Sherwood Forest as a backdrop, even though nobody knows about it but us."

"You mean they will be passing near where Sherwood lies?" Robin asked.

"Sure. The Hoh's on the other side of the Peninsula. They'll have to pass right through the area we came from, and that's where, if I'm right, Sherwood is now."

"Well, then," said Robin, unslinging his bow from his back and drawing an arrow from his quiver. "If your means cannot suffice to take us to Sherwood, we'll have to fall back on less exotic devices."

"You're going to mug the movie company?" Wally asked. "How's that going to help?"

Will Scarlett gave him a wolfish grin, and I could see Will was as cheered as I was by being able to take familiar action. "Why, we'll relieve all but one or two of their horses and carriages and force them to guide us back to this place where the witchlet says we shall now find Sherwood."

"I don't know that I want any part of robbery," Knutson said in churchy tones. I had been unslinging my bow and fitting my arrow, but now I walked over to the man and simply loomed above him—he was of goodly size but still a foot less than my height rather than the foot and a half to two feet shorter more common among my fellows.

Wally grimaced at me. "I don't think you've got much choice, Knutson, unless you'd like to put plane tickets for all of us on *your* American Express card."

Ole was more enthusiastic, but then he was more typical of most of the Norman breed and well suited to theft by his Viking lineage. "A chance to see Robin Hood's men rob," he said, "doesn't just happen every day."

"No, wait," Madrona Warden said. "Look, I think we're getting a little beyond the realm of civil disobedience here, which may not matter to you guys, but the loggers and I have got to live in this century."

"You will not stay our hands, lady," Robin told

her, sounding as dangerous as I have ever heard him sound to one of her sex.

"Me? Oh, lordy, no! I wouldn't dream of it. But I think I'd better help you, like get their plane tickets and stuff, and the movie folks have got cameras so we could all be identified, so I was just going to ask if I could like borrow a disguise or something?"

"Oh, hey, me too," said Ole. The other two loggers looked at him, and he shrugged and said, "You guys don't appreciate historical opportunities when you see them. This is better than World War II battle sites. Besides, I think it may be a dream anyway."

Robin took stock of the situation and ordered Much to peel off his shirt and Hood and Will and Alen to do likewise, and therein dressed the woodsmen from the waist up as men of Sherwood. Friar Tuck, clad as we were in the Lincoln green, drew forth his spare cassock from the sack which he keeps near him in case he needs to pass for the regular sort of cleric to snare some fat bishop. This he gave the witch, who put it on over her more colorful garments, flipping forward the hood to hide her hair.

We stepped forth into the glade, arrows pointed, and Robin cried, "Stand and deliver!"

This was the beginning of more wondrous matters than all of Madrona Warden's magics to date. Though the company of men in green was not large, more men and women were there and these were clad similarly to how the woodsmen had been. Three-legged boxes stood round the glade with shining ropes extending from them to metal cottages set on wheels, like gipsy wagons, though larger. From these came a rumble as of many carts rolling over rutted roads. "Cut their generator," Madrona Warden instructed Wally. "And round up any cellular phones." The rumbling stopped and the lights which had been trained on the false men of Sherwood died, so that the day was at once dimmer and cooler.

"Lady, if you're delivering arrow-grams for somebody's birthday, cute prank but we're a little busy here," said a man with skin as brown as a Saracen's. He spoke through a cone which made his voice somewhat louder.

Robin took it from him and spoke through it, "As I said, stand and deliver. We'll have your purses and the clothing with which you pretend to be men of Sherwood."

"What is this," the Saracen asked, "some kind of terrorist attack?"

"Right," Madrona said quickly. "The Robin Hood Anti-Defamation League takes credit for this raid. Just give us your clothes, your plane tickets, and the keys to the van and we don't hurt you. Otherwise, my comrades will stake you all like vampires."

"Oh, hey," said a young woman carrying a square piece of board on her arm. "We're cool, honest."

Another man behind her beamed, "Oh, the press is not gong to *believe* this. What a stunt! Maybe we can duplicate it when somebody's watching." To Robin and Madrona he said, carefully moving his eyes from one to the other as if unsure who was leading the raid, "I don't suppose your people can let us make one tiny phone call and be back in an hour or so, could you? Just so we'd have time for a press conference."

"Sorry, we're in a hurry," Madrona said, not giving Robin time to answer, which was just as well, I imagine, since the man's words probably made as little sense to Robin as they did to me.

The woman dug into a bag and handed Madrona a packet of rectangular letters with no particular seal. The man handed over his wallet. The actors began stripping off their costumes.

"Look," Madrona Warden told the Saracen, "you guys don't move and I promise, as soon as we're safe, I'll call the *London Times* for you and they can come and find you, okay?"

"That's a deal. I hope your group will be humane enough to just take the cash from our wallets and leave behind personal items and drivers' licenses and so forth."

"They'll be in the van," she promised. And we gathered our booty and followed her into the metal cottage. Robin followed her through one low door that led to the front of the cottage, but after that I did not see them as that front room was enclosed from the rest of the house. As soon as we entered the house, although Madrona had had no time to hitch horses to the cottage, presently there was a great roar and the floor moved beneath my feet.

Much, Alen, and Will took new shirts from the captured garments and others among us traded their old clothing for the new, though there was nothing in all of it to fit me, and besides the new stuff looked to me less durable than the cloth we already wore. No windows were in this caravan but many strange implements of metal and glass.

Many long hours passed, but I slept through some, and at last the cottage stopped and a doorway opened on a vast courtyard where many other wagons and cottages stood before the strangest castle I have ever seen, and the largest. Three of Pontrefact Castle could have fit into it with room to spare, and indeed once inside we found an entire city set around a larger inner square in which people moved about amid a noisome din the like of which I had never smelled or heard in all my life. Alen's baby, forest-bred, began to squall, and though a few of the people stared, most attempted to disregard us as if our demeanor matched theirs, which it did not, varied in aspect as they were.

This castle was not the greatest of wonders I saw or was to see. Carriages, wagons, and cottages moved about on their wheels without the benefit of horses, seeming instead to be powered by lions which roared from within. At any rate, that's what I imagine lions must sound like. Robin explained later that it was some mechanical device that drove them, but he was not clear on the details. These things scuttled like large insects at furious rates of speed. I was relieved, on entering the castle, to note the absence of any wheels from its foundations.

Madrona Warden, having once more abandoned Tuck's spare cassock for her own garb, moved through the village as if she owned it and stepped up to a woman behind a tall counter, handing her the tickets and telling her they needed to be exchanged for ones on the next flight to somewhere called Ceetack. "And may we please have garment bag boxes for the archery equipment?" she asked sweetly. "The filming was running late and we didn't have time to pack it up properly."

The woman looked somewhat relieved at that and took great pains to call two men I assumed were her footmen. Apparently Robin and Madrona Warden had discussed this problem while driving us to the castle, for while still in the castle courtyard they had insisted that Wally, Ole, and Knutson leave their saws behind in the cottage, and the woodsmen agreed that their tools would not be allowed on the "plane." Robin now surrendered his bow and quiver meekly and nodded to us to do the same. Likewise we surrendered our daggers and swords. One of the men who packed our equipment said conversationally, "Fine pieces you've got for your props here, folks. I'll see to them personal. Must have borrowed this lot from a museum."

Robin nodded and smiled, and Madrona Warden folded a bill in her palm and shook hands with the man.

Then followed the greatest enchantment of all. I can scarcely describe it for I know you'll find it impossible to believe.

Madrona led us down a long hall, and through great windows of glass we saw metal birds bigger than mansions fly and perch, fly and perch, and several times we saw people clamoring forward to be swallowed by one of the birds, which connected its mouth to the castle by means of some sort of over-sized straw-like appendage, through which the people fed themselves. Alen's baby squalled even louder but he took the baby from his wife, who seemed faint, and patted the girl's hand, saying loudly for the benefit of us all, "Well, well, 'tis true then, the tales of Merlin's day when a man may take a bird's shape and fly through the air."

Madrona Warden said, "People do it all the time nowadays. Don't be scared. It won't hurt you."

"Not usually," Knutson growled.

I'll warrant among any other band in England— well, in our England of our day—men would have sooner jumped into vats of boiling oil than have walked into the maw of that bird, but we are the merry men of Sherwood and our ladies, too, and you should hear the song Alen made of us as we boldly strode forth into the bird.

Nevertheless my mouth went dry and my knees quaked as I took that last step, but I was shamed somewhat to see a chit of a girl standing there beckoning graciously and smiling. "Oh, my, sir," she said to me, "I can see you'll need to switch and get a bulkhead seat to accommodate those long legs of yours." And she, too, seemed to flirt her eyes at me, but I did not dare reciprocate with a friendly pat to the bottom or any other such gesture in the presence of our Lady Marian.

Soon enough it was clear that this was no natural bird but some mechanical device like those on the ground, for inside of it were seats, albeit inadequate ones, and many diverse compartments and windows little wider than arrowslits through which one could look down on the clouds and sometimes on the towns below and upon the sea. Though at first this made my head as light as it is after I've had a full keg of ale, presently I wearied of the sensation. This was, then, some kind of flying inn, it seemed, for the innkeeper's voice came to us from some hidden panel and the wenches showed us how to strap ourselves to our chairs with belts (presumably so that we would not fall out of their ridiculous little windows and into the sky while we were in our cups) and later they fed us many times. I asked the serving wench when she got off work, just to show that I understood what manner of device this was, and she answered, "Paris," and for a time I was more baffled than ever. But the denizens of the flying inn created a light play on the wall for us with voices as hollow as if they were from the grave and colors more brilliant than real life, so that we passed some time with this diversion.

I even slept at times, but later, when the great mechanical bird device disgorged us, I felt like kissing the ground except that I could not find it for all of the pavement.

Next it was necessary that we reclaim our weapons from a vast dungeon in the bird-inn's new castle, and to reach this dungeon we descended a moving staircase. It took a stern order from Master Robin to keep Alen from riding up the staircase that went up, and down the one that went down, over and over again. With some relief we regained our weapons and Madrona Warden hired another of the lion-roaring carriages, and so we set forth once more to find and reclaim Sherwood.

This ride was not so long as the others, a good thing since the night had come and gone and come again during our journey and I was growing weary of riding in these roaring conveyances and smelling their spoor.

I thought perhaps we had gone back to the land of the Norse from whence Ole, Wally, and Knutson came, for all around us were deep fjords and jagged white-topped mountains bordered by towns lit with thousands of the lights that shone more brightly than any fire and yet contained no flame, such as the ones in the other conveyances.

But soon after we crossed the second great bridge spanning an entire arm of the sea and headed into the toothy peaks that had been before us most of the journey, we found our forest, huddled as if for safety on the valley floor and the lower slopes of the mountains, just beyond the port city called Angeles.

Wally, Ole, and Knutson recognized the forest first, as did Madrona Warden, for despite the full moon all I saw at first were trees. The strangers, being denizens of this region, realized that there were now trees where there had not previously been trees. Then, too, there was the T.R. Maete Inc. conveyance, its lights whirling like an angry ghost in the darkness, as a small group of men stood talking.

"You can let us out here," Wally said. "We'll just report in now."

"The hell you will—" said Madrona Warden, but about that time a banshee wail arose behind us, and looking back I saw that more whirling lights, these an angry red and a fell and chilly blue, chased behind us. "Damn, it's the cops," Madrona said, and sped down the broad smooth turnpike into the forest canopy.

Then it was that I recognized Sherwood, by its fresh smell and the familiar feel of it. I sought to open one of the movable windows to take a deep breath when the conveyance lurched to the right as if one of the horses had broken its traces.

"Uff da!" Ole cried. "Will you look at dem trees?"

I saw nothing wrong with them; in fact, I was pleased that they all seemed to be growing in more or less their proper places as far as I could tell, rather than being disrupted by the structures and confinements of this overcrowded land, but Wally said, "My God, they've grown right up through the highway. Stop the damned car, lady. You can't drive through this. You'll kill us all."

"Screw that!" she growled defiantly, "you'll be bailed out by your company but Robin's band and I will be locked up while you harvest Sherwood Forest." With this she screeched sharply again and wove her way deeper into the forest.

"Hold!" Robin told her. "Lady, if you don't slay us, you will kill these trees."

"Oh, right. I guess we run for it, then."

The banshees continued to wail, and through the trees we saw the flash of lights—white and yellow for the companie, red and blue for the banshee.

Explosions of noise burst through the night.

"Jesus, they're shooting at us!" cried one of the

woodsmen, and the confusion I had felt at all of this resolved itself into a most familiar feeling. Although I saw no arrows, I heard the pursuit and smelled the pursuit and my body leapt forward as does the hind's when it scents the hounds. So ran we all, not stopping to think long enough to become bewildered. Even on this unfamiliar terrain our feet seemed to know the way. Through the streams we splashed and over the ancient log that now bore four new trees on its back we ran, dodging the roots of a lightning-downed oak and startling three deer at the river as we turned up the bank to run back along a rabbit path and through the holly hedge, where the newcomers had to be helped through the thorny leaves in such a way as to keep them from destroying our cover, and onward until at last we came to our camp in the greenwood, where hung the boar Much had slain just the day before and the wool Marian was readying for the dye-pots. For some time the beat of my own heart and the panting of my hard-drawn breath was all I heard, but when these sounds subsided, the banshee wail was no more than the buzzing of an insect in the distance.

Madrona Warden flopped down against a tree and the three woodsmen stood looking at each other, their teeth shining in the darkness.

Madrona said, "Why did you guys run too? So you can go back to the cops and tell them where we are?"

Wally shrugged off her question. "I don't know about anybody else, but I always tend to run when somebody's shooting at me. And T.R. Maete may write my paychecks, but I doubt if he'd pay for a lawyer to get us out of the rap for robbing the movie company."

"That's right," Ole said proudly. "We're outlaws now as much as you." His eyes scanned the leafy ceiling through which the moon was shadowed as it raced across the sky. "This is some forest, huh? My dad used to talk about working in the forest like this. It's what made me want to become a logger—"

Knutson took a deep breath and settled down. Marian was quietly cutting up the boar and making a smokeless fire for cooking.

Madrona Warden said, "Well, it's guys like your dad that made forests like this forest into ones like the one we left back in England."

"Could be," Wally said, and Warden looked surprised but busied herself with magical preparations. An uneasy silence hung over the glade, our men squatting under the trees like hares ready to take flight.

"Have no fear," Robin said to us all, "the Sheriff's men have never yet found our lair and I doubt the lawmen of this age can do more."

"Don't count on that," Wally told him. "They can send in a chopper with an infrared device to spot us— all kinds of stuff. And sooner or later the boss will just chop his way back to us if nothing else. The Germans still want their golf course." He did not sound as happy about it as he once had.

"Well," said Marian, hands on hips, "it's little use to worry over such matters. We can't have a proper roast, but if you spit these pieces of meat, we can all at least have something to nourish us."

Alen groaned. "I couldn't eat anything more after being fed time and again while riding in the bird's belly."

"You'll need more in your gullet than predigested patties of birdfood if you're to be fit enough to outwit these modern sheriffs."

And so we ate again, and I was most happy to do so as were many others, among them Wally, Ole, and Knutson. Madrona Warden, eschewing our feast since the boar retained its face, if not most of the rest of its carcass, busily scurried about the glade, clucking over articles whose significance escaped everyone but herself.

After dinner we relaxed around the warmth of the firepit, as is our wont, and Alen sang his song of how Robin helped him to win his wife away from an elderly knight she did not care for, Tuck told of how we had

bested Robin at wrestling and had given him a dunking, and I told of my adventures working for the Sheriff and of how my comrades rescued me when I was
captured and a condemned man. These stories, old
and familiar to us, took on fresh spice with new ears
to hear them. For that reason, Robin often feasted
friends and foe, just for the sake of an audience.

Even Madrona Warden stopped her fidgeting and
sat down among us to listen, her eyes shining as she
chewed a strand of her lank hair with her somewhat
buck teeth. I fitted the feathers and tip to an arrow
and presented it to the witch, whose eyes kindled
brighter for a moment as she fingered it, then stuck
it in one of her seemingly bottomless pockets. Alen
tuned his lute while his wife rocked their baby and
Marian mended Robin's hose by feel, since the light
of the moon was scarcely sufficient. The smell of the
burning wood and of the new wood was a balm, and
the droning words as sweet to me as breath.

Our guests felt the night's spell, too, and Wally said,
"You know, I wonder if my granddad would have
wanted to keep at being a lumberjack if he'd known
everything he loved about it would be gone so soon.
It's just a job now. Forest like this—hell, I've been in
the woods all my life, and it's just like I never set foot
outside the city by comparison."

Madrona Warden said, "I bet your granddad would
hate it. I've got to tell you something that I don't
admit very often, but it's part of why I feel so strongly
about the forests and the earth and all. You guys keep
talking about how I don't work and I'm overeducated
and everything—did you know my great-grandad was
a sailor and a logger from England who made his fortune selling ship timbers? Everybody in my family has
worked in the forest but my dad. He saw what the
machines were doing and got out. That's what's killed
off your business, boys, is the machines and all the
foreign companies buying up the forest faster than you
can cut it down."

Knutson made a growling sound in his throat and

Marian started to intervene, but Ole took a gulp of the cool ale Robin had Much pluck from the stream for the occasion. "I don't suppose," he said after two more gulps from the jug, "that if the jolly green goddess here can get you and the forest back to England, you might need any more outlaws?"

"Are you an archer?" Robin asked politely.

"No," Ole admitted. "And I'm not much of a man with a staff like Little John, and no wrestler neither. I used to be pretty good at trap shooting, but I don't guess that's any good where you're from."

Robin shook his head regretfully.

Knutson, calmed after a swig from the ale jug, cleared his throat, "My grandad now, he was a wrestler—could dance on the logs, too—nimble man, till he lost a leg. But nowadays there's no need for a man to do such things—too many machines, like the woman there said." He spat into the fire.

As we sat there staring into the flames, it seemed to me suddenly that I could hear the beating of all of our hearts together, as of one accord. Then the beat became faster and so loud that, had it indeed been our hearts, we would have needed to be running for them to beat so quickly.

"There's the chopper," Madrona Warden said.

The moon was suddenly blotted out by another large device—this one more resembling a great insect than a bird. It hovered and from a distance we could hear roaring as more devices sprung to life.

"They'll bring in dirt bikes and horses to find us next," she said. "I guess I'd better try to get you back."

Robin said at last, "Aye," and then to the woodsmen he said, "You're likely lads, all of you, and well-seasoned. I suppose we could teach you the ways of the greenwood if you truly want to leave. I'm sure this land is fair enough if you're used to it, and as you've seen an outlaw's life is precarious enough, but I would not doom anyone to stay here amidst this noise and these horrid great engines if I could make use of him. What say you, lads?" he asked us all.

"Aye," said the merry men, and I added, "I'd include the lass, too, for though her magic goes amiss at times, who knows but what we could use a witch now and again."

She shook her head, however, and smoothed her lank hair back behind her prominent ears. "Thanks, Little John. You're a real pal, but I gotta stay here and save what's left of our forests. I guess it was a dumb idea to expect you guys to help me—the world really has changed a lot. I just don't want it to die."

"I got a wife and kids to get back to myself," Wally said. "At least long enough to say goodbye before I go to the hoosegow."

A voice like that of a drowned giant called to us from the forest, "We know you're in there. Throw down your weapons and come out with your hands over your head."

Madrona Warden drew forth her crystal and her pyramid to draw strength from the moon and motioned us to all join hands. "Oak and ash and thorn, return where you were born—" she began, and pressed the lever on her little box. Grinning, she interrupted the spell to explain, "I bought new batteries at Heathrow." She did not seem to drone on as much as previously, but got to the important bits right away.

As the great wind arose, I saw a small, spotted bird fly overhead and then all else blurred. This time the slurping sound seemed to encompass the whole world and the pop was louder than all of the explosions I had ever heard in all of my life, and I clenched my eyes tight and held on with both fists to the hands beside me, though when I recovered I found my fists grasping the roots on the forest floor. The slurping and the popping ceased, nor was there any longer that giant insect thudding overhead, nor the roar and stink of engines. All that came to me in the silence following so much noise was the calling of nightbirds and the groans of my fellows regaining their feet, the bawl of Alen's baby, and Marian's clucking over her cookfire, which had gone out in the magical wind.

Of Madrona Warden and the three foresters there was no trace, and at a nod from Robin, we Sherwood men fanned out to the edges of the forest. I headed to where I had left the deer so long ago and found it still fresh and dripping blood onto the ground. Beyond, where the white mark had been, and the strange trees, was the familiar great oak I was wont to climb for a lookout. Up it I went and all around I looked, spying the dawn on the horizon. In the view before me, the sun did not have to scale high cold mountains to stretch its paws like those of a warm ginger cat reaching toward the vast leafy acres of Sherwood. It had only to breast the gentle English hills and loll around the rooftops of Sayles, of Barnsdale, and all the other villages of the shire.

Will's horn blew three times its warning then and we converged towards him in time to catch the Sheriff's men, who must have been bewildered to have gone from seeking us in an open clearing to suddenly seeking and finding us in the depths of the properly dense Sherwood where we were more than able to defend ourselves. We harried the Sheriff and his men out of the woods and sent them down the turnpike with our arrows lending their horses' hooves wings.

The incident is spoken of as are the other tales, but lately when it has been told I've found difficulty believing that such a fantastic thing actually happened to us—it's more the sort of tale Alen would make up or the villagers tell to enlarge our fame.

Except that I have retained a lingering feeling of relief on awakening to feel the trees pressing close to each other and sheltering me. Each morning and evening, I have made it my practice to scale the great oak and reassure myself that Sherwood is still vast and encompassing and we of Robin's band safe within. This morning as I dismounted the tree, I heard the whine and thunk of an arrow as it hit the trunk below me. Pulling the tip and the note it bore pinned beneath it from the tree, I recognized the carving of the shaft and fletching as my own.

You may see the note here, for I have kept it to this day, and that evening Maid Marian, who was convent-educated, read it aloud to us all.

"Dear Robin, Marian, Little John, Will, Alen, Friar Tuck, and the gang," it said. "I hope my spell worked out okay and you folks and the forest got home safely. I'd appreciate it if you'd leave us a note under the roots of the biggest old oak—the one that we wound up near when my spell landed us in the future Sherwood. Wally is taking his family to England this summer and he'll be looking for the note.

"He and Ole and Knutson have all been working through their union to try to get the company to cut back on mechanization and foreign sales and to cross-train the loggers in the care and feeding of new trees. They've also been after the so-called pro-timber industry legislators to enact legislation that will help both the forests *and* the men who make their livings there. We'll never see it, of course, but one of these days about four hundred years from now, we're hoping the Olympic Forest will be as full of trees again as it was when I temporarily transplanted Sherwood there. I'm sure you guys are all worried about how we got away from the law—well, all the actors and the director of the film crew we robbed are greenies—environmentalists like me—and by the time I got the problems all explained to them we had generated so much publicity for the movie that they asked for a treatment of the story of what happened to us to make another movie! That's *good* money—we paid them back for everything *and* I had plenty left over to donate to the Olympic Environmental Council. The film people also wanted Wally, Ole, and Knutson to join the cast, since the director thought they looked like the type of people Robin Hood would have wanted with him. Thanks to the movie company's lobbying, the state bought what was left of the forest back from T.R. Maete and the Germans.

"I just want you to know how much we all appreciate all your help—as you know, I'm psychic and my powers told me all along that getting Robin Hood and his merry men to help was the thing to do, and of course my powers were right. Because, in case you haven't figured it out after everything that happened, you guys didn't get forgotten by me or by anybody else. If the Sheriff of Nottingham ever tries to tell anybody you're just a random bunch of punks who've staked out the forest and terrorized the poor people into helping you, you can tell him for me and everybody here in the future that Robin Hood, Maid Marian, Little John, Will Scarlett, Friar Tuck, Alen a Dale (and the missus and the kid, too), Much, and everybody are still talked about just like in your storytelling sessions, and sung about and remembered. Gotta go now. Mustn't waste paper. Wally, Knutson, and Ole say hi of course. Love and hugs, the future reincarnation of Merlin the Magician, Madrona Warden."

Team Effort

by Ed Gorman

After a while I quit knocking on the bedroom door and said to myself, all right if you want to cry go on and cry and get it out of your goddamm system.

Then I went out on the back porch where there was a cold beer waiting for me.

They both looked up when I opened the screen door and stood on the porch and stretched my back and watched a monarch butterfly light on a dandelion. It was late afternoon, when sunlight is rich and dusty and melancholy, and when you hear the first mother on the block start calling her kids in for dinner.

Say what you want, and there are some legitimate complaints about this time mode, this isn't a bad century at all, at least not when you've been with the Force as long as I have and have seen many time modes that are a lot worse.

John had one of those white Styrofoam coolers. Buried in the silver ice were golden cans of beer, like fish swimming below the waterline. I reached in. The cold felt clean and good on such a hot day.

"She still crying?" John asked.

I nodded. "Ever since I told her about the problems we were having with the translator."

Tuck shrugged. "Hell, Robin, lots of expeditions have trouble with their translators. They go on the blink and you tinker around with them and then you get them working right, and in no time at all you're back in your own time mode."

I went and stood on the edge of the porch. This was a nice working-class neighborhood, filled with nice hard-working people who needed help every once in a while with insensitive bosses, mercenary bankers, and drug dealers bent on ruining the tranquility of this pleasant little neighborhood.

That's where the Force comes in—endless groups of Robin and his Merry Band working in endless time modes. While there are thousands of Robins and tens of thousands of his Band members, there are never enough to handle all the work all the millions of time modes require.

We can't do anything that would change history in any significant way, but we can make life easier for common people of good heart. A little at a time. That's sort of our unspoken code.

Which is what Marian was trying to do the other night when she climbed up the utility pole to bring down the five-year-old girl who'd scrambled up there to get her tiny adventurous kitten.

Marian got the girl all right—and the cat as well—and was starting to bring her down when the girl jumped from her arms to grab at the kitten who'd gotten loose again and—

John and Tuck and I worked on the girl for twenty minutes but we couldn't bring her back. Marian stood in the shadow of an old garage that smelled of freshly cut grass and car oil and cried her eyes out.

She held herself responsible, of course, which is sort of an occupational hazard in our line of work.

Then, knowing we could do nothing more for the little girl, we took off running. The Force doesn't want anybody in a given time mode to know who and what we are unless it's absolutely necessary.

For the past two days, we'd mostly holed up in the house. John and Tuck are always interested in the popular culture of the mode we work in, so they contented themselves with television.

I spent most of my time lying in on the double bed with Marian, trying to persuade her that she had nothing to feel guilty about.

I kept telling her that by today we'd be standing in our respective slots in the translator and soon be back in our own time mode where the psychs could give her a purge and make her feel happy again.

Then Tuck set off early this morning to the woods where the translator was stored. He came back much earlier than we expected and announced that the machine wasn't functioning properly, and that it would take awhile for him to figure out what was wrong.

Days, he said.

Marian, just out of the shower, overheard our conversation and fell to sobbing immediately.

She'd been counting on a purge to get her out of her agony.

Now it was going to be awhile.

"She's a nice kid," John said. "I feel sorry for her."

"So do I," I said. "She just lies in there torturing herself. Replaying the incident with the little girl over and over. And always coming to the same conclusion—that she should have held on to the girl much tighter."

Tuck stood up. "Hell, now I'm starting to feel guilty."

"About what?" John asked.

"She's in there torturing herself like you say, and I'm out here enjoying a beer," Tuck said. "I should be in the woods working on the translator."

He stood up, his belly fleshy beneath the colorful Hawaiian shirt he'd come to love. "And that's just where I'm going."

With that, he drained his beer, dropped the empty in the paper sack we kept on the porch for just that reason, waved a goodbye, then walked back to the garage where we kept the car.

"He's a hell of a nice guy," John said. "We're lucky he's on the team."

"We sure are," I agreed.

Then I realized that I was starting to feel guilty myself.

"Think I'll go back in and see how Marian's doing, John," I said.

"Tell her we'll be out of here real soon," John said.

I nodded and went inside. Behind the bedroom door, I could still hear her crying softly. The poor kid.

Vivian

by Midori Snyder

"Give me my bent bow in my hand,
And a broad arrow I'll let flee.
And where this arrow is taken up,
There shall my grave digge'd be."

From the "Song of Robin Hood"

In the early dawn Robin stalked the woods, a small
cloud of steam forming in the cold air as he exhaled.
He heard the quiet crack of a branch, the rustle of
dry leaves and he stopped, his body tense. Slowly he
looked around, searching for the origin of the noise.
A doe edged into his sight, her dun flanks thinned
from the long winter, but her belly rounded with preg-
nancy. She browsed hungrily on a low shrub, her long
neck stretching out as teeth tugged loose the frail
spring buds nestled between the dried leaves.

Robin gritted his teeth and raised the longbow. He
nocked his arrow, the grey goose fletch drawn back
beside his ear. His gaze followed the curve of the
animal's chest, imagining the shaft penetrating to the
heart. The doe snorted as a breeze stirred the branches
of the tree above and water droplets sprinkled her
head. She shook, startled, and then caught Robin's
scent. The two knuckles that held the bowstring back
dug deeper into Robin's cheek as he willed himself to
remain steady. The doe withdrew behind the bush,
seeking cover. Robin stepped forward to keep his target in view. Beneath his foot a twig snapped a loud

warning in the wood. Within a heartbeat the doe leapt from her hiding place and fled.

Cursing, Robin swerved his body, trying to track the rump of the fleeing doe as he let loose his arrow. The hopeful twang was silenced abruptly as the arrow thudded harmlessly into a tree.

Robin hung his head and groaned. Sweat chilled his temples, darkening the curly hair. Damn the greenwood! He swore in frustrated rage. It had turned against him, willing that he should starve from lack of game and freeze with the cold damp of a harsh winter. He looked up angrily and dark eyes, deepset from hunger, stared out at the black and grey trunks of the wintery trees. The leather-brown leaves of the oaks shivered dryly in response.

He had been a fair shot once. Life in the greenwood the last two years had been good, or at least possible. With twenty men he had formed a band of free-foresters, claiming no allegiance to the King's command, or the Sheriff's taxes. They had survived on their skill with the bow, their bravery in the contests against the Sheriff's men, and the goodwill of the people they protected from the worst of the Sheriff's abuses. But the winter had proved hard. Game eluded them, arrows that seemed so sure of their targets suddenly careened wildly as if batted by unseen hands. Wood refused to burn and their camps were cold, wet affairs. Robin pulled his cloak tighter around his shoulders, feeling the winter's damp penetrate beneath the worn wool.

Among the cottages they found a guarded welcome. Grain was scarce, and for people who worked hard on the land it was hard to part with the little they owned to the outlaws that haunted the greenwood. Robin scowled, thinking how in their hunger the cottagers forgot the small gifts of money or the haunch of venison that had appeared at other times from those same outlaws.

Robin retrieved his arrow and began walking again, moving angrily through the woods. He climbed the brow of a small hill where the trees of the greenwood gave way to the fields. At the edge of the forest, he stared down across the fields of Lincolnshire, seeing in the distance smoke rising in a thin grey curl from a cottage chimney. The long road that scarred the landscape was empty. Of late, even the rich had found no reason to pass through the greenwood. Robin and his men had not been able to take even the coin that would have bought them food and shelter for the winter.

Robin's stomach grumbled. He scratched his cheek, feeling how thin the winter had made it. His men were growing discontented. The lack of meat, the lack of a warm fire, had scattered companionship. Petty quarrels broke out frequently, his men choosing to fight each other rather than succumb to desperation. That morning he and Little John had crossed words, and only Friar Tuck coming between them had stayed their fists. Robin had left the camp, determined that he would not return without fresh game.

He sighed, the squared shoulders hunched with cold. The muscles of his thighs trembled, having grown weary from the long morning search for game. The sword at his side felt heavy and useless. "Spring," he whispered, thinking of the rounded belly of the doe. Daily they watched for signs of its coming, bringing with it the promise of warmth and the living green. "Spring," he repeated more loudly, his cold breath clouding around his head.

His eyes followed the rounded hills as the sun lifted from the edge of the horizon. Gold rays slanted across the fields, brightening the dull pewter land to a burnished copper. Robin stepped forward, away from the shelter of the trees, to touch the advancing light. The bright rays of the sun reached him, climbing up his legs, his torso, and his chest. Warmth spread across him, and the light of the sun blinded him as it caressed his face.

Bathed in the brilliant light, Robin's plea was answered. In the muffled damp air, Robin heard the soft trickle of water melting; the quiet sigh of snow settling into the muddy earth. Birdsong sounded from the trees and a gentle moist wind shook the remnants of last year's leaves. Robin opened his eyes and turned to face the greenwood.

For the first time in many months, Robin smiled, his dry lips cracking.

The dull bark of trees shimmered with wetness in the dawn's light. Mist gathered between the black branches and formed a veil of the palest green. When still a boy at Lockesley, his mother had called it the "greenmist." It was the slow waking breath of the greenwood's spirit world, rousing themselves after the winter. The creature Tidy Munn would soon be churning the water of the streams and the fens, driving it over the fields to melt the remaining snow. The Greencoaties, small beings well hidden in the greenwood, would begin unwrapping the brown leaves of their wintery beds. And the tall stately Oakmen would step forth from the trunks of their ancient trees to hunt in the spring morning.

A child's story perhaps, but standing here at the ragged end of a Lincolnshire winter, watching the greenwood misting to life with the breath of spring, Robin could almost believe in its magic. He shook himself, the warm sun on his back freeing the cramped muscles of his shoulders. All would be well, he told himself.

With a sudden resolve he plunged into the woods again to hunt for game. He walked firmly, eagerness driving his step, the longbow slung tightly over one shoulder, the quiver of arrows bouncing lightly across his back. He passed a fallen oak, the leathered leaves of its branches reaching skyward. Robin stopped, seeing the chips of wood that lay scattered about the base of the huge tree. Someone had chopped it down and then left without claiming the wood. New shoots had sprung from the old stump as the oak refused to die. Robin kicked the trunk questioningly. The wood was still hard, dried out from the cold winter air.

Robin rejoiced, for once split, the wood would burn quick and hot, unlike the wood they had saved which had gone soggy and produced sputtering fires that gave off more smoke than warmth.

He'd no axe about him to chop the wood then, but decided to mark a trail that would lead him back to this site later in the day when he had finished his hunting. For now, he decided he would give himself the gift of a fine staff that he could set in a friendly challenge against Little John. He reached up and pulled at a straight branch, one foot braced against the trunk of the fallen tree. He heard the wood groan and then snap as the branch tore away from the flesh of the trunk.

"And what manner of man are you who robs from me?" spoke an angry voice.

Startled, Robin wheeled around, drawing his sword. The torn branch he kept in his other fist like a ready club.

Standing near the base of a tree was a tall man, his face filled with hatred. He wore a cloak of green, the high collar framing a narrow face of deep brown. Broad shoulders arrowed down into a neat waist, and around his waist Robin saw a well-tempered blade that stretched down along the length of a heavily muscled thigh. A huge hand with long, gnarled fingers wrapped around the hilt.

Robin's eyes darted through the bush, wondering how the man came to be here with no sound, no warning of his advance. Behind the man waited a horse, the silver bridle ornate with carved acorns about the cheek strap and the reins hung with the likeness of rusted oak leaves. The horse stood silent as if waiting the word of its master.

"I asked you a question," the man spoke coldly. "Who are you that you would dare rob from me?"

"Rob from you?" Robin answered more boldly than he felt. "You are not the King's forester. And even if you were, it would make no difference to me. I take what I please from the greenwood."

The horse neighed shrilly as the man in the green cloak lunged towards Robin. Robin raised his sword, anticipating the clash of weapons. But the man stopped and drew himself up solemnly. Mist steamed from the man's shoulders with the heat of his anger. Robin stared back uneasily at the green eyes that flashed in the morning light.

"There is no mortal man that owns the greenwood. Neither king nor commoner has claims to these woods. What you take, you steal."

Robin gave a harsh laugh. "If you think to shame me with such words you are mistaken. You are not from here or you would know that I am Robin Hood. I am a lord of thievery. I steal from the King, from the Sheriff, and even you, strange lord, for I can see now by the fat purse hanging from your belt that you have not yet paid to Robin Hood his due." Robin gripped his sword more firmly. He had lost the doe this morning by being over-cautious and waiting too long. He would not lose this second chance for profit.

The man in the green cloak smiled coldly. "My purse is a small bounty for a lord of thieves," he answered. "If you would agree, I would make a contest for a more worthy prize."

"And what prize is that?" Robin asked, curious but wary. In the trees above a flock of crows had settled on the branches. They stopped their preening to stare at him with interest, cocking their heads to one side as they glimpsed him through their black-beaded eyes.

"I would give that which I prize most from my estate. A treasure that has no greater value." He took the fat purse and emptied its contents on the ground. Robin held his breath as from the purse gold coins and three emeralds tumbled to the forest floor. "These are nothing compared to that which I offer from my estate at Kirkley Hall."

Robin knew the name of the estate. It was an old stone house deep in the heart of the greenwood. He had not known that a lord lived there, for the look of it was a tumbled ruin. Still, his eyes could not deny the wealth that now lay scattered carelessly on the wet leaves.

"And how can I be certain of such a contest?"

The man laughed coldly again and he withdrew from his cloak a small gold horn. He blew three sharp blasts. The crows lifted noisily from the branches in alarm, their wings flapping frantically.

Robin stared up at their harsh cawing and their wild flight. As he lowered his gaze again to the man, he gasped. Sitting astride chestnut stallions, two men waited. Like the man, they were dressed in cloaks of green, even their trousers were of green wool. Their faces were rugged, their features resembling roughly hewn wood. The horses were still, and only the steam rising from their flanks suggested they were creatures of flesh. Where had they come from? How had they answered the horn so quickly? Robin's mind crackled with questions and a warning bell clanged in his thoughts.

"I will make these two witness to this contest. And if you win, they are charged with giving you my treasure," the man was saying.

"And if I lose?" Robin asked. "What do I forfeit?"

"If you lose, you must ride the hunt with me as my servant man."

"Is that all?"

The man shook his head. "No. I must know first before we seal the bargain whether you have honor. For a man without honor has blood that runs thinner than water and carries no power to the hunt."

Robin's face flushed angrily. "I may be a thief, but even thieves have honor. I do not steal from the poor, only take from the rich. And I will not permit any woman who travels in the greenwood to be harmed or molested."

"It is enough," replied the man, and with a sudden movement freed his sword from his belt. He slashed the blade upward towards Robin's head, the sword leaving a trail of silvery light.

Robin grunted in surprise and stumbled back, avoiding the rising sword. He lifted his own weapon to meet the attack and the two blades clashed with a grinding screech. Sparks ignited from the swords-point.

Robin scrambled back another step, seeking an even footing. Roots from the fallen oak snaked unexpectedly from the ground and he stumbled again as the man's sword drove him down. Crouching, Robin tried to face his attacker. The man's sword landed a heavy blow on Robin's weapon. Robin screamed as he felt his shoulder wrenched with the force of the blow, his sword arm shoved from the socket with an explosion of pain. Stars lit up in Robin's eyes and he heard the roaring of blood in his ears. He collapsed on the ground and rolled, sensing the fierce rush of air as the man's sword chased him. Robin still gripped his sword, but his injured arm refused to lift the weapon. Robin saw through eyes dazed with fear the bright arc of the sword above him once more. He rolled, instinct rather than courage pushing him away from certain death. The sword came down and the tip sliced neatly through his side. Pain bloomed again in his body, and he cried out as his shirt grew wet with blood.

Through the wild pounding of his own heart, Robin heard the man's triumphant laugh and saw the silvery flash of his sword. Without hope, Robin raised the staff of oak he still clutched in his left hand. The hard wood took the edge of the man's sword. Robin's body shook violently as the oaken staff split, splinters raking his face.

And at once the man's laughter turned to howls. Numbed with pain, Robin gazed up and saw the man stagger backward, the sword dangling from one hand, his face hidden in the crook of his other arm. Robin dropped the shattered staff, and using both hands, raised his sword from the ground. His shoulder throbbed but he ignored it as he forced his sword upright. Only one chance.

Already the man had lowered his arm, tightening his grip anew on his sword. Robin saw the green flash of rage in the man's eyes as he turned once more to Robin's prostrate figure.

Robin heaved his body upward, thrusting the point of his sword into the man's chest. The man shouted with outrage, his arms flailing the air. But he could not stop his body from falling onto Robin's sword.

Robin held the sword steady, feeling the strangeness of the man dying on his blade. The sword drove deep, not finding home, nor the soft parting of muscled flesh, but something different. It cleaved through the man's chest like an ax separating layers of wood, splitting apart the grainy fibers. There was no blood, but a greenmist that boiled in the air around him. Robin gagged as the mist clung to his face, burning cold and wet. It was rank with the odor of rotten wood, of mould and decaying bone. His mind reeled with images of a grave, newly opened in the earth, and himself cast into its depths. He reached out a hand, scrabbling at the dead leaves of the forest floor. He choked in terror as the gold morning light dimmed and a darkness as thick as spring mud was cast over him.

"Robin?" a soft voice called.

Robin stirred, feeling a small hand gently shake his shoulder. He smiled, thinking of Marion. He could see the curve of her cheek, the tilt of her chin when she teased him. Then Robin frowned, knowing that there was something else to be remembered. Something ominous. Dangerous.

Robin's eyes snapped open with panic. He gasped at the air and tried to raise himself up from the ground.

"Stay," the voice urged. "Stay yourself and be at peace." Two small hands rested on his chest, gently pushing him down again.

Robin stared up into a woman's face, her smile sad but kind. Her skin was a pale gold, and he blinked thinking it the light of the morning sun he saw reflected there. But as he lay back, he saw her arms, naked to the shoulders, the same golden color. He stared again at her face and with a start recognized the bright green gaze of her eyes.

He inhaled, releasing the air slowly as he looked around him. He spied first the grey, lichen-covered stones of Kirkley Hall. He was not inside the Hall, but rather lying on a pallet outside the courtyard. He was covered with dark green blankets and he grew gradually aware that his body was dry and warm. Cautiously he pulled aside the blankets and looked at himself.

His brown cloak and white shirt were gone. In their place he had been dressed in the same green wool as the man who had attacked him in the forest. Robin raised himself on his elbow, astonished to discover that his sword arm was healed and that his side no longer bled. He started to lift the shirt when the woman stopped him, urging him to lie down again.

"You are well enough," she said, covering him with the blankets.

"Who are you?" Robin asked.

"You may call me Vivian."

"Do you know what has happened to me? How I came to be here?" Robin asked. He stared in confusion at Vivian. She wore a simple shift of pale green linen but no cloak. Her arms were bare, and yet she seemed not in the least bit bothered by the cold morning air. She moved slowly, as if awakened too early from sleep. Her tousled brown hair had rust-colored streaks and hung around her shoulders in a knotted tangle.

"I know that my father's men brought you here. I know that I am to serve you."

"I fought a man dressed in green in the forest," Robin said trying to remember clearly. "We held a contest. If I won, I was to gain the most valued treasure of his estate, here at Kirkley Hall."

"Is that what he called me?" Vivian said sharply. "His treasure that he bargained away for the hunt.

Arrogant fool." She began to cry, tears flowing down her gold-colored cheeks.

Robin lifted his hand to her, and wiped away the tears. "Stop now. I would ask nothing of you. I've no need of a servant." As he brought his hand back to his chest, he caught the woody scent of tree sap and realized it came from the dampness of her tears on his hand.

"I have no choice, Robin. My father's words have bound me, just as surely as he meant to bind you to him for the hunt had he won instead."

"I am no man's servant," Robin retorted sharply.

"My father was not a man," Vivian said and stood. "He would have used you as all Oakmen use mortals. Blood is important to a good hunt. You would have run for him, like a fox before the hounds."

Beneath the warm green blankets, Robin shivered, hearing the truth spoken in her words, seeing again the hatred in the Oakman's eyes.

He stood weakly and Vivian held his arm until he gained a steady stance. She took one blanket from the ground and wrapped it around his shoulders like a cloak. She took a second blanket for herself.

"Wrapped in the greencloth, you will never be seen either by your enemies, or by the game you seek. Come let us go into the forest and I will show you the deer."

Vivian hoisted his longbow on her shoulder and carried the quiver of arrows at her side. Robin followed, his steps uncertain at first and then growing more confident as he felt the blood flow in his cheeks and his heart beat strongly.

It was still morning when they entered the forest again, and Robin marveled that in so short a time the greenmist had flowed through the woods and brought them to life. The branches of trees were still black and leafless, but the air smelled sweet and pungent with new growth. Snow gave way to the mud and Vivian pointed out to him the bright orange blooms of the lichen set like goblets to catch the spring mist.

Mosses along the trunks of trees turned dark green, and yellowed fruiting stems bowed their heads with beads of dew. The sun slanted through the trees, chasing away the cold breath of winter.

They had not gone far into the woods when Vivian stopped him with a hand just touching his shoulder. She nodded toward a break in the trees. A young stag, his horns still a winter red, entered the clearing. Vivian handed Robin his longbow and arrows.

Robin smiled broadly, excitement threading his pulse as he nocked the arrow. He wouldn't miss this time. He pulled the bowstring back and let loose the arrow. It wobbled slightly in its flight and Robin held his breath fearing failure. And then it landed unerringly in the stag's chest.

The stag reared back his hooves in angry surprise. The tines of his horns crashed against the low lying branches and his bellows filled the forest. He tried to run, but Robin shot a second arrow that landed close to the first. The stag leapt into the air and then landed heavily, the long slender legs collapsing beneath the huge body.

Robin cheered, raising the longbow high into the air. There would be game for the fire. And there would be dry wood with which to cook it, he thought, remembering the fallen tree where he had met the Oakman. He turned to thank Vivian and then stopped, seeing the stricken expression on her face.

She lowered her eyes and he saw the beads of sweat on her upper lip. "Forgive me," she said softly, and Robin thought she meant it for him.

He smiled understandingly at her and clasped her by the shoulder. "The hunt is hard to see the first time. It gets easier." Beneath his hand she trembled.

"The problem now is how to get the stag back to camp quickly," he mused aloud. "I'll dress it here, but there are others in these woods as hungry as my men. I don't want to lose the meat to the scavengers."

Vivian untied a small gold horn from her waist and

handed it to Robin. He recognized it as the horn her father had used to call his men. "Use this whenever you need the assistance of your men. They will answer it, if they can hear it."

Robin took the horn and placed it to his lips. He blew into it, hearing the long shrill notes of the horn soar above the forest. He stopped and was aware of the silence. He blew again and this time when he stopped he heard voices calling to him from the greenwood.

"Robin? Is that you?" cried a loud voice.

Robin smiled widely. "Little John, over here!"

"I told you it would be him," said another voice triumphantly, and Robin recognized Will Stutely.

"It was *I* told you," grumbled a third voice, a little out of breath. Robin searched the trees and saw the black habit of Friar Tuck, his belly breaking first through the bushes.

"In God's name, will you look at the stag!" Little John shouted rushing to examine the fallen beast. He looked around, puzzlement on his broad face.

"Robin?" he called. "Are you still here?"

"Aye, I'm here," Robin laughed. "Can you not see me standing next to you?"

Little John jumped at the sound of Robin's voice so close to him in the woods. Robin let slip the cloak and moved closer to stand by the stag.

"I would never have seen you had you not shown yourself," Little John said, smiling with amazement. "You've a new game afoot, Robin. To wear such a green in the wood. We will all disappear."

"That's why he remains the leader of our band," answered Will with pride.

"Wait, there is more," Robin started to say, turning to look for Vivian. But she was gone. Robin frowned, searching the trees for a sight of her.

"Well, then?" Little John said, already bending over the stag with his knife. He had opened its belly and begun the job of gutting it. Steam rose from the stag's belly as the viscera, glistening like wet jewels, spilled out onto the leaves.

"Don't hold back good fortune, man," encouraged Will, helping Little John to turn the stag's body.

Robin hesitated. For an unknown reason he changed his mind about telling them of Vivian. He looked down at his belt and saw the pouch of money that had once belonged to the Oakman. Seizing it, he lifted it up to show them. "I've money here which I took in taxes off a man not used to paying them," he said with a grin.

"Is that where you got the horn, too?" asked Friar Tuck.

"Indeed. I'll use it from now on to call you, whether for trouble or good news."

Friar Tuck approached Robin. The normally round face had become slack over the unforgiving winter. The skin of his shaven pate was spattered with freckles. He gazed at Robin worriedly and one hand grasped him firmly around the wrist. "The green of your cloak, Robin, concerns me," he said in a low voice.

"It is a good practice in the woods," Robin answered defensively. "Here, take this money and go into Barnsdale. There purchase bolts of Lincoln green wool. We shall all wear it. The better to fox the Sheriff's men."

"There is something in this that is not right, Robin," the Friar whispered. "Tell me so that your soul will not be in danger. For I feel it in my bones that there is something wrong in this."

Robin gave a short, barking laugh. "What you feel, my good Tuck, is your own hunger. I have done nothing wrong," Robin answered with a smile. "I have taken wealth from a man in a fair contest."

"A man dressed in green?" Friar Tuck asked.

Robin's smile remained but he refused to say more.

"Come on, good friar," Little John yelled, "let us see how well you can cook this. It will be a feast in which to welcome the spring!"

Friar Tuck turned away from Robin to help Little
John and Will to bind the stag's hooves to a long staff.
They hoisted it on their shoulders and carried it away
to camp. Behind them Robin fingered the horn and
looked once more for signs of Vivian. Finding none,
he followed his men to camp.

Throughout the spring and into the long summer
Robin and his men found a new life in the greenwood.
The game that had once eluded them now scampered
before their waiting arrows. Friar Tuck had claimed
to Robin that he had never in all his years of hunting
the greenwood found so many wild morels and straw-
berries. The elderberry trees were thick with wide
heads of white blossoms and the good friar watched
them daily, waiting for the heads to turn and become
studded with the small purple berries.

Robin's spirits soared in the greenwood. The sunlight shone only for him, he thought, drowsing in a
shady thicket with the soft buzzing of summer bees.
He glanced up sleepily at the trees, their canopy of
green leaves sheltering him. His face had filled out
during the prosperous summer. His cheeks were
squared and strong, his eyes twinkling with good
humor. He had closed his eyes to sleep again when a
blade of grass tickled his nose.

He woke with a snort and found Vivian sitting
beside him. He smiled at her, surprised as always by
her strange beauty. The summer sun had lightened the
crown of her hair from rust to light brown. Her eyes
were a soft green and her skin the color of honey.

"Is it well with you, Robin?" she asked.

"Aye, very well, Vivian," he answered.

"They say the Sheriff of Nottingham rides the
greenwood today, near the road to Kirkley Hall. I
would bid you have a care."

Robin grinned and sat up. "More than a care, I
think. Perhaps a bit of sport."

And before long, Robin with the sounding of his
horn, had assembled his band together. He had grown

accustomed to Vivian's unexpected visits, and equally
sudden disappearances. But acting on her advice, he
led his men through the woods to Kirkley Hall. It was
as she said. Robin saw the gloomy visage of the Sheriff
of Nottingham, riding through the greenwood, his foresters dressed in bright livery beside him. Robin
laughed quietly to note how close they passed him by
without seeing him, despite the searching looks of the
foresters.

That night Robin and his men feasted the Sheriff of
Nottingham, after first depriving his foresters of their
lives and then the Sheriff of his purse. They fed him
a meal of venison from the King's own deer, and to
add insult to the injury, they served him on the silver
plates that had been stolen from him earlier. At the
next daylight, they tied the Sheriff's hands and legs
and hoisted him over the back of a horse. A farmer,
making his way to Nottingham market, found the
Sheriff cursing Robin's name as he lay face-down tied
to his horse, while the lazy creature cropped the grass
growing by the side of the road. Before the end of
market day, the word had scattered from one mouth
to another of Robin's daring attack on the Sheriff of
Nottingham. And from that night on, in many cottages, the outlaws found a renewed welcome.

The winter came, but still the game followed the
camp. The green Lincoln wool of their cloaks kept
Robin and his men dry, and in the worst of weather,
there were many inns willing to hide them for a night
or two. Robin often looked for Vivian in the woods
when he rambled alone. Sometimes she appeared,
wearing a green dress bordered with the seed down
of milkweeds, and other times she wore a cape of
snow-white wool, owl feathers stitched about the hem.
She stayed with him briefly, telling him news of the
greenwood that would be of use to him and his men.
She showed him where different animals wintered
over, their dens covered by mounded snow. And even
when she wasn't there, Robin always felt her presence
in the snapping of twigs underfoot, or the tired creak

of the oaks, and he knew that had he need of her, she would be there.

When the spring came again, Vivian met him in the woods. She had gathered wild garlic in her apron and gave it to him.

"They say the Sheriff of Nottingham intends to have an archery contest," she told him. "The prize is a golden arrow."

Robin grinned at her. "Then I mean to go and win that arrow."

"I thought you might." She reached into the pocket of her apron and withdrew a small pot of brown cream. "It will stain your skin and give you a good disguise."

Robin laughed and snatching up the pot, tossed it lightly into the air. "I shall go as a poor wanderer. And I shall win beneath the very noses of the Sheriff and his men."

"You will succeed Robin, as always," Vivian said quietly.

Despite the warnings of his men, Robin went to the archery contest. He had it in his mind to win the golden arrow and give it to Vivian. He smiled to himself, standing unrecognized amid the Sheriff's men. Only one other contestant had given him cause to worry. A man with a patch over one eye whose shooting was confident and straight-arrowed. Robin's palms sweat with anticipation. He would have to be better than the stranger.

His eyes glanced up at the stand where the Sheriff and his daughter awaited the outcome of the contest. Robin froze suddenly, recognizing the woman sitting farther back from the Sheriff's daughter. It was Marion, returned at long last from France. Robin's heart soared with delight to see her, her face changed from a coltish girl into an elegant young woman. But there was a still a lively spark of mischief in her, for he saw now in the blue eyes that stared back at him, that she alone had penetrated his disguise. He tipped his hat to her as he took his place in line. She nodded back and then looked away, but not before he had seen the smile that played around her lips.

Robin raised his longbow for the final match. The stranger had shot well. Very well, and for a moment Robin doubted the worth of his own skill to beat the man. There was a fitful breeze. It fluttered the flags of the tents and worried the fletch of his arrow. It would be hard to shoot straight in such a wind. Robin tried to slow the rapid beating of his heart and take careful aim. The target seemed so vague and distant.

In the corner of his eye he glimpsed a face peering at him from the crowds that eagerly lined the edges of the contest grounds. Rust-colored hair billowed in the breeze around a face with honey-colored skin. At once the wind calmed. The target that had seemed so distant became sharp and clear in Robin's mind. He released his arrow and watched it soar, upward first, and then glide down unerringly to split the shaft of his opponent's arrow as the head buried itself in the center of the target.

The roar of the crowd's approval was not half as loud as Robin's own joy.

He looked again to the crowd, but the face he sought was not there.

Later, after his return and the celebration that followed in the camp, Robin walked out by himself through the greenwood. The moon shone brilliantly above the trees, the silvery light dappling the bushes. He walked to Kirkley Hall and in the bright moonlight the stones of the old manor gleamed.

"Well met, Robin," said Vivian, stepping from the shadows of the trees to meet him. "And did you win today?"

"Aye," he answered. "I did." And then he bowed his head sheepishly. "I had meant to bring you the golden arrow as a gift. But in the heat of my victory, I forgot and gave it to another."

Vivian laughed and Robin stared astonished for he had never heard her laugh before. It was a bittersweet sound, without joy. "It were better given to Marion,

Robin. I have no need for golden arrows." As she
approached him, Robin saw an expression of longing
on her face. "I have served you faithfully for a year,
Robin. There is no one in the greenwood who does
not speak well of you. You are a man others will
follow, will love. You no longer need me."

Robin frowned at her words. They made him uncomfortable.

"I would ask one boon of you, Robin."

"Name it."

"It takes courage."

"I am Robin Hood," he answered as if that were
enough.

"I wish to be released from my service to you. I
wish to return to my own life," she said.

"You have always been free to go, Vivian."

"To release me, you must kill me," Vivian said. She
stepped back from him, her arms opened wide.
"Shoot me, Robin, that I may be returned to my life."

Robin's hands chilled and his heart thudded in his
chest. "I will not," he stammered. "No, Vivian, I will
not. I rob the rich to give to the poor and I am protector of women in the greenwood. I can not go against
my own word and kill you."

"I am not a mortal woman, Robin. I beg of you,
release me."

Robin spun angrily on his heel and began to run.
He didn't want to be convinced into so shameful an
act by the look of pleading on her face. "No," he told
himself as he ran, "I will not kill you." Over and over
he reminded himself of his own vows as he tore
through the woods, the branches snapping and cracking underfoot with his fierce stride. But beneath the
firm resolve Robin felt the scratch of doubt. It fes-
tered in his heart like a thorn unwilling to be pulled
free. Until then, he not questioned his good fortune.
Now he asked himself, how much of his skill did he
owe to Vivian? How much of his name, of his success
was her doing? Robin hacked at a bush with his
sword, seeing again the glimpse of her face at the

archery contest. And he knew he battled the rising
fear that in losing Vivian, he might lose his own
future.

"No!" he shouted aloud. "I am my own man. No
servant to any. I will not kill Vivian because on my
word as a man, as Robin Hood, I will not harm any
woman."

As he neared the camp, he heard Allan-a-Dale singing. The smooth tenor voice eased away the sting of
Robin's doubt. Allan-a-Dale was singing of Robin's
victory at the archery contest. And when he entered
the camp again, Robin smiled at the shouts of praise
that greeted him. He belonged here. However it had
happened, he had made a name for himself and nothing would change that.

The years followed and so did Robin's fame,
spreading wide from Nottingham and Barnsdale,
throughout the county of Lincolnshire and to the King
himself. There was no act too daring, or too dangerous, for Robin and his men. They had made a great
sport of the Sheriff of Nottingham, frustrating his
every attempt to bring them to the gallows. And
always, without fail, Robin's arrows with the grey
goose fletch found their mark in the Sheriff's men.

Robin walked the greenwood as if it were his own
estate, the deer his deer and the purses of the wealthy
his own private tax. There was only one change in
him, hardly discernible by the closest of his own men.
He almost never walked the woods alone. Once it had
been his pleasure, but now he avoided it. For it was
in those private moments that Vivian would come to
him. Every time he saw her, she would beg again for
her release.

"Kill me, Robin, that I may return to my life."

"Kill yourself," he replied once cruelly, enraged by
her persistence.

Her face stilled to a wooden mask, her eyes dulled
like stone. "I cannot. My father bound me to you.

Only you can release me. I will stand here before you. It will take no skill of the bow to free me."

"Damn you!" Robin cursed, turning his back to her.

"You already have," she answered bitterly.

It was summer when the word was cried through Nottingham's markets that King Henry was dead and his son Richard the Lionhearted was crowned king. And before the summer was over, Richard himself had come to the greenwood, curious to see if the tales of Robin Hood were true.

They met in the greenwood, and after a night of feasting on the King's own deer, Richard was impressed enough in Robin's skill as a leader to award Robin clemency and the return of his noble rank. To the men that had followed Robin loyally, Richard offered the positions of foresters. They accepted, since no other life but one in the forest held any interest for them.

Robin married Marion in a quiet ceremony, ringed by the trees of Kirkley Hall that had since been turned into a small abbey. He kissed her beneath the spreading oaks, and pledged his heart to her. He promised her a life of peace and happiness.

And they were happy, for a while. But the calm, sedate life of a lord bored Robin, and he soon became restless. He missed the challenge of living in the greenwood, the hard ground for his bed and the openness of the night sky. And deep within his heart, there stirred another pain as the thorn pushed deeper, and he knew he missed Vivian as well.

"The life of a lord does not suit you, my love," Marion said to him on his return from seeing the King. He had ridden hard in the rain and his cloak was soaked and mud-spattered.

He smiled at her. "Is it that easy to see?"

She nodded, her hands on her hips, waiting for him to speak.

He placed his hands on her shoulders and gazed into her troubled eyes. "I have spoken to the King. I want to go to Palestine. To see more of the world."

Her eyes sparkled with determination. "Then I will go with you."

Robin clasped her tightly until Marion laughed, gaily protesting his wet cloak and dripping hair.

He left her to make the necessary arrangements and walked out into the night toward the greenwood. Out of habit, he slung his longbow over his shoulder and carried his quiver of arrows. The rain had abated and overhead only a few lingering clouds scudded across the clearing night sky. The half moon shone brightly.

In the shifting play of shadows, Robin saw Vivian, waiting for him in the garden beside a bush of drenched roses. White petals had scattered on the walk around her feet.

"You go to Palestine," she said, her face downturned.

"Aye," he answered.

She looked up at him and in the moonlight, her eyes glowed green. "Robin, if you leave the greenwood I cannot serve you. I cannot protect you as in the past."

He had been prepared to offer some words of kindness to her, perhaps even reconciliation. But the words she spoke now angered him.

"I have no need of your help," he snapped.

"But I have need of yours," she replied evenly. "If you should die without releasing me, I am doomed forever in this form. Forever. As you say, you do not need me anymore. Then kill me that I might go free at last."

"I am Robin Hood," he said, drawing his cloak tighter around his shoulders against the sudden chilly wind that blew between them. More petals scattered in the air like new snow. "I robbed from the rich to give to the poor and I never harmed a woman in the greenwood."

Vivian raised her hands to her face and cried out one long piercing wail. She fled into the woods, her bare arms flickering in the moonlight like the wings of a moth.

Robin stared after her, pride warring with doubt. He clutched his longbow, his gaze following the ghostly white shadow of her form. He could kill her now, if he chose. But he hesitated and she disappeared into the darkened forest. When Marion's voice called out to him, he turned slowly and left the garden to join her.

Five years later Robin returned from Palestine much aged. The world there had been hot, dry, and full of dust. The color of the landscape, a sun-faded brown, mingled with the red blood of the dying. The battles had been too many and without reason. He had done well, though not any better than any other man. He had received a wound in the side that had taken months to heal. And even now he felt it throb with a cold ache. His hands trembled with fever and his mouth was always parched. But worst of all, Marion was dead. The fever that lingered in him had taken her quickly. He had buried her far from the cool green of Lincolnshire in a grave guarded by rocks and cedar trees. There was nothing left of his life that gave him joy.

Robin had returned to the greenwood in order to recover something of the past; a purpose in his life that he could comprehend amidst his grief. But the greenwood had changed in his absence as well. King John held the throne now, and once again Robin found himself out of favor with the King's court.

He had wandered the greenwood alone for two days, until he came to Kirkley Hall. He saw the grey stones of the old manor and something stirred in his heart. Robin nodded over his horse, feeling dizzy and faint. He slipped clumsily from the saddle and sat in the cool grass beneath the trees, his back to an oak.

A sharp pain in his side caused him to glance down. His white shirt was stained with fresh blood. The wound in his side had opened and begun to bleed. Robin tried to drag himself upright. At once, he felt a hand on his arm, pulling him, helping him to stand.

A nun in a brown habit tucked an arm around him, and half-supporting him, helped him into Kirkley

Hall. Robin's heels fairly dragged across the stones as she led him toward a small cell where a single bed faced a window. She laid him down gently on the bed.

Robin sighed with relief, his tired body sinking into the softness of the bed.

"I am bleeding," he said.

The nun straightened up and pulled back the cowl of her habit. Rust-colored hair spilled from the hood and framed her face. Vivian's green eyes were wet with tears.

Robin gasped, startled at seeing her, and reached his hand to touch her cheek. His hand returned to his chest and he smiled at the familiar woody scent on his fingers.

"You have returned," she said.

"Just," he answered with a weak smile. "I have a wound that has begun to bleed. Please help me."

Vivian shook her head. "I cannot. There is nothing more I can do. The years you were gone have weakened my power. The wound you now have is the one my father gave you so long ago by his fallen oak. I can no longer stop its bleeding."

Robin closed his eyes and turned his head toward the wall.

"Robin," Vivian whispered, and he knew what she wanted to say.

He shook his head, bitterness rising in his throat like gall.

"The pain you feel now is the same that I have lived with since our first meeting." She spoke gently and without rancor.

He refused to look at her. Then he felt her stand, heard her bare feet begin to pace the floor.

"How I despise my life. How my limbs burn in this shape, the soles of my feet cut by the rocks. I long for the peace of the earth, for the sleep of winter, for the sweet silence of the new spring. Robin, do not let me remain thus."

Her pleading stabbed at Robin's heart. The thorn of doubt twisted, causing him to cry out. In desperation, he reached for the gold horn at his side and blew three shrill blasts on it.

"No," Vivian sobbed and fled.

Alone in the room Robin stared hopelessly at the ceiling. If any of his men were near, they would come to him. He would not die alone, nor die tormented by Vivian's pleading.

The steady beat of Robin's heart slowed. The sheets were soaked with blood. On the ceiling of the quiet cell Robin thought he saw his life drawn in the faint etchings of its cracks and seams. He followed the patterns, seeing the tiny flecks of green that resembled Vivian at every turn of the lines.

If he had killed her and she was mortal flesh, he would have dishonored his own vow. He would have failed in his own eyes.

The pattern of the ceiling twisted around the line of a tree, its branches tipped with the buds of new leaves. And if he did kill her, and she was not mortal but an Oakman's daughter, a greenfairy, then he must accept that his accomplishments had been a lie. A lie shaped for the eyes of other men by Vivian's hand.

Would that he had died that spring, he thought angrily, suddenly resentful of Vivian. At least he would have died his own man.

No, his mind retaliated, not your own man. But cursed to be the Oakman's servant, just as Vivian was his servant now. And Robin knew, remembering the look of hatred in those green eyes, that had he begged for mercy, pleaded for release from bondage, the Oakman would have served Robin no better than he now served Vivian.

Robin was overcome with anguish, terrified to look into his heart and pluck out the thorn of doubt. Without the illusion of his deeds, what was he?

"God's mercy, it is Robin!" boomed a voice from the door of his cell.

Robin turned his head slowly and saw Little John.

"I heard the horn. I knew it was you!" he cried and rushed to Robin's side. "But you are wounded!"

"I am dying," Robin answered softly.

"No," Little John groaned and lifted Robin from the bed by the shoulders. He wept, big tears streaming down the sides of his face into his beard.

Robin stared at him, and an easiness settled over the wound in his heart. Love and loyalty. However false his deeds may have been, he had found truth in his companions. He had loved them without duplicity, and in that, he had gained strength.

"Give me my bow and an arrow," Robin said weakly.

Little John propped Robin up in the bed, and held the bow up for him.

Robin stared out the window and saw Vivian standing amid the trees. She was facing him, smiling, her arms opened wide to receive the arrow. His hand shook but he willed it steady. Sweat trickled down the side of his face. This shot must be his own; its aim true.

"Where the arrow lands," he said to Little John, "bury me."

Robin let loose the arrow, hearing its hard twang echo in his ear. The shaft buried itself cleanly in the center Vivian's chest.

As her arms flung skyward, she changed. The nun's habit spiraled around her legs, darkening into the rough hue of bark. Her arms sprouted branches and then leaves. Her head of tousled hair rounded into a burl at the base of two lifting branches. Before Robin was lain back on the bed again, he had seen his arrow fall harmlessly from its target to rest at the base of a young sapling oak.

His breathing was shallow, death brushing the dust of his final thoughts. He closed his eyes wearily. He was aware of Little John holding him, but his mind turned elsewhere. He imagined Vivian, her long roots deep in the earth tangled around his skeleton, clinging protectively to his bones. His eyes snapped open in surprise as he smelled the sweet fragrance of fresh sap in the air. Then he smiled, and closing his eyes once more, relinquished himself to the mercy of the greenwood.

Legends Never Die

by Barbara Delaplace

"Going somewhere, Robby?"

The elaborately casual tone didn't deceive Robby for a moment, and he carefully eyed the tallest of the three boys standing in front of him.

"What do you want?"

He tried to make his voice sound firm, but it wasn't working. Jack and his camp followers, Chris and Tom, had tormented him too many times.

"Nothing, Robby," Jack answered with elaborate innocence. "Just wondering what you have in the basket there, that's all."

"I went to the market." Maybe if he kept his answers short, it would help.

"Oh? And what did you buy?"

"Uh . . . some bread and cheese and eggs." No, he wasn't doing a good job at all keeping his voice steady. He wondered if he could dodge around them and make a dash down the alley. For what seemed like the thousandth time he wished fervently that he was taller and stronger.

"You do that a lot for your mother, don't you? I'll bet you're good at it, too."

He couldn't dodge around them. Chris and Tom had ranged themselves behind their leader, anticipating his strategy. And there was no one else around, worse luck. Jack was very good at choosing the right moment to make his move.

"Let's have a look in the basket and see how good a housewife you are, Robby." The other boys snickered. Robby didn't mind the taunts as much as he did

86

the thought that he was likely to lose the few days'
food he could afford to purchase. With his father away
laboring on the estate of their Norman lord and
money scarcer than usual, food was precious. He
tensed as Jack's hand reached for the wicker handle.

He suddenly realized Chris and Tom were watching
the basket, too, crowding closer to see the contents—
and that gave him his chance. He jerked the handle
away and ducked around them. Then he was running
down the alley with all the speed his twelve-year-old
body could muster.

"Come back, you little rabbit!"

He reached the end of the lane and lunged across
the open grass towards the forest. If he could only
reach the trees before his pursuers . . . Nobody knew
this part of the greenwood better than he did. He tried
to make his legs move faster, his hand gripping the
basket tight, his lungs screaming for more air. Another
few yards. Were they still behind him? He couldn't
hear. The sounds of his own running were too loud.

Just a few more feet—and suddenly he was
through the thick brush screening the forest edge.
He immediately dodged sideways, changing course,
taking advantage of the cover. They might call him
"rabbit" as an insult, but he'd watched how the rabbits escaped their enemies. Not only their speed
saved them, but their zigzag dodging, too. Deeper
in the wood, he changed course again, heading
toward a massive fallen tree. He ran around behind
it, and slid to a breathless halt, letting the basket
drop onto the thick moss carpeting the ground.

His breathing gradually began to slow, and leaning
against the trunk, he listened. They were calling to
one another.

"Can you see him, Chris?"

"No sign of him over here."

"Tom, what about you?"

"He's gone. Let's go back."

"He must be around here somewhere."

Robby swallowed. Jack was the persistent one; the other two always gave up easily.

"Oh, come on, Jack, let's go! We'll get him next time."

"Well . . ." The voices faded away.

Escaped. *For now*, he thought bitterly. *Why can't they just leave me alone?* He pushed back the blond hair that had fallen into his eyes, and wiped his sweaty forehead with his forearm. A plunge in the stream would feel awfully good, and he knew just the place. A secluded place, one that he'd only discovered a few weeks ago. No one would bother him there.

After inspecting the contents of the basket (two eggs would never be the same, but otherwise all was unharmed) he hid it in the junction between the main trunk and a thick branch.

It took him a few minutes of casting about to find the deer trail that went in the right direction. Ten minutes of walking, and he heard the chuckling of shallow water over stones, then saw the glitter of sunshine on water through the trees. A moment later he was at the edge of the stream.

He'd forgotten how lovely it was. Here the stream changed from its meandering course and widened into a deep pool. The edges were shaded by overhanging trees, their foliage forming green draperies at the margin where forest and stream touched. The sun struck through the crystal water at the center of the pool, making bright the pale stones on the bottom and inking in the shadow of a passing fish.

But the water was too inviting and cool to just look at. He hastily stripped and plunged into the pool. And for a while, the bubbling and splashing of the stream was louder than usual . . .

Later, after he'd dried off and dressed again, he lay on the grassy bank in the sun, toying with a smooth rock he'd picked off the bottom of the stream bed. The warmth of the sun and the peaceful atmosphere set him to daydreaming. This really

could be that place they talked about in the village—
the old location of Robin Hood's camp years ago.
The pool, that clearing over there—why, there was
even a pile of tumbled stone that might once have
been a hearth. *I wonder why the clearing hasn't
become overgrown*, he wondered drowsily. *After all,
it's been forty years. Or more.* Forty years since the
outlaw Robin Hood and his band of hard-living followers roamed the forest called Sherwood, dealing
out justice as they saw it, helping protect those who
couldn't protect themselves from the bullying of
those placed in power over them. . . .

His anger and frustration returned. Bullies like
Jack and his cronies. *Too bad there's no Robin Hood
to come to* my *rescue*. It's just wasn't fair. *They
ought to pick on someone their own size*. But of
course that was childish thinking—bullies never
picked on anyone who could fight back. *Only on
someone like me*. The smooth pebble suddenly
smacked into a nearby tree trunk, and he realized he
must have angrily hurled it at the convenient target.

"The last time I threw a rock that hard, I was
furious because the town bully had stolen my only
currant cake," said a resonant voice behind him.

Robby started and spun around. A tall man faced
him, smiling, his white teeth gleaming in the midst
of a short beard. He was dressed in clothing colored
the greens of the forest, and he had the air of someone used to a vigorous outdoor life. A quiver of
arrows and an unstrung bow were slung over his
broad shoulders, and in one hand he held a long
sturdy staff. The other held a fishing rod. "I never
did forgive him for it, either," the man continued.

Robby, embarrassed at being seen when he
thought he was alone, didn't reply. The anger and
frustration must still have been in his face, for the
man's expression sobered and he said, "No, I can
see this is more serious than a currant cake."

"It was my family's food he tried to take. And
I'm *sick* of being bullied."

"And times are hard, and food is hard to come by."

Robby's face again mirrored his feelings. "How did you know?"

"Because your family isn't the only one struggling. I came here to do some fishing. If you want join me, maybe we can both catch some supper."

The boy studied the man. He didn't seem dangerous. *Besides, what could he steal from me—my clothes?* A poor boy's ragged clothes wouldn't be worth much. At last Robby said, "All right. My mother would be happy if I brought home some fish."

"Good!" said the man. "And now, to work." He put down the staff and fishpole, then unslung the quiver and bow and carefully laid them in the grass. Taking up the rod again, he sat at the pool's edge and baited the hook with a chunk of dried meat he took from a belt pouch. Then he cast the line into the water with a practiced flick of the wrist. Robby settled cross-legged beside him.

The man kept his eye on the line, but glanced at Robby. "You said he tried to take your food? The town bully?" The boy nodded. "I take it he didn't succeed?"

"No, I ran away."

"You must be very quick on your feet."

"I can run faster and dodge better than anyone else in the village," Robby said proudly. Then he added bitterly, "Besides, what else can I do? They're too big to fight." His earlier thought returned. "I wish I were bigger! I'd make Jack sorry!"

"Revenge isn't always as sweet as you might think." The man's face held a stern sadness. "Justice is better, justice in the sight of others. Revenge is always solitary, and no one else shares in it."

"I don't care!" said Robby hotly. "It'd be worth it just to get him off my back."

"I don't blame you for feeling that way," the man

agreed. "And if he hurts *you*, I'll bet a copper he makes life miserable for other, smaller children, doesn't he?"

"Yes," answered Robby. "He picks on Timmy all the time, and Timmy's only eight."

"Only eight, eh? Jack sounds like a charming piece of work." He stopped talking as the fishing line began to dart crazily in the water.

"Get ready with a rock, lad—this fellow feels like a big one!" Robby scrambled to pick up a fist-sized rock, and when the man landed the fish on the bank, the boy administered the *coup de grace*.

"Well done! Now let's see if we can catch a couple for you. And since a man should always know who he's fishing with, my name's Robert."

Robert? The boy took in the man's green clothing again, and the quiver and bow lying in the grass. *Wasn't Robin Hood's real name Robert, Earl of Locksley?* He became aware that the man was waiting his reply, and he quickly gathered his wits.

"My name's Robert, too—but my friends call me Robby."

"I'm honored to meet you, sir." They gravely shook hands.

It can't *be! It's been forty years! Robin Hood is dead!* But the hand that had gripped his was warm and strong. *This has to be someone else*, he said firmly to himself. *A forester, that's all. Or more likely a poacher.* Still . . .

"I was just thinking earlier that it's too bad Robin Hood is dead. He'd come in very useful right now," Robby said carefully.

"You never know," said the man cheerfully.

"He's been dead for forty years."

"Well, him or his spirit," said the man with a shrug.

Robby looked dubious.

"Didn't you know? Legends never die. That's part of the business of *being* a legend, after all." The man re-baited his hook and tossed the line back into the water. He glanced up at Robby's wide-eyed stare. "Come, now, lad, don't stare at me as if *I* was a ghost. Ghosts don't need to catch dinner, do they?"

"I suppose not."

"Of course not," said Robert firmly. "And now it's time to catch *you* some dinner. Keep that rock handy."

As they watched the fishing line pencil delicate ripples in the current, Robert continued the interrupted conversation. "It sounds to me time that this Jack should be stopped."

"More than time, if you ask me," the boy replied.

"I expect he's been doing this for years and years?" He paused. "And when you complain to the adults, they just say something like 'Oh, well, I had to put up with a bully like Jack when *I* was young, too. It didn't kill me.' "

"How did you know? That's *just* what they say!"

"Because I'm a very wise man," laughed Robert. "Besides, remember that currant cake? I had to worry about a bully when I was young, too."

The boy looked at him curiously. "How did you solve it?"

"Well, *I* didn't, actually—I was too small at the time. A hero came to my village and taught the bully a lesson he didn't soon forget."

"A hero?" Robby was skeptical. His experience in life suggested there were no such things as heroes.

"You don't believe me, eh?" Robby's arched eyebrow amused the man in green. "Well, maybe I've exaggerated slightly. It was one of King Richard's knights who was passing through. He happened on the bully tormenting a younger boy. Put the flat of his sword across that fellow's behind with enough strength that he couldn't sit down for several days. Looked a proper fool to the whole village, he did, everyone snickering at him. He lost his taste for bullying after that."

"I'm not surprised."

"That was justice, you see. The bully was served as he'd been serving others, and the whole village agreed the punishment fit the crime. That's when I learned justice was better than revenge." Robert's face, which had been full of life, suddenly saddened. "Then, and other times. Lessons have to be relearned sometimes." The line began to jerk the pole. "Man the rock again, Robby!" He drew the pole back, and pulled out a fish even larger than the first. A quick blow by Robby, and it joined the first, lying in the grass. "Is that one big enough for your family's supper?"

"Umm . . . I think one more ought to do it, if you don't mind fishing a bit longer."

"Mind? Fishing's one of my favorite pastimes, lad. And you're doing *me* a favor, you know. If I wasn't helping you catch a meal in the sunshine here, I'd have to be back at my camp, cooking my own. And I hate cooking."

Robby laughed at the droll expression on his face. Then his thoughts returned to their earlier discussion. "I do wish there was a knight around to look after Jack."

"They're not any too common these days, are they? But you said earlier you wished you were bigger and could fight Jack. You *can* fight him, you know."

"*Me?* But I'm smaller than he is. And I don't know how to fight."

"Ah, now, this is where *I* come in. I can show you how to deal with Jack."

"You can?" The look of utter disbelief on Robby's face made the man laugh.

"I certainly can. Once you know how to deal with him, he won't bother any of the other children either, because you'll be around all the time. You and your friends won't have to depend on anyone else."

"But what can *I* do?"

"Well, you're very quick on your feet, you told

me. And I noticed you're quick with your hands. You're just the sort who's good with a quarterstaff."

"I am?"

"You are. I can teach you what you need to know today. All you need are a few basic moves."

Robby's face lit up. This sounded practical. "Do you really think I can fight him and win?"

"I imagine Jack does all his bullying with his fists?"

"Yes, he does."

"Then believe me, he'll be no match for you if you fight him with a quarterstaff, even if you *are* smaller than he is. Let's go to that clearing over there. We can't very well practice thrusts and parries right here without falling into the pool."

They walked over to the clearing, Robert stooping to pick up his quarterstaff on the way. "Now, to get myself a practice staff," he commented while wandering about the margins of the clearing, studying the saplings that grew there. "Ah, here's one that will do nicely." The boy noticed for the first time, as Robert's left hand went to his waist, that a hatchet there balanced the knife on the right side of his belt. "Here, lad, help me bend this one over." Robby helped bend the sapling, increasing the tension on the green wood and making it easier to cut. With a few swift strokes of the hatchet, the man cut down the young tree. Quickly he cut it to length and trimmed off the branches. Then he stood up and flourished it.

"There! Not perfectly balanced, but it's fine for a training session. Now, Robby, come here and let me measure you." Robby stood obediently while the man measured his own finished, metal-shod staff against the boy's slender body. "Right about there. Good." He began cutting down the quarterstaff to fit Robby.

"But that's *yours*," the boy protested.

"Not now. Now it's yours. You'll need a good weapon to fight with, one that's balanced." Robert continued to trim it down neatly. "Besides, who knows? It might give you good luck to use mine." He grinned at Robby, whose surprise was written clearly in his face. "See here? There's my initial 'R' cut into the wood. I carved it one evening by the fire. Now it'll stand for 'Robby,' too."

"But what about you? You can't use the one you just made all the time."

"Nor will I. I have a friend called John who will be delighted to make me another. He thinks I depend far too much on my bow," he added confidentially. "There now—pick it up and see how it feels."

Robby picked up the staff and balanced it in his hands. "It doesn't feel nearly as heavy as I thought it would."

"That's because it's properly balanced—that's what a good staff ought to feel like." Robert picked up the trimmed sapling and stood opposite the boy. "Let's begin. Move both your hands near one end of the staff—not too close together, mind. Now, sweep the staff about knee-height at me." Robby swung the staff. The man leaped over it. "Now, I jumped over it because I knew it was coming. But Jack won't know what you're going to do, so instead he'll have his feet knocked out from under him. And see how far away you are from me? It doesn't matter that you're smaller than Jack, because the staff increases your reach. What matters in using a staff is your speed and agility. And we'll practice enough today that you'll be more than quick enough to handle Jack."

So the lesson went on in the sunlit clearing. The man in green was a patient teacher, and he saw that his surmise about the boy's speed and coordination were correct. Robby was a natural with the staff. And Robby's confidence increased as he learned how to use the extra length of the staff to his advantage, how to give a sudden painful jab in the ribs, how to quickly shift his grip to deliver the sweeping stroke that would knock his opponent off his feet.

The lesson wound up with Robert casting his staff away. "Here now! See if you can stop me from laying my hands on you!" he challenged. He began to circle around the boy. Robby grinned at him and feinted a jabbing body blow. The man reached out to take hold of the staff, intending to jerk it from the boy's hands. Only the staff wasn't there. Robby whipped it away and tried to swipe at his legs. It didn't quite work— Robert dodged out of the way, but not before he'd collected a bruised shin. He roared with laughter. "Well done, lad! If you can do that to me with only a couple of hours' training, you'll be able to handle an ignorant village bully."

Robby smiled with delight. "Do you know, I feel like maybe I can. But," he became more serious, "I'm also nervous."

"That's natural—I'm always scared before a fight, too. Everyone is. The important thing is not letting it stop you from doing what's right."

"I'll try not to. With this," Robby gripped the staff, "I'll be able to show Jack."

"Don't forget about justice, Robby. You use your staff only if you have to. Justice is what I taught you for, not revenge."

"I understand."

"Good!" He clapped Robby on the shoulder. "And now, I have to go. The afternoon's nearly gone, and I have to cook my supper." They walked back to the edge of the stream, and Robert gathered up his gear and his fish. He handed over the boy's share of the catch.

"Thank you for the fish, and the staff. And the lesson. And—everything!" Robby said, belatedly remembering his manners.

"You're more than welcome, sir. I enjoyed it, too." Robert reached out and shook the boy's hand. "We'll meet again." Robby turned as a kingfisher dove into

the water and snared a fish in its beak, then turned
back to Robert—but Robert was gone.

This is crazy. He can't have just vanished. *He must
have slipped away among the trees.*

But there was no betraying crackle of twigs or swish
of branches. *He said he wasn't a ghost. And he was
certainly solid enough when we were practicing.* Robby
wandered back to the bank of the stream and sat down
in the sunlight. *I wonder who* does *keep the undergrowth cut back in that clearing? . . .*

Robby sat motionless for a few moments, then sat
up. The shadows on the bank had grown longer; it was
late afternoon. *I must have fallen asleep,* he decided. *I
dreamed the whole thing.* But no, there was the staff
Robert had given him. And there were the fish for
dinner. That brought him back to reality—he could
ponder the events of the day later, but it was time he
went home.

He gathered his things, then strode down the game
trail to the fallen tree. When he reached the huge
trunk, he knelt and wrapped the fish in some clean
leaves, put them in the basket, and stood up. Basket
in one hand, staff in the other, he headed for the
village. The late afternoon sun was sending burnished
bars of light slanting across the gaps among the trees.
He thought back to Robert's sudden disappearance
again. *He* must *have walked away into the forest. He's
just very good at moving quietly.*

His musings on the afternoon's events brought him
along the path, through the brush at the forest's edge,
and back to the village lane he'd fled down a few
hours before. The birdsong of the greenwood had
given way to the soft clucking of chickens as they
pecked through leavings in the lane. And—his head
came up—over the chickens he could hear the sound
of a child crying. Timmy's voice. And laughter: Jack's
laughter. Robby felt a surge of anger, mixed with
giddy fear. *He* would have to stop Jack; there was no
one else. This time he couldn't run. He put down the
basket and looked at the quarterstaff in his hand. His

thumb rubbed across the carved "R." Robby's jaw tightened, and he ran towards the cries.

They were at the far end of the twisting lane.

As usual, Jack had chosen his spot well. There were no adults around, just the participants in the tiny drama. Timmy was backed against the wall, and there was a streak of blood on his tear-damp face. Jack, Chris, and Tom were ringed around the small boy, laughing. At the sight of the other two, Robby felt uncertainty welling up inside him. All *three* of them? But from someplace within, the thought came: *I have to face all of them together sooner or later.* All right, then, it might as well be now.

He stepped forward and raised his voice. "Leave him alone!"

They turned, surprised. Timmy looked up, his tear-stained face brightening in unexpected hope.

"Why, it's Robby the Rabbit!" sneered Chris.

"Robby the housewife," corrected Jack. "Where's your basket, housewife? Did you drop it the last time you ran away? Better run and look for it, or your mother might give you a spanking." The other two hooted with laughter, and turned back to their victim.

"I said leave him be," Robby repeated firmly. And his voice didn't tremble at all.

"Looks to me like you need a little lesson in who's boss here, housewife." Jack began advancing on him.

Good, thought Robby as he backed away. *I can lure him into the open where there's more room.* His hands on the quarterstaff shifted to one of the grips he'd been taught.

Jack didn't even seem to notice the staff. He simply followed, looking smug at the retreat of the younger boy. Robby the Rabbit was running away, just like he always did. Jack moved out of the alley entrance. Just as soon as he got a bit closer, he'd take care of this little—

Robby's staff jabbed him hard in the ribs. And jabbed again, this time in the stomach. Jack doubled over in pain, gasping. Then Robby brought the staff sharply across his back. Jack went to his knees.

"Robby, look out!" It was the deep voice of a man—Robert's voice!

His shout made Robby whirl around. Chris and Tom were coming towards him. He moved purpose-fully at them, shifting his grip on the staff. When he got within range, he swept the staff low and fast across Chris's shins. Chris went down hard. Robby turned his attention to the final boy, who was backing away uncertainly. A smart rap across the wrist decided Tom, and he fled the scene.

"*Robby!*"

Again Robert's shout alerted him. Chris was about to get to his feet. Another jab in the ribs, and he decided to stay down.

Breathing hard, Robby looked around in surprise. Why, it hadn't been hard at all! He almost laughed out loud at Chris' stunned astonishment. And Jack was peering up at him, fear plainly written on his face. He'd *shown* them!

"Well done, lad!" said Robert. He seemed to have been standing in the alley entrance the whole time. "Handling three at a time is no easy feat. You *do* have a talent for the staff."

Robby smiled proudly at him. "I think you might be right."

"I'll show you more another time. I'd say you've earned it. But now I think you should see to your friend."

"You're right." Robby turned and went back to Timmy. The smaller boy was looking at him with such admiration that he felt embarrassed. "Are you all okay, Timmy? Here, let me wipe that blood off your face and we'll look after that scratch."

"I'm fine—now. Who were you talking to?"

He pointed. "Why, my friend Robert, right over there . . ." Robby's voice trailed away. There was no one there. He ran over to the entrance, and looked down the lane. Robert wasn't there either. Only his fallen opponents, now more or less on their feet, but keeping a respectful distance from him. Odd—somehow, he didn't feel much like gloating triumphantly. Only satisfaction that he'd done the right thing in stopping them. *That* felt good.

He turned back to Timmy. "Well, he *was* here. And he taught me how to fight, too."

"You were *splendid*! Will you show me how?"

"If you want me to. I'm only a beginner, but I can show you what I know." He stared down at the initial on the staff, an initial that he was suddenly certain would not and could not be obliterated. "In fact, I think he'd want me to."

The boys' voices faded as they walked from the scene of battle. And just before silence descended once more, a voice seemed to say "Well done!" in the whispering breeze.

Robin Hood's Treasure

by Clayton Emery

"—almost defiled me! The indignity of it! The nerve! Burned my barn and my castle! Laid hands on me! And stole—*stole*—the last of the money I'd planned for my old age! A pittance to you, no doubt, good Sheriff, but the only bulwark I had against the cold and the wolves of the forest. And now it's *gone!* I say to you, I demand of you, what are you going to do about it! *What?* Tell me!"

"Good lady, I—"

"You don't care! Why should you? You have money. You have wealth. You have silver enough, and gold too, to last the winter. What care you? Eh? *Tell* me!"

"Good lady, we—"

"Oh, it's all very well to talk. That's all you men ever do. Here I am, practically naked as a virgin before the world, and *you* can only boast of catching these ruffians and bringing them to justice! But any real help? *No!* Where am I to get it? Needs I take myself to the forest and beg help from some scurrilous outlaw? He's a friend of the poor and the sick and elderly and the widowed. He's not sitting here in a silver chair swilling wine while—"

"*Madame, I'll get your money back!*"

Nicholas, High Sheriff of Nottingham, was reminded of that Greek king who could never eat his meals for the harpy women who swooped from the skies and shit on his plate. Even his wine tasted sour. The Lady Amabillia, formerly of Three Oaks above Derby (would she be willing to sell her land cheaply? he wondered) hung over him like a gallows tree, alternately wringing her scrawny hands or sketching in the air the horrors she had suffered. Her sleeves brushed against his forehead time and again, no matter how far back he leaned. The Blue Boar's patrons peeked and chuckled. The lady's sleeve dipped in the mustard sauce on his plate, then striped across his forehead. Nicholas clambered to his feet and upset the table. His breakfast, barely begun, landed on the floor.

"Will you, good Sheriff? Will you?" Lady Amabillia cried with joy. Her hands hooked as if to caress his cheeks.

He jerked back and tripped over his stool. "Yes, milady. Yes, I will. I'll have your gold back by tomorrow."

"Will you start right now? Right away? *Now?*"

She swayed back enough that the sheriff could scuttle upright. A boy had come to clean the mess. He held up the sheriff's slice of mutton. It was speckled with straw and dirt and dried dog shit. "Will you take this with you, milord?"

The sheriff's hands shook as he fumbled out a silver penny and threw it at the boy. He scampered for the door with the widow right behind.

Out in the sunshine his men snapped to attention. One let go a milkmaid's waist. One lobbed a tankard behind a tree. Three got up from dicing in the dust. They tightened cinches and untwisted reins.

The sheriff squinted in the light. Nicholas of Nottingham was a short man with flat black hair and beard. He was dressed in a silver-chased doublet and satin-lined cloak and new hose, all in the blue of Nottingham, with the silver-antlered chain of office on his breast. His matching hat had a short peacock feather that constantly intruded on his side vision. The widow clung to his cloak like a swarm of hornets. He grabbed at his saddle pommel and jerked himself astride.

"Which way did they go, milady? I want to get after them as soon as possible."

"Which way? I don't know, I had to flee! But they'll likely come this way, so you go *that* way!"

The sheriff followed her finger. Through Sherwood Forest. Of course.

The widow raised her voice. "One hundred ten pounds it was they got! Almost all gold, except for the silver! Good Italian florins! There were four of them—don't you want to know how many? Sheriff, are you *listening?*"

The sheriff was not listening. He rode as fast as his mount and sour stomach would go.

"We could give more to the crippled ones that crawl in here on hands and knees."

"And more to them little parish churches that have to give to the bishops."

"And more to the orphans. We could do a lot more, Robin."

"A lot more with what?"

"Money!"

Robin Hood opened a sleepy eye and fixed it on his cousin. Green-tinged shafts of light and silver birch pillars gave the greenwood a cathedral air. The morning forest hummed with spring noise. They had to raise their voices above birdsong. "What would you do with more money, Will?"

Will Scarlett intoned, "*I* would give it to the poor."

Everyone hooted.

"Then they wouldn't be poor no longer." Ol Will Stutly recited the old joke. "And we know what you'd do with it."

Scarlett laughed. "And what would I do with it?"

"You'd spend it on lust."

"And malmsey," added Little John.

"And you'd gamble the rest away," added Hard-Hitting Brand.

"And buy food," added Much. He'd been turning the deer on the spit over the firepit.

"And he'd waste the rest," muttered Robin Hood. "Aren't you supposed to be on watch, Brand?"

"This is more interesting."

"Must be powerful boring out there, then."

Will Scarlett nodded. "You're right. I'd spend the money on them things and more. I'd spend it *right*."

"And that's wrong," Robin finished. He sat up straight and stretched his arms. He scratched both armpits and then his beard. Robin had been up since yesterday, visiting Marian who'd slipped out of the nunnery, and they'd spent the night wandering the woods, gathering spring flowers, kissing and hugging, talking. He didn't know if he were ready for the day or not. "When we steal, it's not for us. It's for the poor and anyone else as needs it. We're not the receivers. We're just the vessels, carriers for Our Lady."

"I know some ladies in Nottingham would love to receive some money," said Scarlett.

"You never knew a lady in your life," Little John told him.

Robin picked up his great bow and stretched the string, taking imaginary aim. The weapon fairly hummed. "Gold can't buy anything important."

Will Scarlett clucked his tongue. "But really, Rob. Why can't we keep some of what we steal?"

"You know the answer to that, Will. Because it wouldn't be right. We didn't become outlaws to steal money. We *became* outlaws and that's *why* we steal money. Don't get things backwards. You're always doing that."

Little John rumbled, "But you know, Rob. He's right about one thing—"

"*Ach!*" Robin Hood let his bowstring twang, something he never did. "All this talk about money! I don't remember Jesus talking about getting rich! I seem to remember just the opposite! All we ever talk about is *money!* How many times a week do I have to dig up our treasure chest? Eh?"

Little John rocked his quarterstaff across his lap so the ends thumped on the ground. "Last time you opened it you frightened a mole."

Robin Hood swung his bow in a great sweeping arc. "Would you *look* at this glade? Would you *look* at that lime tree? This cave? These oaks, that were saplings when Our Saviour walked on water? This glade, this forest, yon brook, this way of life we have here— sitting around a tree and lazing the day away and watching the sun come up and *talking* about *nothing* at all—we might as well be steeped in emeralds—"

"In what?" asked Brand.

"—when we could be chained to some plow scratching a furrow across rocks, or a hobbling crippled leper on a pilgimage to Jerusalem, or lost, or alone, or hurt or unloved or without families—all *this*, and you lot want *money*?"

The outlaws looked at one another. They looked at their camp, which showed no sign of human life other than the firepit and Will Scarlett's spare shirt hanging on a bush. They looked at their leader. Robin Hood's shirt and trousers were worn through at the knees and elbows. His leather tunic was scuffed almost white, his belt cracked. Only his deerhide boots, tall and greased, were presentable. Even the feather in his hat drooped. The King of Sherwood was the poorest-dressed among them.

Little John cleared his throat. "If we did keep more of the money, Robin, we could build a chapel."

Robin grunted, his voice tight from pulling his bowstring. "I could build a chapel without leaving this glade. From stone below and trees above."

"We could have a gilt cross."

"Jesus hung on a wooden one."

"What about our arrowheads, eh? You don't find them growing on trees."

"No, I find them hiding in the pack of ironmongers from Kent."

Scarlett said, "Rob, all we're sayin' is—"

"*Enough!*" Robin Hood hopped into the air and landed facing them. "I'm for a walk! Good day!"

He strode off for the woods, the arrows in his back quiver clicking rhythmically. They watched him go.

Will Stutly sucked one of his few teeth. "Much, that deer done yet?"

Scarlett poked his chin with a long finger. "Too bad you mentioned malmsey, John. That's got me thirsty. If we had a few pennies we could walk to the Boar."

"Oh, shut up, Will."

"No, there's nothing like it, Ned, nothing at all. We rise when we please, we hunt the king's deer, we sleep when we're tired, visit whom we please when we please—there's just nothing like it at all. I'd not trade places with King Henry. No king's treasure could amount to a hundredth's part of mine."

"Tell us more, pray." The challenge came from a shadow that filled the doorway. Dust motes whirled around the stolid figure. In a blink the doorway darkened with two more men, then another. Long tapers hung from black hands. They shooed a few peasants past them and shut the door and slammed the shutters. Sunlight and fairy dust were banished outside.

The Blue Boar was quiet. Robin Hood had several bowls of ale under his belt by now. He enjoyed talking to the innkeeper Ned, who'd been the cook in Robin's father's household in the old days. Robin loved to hear stories about his father's careless Saxon tastes and his mother's refined French ones. And of how Ned would make him a berry duff if the boy Robin pestered him enough.

The outlaw chief squinted as the men advanced. Ned the innkeeper moved slowly down the bar, but froze as a man barked. Ned and Robin Hood and the inn's boy, Cnut, waited.

The gruff men were knights, dusty from the road. The four wore leather hauberks with rusted iron plates, scratched Norman helmets, and broken shoes. They carried long knives at their belts and slim swords in their hands, and faces stern from recent sin. A tall thin knight dropped a leather sack onto the planks of the bar with a clank.

The four surrounded Robin where he leaned on the bar. The outlaw stood as straight as he could.

"I said," growled the knight, "tell us more."

Robin squinted again. "More about what?"

The knight used his free hand to punch Robin in the chest.

Quick as a snake Robin's right hand came off the bar and slammed the knight's jaw shut with a *clack!* His left swung wide for the second knight's face or throat—Robin didn't care which, as long as the man fell back. He did, and Robin smashed his shoulder into the man who'd hit him. He clawed for the man's sword. Robin had only his long Irish knife: his bow and quiver hung from a peg on the wall. The outlaw grabbed, but the man clutched his sword tight. Robin had the disquieting thought this plan might not work.

With a toe-popping lurch, he ripped the sword free. It was just in time, for a silver blade swung at his neck like an executioner's blade. Robin shoved his steel into the air and even managed to back the flat side with his other hand. The knight's sword struck his with a muffled *clang* that hurt to hear. It was a solid blow, too solid. Off-balance and clumsy, Robin was knocked sprawling. He tossed the sword rather than cut his face open.

Somewhere along the way he hit the dirt floor with his back, then his head. Someone kicked his foot. Someone kicked him in the ribs. He rocked forward to get clear and almost ran onto a sword blade.

"*Ouch!*"

The tip was dull. It did no more than puncture his tunic and bruise his breastbone. But it stopped him cold. He sighted along the shimmering blade. It seemed to go on forever, like a one-color rainbow. The tip of the sword skipped from Robin's breastbone to just under his chin.

"Don't kill him, Wycliff! He said treasure!"

Treasure? though Robin. *I said that?* His thoughts jiggered like tadpoles in a pond. *Treasure?*

A third knight shouted. "Where is this treasure you spoke of, lout? It means your life."

"Umm . . . Yes, milord."

"It's 'milord,' now," said a man. Robin couldn't see any of them well, up there in the dark of the rafters. "He's scared."

"Hush. Talk! Who are you, anyway? Why are you in devil's green?"

"He looks like a beggar."

"Not with them boots, he don't."

Ned spoke from behind the bar. "He's Robin Hood, the famous outlaw. He robs the sheriff and others on the road. Rich folk. He's got a lot of treasure hidden away, back there in the forest."

"How much?" Someone kicked him. "How much?"

"Oh—" Robin's croaked and tried again. "Oh, some. Gold coins, a double fistful at least."

"No."

"Aye. Some stamped with William's head. Some with Harald's."

The sword at Robin's throat backed an inch. "What else?"

"German pennies. Ecus. Florins. They're all the same, same size and weight. Lots of silver. Fifty pounds if it's a penny."

Ned asked, "Would you lords like a drink while you plan? My ale's fresh-brewed in new vats."

"Aye. That's good." The greedy man, the leader, sheathed his sword. "Rufus, watch him. Don't let him up."

The knights stepped to the bar and took jacks of foaming ale. Rufus spilled ale out the corner of his mouth as he tried to stare at Robin. The outlaw laid his head back on the cool earth and rested and listened. His eyes burned.

Ned talked as if the knights were his best customers. He topped off their ale and asked whence they travelled, what they'd seen, what the news. They bragged about their latest coup.

"We've gained a small fortune just this morning.

Robbed a widow down Derby way. Fired her house and barn. Cooked one of her sucklings for dinner. And got that." He pointed with his jack to the leather sack on the bar. "Sixty pounds if it's a penny."

The man with the sore jaw and fiery temper, Wycliff, laughed. "We left her her son and her virtue. How's that for a bargain?"

The leader choked on his ale. "I wonder where *she'll* sleep tonight?"

"Not in the barn, nor the house neither!" One knight, an older man, wheezed so hard he snorted ale through his nose.

Ned chuckled with them. He hunted back of the bar, then nodded to his boy. "Cnut, run to the house and fetch that cask of special brandy I've been keeping. Let me know if you can't find it."

"Yes, Father." The boy put down his broom and left. A few minutes later he stuck his head in the door. He squeaked, "I can't find it, Father."

"*Gah!* You useless sopdoll." He banged down a pitcher. "I'll be right back, milords. I've something you'll like."

The leader of the knights nodded. The men drained their jacks and refilled them from the pitcher. It was quiet in the room. Robin stared at the blackened beams. He thought it curious no one else came in: someone must be steering people clear. The Blue Boar sat by the road by itself, halfway between Edwinstowe and Nottingham. Ned liked to be alone. They waited some more. The inn's cat, a piebald, slipped into the room and rubbed along the hearthstones.

Wycliff banged his fist on the smooth oak planks. "Where is that fool?"

The leader put down a pitcher. "Hey. I bet he's run off."

From the floor, Robin Hood said, "He's gone for the sheriff. He told me Nicholas was here just this morning, with eight men-at-arms."

Wycliff threw his jack at the fireplace. "Bugger! Let's burn this place to the ground!"

The outlaw said, "The smoke'll attract attention."

Wycliff walked over and peered down at him. "I haven't forgotten you punched me in the jaw."

Robin told him, "Please forgive me that, lord. But 'tis better you slip off quietly into the woods—with me—to fetch that gold. That or fight the sheriff's men."

Rufus gulped the rest of his ale and tossed his jack. "He's right there."

The leader frowned. Wycliff kicked Robin in the side. "There better be lots of gold. A double handful for each of us. You better not be tricking us."

Robin rolled his eyes. "Me? Trick you? I don't think I could. There's plenty. I took it from the Bishop of Hereford himself."

"That's a sin," said Rufus.

"May I get up now?"

The leader grabbed the sack from the bar. He bounced it to feel its weight. "Aye, get up, you scut." He jerked Robin's knife out of his belt and threw it across the room to thud against a wall. "Lead us to this gold. And no tricks."

Robin pushed the door open to blinding sunshine. "Follow me."

"Where're you bound, lad?"

The voice came from the trees. Alphonse jumped like a rabbit struck with an arrow.

One of Robin's foresters had appeared from nowhere. He was tall and broad, Saxon blonde, with a crooked nose and large bony fists. He wore forester's green and a tunic of chain mail scraps, with a bow taller than himself and arrows half as long, and a staghorn knife in his belt. In the green wilderness Alphonse found him more terrible than a dragon.

"A-are you Robin Hood's man, Little John?"

The man reared back and laughed. "Me? No, I'm just a little titch compared to Little John! He's *big*!

Come along and meet him. Are you bearing news or asking for help? You don't act smug enough to have news, so you must need help. Am I right? And stop shaking. Your teeth chattering will scare the deer."

Robin's camp was only a meadow at the base of a tall hill. A lime tree filled the sky and shaded the glade. Oak trees loomed so high they could crush a boy and never notice. A cave mouth in the hillside beckoned to and repelled Alphonse at the same time. Caves led to hell.

Robin's band of Merry Men (as Alphonse had heard them called in songs) lay around like cows in a paddock. There was an older man with a head grey and white like a badger's, a squat and ugly and snaggle-toothed idiot, a smiling rogue in red, a peasant fresh from the plow. Most noticeable of all was a man who covered too much grass. And as he stood . . . Alphonse found himself staring up at the giant's face, silhouetted against the sky like the face of God. The giant had a blonde beard cut like a spade and a long braid down his back. His hand was bigger than the Bible in the parish church.

The man with the crooked nose called, "Someone looking for help."

"Looks more like he's after food," said the man in red. Alphonse had smelt roasting deer. "I'll cut him a haunch before he faints and we don't get our news."

"None of the deer you shoot are ever edible, Will," put in the grey man. "You always gutshoot the poor things and let 'em run. Makes 'em bitter."

"You're just cranky 'cuz you ain't got the teeth to chew 'em with, Will."

"Least when I shoot 'em, they go down and not long."

Robin's cousin cut away a long wide slice of golden-brown venison and juggled it as he rolled it into a tube. He handed it to the hungry boy, whose eyes shone with appreciation.

The man with the crooked nose, Hard-Hitting

Brand, poked Alphonse with a finger. "Your news, boy?"

The boy spoke around a mouthful. "I'm Alphonse, son of Amabillia, widow of Richard of Three Oaks near to Derby."

"Widow Amabillia. We know of her," said the giant. His voice rumbled as if from under the ground.

"We was attacked early this morning. Before dawn. There were four knights tried to get into our manse. They stayed the night in our barn, and when they couldn't get inside this morn, they fired the barn. Then they fired the front door and broke in. They took mother's treasure."

The man in red, Will Scarlett, asked, "How much treasure?"

Little John pointed a finger like the short end of a club. "Tha's none of your business, Will. Go on, lad."

"That's all there is to tell. They took our money. That's what Mother told me to tell y'."

"And she expects us to get her silver back?"

"Gold, it was, she said. Near to ninety pounds. All we had in the world, and now us thrown out in the cold to starve."

Will Scarlett scratched his head. He signalled to old Will Stutly and Little John to move away. He whispered, "I've seen this Widow Amabillia before, and heard more of her. She's the one loses her cattle all the time. Has six head and loses thirteen or more a year. She thinks the pinder works for her. I'll bet if she says she lost ninety pounds it's closer to forty-five. Or thirty."

"You're daft, Will," Little John told him. "Not everyone's a thief like you."

"And she couldn't conjure up four wastrel knights from the ground." Will Stutly scowled. "Still, I don't believe anything until I see it with my own two eyes. We'll set out on their trail. It's what Robin would do."

They walked back to the boy.

Alphonse, skinny and dirty and fifteen or so, gulped

down a hunk of venison a dog couldn't have swallowed. Little John carved off another piece. Will Scarlett sat on his heels across from the boy. "All right lad—you're a bright-looking type, you know that? I hope my little Tam grows up as sharp as you. Why don't you tell us everything that happened. Let's start with descriptions of these knights, their weapons, and their mounts . . ."

The boy's throat tired from answering questions. Finally Will Scarlett said, "That's all very well, but these knights could have gone anywhere."

"But probably they'll go to Nottingham," said Will Stutly. "With that gold weighin' 'em down, they'll be wanting to spend it, and town's the place to waste money. Just ask Scarlett."

"It's as good as any," Little John agreed. "We can take the Black Brook Trail to the Salt Road. Maybe we'll get there before 'em."

" 'Specially if they stop at the Boar," added Scarlett.

"You've yet to pass it by, tha's true," replied John.

"This'll be grand. If we collect the robbers and the money too, that'll do Rob in the eye."

"This ain't a contest. Be sensible. Now let's go. Much, you stay here in camp to tell Robin where we are, or in case anyone else comes. Where are we going?"

Much furrowed his black brows. "Af-ter knights. To Nott'in'um."

"Good!" The giant slapped the idiot on the back. "We'll be back tonight, or maybe not. Rob'll understand."

He caught Alphonse under the arm and picked him clean off the ground, then set him down. "Come on, son. Let's catch these marauders of yours. Maybe we can collect their heads to adorn your mother's gate."

Alphonse choked on his meat but stood ready as the foresters shouldered their quivers and picked up their bows. He stepped out after them, then found himself running to keep up with their long woodsmen's strides.

Will Stutly called over his shoulder, "Where's your mother now, boy?"

"Oh, she's safe. She's asking the sheriff to help."

Before Will Scarlett could say anything, Little John poked him.

"How much farther?"

Robin stopped and turned. Any time they addressed him he stopped, and was slow to start again. "Eh?"

"I said, how much farther?"

"Farther?"

"To camp, you oaf!"

Robin Hood leaned against the bole of an oak tree that reared to the sky. This was climax forest, where the trees had almost ceased to grow. The lowest branches were fifty feet off the ground. The ground was carpeted with oak leaves and nothing else, as clean as if overgrazed by goats. The only moving things were brown moths. High overhead a green woodpecker laughed, the sound eerie.

Behind him had come the four robber knights on their horses. The beasts' hooves were silent on the dead pliant leaves. Only an occasional thud of iron on root sounded in the cathedral of forest. That and the knights' grumbling.

The leader, whose name was Roger, kicked his mount to crowd Robin. He slapped at him with the end of his reins. Robin Hood took it on his shoulder. "How much farther to this stinking outlaw camp of yours? And the gold?"

Robin rubbed his chin. "Oh. To camp, milord. Let's see now . . ." Robin pretended to think. He yawned.

Roger's face turned bright red. He scrabbled off his horse and ripped his sword from its sheath to level it at Robin's belly. "Yes, you goddamned yellow scurvy outlaw bastard mongrel whoremongering fool! Yes, to the camp and the treasure you spoke of, you idiot!

And why are you *yawning*, you dick-headed harlequin? Aren't you afraid?"

Robin waved an apologetic hand. "Of course I'm afraid, milord. Terrified. But I was up all night and I drank my breakfast—we outlaws live to carouse, you know—and—I'm tired."

In truth, Robin Hood had planned to lead these men on a little farther, past this stand of oaks and down a slope to the edge of a fen. There, in the holly and hawthorn, cattails and bullrushes, he had planned to run away from them. Horses couldn't penetrate that swamp without sinking, even if a rider could force them onto the deer trails. But if he did lead them to the fen . . . There would be mosquitoes down there— he and Marian had had to avoid some of their favorite places because of the clouds. It was a warm spring. And the fairies might still be abroad, since they stirred in the spring along with everything else, and their first thoughts were in discomforting humans. And Robin didn't himself like that fen. There were barrows back there, and probably barrow wights. And he was hungry and thirsty and tired, and he didn't feel like running . . .

"No, I'm addled," he said. "T'will be quicker to cut up north and come to camp that way. The trail should be dry by now."

Roger waggled his sword. "So how far?"

Robin scratched his elbow where it protruded from his shirt. "Oh, not an hour's walk."

The knights looked at one another. Clearly, they didn't know what to make of this rogue. Roger jabbed at Robin's chest, scarring his tunic again below the fresh cut of the morning. "Well, let's get to it! We're tired of wandering these damned woods for nothing."

"Me, too," Robin replied. He pointed. "That way."

The men mounted and Robin took the lead. He turned for a slight detour so he could drink from a brook.

He pondered his new plan. He would lead the knights towards camp. He would make noise to alert

the lookout, sing a signal, and his Merry Men would
ambush these knights. They were begging to be killed
anyway.

He hoped the lookouts weren't asleep.

" 'West by northwest. West by northwest.' What
kind of directions are those?"

Cnut, the boy from the Blue Boar Inn, had almost
given up hope of finding Robin Hood's camp when he
saw the smoke. It spiraled up in the middle distance,
white and thick. A cook fire full of grease, he guessed.
Didn't it seem unwise to make so much smoke if they
were hiding from the sheriff's soldiers?

Cnut came to the clearing at the foot of a hill. The
smoke came from an animal carcass—it must be a
deer—that had ignited from too hot a fire.

A man beat at the flames with a stick. His mad
flailing broke the spit and dropped the meat into the
fire. More beating whipped up flames and ash and set
the stick afire. In flailing the stick about, he set fire
to the back of his tunic.

Cnut ran up, snatched off his filthy apron, and
whapped at the flames on the forester's back.

Much the Miller's Son spun around. Someone was
hitting him. He struck back with the charred stick.
The boy tried to get behind him. Robin Hood had
told Much never to turn his back on an enemy, so the
idiot danced in circles. The boy followed, shouting.
Much hit him with the stick and left black streaks on
Cnut's hat and face.

Cnut finally just pushed the forester over to crash
on his back. Then he backpedaled out of range.

Much got up slowly, like a turtle. He tried to
remember what all the excitement had been. He studied the boy, a young boy from town. (Anyone not a
forester was "from town.") "Hail," Much told him,
in Robin's voice. "Wel-come to camp. What do you
want? Why you wear a skirt?"

Cnut panted as he tied his apron back on. "I don't
know. It's not. We need help. Or you do. Not us,

you. There are robbers and they've got Robin Hood.
They knocked him down and kicked him—"

Much remembered. "You knocked me down."

"Y-yes, I did. You were on fire."

"Oh." Much frowned. "What do you want?"

"These robbers, knights, false knights, with horses.
They've got Robin Hood. They took him away."

"Where they take him?"

"Uh, to camp." Cnut looked around. Some crows
had landed on the lower branches of an oak tree to
investigate the meat smell, but that was the only activity. "To here, we thought. To get Robin's treasure."

"'Rob-in's trea-sure? What trea-sure?"

"Uh, I don't know. Don't you know about his
treasure?"

Much shook his head gravely. "You hungry? Boys
are always hungry."

"N-no, I'm not hungry, thank you, milord."

"I'm no man's lord. I'm Much the Mill-er's Son. I
get you some food."

Much drew a slim knife and dragged the smoulder-
ing deer clear of the fire. He poked around, hacked
with his knife, used his hands and tore a bloody chunk
loose. He dropped it on the grass, speared it, brushed
it off, finally presented it to the boy with black fingers.
"Eat. Sit. Wel-come to camp."

Cnut took the meat and sat cross-legged on the
grass. He tried to nibble at the lump. He wondered
how it could be raw and burned black at the same
time. He closed his eyes and bit deep, tried not to
spit it out.

Much sat across from him, too close. He dandled
the sharp knife in his hand. "Why you come here?"

Mouth smeared with blood, Cnut started, "I'm the
slops boy at the Blue Boar Inn. This morning—"

"Boars are black," Much told him. "With grey—"
he plucked at his hair and pulled it around to look at
it, "—hairs."

Very slowly, not eating his meat, Cnut explained
what had happened to Robin Hood. It took a long

time. In the end he said, "So Robin Hood is coming here—I think—with the bad men. Here. No, not yet. They're *coming*—to steal your treasure. Robin's *gold*."

"Gold!" Much exclaimed. He got up and ambled off towards the cave. Cnut threw his meat into the bushes, wiped his hands on his singed apron, and followed.

The boy crept into the cave after the idiot. The inside of the hill was very dark after the sunshine. He waited for his eyes to adjust. He smelt water and dry stone. The cave was surprisingly large, the ceiling higher than he could have jumped. Some bulky objects—barrels and sacks and a chest or two—were stacked at the back. That was all. This was an outlaw's life? Living with idiots in caves in the woods?

Much knelt at the far side of the cave without any light. Cnut heard digging. Much moved something aside, stomped dirt flat, picked up the something and headed out. Cnut got out of his way.

Back on the sunny spring grass of the clearing Much brushed dirt off a small wooden box. It was iron-bound, riveted to be strong, with a hasp but no lock or even peg. Much pried up the lid and something sparkled brighter than the sun.

It was silver and some gold, more than Cnut had ever seen, even working in an inn all his life. There were fat Norman coins with Stephen and William's heads, and older coins with faces he didn't know. There were coins stamped with city walls. The silver was black with tarnish, but thick and round or cut square. When Much closed the box it seemed like sundown.

"Robin's gold," said the idiot.

"Well, Much, I don't know what you should do with it. Except hide it, maybe. Those robbers are coming soon. They should have been here by now." Cnut gulped. The sight of all that money and the thought of marauders coming to steal it unnerved him. "I have to go, milord."

Much stood up and picked his nose. "You hun-gry? Boys al-ways hun-gry."

The boy shook his head. "No, no thank you. I'm full from that venison I had. Really."

But Much headed back towards the firepit. "Non-sense. Boys always hun-gry. Can't send you 'way emp-ty." He shooed crows away from the scorched wreck and ripped another hunk loose. He picked up the deerhide from the grass, shook off the ants, wrapped it up and gave it to the boy.

"Thank you muchly, uh, Much. Will you hide that treasure? It shouldn't be left out."

The idiot stood over the box. "Hide it. Hide it. Hide it where? Hey, where you go?" Cnut had made his getaway.

Eventually Much picked up the chest, set it on his sloping shoulder, and settled it into place.

He marched off into the woods.

"I know you lot don't appreciate the forest. You'd rather a town. Bright lights, alehouses, painted women. But it's a *lovely* place to be. There's no other spot on earth like it. Not a one. Why just *look* at those trees, would you? Just *look* at them! Other men see only the wood in them, that they'd fell and cut out the heart of, but I say they're *beautiful*, God's *finest* works—"

"Would you shut up with your drasty speech? You'll drive us all mad! You talk and talk and talk and say nothing!"

Robin Hood turned in complete innocence. The four knights scowled at him. Or three did. The fourth, the old man, clung to his saddle and panted. Robin calculated. They were past the lookout's post, so the Merry Men knew they were here. He hadn't hailed or blown his horn, so they expected trouble. A signal would cap it. He asked, "If I mayn't talk, may I sing?"

"*No!*"

Robin had already launched into "Pour Mon Coeur." "*At-tend-ez moi, les pe-tites—*"

The lead knight spurred his horse and swiped at
Robin with his fist. The outlaw sidestepped by moving
close to a tree trunk. The knight cursed him. "Shut
up and *move!*"

Robin Hood shrugged and walked. With every pace
he expected the *zip* and *thop!* of an arrow hitting a
man or horse, and he tightened his belly for the dash
for cover. But one step followed another, and eventually he could see the bright green-yellow of the camp
clearing. Then he was in the open and the horses were
snorting behind him.

The King of Sherwood stood and stared at the
empty camp. The only thing out of place was a misshapen burned deer on the grass. Nothing moved.
What the hell?

Roger walked his horse beside Robin. "Well? Fetch
out the treasure!"

Robin Hood scratched his beard with his thumb.
"*Go!*"

"Yes, milord." Robin hitched his belt and started
for the cave. Oh, well. He'd give them his gold and
bolt for the woods if necessary. If he could find the
Merry Men, they could maybe hunt the knights down.
Or maybe not. He could always steal more gold.

Robin chirped as he crept into the cave, but there
was no answer. Roger bustled in behind him, leather-
and-iron armor creaking and squeaking. The tall
Rufus came after and thumped his head on the
entrance. But that was all. Wycliff the Quick-Tem-
pered stayed outside, as did old Tomkin. Wycliff said
nothing, but Tom carried on about "caves ain't no fit
place for men. Devils' territory, that. Y'ud be mad to
venture in there . . ."

Robin Hood reached for his belt and found his
sheath empty. "Borrow your knife?"

Roger squinted in the dark. He'd drawn his sword.
"D'ya think I'm a fool?"

Robin didn't answer that. He poked around and
found an iron spoon. "Never mind."

He felt with his hand for the spot. There it was,

tamped down in the shape of feet in deerhide soles. He dug. The earth seemed looser than it should be. He hadn't been at this chest in weeks. . . .

His spoon scraped hard dirt. The hole was deep now. He stopped. He felt around. He poked the soil on either side of the hole. It was tough, undisturbed.

Robin Hood sat back on his heels. He scritched his beard.

Behind him stood Roger and Rufus. Their sword blades shone dimly in the yellow light of the cave mouth.

"So where's this gold?"

"Christ, what a day! *Bloody* woman."

The Sheriff of Nottingham rode the skirt of Sherwood Forest, going west. He had more taxes, more rents to collect, more business to transact. He smiled at the thought. And if he should meet the robber knights, well and good. His men could capture them, and he'd impound their money. "But it would be just my luck to meet bloody Robin Hood and his bloody Merry bloody Men—"

He heard a *zip* and *thop!* and blinked. An arrow shaft stuck out of his horse's breast just in front of his foot. How did that—

His horse took another three steps, died, and collapsed. His nose banged the dirt road, his neck twisted, his body slumped at an angle. Nicholas of Nottingham followed, tumbling out of his high Norman saddle. He landed on his back knowing his clothes would be filthy. Then the sky darkened.

A hand came down and caught the sheriff by the doublet. Nicholas was plucked up off his feet as he hadn't been since a child.

Little John propped the sheriff on his feet. The forester was impossibly tall, making Nicholas feel even smaller. He grinned. "Hail and well met, good Sheriff. Master." The giant laughed, then laughed some more. "How're your home and your lovely wife? Hired a new cook, or any more servants?"

Nicholas scowled. It was not so long ago that Little
John, then unknown, had entered his service, cleaned
out his kitchen, and lured away his cook. Later he'd
tricked the sheriff into attending a feast in the greenwood. Nicholas had eaten off his own plate, been
served his own wine by his own cook, and then been
robbed for dessert.

More foresters held bows with arrows nocked and
pointed at his soldiers. Nicholas found his temper rising. Here was Robin's cousin, the laughing Will Scarlett, who prowled Nottingham as a cutpurse named
Badger. Here was Hard-Hitting Brand, a tall man
often mistaken for Little John (by anyone who hadn't
seed the real thing). And here was old Will Stutly,
whom the sheriff had tried to hang, but whom Robin
Hood had snatched from under his nose.

Brand pointed. "No word for Reynold Greenleaf,
Sheriff?"

Will Scarlett laughed, "Isn't it Reynold John?"

Little John smirked. "Or Little Greenleaf?"

Will Stutly grinned a gap-toothed grin. He rasped,
"And have you reconsidered joining our band?"

The foresters laughed, Brand and John and the two
Wills and a man named Simon. Little John finally
wiped his eyes. "You ought to teach your men proper
archery, Nick. Them crossbows are too slow to
engage, and they look so helpless."

The soldier at the forefront burst out, "Only cowards strike from cover!"

Simon darkened. "*Cowards?*"

Little John waved a hand. "Don't be touchy,
Simon. They always say that. We're forever killing the
sheriff's men, and they're sensitive about it."

Nicholas brushed at his cloak. "Did you have to
kill my horse? They cost more than the soldiers, you
know."

The giant shrugged. Besides his quiver and bow
across his back, he held a quarterstaff taller than himself, thicker than the sheriff's wrist. "All you lot do

is complain. Next time we'll knock you out of the saddle and spare the horse."

Nicholas shuddered, then froze as the giant continued. "Now hand over the gold."

"G-gold? What gold?"

"Or silver."

"I, uh, I haven't any—"

Little John shook his head.

Nicholas sighed. "It's in the saddlebags."

Little John waved. "Scarlett, fetch it." Will untied the saddlebags and bounced them on the road. They gave a muted *chink*. Little John stuck out his hand. The sheriff produced his purse from inside his shirt.

Nicholas asked, "How did you know I had money?"

Scarlett laughed. "You always have money."

Little John added, "And you're not supposed to even be in Sherwood. This ain't sheriff's territory."

"I can ride the roads!"

Will Scarlett slung the saddlebags over his shoulder. "You gonna do like Rob does? He always splits it and gives half back."

"Robin ain't here."

Stutly croaked, "Besides, he lied. He said he didn't have no gold."

"Oh, that's right." Will nodded at the soldiers. "Do we rob them?"

Little John answered. "No. We're too cowardly to go near fighting men. Besides, anyone takes up soldierin' needs money bad." The sheriff's eight men fidgeted in their saddles but said nothing. He told the sheriff, "That's all. You can go. Oh, did you hear about four knights robbed the Widow of Three Oaks? We're hunting for them."

Nicholas grit his teeth. "I heard. I met her. We're hunting, too."

"Oh, good."

The sheriff's eyes blazed at the foresters. "One of these days . . . I'm going to catch you lot and *hang* you all!"

Simon was stunned. Stutly was smug. Will Scarlett nodded. "Fair enough."

Nicholas, High Sheriff of Nottingham, stalked back to the last man in line. "Get off that animal, you idiot! I need it!" The soldier got down and the sheriff mounted. "Start walking!" Head high, he led his troop down the road. The dismounted soldier walked around the outlaws and the dead horse, swinging his arms.

Little John laid his staff down in the road, broke the laces on the saddle bags, and dumped out the money. He whistled at the bushes. "Alphonse! Come here!"

The widow's son crept out of the bush. He looked at the retreating entourage. "Is that always the way you rob people? The sheriff?"

Scarlett stacked coins in piles of ten. "No. Sometimes we make fun of him. Look at this, son. How much did your mother lose?"

Alphonse gulped. "Near to ninety pounds, is what she said to say."

"But how much did she lose?"

"Uh . . ."

Scarlett glanced at Little John. The giant shrugged. "Count out ninety and give it him. Near enough is close enough."

But when it was counted out, there were only eighty pounds in gold and its equivalent in silver.

Little John straightened up. "Eighty's almost ninety. Good." He squinted at the sun, scratched the base of his braid. "Not yet noon and we've recovered most of the widow's money. Robin will be pleased."

Scarlett grinned. "We're one up on Rob."

"This ain't a contest, I tell you. Alphonse, why don't you get along home? Your mother'll be frantic over the loss of that money, and glad to see this. We'll chase after those knights, but they could be anywhere. We'll send word if we get lucky."

"What will you do if you catch 'em?"

Little John kept pulling at his braid where it caught on the bowstring. "Depends what they do. If they surrender, we'll march 'em into Nottingham for the sheriff, I guess. If they act up, we'll stack 'em by the side of the road for the wolves. You lot ready?"

Scarlett said, "You're the one talking and fussing with your hair."

Little John frowned. "I see what happened. Robin was born first and got all the brains in the family."

Will grinned. "That's right. I got all the looks."

"Must be one ugly family. Let's walk."

Alphonse went west, and they set off south.

Simon asked, "You think Robin's back in camp yet, so we can tell him what we did?"

Little John reached for his braid and turned the gesture into another shrug. " 'Less he stopped for a nap."

Robin stood up in the dusky cave and brushed off his trousers. Because of the holes in his knees, most of the dirt fell inside his pants legs and down his deer-hide boots.

"Well?" demanded Roger. "Where's the gold?"

Robin turned around slowly. "I forgot. I had one of my men fit it into a niche here."

Rufus asked, "What's a niche?"

"Up here." In the gloom Robin walked to a wooden rack suspended from the ceiling by pegs. As the robbers pressed behind, he caught at something and brought it down. It was long and wrapped in deerhide. Robin tussled with the wrappings, turning around in the process.

Rufus pressed closest. "What is it?"

"This!" Robin spun around and shot out his arm. Rufus gave a grunt and dropped his sword.

Roger slapped his shoulder. "What are you doing, you fool? Pick that up!"

Rufus merely clutched his middle. Robin Hood danced backwards and tossed the wrapping aside.

Robin Hood laughed. "Roger, you false pig! Let's see you use that sword!"

In the half-light, the knight could see Robin Hood

facing him down a length of steel. He bore a long tapered sword with a wheel pommel and wire-wrapped handle. It was a Norman sword, Robin's father's. Robin Hood shuffled forward and swiped at the knight, who only just jerked out of the way.

"I was trained by Will Stutly, who fought in the wars of Wales and taught King Henry a thing or two." His voice was gravelly from a bellyful of adrenalin. He took another swipe and Roger jumped again. Rufus coughed, face down. The outlaw chief had punched a hole through his midriff. The scent of hot blood, like iron ore smelting, filled the cave. Roger turned and bolted.

He popped out of the cave and pelted for his horse. Dismounted, Wycliff and Tomkin were caught by surprise. "What's happened?" "Where's Rufus?"

Then Robin Hood appeared in the cave mouth waving a bloody sword. *"Yaaaahhhh!!! Git! Git! Hyaaahhh!"*

Spooked, the two knights snatched at their cantles. Roger and his mount were already entering the forest, going much too fast. Wycliff slammed into the saddle and rammed home his heels. His horse banged Rufus's, which whinnied and shied aside to trot into the woods.

Robin shouted and waved. He had no plans to fight them all. But as the last knight, the old man, finally got mounted and moving, Robin spotted something. Tied behind his saddle was the leather bag from the Blue Boar. That would be the widow's money.

"Oh, no, you don't!" Robin caught up to the horse before it set its back hooves. He swung the sword wide and cut a back leg to the bone.

The horse screamed and reared. The man screamed, too. Robin swung again and chopped the beast's leg below the fetlock. The horse slewed sideways, stumbled, and crashed to the earth. Old Tomkin crashed along with it. He was quick enough to pull his leg clear so the horse didn't pin it.

The horse shrieked and kicked. It chopped the forest loam into powder. Robin Hood skipped to its front and chopped the windpipe, then jumped aside to avoid the spray. The beast thrashed and fell still. The round brown eyeballs glazed over.

Robin Hood stood back and signalled with his thumb at Tom. "Can you get up?"

Tom was shaky but upright. He nodded, his mouth open and dry.

Robin waggled his thumb again. "Then drop your sword belt and get out."

He was gone in a moment, hobbling off down the trail after his companions.

Robin Hood stood for a while, breathing deep and wiping his forehead. Eventually he cleaned his sword on the dead horse's tail. He unstrapped the saddle and tugged it clear. The leather bag contained gold, right enough, though not more than twenty pounds by a quick count.

Robin wondered about that: hadn't they bragged there was sixty-some? Could they have spent some, or hidden it? He thought about carrying the gold into the cave, but he'd had a treasure there and it was gone. He stashed the bag under some bushes instead.

He hauled the dead knight out of the cave, and for lack of a better place, stacked him with the dead horse. "What a waste," he remarked to the air. "Can't eat either."

He fetched out his scabbard and baldric and hung them on. He strung his old bow, found a spare quiver and filled it with arrows. He catfooted after Rufus's horse, crooned and cooed to it. "You're a valuable piece yourself, aren't you, hmmm? That's right. Good fellow. Animals are smart. They don't chase after money, do they?" After some nose-patting and neck-rubbing, he got mounted and settled.

"And where do we go?" Robin asked his new horse. He yawned. "I thought I wasn't sleepy. Well, let's see what transpires on the road. It can't be any more busy there than it's been here."

*   *   *

"Hello? *Hello?*"

Alphonse had found his way back to the camp largely by luck. Robin Hood's camp was far from the road, but all trails seemed to lead there.

The camp was a riot. The deer he'd partaken of earlier was a scorched heap on the grass. Nearby was the carcass of a horse, slashed in several places, its saddle torn loose. A knight lay dead next to it. Crows picked over both, but flew off at his approach. With his heart pounding to burst, Alphonse came close enough to recognize the man. It was one of the wastrel knights who'd burnt his mother's barn and home.

The boy's hands shook as he opened the saddlebag full of gold. He had carried it first in one hand, then the other, then behind his back, then in front. It worried him terribly to be carrying this much money. It felt obscene. Especially since he didn't deserve it.

Alphonse had a good heart, inherited from his deceased father. The boy knew well his mother hadn't lost "near ninety pounds" but more like thirty. She'd hoped more would somehow find its way home. It might have, except that Robin Hood's men had thought Alphonse dishonest. With a pride that can only come from poverty, he'd prove them wrong.

The widow's son counted out stacks of ten coins each, as he'd seen Will Scarlett do, then piled four stacks back into the saddlebags. His mother would be pleased enough to receive ten extra pounds.

The rest of the gold stood stacked on the grass, glittering in the sun. Alphonse hunted for inspiration. The crows circled overhead. Flies thickened. The forest glade was oppressive. Where to hide the money? Not the cave—caves led to hell.

He spotted the saddle. He scooped up the gold and swept it underneath, covering it completely. Then he grabbed the sheriff's saddlebags and scampered for the woods.

"The rats. The shits. The bastards."

Old Tomkin had run for most of a mile before his

breath gave out. He leaned against a giant oak and clutched his chest. Cool air burned his lungs. He tugged off his heavy helmet and threw it in the bushes. A hell of a thing, running. No wonder God invented horses. They'd run off and left him, all of them. He started as a covey of quail raced by on tiny legs. Christ, what a place, this forest. "The dogs. The pigs—"

He squinted at his backtrail. There was no one in sight, but there could be any second. Best to keep moving. That Robin Hood was a killer. Teetering from tree to tree, he stumbled off down the path.

And stopped. Up ahead—damn!—was another of Robin Hood's outlaws, dressed like the devil in green. One before, one behind, no way to leave the trail without getting lost. . . .

But that one was carrying something on his shoulder. A chest. A small one for gold.

Tomkin wiped his face and checked his backtrail again. No sign of Robin Hood. No sign the fat forester before had heard him. Tom drew his long knife.

Much the Miller's Son rolled down the trail towards the road. He had a walk all his own, like a crippled duck, but he covered ground quickly and never tired. *Get to the road,* he thought. *Find Robin . . . and then . . . do something. . . .* Robin would know.

A thumping sounded behind him, feet on the forest floor, coming fast, and he stepped out of the way.

Charging like a demon let loose from hell, knife held high, on his last breath, Tomkin sailed towards the idiot. Much discommoded him by side-stepping, and further so by leaving his foot in the path. Tom stumbled on it and crashed full length on the ground. His knife flew away and slithered under the oak leaves that lay everywhere.

Much the Miller's Son helped him up.

"You hurt?"

Tom was surprised at the idiot's strength. "No, no, I'm not hurt. Uh, are you?"

Much checked himself slowly. "No."

"Oh, good. I was afraid you'd fallen."

"No."

Tom pointed. "Uh, what's in the chest?"

Much turned halfway around peering at it. "Treasure."

"T-treasure? Real gold?"

The idiot frowned.

Tom brushed at his clothing. "I, uh, lost my knife. D'ya see it?"

With his free hand, Much drew his own knife and pointed it at Tom. "Knife like this?"

"Uh . . ."

Much suddenly jerked the knife sideways, just missing Tom's arm. Then he jerked it back in Tom's direction. "You take mine. Every-one needs knife."

Tom gingerly took the blade away and shoved it in his own empty sheath. "Right. Thanks. That's better. Uh, if that's really treasure—I mean, uh, Robin's sent me to take that treasure from you—for you."

"Oh." So Robin had known what to do. Much shoved the chest at the robber, who caught it awkwardly.

Tom grunted. The box was heavier than Much had made it look. It must be chock full of gold. He scouted the trail again, then set the box down. No harm in checking.

He pried back the lid and had to shield his eyes. Even under the green roof of leaves the sun jumped around in the box. Tom grinned so wide his face hurt. "It is! It's gold!" Then he remembered Robin Hood's man.

Much grinned, too. "Gold can't buy any-thing 'portant."

"What? Never mind. Let's . . . lighten the load some. No use hauling the box."

He was hot anyway. He shucked off his hauberk and his shirt. He laid the shirt on the leaves, then dumped the coins onto it and pitched the box. He stirred the treasure with his hand. The coins made a lovely liquid sound, a friendly chuckling noise. He stuffed some into a pouch to spread the load, then gathered the corners of the shirt, made sure there were no leaks, and slung the sack on his back. He staggered as it hit.

Much asked, "I help carry? I strong. Strong as Little John at arm wrestle."

"No." The old man shook his head and staggered again. "No, thanks, lad. I'll manage. You run along back to—" Wait. He couldn't point him towards camp. He'd run right into Robin Hood. "You better come with me for a while, lad. Keep out of trouble. What's your name?"

"Much the Mill-er's Son. 'Sher-wood ain't much with-out Much.' "

"Much. Good. I'm . . . Peter. Come along now."

So Tom, or Peter, hunched now and rolling like Much, set off down the trail. The unencumbered idiot followed, happy as a dog after its master.

"If you'd gone *into* the cave we could have killed him there!"

"And if you *hadn't* gone into the cave there'd still be four of us!"

"Afraid of a cave!"

"Stupid enough to be taken in the dark!

"*Idiot!*"

"*Fool!*"

"*Coward!*"

Wycliff jerked his tired horse to a halt. He grabbed for his sword. "No man calls me coward!"

Roger clutched at his own hilt. He had to drag his horse backwards, for there was no room to swing. The Nottingham road was very narrow here, overgrown at the sides from neglect. "No man calls me *fool*! Defend—"

His horse snorted.

From out of nowhere, Little John said, "You're both fools. *And* loudmouths. Let's call it even."

The giant—he was the biggest man the knights had ever seen—filled most of the road. He held a quarterstaff lightly across the horses' throats. He smiled at their discomfort.

Roger was furious at the impertinence, Wycliff blind with anger. They both raised their swords. Roger snarled, "You *scut!* I'll—"

A cord snagged his throat. His Adam's apple was wrenched out of joint as an irresistible force tugged him backwards. The knight tumbled out of the saddle and landed hard on his head and shoulder.

Sprawled in the road, Roger and Wycliff rubbed their throats and gagged curses. Facing them were more outlaws in green. Their bows had been slipped over the knights' heads while the giant distracted them. Will Scarlett examined his bow, then used it to rap Wycliff on the helmet.

Tonk! "You cut my string with your blade." *Tonk!*

Snarling, Wycliff dove for the outlaw. Scarlett skipped aside and let him pass. The mad knight plowed into old Will Stutly and both went sprawling.

Will Stutly growled on his own as the knight pummeled him. Will didn't bother to call for help—he knew better. He tossed his bow and jammed both thumbs into the knight's eyes. Hard-Hitting Brand crashed a fist onto the side of Wycliff's neck and knocked him loose. Brand stamped on the man's back and snatched away his knife. The outlaws tied his hands with the broken bowstring.

Roger felt a rap on his helmet. He looked up, and up.

Little John pointed at the saddles. "Where's the widow's gold?"

Roger swore. "We lost it. One of our men—old Tom—ran off with it." He watched Wycliff thrash on the floor like a suckling pig. Why had he taken up thieving with these three: one mad, one stupid, and one decrepit? Next time he'd enlist real men-at-arms.

The giant rested his quarterstaff on the ground and rolled it between his hands as if drilling. "Hmmm . . ."

Scarlett grinned. "This puts us up even more on

Robin. We've robbed the sheriff, paid back the
widow, and now captured two of the knights."

"This ain't a contest, I tell ya. Where'd the old man
get to?"

"I don't know. Away."

"Where's the other one, then? There was supposed
to be four of ye."

"He ran off, too."

"Is that so? But no widow's gold, eh?"

"No. And I don't care anymore. Damn you all."

"Hmmm . . ." Little John sped up his drilling. "I
don't think I believe you. But this can work out fine.
Robin didn't get any gold yet, but we will."

Scarlett laughed. "I thought this wasn't a contest."

"Hush. Let's pack up this baggage. We'll take 'em
to Nottingham."

Stutly grunted. "Nottingham? What for?"

"We're going to stuff 'em into a wine press and
squeeze out gold."

Scarlett grabbed Roger by the shoulder. "That
makes sense."

Roger gasped as his shoulder was wrenched. Wycliff
chomped grass. "Are all you bloody outlaws daft?
What's wrong with you? What are you talking about?"

"You'll see. Get up. I'm thirsty."

Will Scarlett slammed the knight belly-down across
his own saddle. "See? He's not daft at all."

"Mother! Look what I have!"

Amabillia, the Widow of Three Oaks, poked a maid
in the shoulder as the girl stirred an iron pot over a
fire. All around stood the burned wreckage of her
house. She stopped in mid-poke as the boy held a bag
aloft.

Alphonse trotted to a halt. He panted, "Here,
Mum. Here's the gold. From Robin Hood's men." He
thrust the bag into her hands, glad to be rid of it.

The widow blinked at the heft. She set the bag on
a fallen timber and counted the coins.

"This isn't our gold. There are no florins. It's someone else's. Though we'll keep it. Where did they get it? Was it Robin Hood did it?"

Alphonse nodded and wiped his cheeks. "Aye. His Merry Men . . ." He told her about their intercepting the sheriff.

Amabillia smiled a cold smile. "That's fun. I set the sheriff on the knights' trail, but I knew he'd slough it off and run for Nottingham." She cackled some more, then turned to the cook. "Never mind that. Dump it out. We'll leave now."

For the first time Alphonse noticed the two pack horses hung with sacks and ironware. "Mother, where are we going?"

"Where do you think? Use your head, Alphie." The widow circled the horses and tugged at knots. Three servants watched her with slack hands. "We're going to live with your Aunt Alditha in York. There's nothing for us here. Now that we have the gold."

Alphonse looked about at the ruins of the manor and barn, at the tumbledown cottages, at the weedy fields. He pointed to things at random. "We're leaving? But I've lived here all my life! What about our home? What about the land?"

Amabillia struggled to mount a horse already piled high. "Oh, for heaven's sake, Alphie! Shut up! It's only land. Nobody wants that. It's not worth anything. Now come on!"

She kicked the horse with her skinny heels, and the beast lumbered forward. The servants trailed, leading the other horse.

Alphonse took one more look around, then followed.

"After we get the money, can we spend it on wine and debauchery?"

Little John pointed to the robber knights trussed on the floor. He answered Will Scarlett. "Are you sure you shouldn't be on the floor with those two?"

The Merry Men waited in the dust-speckled dimness of a barn on the outskirts of Nottingham. They ate and rested, lazy with the long day and spring warmth.

Barn swallows turned circles that brushed the rafters and skimmed straw from the floor. The knights' horses chewed hay. One kicked his hoof regularly against the outer wall.

Scarlett carved his initials in a post with a wicked knife. "Those two don't know anything about debauchery. I can tell 'em about debauchery. When I go out to debauch, I have a good time. They probably just get drunk and beat up someone small. By the time they get to a whore they'd pass out. Did you ever see two more sour faces?"

From the loft Hard-Hitting Brand called, "Here he comes with the blacksmith."

"Anyone else?" asked Little John.

"Nope. Just a smithy and two apprentices."

"Well, keep an eye out all around. He may have told the sheriff's men to come later, when we're negotiating hot and heavy."

"Right."

Scarlett brushed away shavings to see his handiwork, yellow etched in brown. "You doing the negotiating?"

Little John rumbled, "No. I'm goin' to leave it to Simon here, only because we don't have Much to talk for us." Simon blinked, but the giant waved a hand at him. "Just joking, lad. I'll do the hagglin'."

Scarlett touched up his graffiti. "You sure you don't want me to?"

"I'm sure."

"Fine. You handle it. I'll keep quiet."

Little John snorted.

The owner of the farm, a merchant, knocked at the door and then crept in. With him was the Nottingham blacksmith, a short solid man whose long tunic had burns in the front. He carried an iron box. His two apprentices, a thin boy and an older journeyman, carried steel pokers.

The Merry Men shuffled about in the tight barn to make room. Little John signalled to shut the door, and for the blacksmiths to put down their pokers.

"You won't need those. We're not here to rob you." The boy breathed easier. The journeyman seemed disappointed.

The blacksmith set down the box and put one foot on it. "So what have you?"

The giant forester squatted and unfolded a hauberk. On it lay all the knights' accoutrements. The knights themselves wore only gambesons and rope.

"Two swords, two long knives. Baldrics—this one ain't got a crack on it anywhere—scabbards and sheaths. Tooling, here. Their shoes, one pair with double soles. Hauberks, one with copper, one iron squares, good solid rivets. Norman helmets. Some kind of a locket here, must be silver, and a cross of whatever this metal is—bronze, is it? Someone's been to a shrine, though it din't do him any good. Plus them two nags. And their tack."

The merchant, the owner of the barn, cleared his throat. The giant gave him a gold mark for fetching the blacksmith.

There was a very long space as the blacksmith checked over the booty. He unsheathed the swords and tested their edge. He rapped them together to hear them ring. He picked at the handles to learn what kind of wire wrapped them. He scrutinized everything the same way. Then he checked the horses. He counted their teeth, stared into their eyes, pressed his ear against their chests and bellies, poked their frogs, peered under their tails.

Finally he rocked back on his heels and rubbed his throat. "All of it?"

Little John nodded. "We can't use it."

The smith probed the barn with his eyes. "Forty pounds."

"*Forty pounds?*" Will Scarlett bounded off the stall railing and landed in front of Little John. "Forty pounds? Are you *mad?* God's fish and teeth, one of those damned helmets *alone* is worth forty pounds! Where in the hell did you get a figure like *that?* Forty pounds! Christ's sweet tree, it'd take you three months to make *one* of those hauberks, and you'd be glad to charge some idiot fifty pounds for it *alone*. Did you hear the ring on those swords? One of 'em's got to be Milanese or Damascan, and *you're* offering us forty pounds for it? The *knives* would be worth forty pounds even *without* the sheaths. You *Jew!* You Saracen *pirate!* You tax-collecting, wine-nipping, cheese-paring, gold-shaving—"

Little John interjected, "We'll take it."

Red-faced but silent, the blacksmith twirled the barrels on the lock and opened the chest. Shielding it with his body, he extracted forty thin coins and stacked them on the floor. Little John packed them into his purse. All the while Will Scarlett ranted and raved and waved his arms in the air. " . . call *us* thieves! *Simpletons,* maybe! *Fools!* Children wandered to the woods! But *thieves?* You need a *town man* to teach you about *thievin'* . . ."

The blacksmith ordered his apprentices to tie everything onto the saddles of the horses. Then he led them out, not directly towards the town gates, but along some oblique route. He didn't say goodbye.

Will Scarlett wasn't through. ". . . can't *believe* you let it go at forty pounds, John, and *clipped* ones at that! Have you lost your *mind?* We were robbed, plain and simple, same as we hoist the sheriff! We could've shopped around. We could've gotten three smiths here, pitted 'em against one another, gotten a fair price. But *no*, you had to give the stuff away! We could've gotten two *hundred* pounds—"

Little John grinned. "It's worth a hundred to see you hop like a frog in a pot."

Scarlett glared. "Forty needs a hundred sixty to make two hundred."

Little John picked up his quarterstaff. "Does it? I never was one for numbers. Get over twenty sheep and it might's well be a thousand and one, and half of them wolves. Get you up, you lot, we're for the woods."

Will Stutly creaked upright. He rubbed the small of his back. "What about them?"

The giant regarded the knights. Through the exchange, as their worldly goods had been auctioned away, they had glared and chomped on their gags. John scratched his jaw in imitation of Robin Hood. "Can't sell 'em. Can't eat 'em. Can't leave 'em here, 'cause that'd get Paul in trouble. Hmmmm . . ."

A little later the Merry Men approached the tall broad towers that were the gates of Nottingham. Slung from Little John's quarterstaff, between John and Hard-Hitting Brand, were the two knights. With hands and bare feet in the air, their gambesons hung slack. Their rumps shone in the sunshine. Women in the fields pointed and laughed.

The foresters stopped in the road outside crossbow range. The sheriff's guards, in blue gypons and soup-bowl helmets, had already gathered at the gate—they could spot Lincoln green a mile off. Little John dropped the knights in the road and slid his staff clear. "Hoy! Captain of the guard!"

The captain cupped his hands around his mouth. "What d'ya want?"

"These here are the false knights robbed the Widow of Three Oaks by Derby! Give 'em to the sheriff with our compliments!"

"Compliments of who?"

"Don't be thick!" the giant retorted. He pointed with his thumb at the guards and asked Will Scarlett, "Relations o' yours?"

Robin's cousin snorted. "'Maybe. My father went into Nottingham a lot. But none of them—thick as they are—would trade away two liveries and horses for forty pounds."

Little John shrugged and started down the road towards Sherwood. His quarterstaff on his shoulder stuck out six feet behind him. "I suppose not. Next time, you do the negotiating and I'll be the one to keep quiet."

*   *   *

Old Tomkin sat down by the side of the path to rest. He kept the gold in his lap with one hand on it. He grimaced at Much, who had followed him for miles. "Awful hot today, ain't it?"

Much pointed up. "Sun's out."

"Aye. Makes it hot. But my hands are cold. Funny." Tom wheezed and rubbed his chest. "Can't get my breath, neither. Not as young as I used to be. M' ribs feel squashed."

He tried to shift the gold in his lap, but it was too heavy. He shifted himself instead and winced. "You don't need to keep me company, lad. I can fend for m'self. You just run along now. I'm going to just rest here, maybe take a nap . . . Awful hot. Makes me chest . . ."

His head sank back and he lay still. Much sat down beside him to wait.

He waited a long time.

Much grew hungry. He poked the old man gently on the leg. He was stiff. The idiot poked the man in the eyeball. He was dead. Much knew what death was.

He scratched his upper lip for a time.

Eventually he picked up the shirt full of money. He started walking towards the Blue Boar.

"Because we still owe the widow ten pounds, that's why."

"We don't owe her nothing. You know and I know she lies like a flounder—"

Little John walked fast and everyone struggled to keep up with him. The deep woods were warm and buzzy with late-day heat. Pale green translucent leaves unfolded almost as they watched. Lizards basked in sandy patches. Digger wasps bored by, heavy with eggs. "No, we don't know that. She's supposed to have ninety pounds and we only gave her eighty. That leaves ten we owe her, if my countin' is right, and you'll probably tell me it ain't."

Will Stutly croaked, "Slow *down*, John! For Christ's sweet mercy!"

The giant stopped altogether. The five foresters stood in the middle of the road trying to catch their breaths.

Little John explained, "We're giving her ten pounds, and that's all there is to it. If you want to argue, take it up with Robin. You know he's funny about honorin' women. Are you going to tell him we shorted a widow in need?"

Scarlett sliced at the iron-red head of a foxglove with his knife. He said nothing.

"Right then. Anyone doesn't want to go with me to Three Oaks can return to camp. Well? Right then. Let's go."

"Slowly," said Stutly.

"Slow it is. I'm easy."

Another two hours' of shortcut brought them to Three Oaks. The ruins stank of damp ashes.

Simon said, "There's no one here."

Will Scarlett said, "No. There isn't."

Brand pointed. "Fresh horse turds here."

Little John scratched his beard. Then stopped.

The Sheriff of Nottingham and his men stood up from behind the wreckage of the hall. Four soldiers covered them with crossbows. The other four were behind.

Nicholas grinned like a wolf. "The tables are turned. I took your advice, *Little* John. Our crossbows are cocked and nocked this time."

Little John frowned. "Where are your horses?"

"Far down the road, west. I didn't bring them anywhere near here. Shall I shoot you now?"

Little John drilled his quarterstaff into the ground. "Shoot as you please, just don't tell Robin we walked into your trap."

Will Scarlett asked, "How did you know we'd come here?"

The sheriff put his hands on his hips and puffed out his chest. "I knew it because— Stay there, Will Stutly!

I like you in a covey. It makes a smaller target. I came here—"

The giant stopped his drilling. He thumped his staff on the ground. "Do you want your purse back?"

"That and my eighty pounds. I—"

Little John dragged out his purse and hefted it, making it look heavy. Will Scarlett snatched it away. "Let me give it to him."

Robin's cousin dumped the contents of the purse into his hand. Coins spilled into the blackened grass.

"Here now," called the sheriff, "you fool! Give me that—"

Will Scarlett whipped back his hand and flung the coins. Gold and silver sparkled in the air and pelted the sheriff and his men. The sheriff ducked. His men grabbed at the air with their free hands.

Little John spun around and slung his huge quarterstaff by one end. Crossbows *thunked*. The staff hummed through the air and slammed into two soldiers behind.

Will Stutly hopped backwards into Simon, jostling him out of the way. Another crossbowman shot. The bolt sizzled overhead. The other took aim, too late. With arthritic hands Old Will nocked an arrow, half-drew, and loosed before the man could pull the trigger. The long arrow caught him in the upper chest. He cried out and folded, dropping his crossbow to clutch the shaft.

Will Scarlett followed his gold-throwing with a knife. He aimed for the one man who'd kept his head. The soldier ducked. By that time Hard-Hitting Brand was over the wreckage and among the soldiers. He slung his fists and bowled men over. He made sure their crossbows went flying.

"*That's it!*" Little John cried. "*Run!*"

The giant grabbed Simon by the shoulder and spun him around towards the road. Scarlett was already there with an arrow nocked. Will Stutly looked for a ready victim. Brand caught at the old man as he ran past. "Come on, Will!"

"Always hurryin'." He pegged his arrow at the most alert soldier and scuttled along.

Ten minutes later and many trees deep into the forest, the outlaws stopped to catch their breath. They were built for walking, and not running.

"Fine thing," Scarlett gasped. "You get robbed selling the knights' tackle—and then robbed by the sheriff."

"If you hadn't been arguin' about money—" wheezed Little John, "—we would'a spotted the sheriff hiding."

"If you had listened to me—we wouldn't have come—in the first place."

"You came along. I gave you a choice."

"I don't care about the money anyway—I just like arguin'." He grinned. "You still going to give the widow—ten pounds when you see her?"

Little John huffed. "No, I'm going to give her you. If she's travelling the roads, she'll need an ass. Let's get back to camp. We've done enough today."

"What *have* we done?" Simon asked.

The giant snorted. Lacking his quarterstaff, his hands clasped and unclasped. "We'll figure it out later. Let's go."

Stutly cursed. "Always hurrying."

"If you lot could *shoot* better, we wouldn't have this problem. Damned slippery outlaws. Cowards. Why *didn't* you pot them? We'd be out a few headaches, or I'm a fishmonger."

The sheriff berated his men in a flat uninterested monotone. His soldiers clutched their wounds and grit their teeth and said nothing.

"We'll have more practice, I can assure you that. Up before dawn, now that the days are longer, out there in the sun until you can knock a mosquito off a squirrel's ear. Eighty pounds down and only thirty-five back, and— Who's that up there?"

Much the Miller's Son plodded down the road with a sack of treasure over his shoulder, the same as when he'd carried grain and flour for his father, the same as when he'd met Robin Hood. He waddled along and thought about . . . about . . . wherever he was going.

Whiff! Something plunked in the road alongside him. He stooped slowly and picked it up. Was it a snake? A bird? No, it was . . . a crossbow quarrel. Another slapped the earth nearby and spattered dirt in his eyes. Who was? . . .

Much saw the sheriff's men thundering towards him. He knew these men. They were bad. What would Robin do? He heard his leader's voice. "Run, Much! Run!"

Much dropped his sack and ran for the deepest, most tangled bushes he could find.

Moments later the sheriff dismounted in the road, exulting. "It *was* one of Robin Hood's men! Look at this silver! No, get away! I'll get it!" Nicholas scraped the muddy coins together onto the filthy shirt that had carried them. "Well, it's not such a bad day after all. Robin's treasure come home! We might even celebrate when we get to the Boar."

The sheriff remounted, the money on his lap. "Now, let's—"

There came a *zip*! and *thok*! The sheriff's horse gave a grunt and stumbled, squealed, fell.

Nicholas grabbed at the beast's mane as it collapsed in the road. This time he got clear without tumbling in the mud, but he dropped the money.

"*Sheriff!*" the voice echoed all around.

Nicholas raised his arm. There. Down the dappled leafy tunnel of road sat a lone rider. Long arrows at his back and a long bow held ready marked the silhouette. The sheriff tried to hide behind his men's mounts. His men were already in the bushes. Another arrow thudded into the horse carcass. The arrows were impossibly long, as if hurled by God. "*Hold still!*"

Nicholas stood still, alone. His mount twitched, then sighed with finality. The sheriff sighed, too. "Twice in one day."

He brushed back his brocaded sleeves and called down the road. "Who are you?"

A laugh.

"Goddamn him." In the brush his men cranked their crossbows—those who could. The sheriff cursed some more. Robin Hood was outside crossbow range, but not, obviously, long bow range.

"Keep still."

The sheriff cupped his mouth. "What do you want?"

The distant figure bobbed. "Today? Money! I've something to prove!"

"I don't *have* any—"

Ziiiiip! Something snatched at the sheriff's sleeve. He could see the red satin lining of his doublet where there should have been only blue. Sweat broke out on his forehead. But this was gold at stake. He tried once more. "Your men have already robbed me once!"

"I believe you!" Another laugh. "Truly!"

"Then why do you think I have any money now?"

"You always have money!"

The sheriff wanted to cry. "Goddamn you, wolfshead! You've no right!"

"You don't like it, become a shoemaker! Now I've had a long day, Sheriff. Leave your money and go. Your men can keep theirs."

Nicholas shook his head. He tugged out a purse (Little John's) and set it on the saddlebag. He pointed. "It's all here!"

The archer waved a long bow. "Our Lady thanks you!"

Unable to go forward, Nicholas of Nottingham mounted yet another horse and turned back towards nowhere. It didn't make any difference which way he went today.

Robin Hood dismounted and tied his horse to a branch. He moved away, crouched, and waited for thirty minutes. Finally he walked around wide, back to the road. He watched for soldiers, but they couldn't hide in his woods. He took the purse, the saddlebags, and a shirt full of mostly silver.

He took the saddle as well. "Should be able to sell this to someone."

"Hoy!"

Little John and the rest sat under a tree, just lolling, not talking, when Robin Hood staggered into camp. He came up to them and dropped several loads: saddlebags, a pouch, a shirt full of money, Little John's purse.

Little John frowned. "Where have you been?"

Robin went for a drink at the stream. "Out and about. Adventuring. Where have you been?"

"Nowhere."

"You've sat here all day?" No one answered. "Surely that's not possible. The sheriff told me you robbed him once."

Little John and the others just stared at the pile of loot. Robin Hood went behind some bushes and produced yet another bag to throw on the pile.

The giant said, "Well . . . we did that."

Robin flopped down on the grass, but grunted and reached into his shirt for more money. "I forgot. I sold a knight's horse and saddle to Ned for forty pounds, and threw in the sheriff's saddle for free." He slapped his friend on the knee. "Now come, John. Tell me what you did. Please."

"Well . . . we captured them robber knights."

"Oh. Good."

"We delivered them to the sheriff."

Robin plucked up a blade of grass to chew on. "Good."

"And we recovered the widow's money and gave it to her son."

"Good. Very good."

"Is that all you can say? 'Good'?"

"No. Tell me the rest."

They did. Robin listened, then said, "You want to hear what I did?"

No one answered, so he told his story. He finished with, "And on the way back, on the Meadow Trail, I found the oldest robber dead. Just fell over, I suppose. He had a purse on his belt. So that's it. I must have been picking up after you all day."

He laughed, alone. Everyone else was quiet. Robin asked, "How much money did you get?"

It stayed quiet.

Little John rocked his makeshift staff to thump the ends on the ground. "I wonder if anyone else is forming an outlaw band in this forest this year."

Robin laughed. "What? What are you talking about?"

Stutly lay on his back with his eyes closed. "I'm hungry. Do we have to eat that horse? The meat'll be bitter."

Robin Hood went on. "You don't have to fret about anything you did, John. Getting the widow's money was wonderful. Selling the knights' tackle in Nottingham was a very clever idea and an apt punishment. And the sheriff robbing us is a great joke. Getting away safe is even better." The way he said it, so jolly and gay, made the Merry Men feel much worse. "By the way, how much did you get for the tackle?"

Will Scarlett piped up. "You won't believe, Robin. This one here only got—" He stopped, shrivelled under a murderous glare from Little John. "Uh . . . John got near to a hundred pounds for the knights' gear. Just the gear alone. The horses we—uh—gave to the boy to give to his poor widowed mother to keep her from the cold."

"Horses to keep her from the cold? What are you babbling about? And hadn't you already sent the boy on his way with the money? No? Well, it doesn't matter anyway . . ."

Simon called, "Here's Much."

The foresters watched as their idiot friend rolled out of the woods and up the small slope towards them. Much the Miller's Son walked right by the dead horse and knight without blinking. He sat down with a thud. He greeted everyone by turn, as if he hadn't seen them for weeks. "Hul-lo, Rob-in. Nice to see you back."

"Thank you, Much, thank you. It's good to see you and good to be back. But where have you been?"

The idiot pointed towards the woods. "Out."

"What were you doing?"

"Walk-ing."

"Good. Walking is good. But Much, did you dig up our treasure?"

"Trea-sure?"

"Gold?"

"Gold!"

"Yes, Much. Gold. Did you take it?"

Much nodded. "No. Dead man took it. In a skirt."

"What? You mean a shirt? This shirt here?"

Much patted his thighs. "Skirt."

"Who was he?"

"Peter."

"A dead man, named Peter, wearing a skirt, dug up our treasure?"

"Yes."

Simon shuddered. "Maybe he met a saint. Maybe it's a miracle."

Robin grunted. "It'll be a miracle if we figure this out."

They talked some more, but eventually gave up. Robin Hood said, "I'm sure—fairly sure—part here is our treasure. I think I recognize this cracked penny. And I know some of this is the sheriff's money and some is the knights'. And we've paid back the widow, so that's fine. It's all fine. But where's the lesson here? What have we learned from all this?"

It was as quiet as it would ever be in the Sherwood glade.

Robin laughed again. "What? So quiet? Will, you're never at a loss for words. Where's the lesson here?"

Will Scarlett stood up. He looked at all that gold and silver, then at his fellow foresters. "The lesson, Rob? The lesson . . . The lesson is this. That money just isn't important—"

"Good, Will! Finally!"

"—because it's so damned plentiful in Sherwood it practically grows out of the ground."

The Merry Men laughed.

Robin Hood frowned. "I give up. You lot are hopeless. Let's go get some ale. I'll buy."

Will Stutly let out a groan. "*Walk* to the bloody Blue Boar? Again? After all the walking we've already done?"

Scarlett told him, "It's for a drink, Will. You won't have to kill any soldiers along the way."

Robin caught Will Stutly by an arthritic hand and hauled him up. "But before we go, let's get that saddle into the cave so the foxes don't chew on it. Later on we'll—"

Simon shouted. Underneath the saddle lay a pile of gold coins that sparkled in the late evening sun.

Robin Hood blinked. "Where did *this* come from?"

No one knew.

"Aha! Sheriff! Here you are! Drinking in a tavern when you should be on the road!"

Nicholas, High Sheriff of Nottingham, wrapped his hands around his tankard and dropped his head on the grimy table. He knew that voice. It was Amabillia, Widow of Three Oaks above Derby.

"Is this where you've been all day? Sitting here, a disgrace, while robbers ride the highway free as the air? Haven't you been after them? *Answer* me! *Talk* to me! *Where's my money?*"

Robin's Witch

by Nancy Holder

It were a night of whispers and a hooded, horned moon; and Robin and his men ate their venison like the thieves they were: with haste and a shattering relief that they'd survived, hands and feet and all intact, to dine in the chilly oak forest that was their home. None had fallen beneath the sheriff's arrows; for once, a raid had yielded up no outlaw pelts for the king's fee.

But their numbers were dwindling, and Robin knew his men were scarcely his any longer. The pickings along the Great North Road were no longer fat and easy; there were tales spread about the Hooded Man and his followers now, and many who yearned to bring him down—for the coins, and for the boasting.

Though 'twas bandied about that he was a dryad's son, or the heir of Herne, the forest god, the nobles knew who and what he was—a simple yeoman, whose only magic was his cunning. And yeomen could be hunted and shot, or hung in the square as an example to the other lawless men who roamed England. This they knew, and this Robin Hood knew. And this his men knew, and so they quitted him in these dark times and went home, to their miserable villages and hamlets, to till the soil like oxen for their betters. But a wretched life were better than glory as a dead man, at least for most who had once believed the legends of the Hooded Man were true.

Now, when he was almost alone, Robin knew he needed the legends to be true. If he were a dryad's son he didn't know it; and if he could fly through the night like an owl, he had yet to be aware of it. A yeoman was all he was, and not even such a worthy as one who stole from the rich to give to the poor. That, too, was a tale oft told, because he had once aided a knight the Church had sought to ruin. It was hatred of priests and priors that had moved him, not the plight of the mistreated man.

Ah, well, then. He lay on his back, chewing tough venison, and pondered the stars and their courses. His heart pounded sluggishly, for he was afraid; some nights he wondered if one of his own band would cut off his head for the sake of the bounty.

An owl hooted once, twice, three times. A wind whipped his hair and the edge of his jerkin. The earth was damp and cold.

The bird hooted again. Robin swallowed down the meat and stretched out his arm for his ale. The golden cup was loot from a fat abbot who'd wandered through the forest and lied about the size of his purse. He'd been invited to dine, and then to pay for his share of the banquet; and when all the gold coins had spattered like acorns at Robin's feet, he'd taken the golden cup the abbot had prized most, though the abbot swore it were a communion goblet from the abbey. Robin, though a cutpurse, were a pious man, in his own fashion—none lived who was more devoted to the Virgin—and he had known this to be yet another lie. Now, though, his hand trembled when he brought the goblet to his mouth.

He needed protection, and he had prayed to his sweet Lady, and She had given him none. Had even crept into St. Mary's at Nottingham to beg Her help, though it meant his life if he were caught, and She ignored him. Perhaps he had stolen a holy cup after all, and She were angry for the sake of the monks.

The owl hooted again as he drank. He closed his eyes—

—and saw, against the moon, streams of hair blowing madly in the wind, copper and crimson; and eyes slanted like a cat's, and a half-clothed, woman's body that writhed in the storm, pale and supple and young.

He sat up, knocking over the cup. The earth sucked up the ale. The owl sang and flew from the oaks toward the open road.

If his Lady would not help him, he would find another who would. He would steal the witch-woman, Marian, from her master, Prince John.

"John!" he cried to his lieutenant. "Scarlet! Make haste!"

It were not an easy task. They rode by the caped night to Barnsdale, where John kept a sheriff, who kept the witch-woman, and where, 'twas said, she fashioned potions and amulets that kept the prince and his minions safe. Folk told of her ability to look straight at a man and know if he forsook himself or no; and that the sheriff had sent more than one man to the gallows based solely upon her judgment. When she walked in the streets, men, women, and wee children crossed themselves and lifted their gazes away from her; and none dared walk in her shadow. She was feared; and the feared were also hated; and so she remained in the garrison nearly all the time.

Thus, Robin supposed she would be difficult to capture. Once he and the raiding party—the most trusted of his followers—reached sight of Barnsdale, they hied themselves to a forested hillock to study the keep and to plan their strategy.

But she walked freely! Though the wind blew the birds from their nests, and frost wrinkled the fair faces of the ponds and lakes, the witch sauntered along the battlements, climbing the merlons, stepping down to the embrasures, sure-footed as a royal stag. Her gown flew about her like wings, revealing her white legs and arms, and she moved so slowly Robin wondered if she knew what she was about, or if, perhaps, she herself were enchanted.

They watched for three nights, and each night she glided along the walls. And on the fourth, with the

sharp bite of snow in the air, they stole into the yard
and up the staircases. Their feet were soundless upon
the flagstones; they moved like ferrets, stealthy in
their thieving business.

Scarlet, Much, and John kept watch while Robin
crept up to the topmost crenelation; the moon had
waned, and only her shadowed form illuminated his
way. He could not see the stone beneath his feet. In
the dim mist, a figure floated on a vast plain of nothing beyond him; and as he hefted the sack over his
wrists, he prayed to the Virgin—though She continued
to ignore him, Her most devoted and courtly lover—
that this was indeed the witch and not some guard,
and that his mission would find him home in the forest
with a potent new weapon, and not hanging on a gib-
bet at dawn.

He drew closer to the figure. An owl hooted in the
distance and he took it for a sign; for had he not heard
such a bird when the idea came into his head to steal
the witch? He ran forward, his breath in his throat,
and threw the bag over the figure's head, and hit it
once—not too hard—and caught it as it crumpled with
a gasp.

Then over his shoulder he hoisted the still form,
marking its lightness—if it were not a woman, then
'twere a boy, by the wounds of Christ. He ran, and
the others saw him, and they motioned to him that it
was safe.

And as they stole down the stairs and across the
yard to the gatehouse, there Robin's heart stopped,
for the moon winked from behind the clouds. A movement caught his eye, and as he shifted his attention,
a long white arm draped across his shoulder, and long
tresses of red tumbled from beneath the hood. Despite
his terror, he rejoiced: he had her.

The moon hid herself again, and the guards drew
themselves into their cloaks and argued about Jerusalem and the king and the prince, and the thieves
dashed to the road and to their horses.

It was not until they were well away, and on the

Great North Road, that he dared to pull away the hood and look upon her. She lay still in his arms as he drew up his horse. Her features were sharp, her hair as red as only a sorceress's could be. Her lips were gathered in the smile of untroubled sleep, and Robin stirred. She were as beautiful as it was said she were powerful. Now he must bend her to his will and make her help him. For who was to say she would not strike him dead the moment she awakened? Or if she took flight like a falcon and whistled for her master to come and seize the outlaws?

Of a surety, he'd gone to the wise woman who dwelled in the neigh of the Kirklees Abbey (whose prioress was a kinswoman of his, and loyal to him; and had agreed that he must seek help from other than the Virgin at the moment). The wise woman had given him amulets and talismans to shield him and the others from the powers of the witch, but with one as mighty as she, who was to say that they would work?

And who was to say how a common thief could persuade a vassal of the regent to throw down her oaths of fealty and rule the forest with him?

All this Robin had considered, and he knew his hopes were bleak. But he were a bold man, though some called the measure of his bravery madness. Large deeds made large men; and to the world outside the forest, he were a giant. Perhaps she would be swayed by the stories and fall prostrate and beg his mercy. Or perhaps she would be intrigued to meet the famed outlaw himself, at last.

Or mayhap she would survey the raggle-taggle band left to him, and know that desperation had brought him to her, and she would laugh, and kill him herself with a wave of her arm.

That wild, red hair, streaming like a tourney pennant in the wind . . . on they rode, Robin, the hooded king of the forest, and the witch-woman, Marian, his spoils, his plunder.

* * *

Anon they returned to the shield of the oaks. No
one was on the road yet, following after: the theft had
not yet been discovered, or perhaps the snow, falling
now, had hidden their tracks. Robin pulled up his
horse and one of his followers ran to care for it, catching the fine bridle he had stolen from a merchant.

John strode over on long legs, and after a moment's
hesitation, held out his arms for the witch-woman who
still swooned across Robin's saddle. But Robin knew
it were a dangerous thing for any man to handle her,
and so he dismounted with John's help, the woman
still in his capture. He were the *seigneur*; his the task
to ken the danger of her presence.

A fire burned brilliantly through the snowflakes;
Robin strode toward it with his burden. Many of his
men, apprised of the purpose of his raid, moved away
from the warmth and shivered in the shelter of thick
branches, safe in one another's presence. Others,
braver, paled as Robin set her down close to the fire
and called for mead. He took one of her hands and
rubbed it briskly. Soft it was, and small; but he was
not deceived. He knew she were powerful, and that
if she chose, she could strike him dead with a glance.

The drink came and Robin paused, wondering if
she would waken of her own accord, and beginning
to worry that he had struck her too hard. Such a beautiful face, such lips, and that hair . . .

Her eyes flew open, widened, found his. They gazed
at one another; and then she smiled, took the cup in
both her hands, and lifted it slightly.

Then she drank.

In the tree, the owl hooted. It swooped from its
perch and glided through the snow toward Kirklees,
where the prioress stood by an opened casement, waiting. It fanned its wings against the moon and sang to
her, and she smiled.

Witches there were, and druidesses, too, though the
Church had long ago scattered them into hiding. And
some had become dryads, and borne minor gods, and

some had taken veils and called themselves the brides of Christ.

Men might reign in England, but women ruled.

And once the witch-woman had purified the prioress's kinsman and ennobled him, and he had fulfilled his godhood as a prince—of thieves, yes, but a true, good prince—they would do as they had done in the days of the full glory of the mistletoe and oak. There was a knife, and she herself would do it. And though he would believe himself betrayed in the end, that she had murdered him under the guise of bleeding him to heal an illness, in truth she would grant him immortal honor, and give her people a martyr. A sacred king of the greentime, as the druidesses and druids of the old times had promised, and provided. And how the land had flourished then!

This Robin's witch knew, and this the prioress knew.

The owl hooted and flew away. The prioress shut the window, and waited for the greenwood to blossom beneath the snow, and to grow, and to yield the harvest.

Avant Vanguard

by Laura Resnick

Robin Hood strode boldly through the woods as the gay sunshine of a fresh summer morning played upon the dewy leaves of Sherwood Forest and a soft breeze tickled the long, lush blades of grass in the glens, glades, and meadows.

"All right, I think I've got it," said Little John, tramping heavily behind him.

"Don't tramp," Robin snapped. "Creep, stalk, tread, sidle, slink, rove, ramble, roam, or perambulate, but *never* tramp. We're supposed to be outlaws, for God's sake. Do you want the Sheriff of Nottingham to hear you coming from a mile away?"

Will Stutely rolled his eyes. "Don't mind him," he whispered to Little John, who was looking quite hurt. "He's been this way ever since he found out they've started singing ballads about him."

"What do you think you've got, John?" Robin called absently over his shoulder. He perched on a sturdy, moss-covered log, seized a thick vine, and swung agilely across a burbling brook.

Little John and Will Stutely watched as he postured on the other bank. "Top that, if you can," Robin dared them smugly.

Will sighed. "I think I'll just use the bridge, if it's all the same to you, Robin."

After the two merry men had rejoined their fearless leader, Little John continued his much-broken train of thought. "Just let me make sure I understand before we get to the highway. We rob from the rich and give to the poor."

Robin clapped him on the shoulder in good fellow-ship. "Well said, John. You learn quickly, little friend." He chuckled merrily at his own sterling wit, for Little John, as everyone knows, was big. Really big. We're talking gargantuan. He was, shall we say, the Hollywood Bowl of Englishmen.

So Will Stutely suggested they get on with robbing the rich and all that, which they did. They proceeded to the highway—which is a pretty grand name for what was basically a dirt track leading south from Notting-ham—and hid in the bushes, waiting for a rich man to come along.

By and by, one did indeed appear, riding a pure white horse that wore a new bridle with shining brass studs on it and a red plume sticking out of the head-band. The man travelled with only a small escort of four lazy-looking men-at-arms. Robin's brave heart thudded wildly—what a prize!

Well-camouflaged in their suits of Lincoln green, the merry men were upon their prey before they had even been spotted. It was only the work of a moment to unseat the four men-at-arms. With a gentle prod from his flashing sword, Will Stutely encouraged them to prostrate themselves upon the road. Robin turned to face their lord and master.

"Whom do I have the honor of addressing?" he asked the stranger in that courtly manner about which all the troubadors were singing these days.

"I am Jacques de Vanguard, Earl of Wessex. Out of my way, you ruffian!"

"Knowest thou who I am, my valiant lord of Wes-sex? Methinks mayhap thou knowest not."

"Why's he talking like that?" Little John demanded.

"In case a troubador should happen to be within earshot," Will muttered.

"Of a highway robbery?" John blurted.

"So! This is a stick-up, is it, you robbing hood?" exclaimed the earl.

"It's *Robin*," said the outlaw irritably. "*Robin* Hood."

"Ah," said the earl, stroking his bearded chin as his magnificent horse pranced nervously. "So you're that devil who's giving the Sheriff of Nottingham such a hard time."

Relieved to have been recognized at last, Robin replied, "Indeed, I am that fellow, sir. And these hearty lads be my merry men."

"Well, *that* one can only be Little John," said the earl, stealing Robin's thunder. "And I suppose the blond one is Will Stutely."

Robin frowned. "How did you know?"

"Do you suppose *you're* the only one people sing about?" the earl answered.

Slightly flustered, Robin continued, "Well, then, my lord, you know why we've so boldly interrupted your journey."

The earl began to look a little wary. "You're making a grave mistake," he said carefully. "You'd better reconsider this."

Robin eyed the earl. He was a fine-looking fellow, about thirty-something, with thick brown hair, clean features, a proud bearing, and wearing the finest raiment Robin had ever seen. Robin was about to speak again when Little John preempted him.

"What's to consider? We rob from the rich, and you obviously qualify. Hand over your purse!"

Robin glared at John. He usually led up to the actual robbery with a great deal of flair, paving the way with talk of the masses of unwashed poor, the merry men living in Sherwood Forest who had to be fed, and the evils of the Norman nobility.

"My dear boy," said the earl, "I am a favorite at court. 'Twould be utter folly to interfere with me. Don't even think of it."

"What, ho! My lord imagines himself to be above justice!" Robin cried, eager to get things back on track. "But here in the forest you will find, my lord, that no man may escape that scale-bearing maiden."

The earl sighed rather heavily. "Look here, boys, let's be reasonable, shall we?" He removed his heavy purse from the folds of his cloak and hefted it in his palm. "There's enough gold in this bag to keep the three of you eating, drinking, and wenching merrily for the next six months. What say I simply hand it over, and you disappear? No bloodshed, no trouble."

Robin circled the earl's prancing steed, his brain working with its famed lightning quickness. "A man must possess a great deal of wealth to part so willingly with a purse full of gold," he suggested slyly.

"Money I have aplenty," the earl conceded. " 'Tis time that I lack. I am charged with an urgent mission for His Royal Highness, and I frankly have no time to squander in a skirmish with a few roadside thieves."

"Thinkest thou we are but thieves?" Robin cried, quite pleased with the effect he made by dropping his voice suddenly on the last word.

"I do believe you said something about robbery?" the earl said dryly as he swung the purse away from his horse and tossed it to Robin. "Come now, away with you. There's your gold. Let my men go."

"Hold, Will!" Robin ordered. He tossed the bag of gold over his shoulder with a casual disregard for its contents, ignoring Little John's look. "If only you Norman lords were as free with your gold as you are with your contempt," he sneered.

Jacques de Vanguard frowned. "I believe I *have* just been rather free with my gold. Now, if you'll pardon me, I really am in a great deal of hurry, so—"

"Pardon you, my lord? *Pardon*?" Robin practically spat the word. "Pardon you for the misery of Saxon peasants, for women widowed by the toils of poverty, and children left to starve?" He rolled on, pleased to have found a suitable moment for his most famous speech. "Pardon you for babes that cry for want of milk while the children of nobles grow fat? Pardon you for land stolen from its rightful owners, for fields gone fallow and swallowed up again by the forest? Pardon you for common men condemned to death just for hunting to feed their families, because kings choose to keep the deer for their own careless sporting pleasure while their subjects die of hunger and misery?''

Robin stalked forward in magnificent anger, seized the bridle of the earl's white horse, and snatched the reins away from him with a vicious tug. "And there you sit," he growled accusingly, "a well-fed, contented, wealthy Norman lord. Let me ask you just one question: how do you sleep at night, my lord? How do you *sleep*?"

"I sleep exceedingly well," Jacques de Vanguard said in all seriousness. "My wife and I have an excellent new feather tick made by that marvellous Italian chap, Sealio Posterpedio. Now, without wishing to seem rude, I really must be on my way."

As the earl attempted to take up the reins again, Robin snapped them so hard they broke. "Have you no shame, man? Think of what you are!" He usually had people stammering apologies, denials, or pleas by now. The Earl of Wessex, however, merely looked as if he resented being distracted from the task he was meant to perform for John Lackland.

"Think of what I am?" the earl repeated. "I am a Norman lord, as you have so cleverly pointed out. May I go now?"

"And have you no regrets?" Robin pressed, wanting to get *some* kind of ballad-making material out of this day.

"Regrets? Heavens, no! I daily thank the good Lord for making me an aristocrat rather than a miserable peasant."

Robin started to feel frustrated. This was the point at which the earl was supposed to say he regretted all the wicked things he'd done, offer up his fortune to Robin, and promise to spend his life atoning for his sins. Everyone who said it was lying, of course, but it still made for a good day's work.

"Now, see here, Robin Hood," said the earl. "It's the bloody twelfth century. Considering the choices I've got—to *starve* the masses or to *be* one of the starving masses—what would any sensible man do?

Lest you should think me selfish, let me add that I've got a wife and family to consider. If only for their sake, it's best that I be a nobleman, even if that does mean I'm obliged by tradition and social custom to squeeze the blood out of the poor."

"But that's monstrous!" Robin insisted, quite forgetting to be urbane.

"It's simply realistic. Face facts, my boy. There's not likely to be a labor government in power in England for, oh, I'd say seven or eight centuries. So we're just going to have to make the best of things in the meantime. In my case, that means being an opportunistic Norman lord. Naturally, I'd like it to be otherwise, but . . ." The earl shrugged. "What can I do? My hands are tied."

Robin raised his head quickly. "Not yet, they aren't," he said, making his voice sound ruthless and sinister.

"I beg your pardon?"

"And well you should, you cur!" For a moment there, the earl had sounded so convincing that even Robin had felt a sense of futility about this whole business of robbing from the rich and giving to the poor. He now vented his spleen on the earl, pulling him roughly from his steed, jumping on top of him, and tying his hands behind his back. Will Stutely and Little John handled the men-at-arms in the same way, and soon the lot of them were lying in the muddy road like trussed chickens.

After a thorough search, Robin discovered several bags of silver and a few jewels. There was also a written document with an ornate wax seal on it. He couldn't read and had no interest in palace intrigue, so he paid it little heed and could never recall later what had happened to it.

As Robin and his men mounted three of the horses, intending to lead away the remaining two, the earl cried, "Stop, you fool! I am on urgent business for Prince John! You don't know what you're doing! This will *ruin* me!"

Robin and his merry men merely laughed, pleased to have gathered five horses and some riches today, since nothing worth singing about had occurred.

The seasons turned, cool rain turning to cold rain and eventually to freezing rain, and Robin continued his great mission, robbing from the rich and giving to the poor, who were multiplying at an astonishing rate, at least around Sherwood Forest. Indeed, since Robin had become so popular in song and story, the poor actually seemed to be *migrating* to Nottinghamshire. So there was no lack of work for the merry men.

It was deep in the dead of winter, then, when Robin approached a particularly dreadful-looking hovel in the most desperate and desolate quarter of the town of Nottingham. Seldom in his entire career of giving to the poor had he seen such a miserable dwelling.

"These people will rejoice indeed to see me," he said, wishing a troubador were there to see the welcome he would receive. He must give more thought to Friar Tuck's suggestion that he hire one to accompany him regularly around the countryside while he robbed and gave.

"Hello, in the house!" he called out. "Be you poor, honest folk of humble and worthy demeanor?"

A rather comely, if filthy, woman appeared in the doorway. She was about thirty-something, with proud carriage despite her humble station in life. "Aye, pilgrim, poor, honest, humble, worthy, and more. But if you've come abegging, I'm afraid we've naught to give you. We've nothing in the world anymore, not since some rascal destroyed my husband."

"Destroyed your husband?" Robin's heart ached for the poor woman. "Then you are a widow?"

"Nay, but I might as well be. My husband is a broken man." She gestured to their surroundings. "It has broken his heart to be able to provide no better life for us."

"Indeed, madam, 'tis for that very reason I have come here today," Robin intoned. This was going very

well! "For you see, I have here a sack of gold, and
'tis all thine, if thou dost but desire it."

The woman looked suspicious. "Why are you talking like that?"

Robin chewed his lip for a moment. "There's gold
in this bag, I say! Enough to elevate you from your
poor miserable state and put food in your children's
bellies." He paused. "Er . . . You do *have* children,
don't you?" It would add that final touch of poignancy
to the song they would sing about this encounter.

"I have five daughters, sir. *Five.*" She rolled her
eyes.

"Five?" Robin counted his bags of gold, then asked
a little wanly, "I suppose you'll want dowries for all
of them?"

She spread her hands. "How else will they make
good marriages in this harsh world? And then there's
my aging mother . . ."

"Sick, is she?"

"She'll die without a doctor. But the nearest doctor
is a three-day walk from here . . ."

Robin totalled the family's liabilities in his mind.
"A heartbroken husband, a care-worn wife, five
daughters in need of dowries, and a sick, aged mother
. . . Oh, it's too good to pass up! Madam, you must
be the neediest family in all of Nottinghamshire. I
want you to take *all* my bags of gold. And my horse."

The woman looked stunned. Overwhelmed. Utterly
speechless. She staggered forward. Her small feet
wrapped in pitiful rags slipped pathetically in the snow
and ice. Robin felt renewed as he realized how thor-
oughly he had just changed the lives of these miserable, downtrodden people. "God, I love this job!" he
exclaimed.

The woman sank to her knees before him, kissing
his hands and his feet, half-formed phrases of thanks
tumbling from her chapped lips the whole while.
Finally, Robin hauled the woman to her feet and suggested she lead the horse and its burden of riches into

the hovel until her husband returned from—as she
told him—his fruitless quest for employment.

The woman complied. Just as she disappeared
inside, Robin heard the thundering sound of horses
approaching at a gallop. He whirled to face the new
arrivals. It was that fiend the Sheriff of Nottingham,
accompanied by a dozen soldiers!

"Robin Hood!" cried the Sheriff. "My sentries
informed me you were seen prowling about the town!
I arrest you in the name of—"

At that very moment, Will Stutely's arrow whizzed
past the Sheriff's nose, causing his horse to rear and
giving Robin an opportunity to slip into a narrow,
crowded street. The chase was on!

Now, Robin may have been a bold and impetuous
fellow, but he wasn't so great a fool as to roam around
without a bodyguard. Four of his merry men had followed him to town, and they now dispersed the Sheriff's men with a deadly round of arrows. Consequently,
it was only the Sheriff who pursued Robin through
the impoverished back streets of Nottingham, and
when Robin knocked the Sheriff off his horse and the
two men faced each other at sword point . . . well!
The fight that followed, combined with the story of
Robin giving all that gold to a starving family with
five daughters *and* a sick old woman, made for songs
and stories that kept the miserable peasants warm for
the rest of the winter. It was a shame that the cowardly Sheriff of Nottingham got away from Robin
safely, but then you can't have everything.

It was nearly a year and a half later that Robin
Hood and Jacques de Vanguard met again. In the
meantime, things had been hotting up in Sherwood
Forest. The Sheriff of Nottingham had commissioned
special units of crack troops to ferret out and destroy
the band of merry men, the peasants were migrating
to the shire at an even faster rate than before, and
Prince John had been caught in unnatural acts with a
Bolshevik. What with all the close escapes, inquisitive

troubadors, and general excitement, Robin had nearly forgotten all about the Earl of Wessex.

It was on a fine afternoon in late spring that Robin Hood, Will Stutely, Little John, and a large band of merry men concealed themselves beside another highway, this time awaiting the caravan of the Crown's tax collector. The caravan was reported to consist of carts laden with fabulous sums of gold, silver, and jewels, as well as horses, donkeys, cattle, sheep, and other livestock, and silks, spices, and perfume.

It would be the richest prize Robin Hood had ever seized, and since the caravan was following a route far from Robin's usual haunts, he expected to take it completely by surprise. The bold robbery could elevate Robin to new poetic heights, so he wanted everything to go perfectly today.

When the caravan approached, the merry men executed Robin's plan with brilliant precision, disabling half the mounted soldiers who guarded the treasure while leading the other half straight into an ambush. Calculating his moment carefully, Robin seized a thick vine and swung from the treetops down to the highway, landing directly before the tax collector's horse just as all the excitement was dying down and everyone's eyes could turn immediately upon him. He was so glad he now had a troubador on retainer!

"Greetings, my lord tax collector," Robin cried. "Knowest thou who I am?"

"No, of course I—" The man paused in mid-sentence. Then his jaw dropped and his eyes bulged. He made a gurgling sound and said, "My God, it's you!"

Robin stared, realizing the man was familiar to him. "The Earl of Wessex?" he guessed. The man looked older and more care worn than he had upon their last meeting, but it was undeniably the same face. "But I thought it was some new fellow—the Earl of Bilbury or something—who was to lead the caravan today."

"The *ex*-Earl of Wessex," Vanguard said in a somewhat strangled voice. "These days I'm the Earl of *Mul*bury."

"No kidding?" said Robin. "Small world, isn't it?" A moment later, he frowned and said thunderously, "Then you didn't learn your lesson, did you, my lord? Last time we met you were simply bleeding the peasants for your own purse, but now you ransack their homes and farms on behalf of the Crown!"

"You're as headstrong as ever, I see," said the earl. "May I point out, dear boy, that the poor very seldom have sacks of jewels, cloaks of ermine, and fatted calves to pay to the Crown. Most of the goods in this caravan were taken from your friends the evil Norman lords." He paused. "I don't suppose that makes a difference to you?" he asked hopefully.

Robin threw back his head and laughed lustily. The merry men, recognizing their cue, did the same. When the hilarity had died down, Robin leaped upon a tree stump and exclaimed, "And what should you care, my lord? This time the wealth I seize on behalf of the poor is not even thine own. Although," he added, "you don't seem to have suffered at all from our last encounter. Your clothes and horse are as fine as they were when last we met upon the highway."

"A fat lot you know," the earl snapped. "You ruined me that day, and condemned my family to misery and starvation."

Feeling his oats, Little John used his knife to slit open Jacques de Vanguard's purse. As gold coins spilled to the ground, he boomed, "If this is poverty, friend, I'll gladly share it with you!"

Everyone burst out laughing again except the earl and Robin. The earl undoubtedly had his own reasons for scowling, but Robin was incensed that John had once again stolen one of his favorite lines. It was becoming a bad habit. How often had he told the big oaf to write his *own* material?

Intending to take control of the situation, Robin stepped forward, and raising a hand to silence the merry men, he said, "See here, friend! You call *this* ruination?"

"No, you fool," snapped the earl. "I've managed

to regain the favor of His Royal Highness, Prince John, who is not, shall we say, the most forgiving and understanding man in all the land."

"I don't follow you, friend," said Robin, feeling rather curious. This guy really got around.

"I'd rather you said, 'I don't *rob* you, friend,' " said the earl. Everyone laughed again. Robin decided to let the nobleman have his little jest, since the merry men would get all the gold.

"But how did losing a bag of gold and a few horses ruin you and your family?" Robin persisted.

"That sealed document you so carelessly took from me that day on the highway was a top secret communiqué which, had it been delivered to Prince John in a timely fashion, would have undoubtedly helped him succeed at last in his quest to become the unquestioned king in favor of his brother Richard, his nephew Arthur, and the half dozen or so of his other relatives who are after the crown."

Robin sat down on the stump and made himself comfortable. Swinging his legs back and forth, he asked with interest, "And you say John Lackland was not very understanding or forgiving about your mishap on the highway?"

The earl's handsome face darkened. "No. I had been promised a dukedom if I succeeded in my mission for the prince. When I failed, managing to get myself robbed and humiliated by an ordinary highwayman, my lands and castles were confiscated, my money desposited in the prince's own coffers, my horses and livestock given to the Bishop of Ely, and my title rescinded. I was also locked in the Tower for three months and beaten regularly." He shook his head and shuddered at the memory. "In short, within a day of being robbed by you, Robin Hood, I became a destitute peasant, unable to provide even food and a decent shelter for my wife and family."

"Oh, this is a sad story," cried Little John, his big red face crumpling in sudden sympathy. "Robin, you never told me things like this could happen when we robbed from the rich!"

"John does have a point, Robin," added Will. "We're supposed to be *giving* to the poor, not creating *more* of them."

"Our friend has not yet finished his story," Robin reminded the merry men. "For, as you can plainly see, he is once again far from being a humble peasant."

"I have to admit that I cannot take full responsibility for my current good fortune," the Earl of Mulbury admitted. "In fact, I was quite unprepared for the life of a working man. I had been without employment for months when, one cold winter's day while I was far from home, a stranger appeared at my wife's door and gave her many sacks of gold. It was enough gold to buy a new title, new horses, new weapons, *and* put aside a dowry for each of my five daughters. I know it sounds extraordinary, but I swear to you—"

He stopped speaking as Robin burst out laughing. "But it was *I* who gave that money to your family. You mean you didn't know?" His eyes widened with sudden understanding. "No *wonder* that bedraggled woman and her five daughters never came to Sherwood Forest to thank me. They didn't know who I was!"

The earl was astonished. And, far from expressing a proper measure of gratitude, he was distinctly annoyed. "And had she known you, you brigand, she would have refused every last ounce of the gold you gave her that day. Damn it, you're the common thief who ruined us in the first place!"

"There's gratitude for you," Robin sneered. "Since you find your newfound wealth so distasteful, my lord, my merry men will obligingly remove it for you. Take the gold, lads, and the silver, the jewels, the livestock, the ermine cloaks—everything!" Robin pulled the sputtering earl off his horse and added, "And I, my lord, will be only too pleased to relieve you of your fine velvet clothes and your costly horse."

As Robin Hood and his merry men rode away from

the destitute, humiliated, and half-naked earl, he called out, "Be sure to give my regards to Prince John!"

It made for a good finish to the songs that started circulating the following week.

It wasn't long before Robin started hearing sad tales of a fallen nobleman who was now living once again in the foulest corner of Nottingham with his wife, his five daughters, and his always-ailing but never-quite-departing mother-in-law. Robin stoically ignored the stories and concentrated on his work. Nottinghamshire was now drawing an enormous number of immigrants from India and Africa, as well as the usual crowds of starving peasants from neighboring countries. Handing out gold to all of these people was becoming such a booming business that Friar Tuck now constantly nagged Robin about incorporating and setting up a board of trustees.

The troubadors continued to praise Robin Hood in song and story. Robin had heard tales about a particularly interesting quartet of lads who nightly drew vast crowds of screaming women to their sing-alongs. They had named their group after some sort of insect and, according to gossip, hailed from Liverpool. Robin hoped they would pass through Sherwood Forest one day so he could hear them. One of the disadvantages of being a nationally celebrated outlaw was that he couldn't get out of the forest much these days.

As the tales of the ex-Earl of Mulbury persisted throughout the winter, Robin began to grow concerned. Due to his five daughters, his desperately unhappy wife, his ever-lingering mother-in-law, and his impeccable manners, the ex-earl had become a figure of considerable sympathy in the shire. In fact, some said Robin Hood should have been a sport and forgone robbing him the second time.

When the stories starting multiplying in number, each one more unflattering toward Robin than the last, he decided it was time to take positive action.

Cleverly disguising himself as a common shepherd, he stole into the backstreets of Nottingham once night and sought out his ubiquitous nemesis.

The earl's current abode was another miserable hovel, and Robin supposed that maybe he shouldn't have left the earl quite so destitute. Stealing the tunic off his back had obviously been going too far. Firm in his resolve to correct his mistakes, Robin entered the earl's home.

"Jacques de Vanguard?" he queried in the dim light of a peat fire.

Five young girls squealed at his sudden appearance in their home, an old hag in the corner cackled then moaned, and the woman Robin recognized as the earl's wife cried, "My God, it's you!"

"Oh, no! What are *you* doing here?" grumbled the ex-earl. "I've nothing left for you to steal, young man, unless you're here because you forgot to swipe my jockey shorts when last we met. And the name's changed now, too. These days I'm just ordinary Jack Vanguard."

Robin cleared his throat. "It, uh, it has a ring to it, Jack."

"Well, what do you want?" Vanguard demanded.

Robin reached inside his humble shepherd's cloak and pulled out a fat purse. "Now that you're one of the poor again, I've come to give. There's enough gold in here to buy a better hovel, get medicine for your mother-in-law, and feed your family for the rest of the winter."

"Buzz off," said Vanguard.

Robin blinked. "What?"

"Get lost. Go away. Be gone with you." Vanguard leaned forward and added, "Scram."

Robin decided Vanguard must not have heard him correctly. "See here, Jack. There's gold in this bag, I say." He shook the bag so that Vanguard might hear the coins jingle. "Take it and be blessed by the prince of thieves."

Vanguard threw up his hands in exasperation. "Why are you doing this?"

"Well, it's my job. I mean, you must understand by now. I rob from the rich and give to the poor. And you're poor again, so . . . Look, Jack, this gold is pretty heavy, and I've carried it all the way from Sherwood Forest, so do you think you could—"

"Absolutely not! Are you trying to ruin my life?" Vanguard snapped.

"I'm trying to help you!" Robin protested.

"You really want to help me?" Vanguard demanded. Robin nodded. "Then I'll show you how to help me. There's the door. Use it."

"But . . . but I don't understand. You surely can't *like* being a miserable destitute peasant with no hope of anything except the hereafter."

"I'm not crazy about it," Vanguard admitted, "but what I hate even more than I hate being a peasant is being humiliated by some cocky adolescent gang leader on the highway every time I've got a few quid in my pocket. Do I make myself clear?"

"Now see here—"

"So you give me a bag of gold today and I go back to being rich tomorrow. What then? How long before you rob me *again*? How many times do you think Prince John is going to let me off the hook with a simple demotion, a few months imprisonment, and some relatively mild beatings? Next time I screw up on account of *you*—and we both know there'll be a next time—I fully expect to be beheaded. So just take your gold and go, Robin. Go ruin the life of some *other* evil Norman lord. I have no intention of becoming your perpetual victim."

"But I can't just leave you like this." Robin's brow furrowed as he thought long and hard. "Look, maybe we could work out an arrangement. Maybe I could promise not to rob you again if you promised not to oppress peasants, or something like that."

"Forget it, Robin." Seeing the dismay in the outlaw's expression, Vanguard sighed and added, "Look, maybe your intentions are good, but you're ruining my life. I can't take all the stress. My analyst says I can't go through another lifestyle change so soon without destroying all the progress I've made since being released from the Tower."

Stricken with remorse, Robin Hood sank to the floor. "What have I done?" he cried.

Realizing that the bandit was truly distressed, Vanguard's wife pulled Robin a little closer to the fire and handed him a nice steaming cup of hot water (tea not being available for several more centuries). "Poor Mr. Hood, you mustn't be so hard on yourself. It's not so bad, really. True, we have nothing to eat, only these rags to wear, just this one miserable, drafty room to live in, and the Sheriff of Nottingham bleeds us for taxes, but it's not as if things couldn't get worse."

"I feel just terrible about this," Robin said piteously.

"Now, look, Robin," Vanguard said consolingly. "We've got a little neighborhood watch committee forming, my wife belongs to the ladies' sewing circle, and my oldest daughter has met a charming ditch digger who doesn't even care that she has no dowry. All in all, it's far better than a career of being regularly robbed on the road then thrown into the Tower, believe me."

"But you must want more out life than this!" Robin cried, gesturing to their miserable surroundings.

"Well, of course we do," said Vanguard.

"But Jack doesn't want to go back to being an earl," said Mrs. Vanguard. "It's just as well. He was working sixty and seventy hours a week, the poor dear, getting up early, going to bed late, no time to exercise, grabbing fast victuals instead of sitting down to proper meals. And if I ever saw him more than two days running, I can't remember it. Always on the road, he was." She laughed prettily. "But of course, you of all people know that."

"But, my lord . . . I mean, but, Jack, you're just

not cut out for the life of a humble peasant. You discovered that the last time you tried it."

"Oh, I'll think of something," Vanguard assured him. "But enough about me. Let's hear all about you. What have you been up to since last we met?"

"Oh, you know, the same old stuff. Robbing from the—"

"Yes, yes, I know all about that. But I hear there's talk of a girl now."

Robin blushed. "Maid Marion," he admitted. "We want to get married, but it's tough to plan a wedding when there's a price on your head."

"Yes, I suppose so," said Vanguard.

"Well, perhaps we could help you," suggested Mrs. Vanguard.

"Help me? How?"

"If there's one thing nobles know about, it's planning parties, Mr. Hood. I'm sure that for young people like you a wedding seems like such a major undertaking, but to an experienced host and hostess like my husband and I—"

"No problem at all, Robin. It'll help take my mind off my troubles," Vanguard added. "Mrs. Vanguard can arrange the food, the bridal clothing, and the floral arrangements, and I'll arrange for a suitable dance floor in Sherwood forest, the musicians, and the transportation. I hear you've already got your own priest?"

"Yes, but I can't ask you to—"

"Please, Robin, it'll be our pleasure," insisted Mrs. Vanguard.

"In fact, it'll probably only take us a week to organize everything. And it's not as if I have anything better to do."

"Then you must let me pay you for this," Robin decided.

The Vanguards objected at first, but eventually Robin made them see that accepting a fair wage for honest work wouldn't in any way put them in danger of becoming aristocrats again—in fact, it was positively contrary to aristocratic behavior. Having settled matters to his satisfaction, he once again returned to Sherwood Forest, pleased to be able to tell his betrothed they were finally going to have the fine wedding she had always wanted.

Robin Hood's wedding to Maid Marion took place that spring and was an enormously popular success. The Vanguards, who did such an excellent job of planning the whole thing, had even managed to engage the quartet from Liverpool to play at the wedding before they went off to spend six months playing in some hovel in Hamburg. Maid Marion was a little miffed, since the fab four sang ballads about girls named Rita, Michelle, and Yoko, but none about her. Otherwise, however, the day went so well that two more of the merry men hired the Vanguards to plan their upcoming weddings.

By the end of summer, the Vanguards had organized and catered so many weddings that they had stockpiled a tidy sum of gold.

"Are you going to try to buy back your title with all that gold?" Robin asked Jack Vanguard one day.

"Hell, no. Catering weddings is the first peace and quiet I've ever known. I'm reinvesting our profits in the business. Mrs. Vanguard would like a bakery of her own, so we can provide our own wedding cakes and petit fours rather than relying on those crooks in Bread Street, and I'd like to buy a bigger cart for transporting wedding parties around town and out to Sherwood Forest." After a few more minutes of explaining his plans for expanding the business, Vanguard said, "And what about you? How's the highwayman business these days?"

"Well, you've hired so many waiters, bus boys, carters, grooms, cooks, and seamstresses that there aren't as many starving peasants to give to as there were last year, but I suppose the merry men needed the break anyway."

The Sheriff of Nottingham, however, still planned to destroy Robin Hood and the merry men, so the troubadors still sang ballads about mad chases, heroic

duels, and hairsbreadth escapes. Only Robin seemed
to notice that the number of starving peasants continued to dwindle.

"Surely you can't be providing work to all of
them?" he said one day to Vanguard.

"No. Geoffrey Shoemaker has gone into mass pro-
duction and has about one hundred men and women
working for him round the clock. What with all the
out-of-towners coming to Nottingham these days to
talk to me and Mrs. Vanguard about planning their
weddings, Master Sheraton has had to expand the inn
to almost twenty rooms. Naturally, most of those
crooks in Bread Street have caught on to my family's
success and are opening little catering businesses of
their own. A couple of new banks moved into town,
and when one of them came up with this new idea of
twenty-four-hour banking, naturally the others had to
follow suit to stay in competition." Vanguard sighed
as he poured more spiced wine into his and Robin's
imported goblets. "The old town is changing, Robin."

"You sound unhappy about that," Robin said.

Vanguard shrugged. "Well, naturally, I'm as
pleased about all the prosperity as anyone else. It
seems like only yesterday that everyone around here
except the nobles was starving and had no hope of
survival except for you."

"Yes," Robin said a touch morosely. He was stealing as much as ever, but it was becoming awfully hard
to find anyone who really needed his booty.

Vanguard gestured to the walls of his remodelled
hovel. "We've made a good life here, but the city is
getting too crowded. It's full of strangers and trouble-
makers. I worry about my children's education, not to
mention their safety." He shook his head. "You might
as well be the first to know, Robin. Mrs. Vanguard
and I have decided to move."

"Move!" Robin exclaimed. "But this is the twelfth
century! No one simply *moves*."

"No one catered weddings or advertised in the

Saxon Chronicle until I did," Vanguard reminded him. "Don't pester me with precedent."

"But where will you go?"

"The suburbs."

Robin gave him a puzzled frown. He knew every inch of the shire, but he had never heard of this place Vanguard intended to go. "Where exactly are these suburbs?"

"They're just outside of town. Since we'll be the first to move there, we should get a pretty good deal on a plot of land."

"But what about your catering business?"

"Oh, we'll get used to the commute in no time. In fact, Ian Carter has been talking about sending a cart back and forth for us every day for a small fee, once a few more families have moved out to our neighborhood." Vanguard nodded decisively. "We'll build a nice little three-bedroom house with a two-cart barn, the school district is bound to be better, and God knows the taxes will be better. The Sheriff of Nottingham is too bloody lazy to go all the way out to the suburbs to hound us for taxes the way he does here."

As Vanguard had predicted, once he and his family had moved out to the suburbs, many of the other folks from Nottingham began to do the same. One day Robin slipped stealthily into the poorest district of town, his cloak concealing bags of gold he intended to give to the poor, only to discover he couldn't *find* any poor. He searched hovel after hovel, only to find they had all been abandoned.

Never once to take defeat and disappointment lying down, Robin then crept into the section of town now inhabited by the upwardly mobile poor, as opposed to the hopelessly starving poor. Upon spotting Jack Vanguard's eldest daughter, Florence, supervising a number of workers in front of the tumbledown church, Robin approached her with a feeling of utter bewilderment.

"Why, Robin!" cried Florence, recognizing him immediately.

"Shhh!" He glanced around warily. "Don't you know there's a price on my head?"

"You haven't heard, have you? The price on your head has been lowered by eighty percent. Considering the fight you would put up, most soldiers and bounty hunters figure it wouldn't be worth the effort of capturing you," she informed him cheerfully.

Robin was stricken. "*What*? How could the Sheriff have lowered the price on my head? I'm Robin Hood, the bandit king, the prince of thieves, the—"

"Well, Robin, you really haven't stolen much for the past year. In fact, word is that you're still trying to give away gold you stole *last* year," Florence explained gently.

"There's nobody to give it to anymore," Robin said defensively. "Everybody's working, everybody's got a little pension plan or nest egg, all the suburban communities are organizing committees to prevent the Sheriff from taxing them as heavily as he used to, should he ever work up the energy to go out there and try to take away their money." He threw up his arms in exasperation. "I mean, I'm as committed to my mission as ever, but how the hell am I supposed to give to the miserable, starving, downtrodden masses if there *aren't* any? Tell me that, will you?"

"Have you ever considered another line of work?" Florence suggested.

Robin plopped down dispiritedly on a stone bench. "I'm a highwayman, Flo. It's all I know." He shook his head sadly, then looked around him. "What's going on here anyhow? Who are all these workmen?"

"We're building a new community center," Florence explained. "There'll be a section for sports and recreation, a small medical facility for the poor—"

"What poor?" Robin sneered.

"—and an educational foundation. It's being funded by all the people in the suburban communities who've done so well with their services and businesses. Maybe you'd like to make a contribution?"

Having no one else to give it to, Robin gave her

all the gold concealed on his person and returned to Sherwood Forest and his wife Marion.

Although Marion had shared Robin's vision in bygone days, she was now growing restless. Everyone they knew had three bedrooms, a couple of carts, and a new kitchen, she complained. Times had changed, Marion kept insisting. Robbing from the rich and giving to the poor was becoming old-fashioned. Worst of all, it was hard for Marion to hold her head up at bridge parties, knowing how everyone feared the lingering possibility of being robbed on the highway by their old hero Robin Hood.

Another year went by, and the merry men started deserting Robin when he adamantly refused to let them spend their piles of gold on themselves. Some went off to seek adventure in less affluent counties, some got married and moved to the suburbs. On the day that Robin realized that no one had sung about him in a very long time, and never would again, he went to see Jack Vanguard.

"How's your mother-in-law?" Robin asked.

Vanguard grunted. "Healthy as ever. I can forgive you for robbing me twice, but I may never really forgive you for saving her life."

"How's the rest of the family?" Robin asked, hoping to put Vanguard in a more affable mood.

"I'm giving my third daughter and her boyfriend a condo in town for their wedding present," Vanguard said with fatherly pride.

"I thought everyone was moving *out* of town," Robin said dully.

"Hey, kid, you've been in that forest for too long," Vanguard said good-naturedly. "Everyone *did* move out. Now all the young folks are moving back *into* Nottingham, renovating all those old tumbledown hovels that we said good riddance to." He shrugged and grinned at Robin. "Go figure. So what brings you here, my friend?"

Robin scuffed the ground with the toe of his boot. "I'm thinking about giving up highway robbery, Jack."

"No! Really?"

Robin nodded. "It's just not the same anymore. Nobody has any *ideals* these days, Jack. Back in the old days, peasants would fall to their knees and sob with gratitude when I showed up with bags of gold that I'd risked my life to steal from the rich. Poets praised my feats of daring, and troubadors wrote ballads about me every week." He sighed. "Now there's no one to give gold to, so there's no point in stealing it. Just for old times' sake, I robbed a group of the Sheriff's men last week. Do you know the new recruits have never even *heard* of me? What's more, when I gave the money to Florence for her new medical center, I discovered that the sum I donated was less than half of what Master Sheraton gave her that same day as a tax write-off."

Vanguard nodded, his face showing a certain amount of sympathy for the fading bandit. "It's definitely time to move on, Robin. Have you thought about what you want to do?"

Robin shrugged. "What can I do? Life in the forest is all I know."

"Planning parties was all Mrs. Vanguard and I knew," Vanguard reminded him. "Capitalize on your assets!"

"Huh?"

"Stick to what you know," Vanguard clarified.

"What would you suggest?"

"Well . . . with a little cooperation from the Sheriff of Nottingham, I think we could work out something very interesting," Vanguard suggested.

"Join forces with that swine? Never!" Robin cried.

"Robin, be reasonable. For a small cut of the profits, I think we could convince him to take the price off your head and let you operate without government interference."

Robin squinted at Vanguard. "What exactly do you have in mind?" he asked at last.

And so it was that, with a little help from the Vanguards and a little loan from Barclay the moneylender,

Robin Hood quit highway robbery and began his new career. In due time, he was pardoned by the king, who appreciated the foreign tourism he brought to England. And, living happily ever after, Robin reinvested his profits in the business and became a regular advertiser in the *Saxon Chronicle*:

"Now booking for weekends and holidays: The Sherwood Forest Resort. Meet you host and hostess, the famous Robin Hood and his lovely Maid Marion. Mingle with the merry men, fraternize with the fabled Friar Tuck, put your strength against Little John. Lessons in archery, banditry, basic forest survival, and vine swinging.

"All meals provided in the healthy open air of Sherwood Forest by the popular Vanguard Catering Company, followed by evenings of song and story, with special holiday appearances by a quartet of troubadors recently returned from the continent.

"Join in a highway robbery, duel with the Sheriff's men, relive the days of high adventure—and all at no risk to yourself!

"Reserve now and receive a free annual visit from a certified Sherwood Forest Troubador who'll keep you abreast of all the new features and upcoming events at the Sherwood Forest Resort!

"Please note: a portion of your non-refundable deposit will go directly into the Robin Hood Fund for Disabled Highwaymen."

Robin in the Mists

by Steve Rasnic Tem

Knowing that his band virtually fed on elaborate tales of adventure, Robin was always eager to enthrall his good stout yeomen with the details of any encounter of action or mystery. Save one. This particular tale, begun one night after his men had drunk themselves into a deep sleep, he locked forever inside, until and including that day when with Little John's aid he would let fly his final shaft.

The greenwood had been a blackwood that night, still and colder than at any time Robin could remember; so cold he wondered if even the prodigious amount of drink could keep the ice out of the bones of his sleeping men as they lay asleep under a giant oak's boughs. Unable to sleep, he crept softly from body to body, laying animal skins over the death-like figures, moving among them like a wolf or a badger. He halted at the end of the circle, below the edge of the great tree's reach, and stared down at the mottled mass of beasts his band had suddenly become, snapping and growling in the cold grip of dreams.

"I feel a dream myself," he said softly to the icy dark. Wondering, Robin looked back across the masses of fur, looking for his own sleeping head, but could not find it in the cold damp mist which now filled the spaces beneath the trees.

Neither could he find in any of this vision the forest he knew so well. No sanctuary here, no familiar wood where the flowers bloomed forever and the birds always sang. No plenitude of bright spirits. No abundance of game. Here the rains were stark and chilling, turning to snow beneath his tired gaze. Here the forest was endless, unknowable, and abundant only with winter.

Though it should have seemed impossible, Robin suddenly knew that this winter had developed harsh beyond all bearing for the outlaws. The ice which now filled the wood had begun to grow razor-sharp in his belly weeks ago. The images of Little John and Friar Tuck suddenly floated up out of the white vapors, laughing and drinking—the flames of their spirits bright in these dark woods. Robin was filled with a sadness at this vision, for their images felt too much a memory now, too soon to be lost, too near ghosts of themselves. And yet still they caroused with the others in his misty dream; good fellows all, bellies full of game and throats full of song to ease the too-quick passage of their meals. They had always depended on him for the best game to be foraged from the great wood, but this cold season he had failed them miserably. Their images began to fade, as if finally acknowledging their starvation.

A change in light, as if the misted moon had suddenly grown expansive, made Robin shift his gaze to the nearby hill. A great white hart had appeared upon the crest of this clearing, and Robin could sense the hot, angry blood of it coursing as it pranced back and forth below the huge yellow moon. His long bow was in his hand, and his feet were moving him toward the hart's bold dance.

Be still was the message he sent, not to the hart but to his own blood, which he sensed flowing wild and overly full in his veins, as if ready to break the bounds laid upon it by his flesh. With this fullness of blood came a rising anger and an impatience such as he had not experienced since his youth. He prayed such reckless anger would not spoil his shot. In such a harsh season, the hart's meat was life itself for his band.

"You shall die for my taste of you . . ." he whispered into the goose feathers as he let fly the bolt toward the deer's great heart.

There was a stillness and a slowing of the world, as always occurred when Robin took aim and released a bolt. He stared into the shadowed gaze of the deer, prayed his arrow on its way, and watched as the mists wrapped the deer until only its head, then only its dark gaze was visible. Snow suddenly filled the mist, and the moonlight turned it into a cloud of stars.

Then the hart was gone, and Robin's fingers stung from the cold.

A male deer can be a swift thing surely, but Robin had never before encountered the likes of this. He knew he could not have missed, for he had felt that self which travels in dreams fly with the arrow and pierce the chest of the deer. But when he ran to the crest of the hill, there was no sign of his deer. He stepped slowly around the clearing, unleashing his eyes and ears to explore the gray edges and black hearts of the surrounding trees and the regions between. But there was no motion of escape as far as his poor senses might detect. He would have gone back to camp, thinking the beast's escape was deserved, if he had not been so worried over the health of his companions.

Robin sensed a change in the forest's light once again, and turned his head to see a trail of white mist rising out of a ground dead with leaves and damp black branches. There, beyond a row of slanted trees, the white hart solidified out of the milky fog, its head turning to return his gaze as if in mockery. The deer's chest rose, and Robin could see his arrow wedged there before it appeared to float back out of the creature's fair hide and burst into flames, becoming a gray line of ash which broke in two then tumbled slowly to the ground.

He should have turned back then, he knew, returned to sleep with his companions where his body even now lay; for surely he was a mere nightmare of himself, and the true Robin lay dozing in his white mist of drink. But he did not, for dreaming or no, his men still lay on cold ground with empty bellies.

Robin had no hope of outrunning this magical creature, certainly, but could hope to outwit it with his near-animal knowledge of the trails. He forced himself through thickets of harsh brush where there were no trails, his eyes open for the mist, his heart full of rage for the deer, his tongue eager for the taste of its blood. Since a youth, Robin had taken what he wanted and given away what he had wanted. Long had the greenwood and all its creatures been his to order and dispose. He had been both the stern father and the champion son, the yeoman's god and the Sheriff's devil. His blood ran fast with a forest's worst savagery, and hot with a man's strongest feeling.

Robin followed the deer into another clearing, this one broad and flat and layered with a carpet of black leaves now silvered over with ice. The moon hung fully exposed here, reflecting off the icy leaves so that a resemblance to a wide lake was created. Robin hesitated, watching as the deer leapt through its own halo of brilliant white mist, through layers of shadow, and into the dark air above the silvered leaves. It floated there a moment, its head bold and upright; then it began to fall, its front legs straightening, pushing forward, as it descended to the carpet of reflecting leaves, then through them, passing through the vague barrier of ground, its legs disappearing, its long belly, its broad chest, its proud head. Thus the hart vanished completely, leaving the delicate iced surface unruffled, only a soft smoke settling out of the night above it like sediment in a tankard of ale.

Robin was sorely tempted to follow the hart out onto this mockery of water, a temptation which disturbed him deeply. For standing at the edge of the silvered skim of leaves, he was able to gaze lengthily into its depths, and saw his good dead yeomen killing their enemies, and the friends of their enemies as well, in ways more like butchery than the combat of noble men—severing limbs from torsos and freeing heads from the jealous tethers of their necks—and there was he, too, as a younger, wilder bowman, with his long shafts making sieves of the bodies of those who opposed him.

Robin tore himself away from these unpleasant visions in time to see the deer rising up once more out of this fanciful pond, shaking itself off and spraying the clearing with a disturbance of leaves both shiny and black. He might have lost his quarry then, if the hart had not waited at the far edge of the clearing while Robin made his way around its bank. But once within arrow-shot, the beast leapt and was gone further into the twisted dark trunks of the other side.

As the deer led Robin deeper into these great woods of night, he found himself puzzling over the awkward strangeness of his surroundings. For Robin knew the greenwood better than he knew any man, and yet here were stretches and rises and twisted clearings and odd groupings of timber which were completely unfamiliar to him. The weather here was far more harsh than before, despite the increased height and thickness of these tree trunks he would have thought capable of blocking the worst of storms. Flying ice pierced his cloak and leggings, leaving him bleeding. Black damp spread from sodden ground through flesh into bone. Cold winds stripped him of protection and wrapped him in garments of their own ill fashioning.

Yet all this hardship of travel only made the need for a taste of the pale flanks of the hart—glimpsed rarely, but still glimpsed—all the more desperate.

When the hart once again paused some distance away, as if cautious of Robin's losing sight of it completely, Robin returned this gesture with similar caution. He paused as well, standing with bow at the ready. After a moment's stillness, the hart turned and came further in Robin's direction. Robin permitted his bow to drift up before him. As the deer crept into Robin's range, an arrow found its way onto the nock, although Robin had no recollection of putting it there.

The deer stood its ground, waiting. Robin breathed out slowly, and the arrow went with his breath and warmed the cold chest of the hart with its piercing affection.

Robin held his breath, waiting for the hart to vanish. Instead it appeared to grow taller with the agony of the arrow at its center. Its head lengthened, its horn rising into a tall helmet framing startling silver and red eyes. A long white beard poured out of the base of this helmet, wrapping the body and its dark robes and trawling the ground for secrets like a thing alive. A narrow pink mouth glowed for a moment at the center of the helmet, then appeared to turn upside down as it began to speak.

"You hunt well, fair Robin. But hunters do not always seek what it is they find."

"I hunt meat for my band. I would beg that you forgo the riddles, however. If it were philosophy I'm needing, then I can always find it in some good ale."

"You have come a long way, Robin. As have I, to show you these things."

"This is not your home, noble hart? It seemed a likely spot for someone so . . . changeable."

"No. This is *your* home."

"Mine? I live in the greenwood, with my loyal men."

"You live *here*, as have you always. In the cold, and in the angry dark."

Robin shifted uneasily, stroking the goose fletching across his arrows. "This is madness," he said. "A dream. Too much drink. Too much song. The greenwood was never so dark, so empty of fair game."

"It is your greenwood all of songs and mornings which is the dream. The fantasy of an outcast, a tale told by a hot-headed outlaw."

"What is your tale, then, fair hart? Or shall I say magician? Or wizard? I have heard from the knights of one such as you . . ."

"My name is unimportant. It is what I have seen, what I shall see."

"Your tale, then?"

"This morning I came upon the grave of a man recently buried. From the depths of this grave I heard a distant squealing, like that of a pig. Fearing that the poor man had been buried alive—there is so much ignorance hereabouts, I am always aware of such possibilities—I used my staff to uproot the burial. I found the man's corpse, and was curious to find that the dead man had quite devoured his own clothing."

"Curious?"

"Aye, wouldn't you be?"

"Oh, that and more. But curiosity seems an unusually mild response, is what I meant."

"I fear little excites me anymore, fair Robin."

"And yet everything excites me, magician."

"Aye, and too much it would seem. First, there were the King's foresters when you were a mere youth. Fifteen of them, I believe. When one welched on a wager concerning a shooting contest, you, I believe the song goes . . .

took up his noble good bow,
And all his broad arrows all amain;
And Robin being pleas'd, began for to smile,
As he went over the plain.

And smiling so gaily, you proceeded to shoot all fifteen."

"That is not how I remember it, magician. This story about the buried corpse, what does it mean? I do poorly at riddles."

"And what does your story of the fifteen foresters mean, Robin? Or when your good men Little John and Much the Miller's son cut off the head of the monk's page so he might not witness to the Sheriff? Or when you yourself cut off the head of Guy of Gisborne, planted it on your bow's end, then took up the knife and mutilated his face so that no man born of woman might know whose it was? What does that story of Robin Hood, outlaw among men, mean?"

"There is no justice, magician. You tell too many tales." Saying this, Robin took up the bow again and began to shoot at the figure before him, filling the cold air with his shafts, anxious that this lying magician make no escape.

"Here, Robin," the magician said from the top of a great tree. "Perhaps stones would be more effective. I will wait here until you gather some."

"Keep that promise and I will join you soon." Robin crouched and began searching the ground for the sharpest stones, clawing like a desperate animal in order to pry them from the frozen ground. "While I search, what other lies might you have to tell?"

"Oh, there are many events about the land you may have failed to notice while in your greenwood of eternal summer. There have been several severe winters of late, and a flood or two, the usual sheep and cattle plagues. Many of the smaller towns are in ruins, the land having taken over them once again. Tall grass grows in a surprising number of streets. The markets are closed and the crops do poorly."

Robin stood with a particularly vicious stone held firmly in his palm. He watched the tree for movement, then tossed the stone into its dark center. "So what do the poor people eat?" he shouted.

"You missed," the voice in the tree replied. "But I congratulate you; you were quite close. The poor have eaten fairly well, actually. I know they would appreciate your concern, and your charity. Currently they consume cats, dogs, dove droppings, and their own children."

"You tell a good story, magician," Robin said as he tossed another stone into the darkness. He was answered by a satisfying thump. A shadow fell from the tree and lay still. Robin strode over cautiously, his hand on the knife hanging from his belt, the knife he had once used on the face of Guy of Gisborne.

He turned the body over. The magician stared up at him with a face half-man and half-deer, his thin lips virtually hidden by a long snout of pale, soft nose. "You throw a good stone, Robin," the narrow mouth whispered.

"But your story of the corpse in its grave and how the man had eaten his own shroud. What does it mean? I bested you—now reveal the riddle."

"There is no riddle to it, fair Robin," the voice replied, although the magician's lips were no longer moving. "Look to your own body."

Robin gazed down at his hands where they held the magician's robe. Great boils had suddenly appeared in the flesh about his knuckles. Robin let go of the robe and stepped back. He felt a sudden discomfort beneath his arms and threw off his own cloak, pulling his shirt away from his hot, sticky chest. A large knob of softness had filled his armpit, and he could feel another the size of an egg growing in his groin. Now minute and numerous black spots spread in all directions across his skin, like an infection taken from the magician's dark, night air. He turned back to the still form, but the magician was gone.

"Stop this!" Robin pleaded with the night. "I did only what I must!"

"What you felt you must . . ." the night said back. "That much, certainly, is true."

"How do I stop this dream?" he shouted, covering his face with blackened, sore-ridden hands.

"To stop this dream," the fading voice in the night replied, "you merely create another. Dream of an endless summer in the forest, fair Robin, where flowers bloom forever and the birds are always singing. Where ale and beer flow like water in a brook, and outlawed men are always fair, and always just."

The Locksley Scenario

by Brian M. Thomsen

"Oh! Excuse me. I must have made a wrong turn somewhere."

The fox had entered my office and didn't seem to know what to make of it. Perhaps vixen would have been a better handle. A long, blonde, and leggy vixen at that.

"I'm looking for Mouse Chandler, the private investigator. Is he around?"

"You're talkin' to him. What's up?"

She stopped dead in her tracks, trying to hide with her lacquer-tipped fingers the creeping embarrassment that crept its way across her face. She still didn't believe what she had heard. "You're Mouse Chandler?"

"Yeah. That's my password, don't wear it out." Over the years I've grown accustomed to this sort of reaction. For some reason John and Jane Q. Public had a hard time getting used to a myopic, pencil-necked nerd as a famous detective, but I haven't had a dissatisfied customer yet. Taking a ballpoint pen from my handy plastic pocket-saver and the canary pad from my coffee-stained desktop, I motioned for her to have a seat and readied myself for just the facts.

"What can I do for you? Time's short and it's not cheap."

She eased herself into the hot seat and began to spill her guts. "My name is Marion Gisbourne, soon to be ex-wife of Donald Gisbourne. You may have read about our impending divorce in the newspapers."

It had been impossible not to have heard about this

little breakup: storybook romance to happily-ever-after marriage that went to pieces when wife discovered hubby playing "Press enter ( )" with some magazine cover bimbo. Despite a current downtrend in the economy, Gisbourne had to be worth millions, half of which would soon be awarded to the lovely lady on the other side of my desk.

"Sure, I've read about it. Inside of a few weeks you'll be a fun-loving single with enough cash to buy a Japanese entertainment conglomerate. How can I possibly help you? Normally you hire a guy like me to get the goods on Mr. Ex. You caught him with his pants down. Case closed."

She opened her Halston handbag and handed me a sheet of paper.

"Yes, case closed," she countered, "except for one little thing. Read this."

The paper was a court-certified audit of the assets of Gisbourne Industries, sole shareholder Donald Gisbourne. Well, lo and behold! Things weren't as rosy as one might have believed for the Don-man. Total net assets 1.6 million, a mere fraction of what was reported in last year's *Fortune* article.

I now knew why she was here, but decided to play dumb just for the fun of it. "So what. Things are tough all over. The recession you know. 800K ain't half bad."

"800K is a pittance!"

I'd gotten her anger, and she was beginning to show a little of the kind of spark I liked to see in a blonde firecracker.

"Donald is worth a hundred times more than that." I countered. "That's not what this paper says." I began to realize that it was about time to end my little game.

"It's what I know!"

She had gone from rage to flustered and would soon be in tears. I jumped right in to save the day. "And that's why you need me, right?"

"Right. They say you're the best, and I'm willing

to pay for it. I only have forty-eight hours to appeal
the settlement," she explained.

I eased the computer keyboard from its place in my
top drawer and swung the arm of the monitor into
place. "No problem. Just answer a few questions.
Husband's full name?"

"Donald Travis Gisbourne."

"Business phone?"

"989-5342."

"Accountant's name?"

"Howard Kirschbaum."

"Phone number?"

"898-7521."

"Any other money merlins in his employ?"

"Just Gary Reuben, but he works with Howard."

"Same office."

"Yes."

"Does your husband use AT&T or Sprint?"

"AT&T."

I restored the keyboard to its proper position, and
moved to usher the now-bedazzled Marion from my
office saying, "That's about it. Check back with me
tomorrow at about this time."

She began to fluster again. I guess the Fifth Avenue
crowd hadn't prepared her for a real no-nonsense type
like me.

"But surely you need . . ."

"No problem, toots. You need evidence of his real
net wealth. He's obviously hidden it somewhere, and
that information must be in his database. All I have
to do is get inside the good old Gisbourne Industries
databank, find it, copy it, and give you the evidence.
Right?"

"Yes, but the system has safeguards. Two other
auditors tried to get inside but came up with zip, and
I only have forty-eight hours left."

"Which is why you came to me, right?"

"Well, yes, but—"

"So get out of here and let me get to work. Just
check in tomorrow, like I said."

Her last question was the usual one.

"But what about your fee?"

Closing the door and catching one last look at her million-dollar gams, I answered, "Don't worry. I'm sure you'll cover it somehow."

Most people don't realize that the Philip Marlowes and Mike Hammers of yesteryear are the hackers of today. Information is what everyone is after today, and retrieval is my expertise. I've yet to meet a security program that I couldn't crack with one of my well-chosen scenarios. All it takes is a little time and a doorway; and what better doorway to start with than a phone number?

A quick AT&T cross-analysis of the phone logs for both Gisbourne and his money man yielded a single recurrent path to follow. 7437963. Bingo! The active line 743-7963 (which I will call SHERWOD) is the access line.

Here we go:

SUBJECT: Gisbourne Industries, Inc.

PURPOSE: Full audit of assets including those coded access denied.

Record and copy all obvious and secret security locks.

Record all financial records.

DATA TO BE DOWNLOADED AND SAVED AS IT IS ACCESSED.

If SHERWOD is the place, then Locksley has to be the scenario.

LOAD PROGRAM LOCKSLEY
ACCESS SHERWOD
ENTER R. HOOD
WELCOME TO SHERWOOD

One fine day Robin Hood was making his way through Sherwood Forest when he was stopped by a messenger from King Richard the Lionhearted.

"Good sir," said the humble messenger, "are you Robin Hood?"

"Yes, I am, good sir," said Robin. "What tidings do you bring from His Royal Majesty?"

The messenger read from his scroll. "His Majesty wishes you, the honorable Robin Hood, to assist him in an audit of the accounts of the sheriff of Nottingham. It is believed that the knave has been absconding with royal funds, hiding them somewhere for his own use later on."

"Then I must go to Nottingham," said Robin.

ENTER NOTTINGHAM TOWNSHIP

Robin entered the township of Nottingham. Immediately recognized as the forest lord of Sherwood due to his lincoln green suit, he was set upon by two of the sheriff's men, his body riddled with arrows, and his lincoln green suit stained blood-red.

[Oops! Back to line 10]

ENTER NOTTINGHAM TOWNSHIP

Robin, dressed in the robes of a Nottingham monk (clothes that were loaned to him by the fun-loving Friar Tuck to obscure his suit of lincoln green) entered the township of Nottingham.

Robin came upon two of the sheriff's men.

"Go with God, and bless the king," said Robin.

The two sheriff's men ignored him.

Robin proceeded further into Nottingham township.

Coming upon an inn, Robin decided to stop and sup and gather information.

After ordering an ale, Robin engaged the bartender in conversation.

"How fares taxes in these parts?" inquired Robin.

"Same as elsewhere, stranger," said the bartender.

"Higher than some places I hear," pressed Robin.

"For a stranger you talk too much," said the bartender, who cudgelled Robin, breaking his head, and turned his body over to a band of brigands.

[Back to line 17]

ENTER ALLEN-A-DALE

Coming upon an inn, Robin recognized his friend Allen-a-Dale, who was playing some tunes on his lute to pay for his supper.

After ordering an ale, Robin engaged the bartender in conversation.

"Hi. I'm a friend of the minstrel's," said Robin to the bartender.

"Aye, he plays well enough but perhaps a bit too loud. It is hard to think straight with the sounds of such merriment," said the bartender.

"Aye, yes," agreed Robin. "How fares taxes in these parts?"

"Same as elsewhere," said the bartender.

"Higher than some places I hear," pressed Robin.

"Perhaps, but isn't the music grand?" said the bartender.

"Surely enough," said Robin, who thanked Allen for his help, finished his ale, and proceeded further into town.

ENTER NOTTINGHAM TOWN SQUARE

As Robin Hood entered the town square, he became aware of a tingling presence in the air as if an electrically charged fog had enveloped him.

Pressing on, he decided to ask for directions to the sheriff's castle and keep.

"Good fellow," he asked a peasant, "where is the sheriff's castle and keep?"

The peasant smiled and said, "Otn oto arf romf ehre. Stuj ndeboy het atom." And continued on his way.

Robin was confused by this unexpected foreign tongue and decided to try a second peasant. "Good sir," he asked a second peasant, "where is the sheriff's castle and keep?"

The peasant smiled and said, "Otn oto arf romf ehre. Stuj ndeboy het atom." And continued on his way.

Robin, more confused than before, decided to return to the inn to seek help. The crowd had gotten loud and rowdy.

"Tawh si uroy easuplre?" asked the bartender.

Robin was even more taken back from the gobbledygook he heard coming from the bartender, who had previously been a master of the King's English.

"What did you say?" asked Robin.

The bartender, spotting him for a foreigner, cudgelled him, breaking his head, and turned his body over to a band of . . .

[Back to line 24]

Robin was confused by this foreign tongue and decided to enlist the aid of one of his merry men, who was a legendary linguist.

ENTER WILL SCARLET

"What ho, Will!" said Robin.

"What ho, Robin!" said Will. "How can I be of service to you?"

"The people of Nottingham seem to have been enchanted so that they now speak a tongue other than the King's English," Robin explained.

"It is possibly just a language scramble spell," said Will. "Everything will remain scrambled until the loop is broken. Observe."

And with that, Will turned his attention to a passing young peasant.

"Good sir," asked Will, "where is the sheriff's castle and keep?"

The young man smiled and answered, "Otn oto arf romf ehre. Stuj ndeboy het atom."

"Nkhta uyo, odgo irs," returned Will.

The young man answered, "You're welcome, good sir," and continued on his way.

Turning back to Robin, Will said, "You should have no further problem with their language. The loop is broken."

"Thank you, Will," said Robin.

"You're welcome, Robin," said Will, who promptly returned to their Sherwood Forest hideaway.

"Fair maid," Robin inquired of a passing young woman, "where is the sheriff's castle and keep?"

The maid smiled and answered, "Not too far from here. Just beyond the moat."

"Thank you, fair maid," said Robin.

"You're welcome, good sir," said the maid, and continued on her way.

Robin set off in the direction of the moat.

ENTER NOTTINGHAM AT THE MOAT

Robin approached the moat and decided to cross it by means of the drawbridge. Setting foot on its hard wooden surface, Robin continued on until he was almost halfway across, whereupon he was picked off the bridge by the jaws of a huge sea serpent who quickly pulled him down into the deepest realms of the moat where he soon became the serpent's next meal.

[Try again. Back to line 38]

Robin approached the moat and decided to cross it by taking a running jump and leaping across to the other side. Robin ran, leaped, and fell into the middle of the moat where he soon became the next meal for the moat's sea serpent.

[Back to line 38]

Robin approached the moat and decided to survey the situation carefully. He decided that he needed some assistance and summoned Little John to his side.

ENTER LITTLE JOHN

"What ho, Robin! How may I be of help?" asked Little John.

"You were once with a circus, were you not?" asked Robin.

"Yes," replied John. "I was a strongman and an acrobat."

"Then I will enlist your services in crossing this moat," said Robin.

Robin took a running start and began his leap across the moat with a final leg-up and boost from the very able Little John. He crossed the moat easily, quickly entered the sheriff's castle, and approached the keep.

ENTER THE KEEP

ENTER THE SHERIFF

"Ah, Robin, I've been expecting you," said the sheriff. "The King must have sent you for an audit, but as you can see all I have in my keep is 800K pieces of gold. No more, no less."

All Robin could see was the 800K pieces of gold, but he could feel the presence of even greater wealth somewhere. Striking the base of the gold's container with his staff, Robin recognized a hollow quality to the sound it made.

"You have been holding out on your king," said Robin.

"Prove it," said the sheriff, who lunged forward with his sword.

Robin quickly sidestepped the lunge, and cudgelled the sheriff with his staff. The sheriff passed out.

Robin quickly moved the gold aside and broke open the base of the container. The container's base had obscured from view a tunnel that led to a cave in a far-off land.

Robin travelled quickly, and came upon a darkened room. Upon entering it he was killed by an ogre, who . . .

[Back up two lines]

Robin travelled quickly and came upon a darkened room. Lighting a match and turning his staff into a torch, Robin quickly surveyed the contents of the room from the doorway, never venturing over the threshold. He accounted the wealth of the chamber at close to two million gold pieces, and then continued down the hall where he surveyed ten similar chambers in the same manner.

His mission accomplished, Robin returned to Sherwood and reported back to the King.

EXIT PROGRAM

A Locksley scenario with a Robin Hood RPC never fails (particularly when backed up by the merry men: the "Tuck disguise-a-probe," an "Allen-a-Dale distraction program," the "Will Scarlet translation cipher," and the "extra-charged Little John mobile auxillary power surge unit"). I like to think of it as robbing from the rich and giving unto others that which is rightfully theirs, minus my fifteen percent commission, of course.

I transferred my cut from the Gisbourne account (no one would ever notice; not Gisbourne, nor the IRS), and on the next day handed Marion the report and waited for the fur to fly.

The headlines pretty much said it all: MARION A MAID AGAIN; TEN MILLION DOLLAR SETTLEMENT. The Swiss accounts, the points on the South African and Tokyo exchanges, and the interest on the loan they made to the U.S. government spoke for themselves. It was all there in black and white.

I never saw Marion again. That's the way it has to be. Her world was Fifth Avenue society, mine was Silicon Valley. She shopped at Tiffany's, me at Modems R Us. It would never have worked out.

Life for me is just a romp through Sherwood. All the world's a game, and if I play my cards right, I may wind up as High Score.

Till the next game—*ciao*, baby.

The One-Eyed King

by Nancy A. Collins

Robert Fitzooth, Earl of Huntingdon, Master of Locksley Hall, known to Saxon and Norman alike as Robin Hood, stood atop the ramparts of his castle and surveyed his forest.

Not a year ago he had been an outlaw, an enemy of the state, hunted by the Sheriff of Nottingham's men like a fox in the wood. He had been stripped of his lands and chattels, his ancestral home given over to that Norman codswallop, Sir Guy of Gisborne; he and his men forced to make their home amidst the sheltering bowers of Sherwood Forest.

There had been much blood and suffering along the way. He had lost his closest and oldest friend, Will Scarlet, to Prince John's treachery. And he, in turn, had snuffed out Gisborne life's in repayment for his companion's death.

But all that was over now, erased by a wave of King Richard's royal hand. Robin was once more master of Locksley, and legally married to the Lady Marian. His outlaw band, the famed "Merry Men," had disbanded to the four winds—save for the most loyal of his followers, who now served him as stewards.

Still, Robin had hoped that King Richard would have remained in England longer, keeping his heel firmly planted on his younger brother's neck. But three months had not passed before the Lion-Heart was once more on the road to Damascus.

Robin tried to be philosophical about his protector's flagrant distaste for the more mundane aspects of being king. While he did not care for the yoke of

Norman rule, if he had to submit to a Norman king, one that was never around was preferable to one that *was*. Still, it worried him that Richard had yet to sire an heir. Should a heathen arrow find its mark, England would once more find itself in Prince John's ungentle hands. But next time he would not be regent.

"Robin, my husband. What is wrong? You seem so—sad."

Robin turned to look at his wife, who had joined him on the rampart. The wind ruffled the white silk wimple and coverchief framing her heart-shaped face, and Robin was once more amazed that a woman of such loveliness had consented to be his.

He smiled wanly and shrugged, returning his gaze to the forest. "I guess I'm just . . . homesick."

"Homesick? But you *are* home, my husband! Locksley Hall has been in your family since before the Conqueror."

"I meant I miss Sherwood."

"Ah." Lady Marian slid a slender arm about her husband's waist and laid her head on his shoulder. "I know what you mean. Sherwood was as much home to us as any house built of stone. It sheltered us and fed us, like a mother does her children."

Robin pulled her closer. "I am pleased you understand. It is not that I am unhappy here with you . . . it's just that I miss the old days. In the forest."

Lady Marian's voice was gentle but firm. "Those days are gone now, Robin. You have won all you fought for."

"Not all."

"But enough. Come, there is an edge to the wind, my husband."

Robin hesitated for a moment. "You know, I was born in those woods. Or so I was told."

"Come inside, Robin, before you catch your death."

Little John frowned at the trembling forester. "You are sure of what you saw?"

"As sure as Christ died and walked again," the forester replied, wiping a hand across his lips. "I left my oldest boy to watch the spot, least someone disturb it."

"And you say this man was a monk?"

"Aye. At least he wore a monk's habit and tonsure."

"Come with me, then." Little John's huge, calloused hand clamped around the forester's upper arm. "We'll soon get this madness straightened out."

Little John dragged the nervous forester through Locksley Hall's winding corridors until he came to Robin and Marian's private chambers. He rapped his knuckles against the heavy oak door, using a code devised during their days spent in Sherwood Forest.

The door opened a crack and the Lady Marian peered out at them, frowning first at the forester then at Little John.

"What is it?"

"I must speak to Robin."

Marian was about to say something when Robin Hood appeared behind her, pushing open the door. "John! Is something wrong? Please come in."

Little John brushed past Marian, dragging the frightened forester in after him. "This is Ned, one of your foresters. He claims . . . well, it's best that he tell you."

Ned stood transfixed, gaping at the famous outlaw lord.

"Well, get on with it, man!" roared Little John, thumping the awe-struck forester on the side of the head with one bear-like paw.

"Leave the fellow be, John!" scolded Marian. "He'll tell his tale in good time."

Little John grunted and folded his arms over his chest.

"I . . . I was out in the woods with my boy, Marcus, when we come upon this monk."

"Monk? Do you mean Friar Tuck?"

"Nay, milord. I've seen the good friar in church, taking confessions. This priest was tall and thin, where's Friar Tuck is short and fat. He was resting on the side of the road, dressed in a cassock the color of ashes. When he sees me and my son, he lifts a hand in greeting and asks if we were in the service of the Earl of Huntingdon, known as Robin Hood. When I says yes, he says there's something I should see off in the woods, just off the footpath. Something of importance to you, milord."

"Me?" Robin scratched his chin-whiskers and exchanged glances with Little John. "Did you do as this monk asked?"

Ned the Forester turned pale and licked his lips. "Aye. Although now I wish we hadn't. When we returned to the path, the strange monk was gone. I hurried here as fast as I could."

"And what did you find?"

The forester closed his eyes, and for a moment Robin wondered if the man was going to swoon. "It was horrible, milord! Too horrible to speak of in milady Marian's presence."

"Very well. Then I shall travel to this place and see things for myself."

It was a hour's ride from Locksley Hall before they came to the spot where the mysterious priest had spoken to Ned the Forester and his son. The boy was still standing by the side of the road, looking pale and anxious.

"Marcus! I thought I told you to stay in the clearing," barked Ned.

"I couldn't stay there, father. I tried, but the *smell* . . ."

Robin sniffed the late afternoon breeze. The reek of death was heavy on the air. He dismounted and gave the reins of his horse to Ned's son to hold.

"You did well, lad. Don't worry," Robin murmured, clapping a hand on the boy's shoulder.

The forester lead them away from the road, along a narrow pig-path through the brambles and undergrowth. The farther they went, the heavier the smell of death grew. Five minutes' walk from the main road, they found themselves in a small clearing.

The first thing Robin noticed was the cold campfire in the center of the clearing. Then he saw the corpses.

"By the Rood!" swore Little John, his ruddy face suddenly leeched of color.

There were three of them: a man, a woman, and a child. Each had been nailed, spread-eagled, to a tree.

The man wore the tattered remnants of an abbot's gown. He had been throttled by his own rosary with such violence the beads had become embedded in his flesh. He'd also been gelded prior to being disemboweled.

The outrages done to the woman made those inflicted on the abbot look mild. She, too, had been of the church, judging from what little remained of her habit. She had been nailed to her tree upside down, her privates cut out and her torso split open like a dressed deer. Her breasts were missing, the abbot's severed member shoved in her mouth.

But the boy—the boy was the worst.

The final victim was facing the tree, as if embracing it. Countless shallow cuts marred the dead boy's naked back and buttocks. Whoever had tortured the unfortunate child had finished his work by taking a burning branch from the campfire and thrusting it between his victim's hams.

"How *dare* they?!" roared Robin, turning his back on the carnage and kicking at the remains of the murders' campfire, scattering ashes everywhere. "How dare they defile my woods with such evil? Sherwood is *my* province, and I shall not tolerate such wanton cruelty and bloodshed while I still have breath and strength!"

Little John frowned. "Robin, do you think Prince John had a hand in this?"

"Prince John may be a vicious back-biting ferret, but he's not fool enough to molest the Church in such an outrageous manner. Whoever did this—and judging by what's left of their camp, there were several of them—swears allegiance to none, neither State nor Church."

"Outlaws?" whispered Little John. "You're saying outlaws did this?"

"Don't look so heart-stricken, my friend. The outlaws who committed these atrocities were never Merry Men."

"But who—?"

It was then that Robin spotted a piece of folded parchment amongst the litter of torn garments at the foot of the dead abbot.

"What is it, Robin?" Little John asked, looking over his leader's shoulder. While he could sign his name, John Little was as illiterate as every farmer's son.

"It would seem to be a letter. Addressed to me."

To Robert Fitzooth, The False Earl of Hunting-don, Usurper of Locksley Hall, Known As Robin Hood.

Greetings, Brother!
It has been thirty years or more since last we suckled at the same teat. In that time, we who shared the same womb have walked very different paths indeed. News of your adventures have reached as far as my own domain, here in Modred's Wood. It is even rumored that thick-skulled sodomite, Richard, has returned to you our ancestral lands and titles.

I weary of living the life of a shadow, dear lost brother. I feel now is the time for me to come forward and claim my rightful inheritance.

You, little brother, are a pretender. I am the firstborn son of William Fitzooth and the Lady Joanna, not you! If you do not promptly relinquish your claim to my lands and title, I shall wreak upon your house the same fate these worthless fools suffered. And if you do not believe my tale, go to our uncle, Sir William Gamwell, and ask him the truth. If you then decide to deny me what is mine, then woe to you and yours, my brother!

Thomas Fitzooth, True Earl of Huntingdon, Rightful Master of Locksley Hall, Known As Tamlane the Dragon

"What does it say, Robin?"

"Nothing, my friend. But perhaps it would be wise for me to pay a visit to my uncle, Sir Gamwell."

Sir William Gamwell, Lord of Gamwell Hall, sat and studied the grim letter his nephew had produced, stroking his white beard.

"I have heard tales of this so-called 'Tamlane.' He is a most foul and black-hearted brigand."

"Is—is what it says true, uncle?"

"Aye. Were that it wasn't!"

Robin stared at his hands for a long moment before blurting out his question. "Why was I never told that I had a brother?"

Sir William heaved an old man's sigh. "It happened such a *long* time ago, my boy. And, besides, talk of it upset your mother so." He motioned for one of his servants to pour wine into his and his nephew's goblets before dismissing him from the room.

"But my poor sister is fifteen years in her grave, and I see no point in keeping silent now. It is a long story, Robin. And not a pleasant one, I'm afraid. . . .

"You are, no doubt, familiar with the tale of how your mother and father came to be such?"

Robin laughed. "Of course! Mother never tired of telling it! Father was the son of the Baron of Kyme, a Norman nobleman. Mother was the only daughter of Sir George of Gamwell, a Saxon knight. Grandfather George forbade them to see one another, but they were married in secret.

"When my mother became great with child, she begged my father to hide her in Sherwood Forest, for fear of what Sir George would do. When Sir George realized what had happened, he went into the woods to search for his errant daughter, determined to have her Norman lover's guts for garters. But when he came upon them at last, my mother was busy bringing forth their child. When Sir George saw his grandson—that is, me—he lost all interest in wreaking vengeance on William Fitzooth, and welcomed his son-in-law into his home and family."

"Mostly that's true," grunted Sir William. "The bit about your parents hiding out in the woods and my father being madder than a baited badger is right enough. But you were not the babe that turned Sir George's rage away from your parents. That was your twin brother—your older brother—Thomas.

"In those days, Sir George kept a young priest at Gamwell Hall as confessor for the family. He was a tall, lean fellow by the name of Garth. Garth was an odd one, even for the clergy, always keeping his hooked nose buried in scrolls. He was learned though, and my father respected him for that. He could read and write in Latin, Greek, French, Hebrew, and a few other heathen languages. Still, there was something . . . odd about him.

"As for you and your brother—why, you were identical as two peas in a pod! Even your wet-nurse had trouble telling you apart. So she took to tying a bit of ribbon about your ankles: green for Robin and black for little Tam.

"On your first birthdays you were to be taken to the nearby abbey, as it is the custom, so the abbot could baptize you properly. But the day Sir William and Lady Joanna were to leave, the wet-nurse found only one child in the cradle. And to make matters worse, the ribbons had been removed from the infants, so there was no telling which child had disappeared.

"Well, Sir George had Gamwell Hall turned upside down, but no trace of the missing twin was found. It was soon noticed that Father Garth was nowhere to be found. Sir George ordered that his rooms be searched. . . ." Sir William shook his head sadly. "It seems my poor father had been playing host to a serpent at his bosom. Inside Father Garth's room were found occult artifacts of unwholesome origin. It was evident by what was found that the priest had become a necromancer, turning his back on Mother Church in favor of the dark arts.

"Your mother took the news very hard. As everyone knows, witches and warlocks use the rendered fat of babies to anoint themselves for their midnight meetings with Satan, the Prince of Lies. It was obvious that poor little Thomas—at least the wet-nurse insisted that was the twin missing—had met such a cruel fate at the hands of the debauched priest.

"Your father, grandfather, and I decided to make things easier on your mother by not dwelling on little Thomas' kidnapping. In time, Joanna got over her grief and came to focus her love and attention on you, Robin. If she ever mentioned little Thomas' name again after that first year, I never heard it. Still, I know she kept a place in her heart for her lost boy, up to the day she died.

"Since then, no one has seen or heard of Garth for well over thirty years. Now you say he was spotted creeping about Sherwood. I don't like this, Robin. Not in the slightest.

"Perhaps we underestimated Garth's perversity. Indeed, if a simple infant sacrifice was all he wanted, he could have stolen some hapless peasant woman's brat, and no one would have been the wiser. If this Tamlane the Dragon is indeed your long-lost twin, then that bastard of a priest has indeed raised up a monster deserving of Hell."

"You say you've heard of this 'Tamlane.' Why have I not learned of him before now?"

Sir William gave a dry laugh. "The last year or so have been rather busy ones for you—have they not, nephew? Between dodging the Sheriff of Nottingham's men and outfoxing Prince John, I doubt you have had time to keep afoot with the latest gossip.

"What little I have heard of this brigand has been grim, though. Tamlane the Dragon is a murderer, rapist, thief, poacher . . . In short, everything you and your Merry Men chose to shun, he has embraced wholeheartedly. He revels in pain and torture.

"It is said that he and his band of cutthroats, who call themselves the Dragon's Teeth, raided an anchorage, raping the holy sisters. When they were finished, they then sewed the nuns shut, so that they would be unable to deliver themselves of whatever issue might have been spawned on that black day."

"God's mercy! And this monster is my *brother*?"

"Perhaps. Perhaps not. There is only one way you shall ever find out the truth, Robin. You must go and meet this Tamlane. And, if it is true that he is your blood—you must kill him."

"Uncle!"

Sir William leaned forward, his eyes hard as beads, and thrust a bony finger at Robin's chest. "This is no time to be fainthearted, boy! If Tamlane is indeed Thomas Fitzooth, *he* is the rightful heir and master of Locksley Hall, not you. And I would fain suffer the stones of the Vatican be washed in my blood than suffer such a creature tarnish the family name!

"I loved your mother as only a brother can. It would have broken her heart to discover that her poor, lost little Thomas had been twisted into a murdering ogre. And as to you; the threats he makes in this letter to you and your loved ones are quite clear. Could you suffer their falling into the hands of this monster, knowing you could have prevented it?"

Robin was silent for a long time. There was much for him to contemplate: the discovery of a twin brother he never knew he had, the threat to his family and friends, the possibility that he might soon find himself contemplating fratricide. But what else could he do?

"I ride for Modred's Wood come the dawn."

Robin squatted in front of the fire, feeding tender to the struggling flames while chewing a strip of jerked venison. He had been gone from Locksley Hall for two solid days, and his bones ached and his spirits were weary. Normally, traveling the woodlands gladdened his heart, but he had long since left the familiar bowers of Sherwood Forest.

He was in Modred's Wood, and it was as different from Sherwood as night is to day. Where Sherwood was full of deer and other game, Modred's Wood seemed bereft of anything but predators. Earlier that day he'd spied a wolf between the trees lining the path. Had he not been handy with his bow, the beast would have set upon his mount.

Even now he was aware of the eyes of myriad wild things watching him from outside the ring of light cast by his campfire.

So this was where the Dragon's Teeth made their home: a place of stagnant bogs and vicious beasts. Perhaps it was just his frame of mind, but it seemed to Robin that Modred's Wood was a blighted place. The smell of fungus was strong, as was another, less recognizable, odor.

Robin heard an owl calling to its mate in the darkness. At first he thought nothing of it, then he realized that he had gone all day without once hearing the song of a bird. He got to his feet, his hand resting on the sword sheathed at his side. But it was too late.

They came out of the woods, as silent and quick as a pack of wolves on the hunt. There were at least six of them, armed with short swords and cudgels. Before Robin could make a move, the largest of their number hurled a net over him, pinning his arms to his sides.

Robin cursed and struggled to free his sword from its scabbard, but it was no good. The bandits descended on him then, whooping and screeching like wild animals. One of them struck Robin behind the knees with his quarterstaff, knocking him to the ground. Dozens of blows rained down on the helpless man, the bandits yowling their delight at the sight of blood and the sound of his groans.

"Enough! Do not kill him—yet."

Robin's attackers froze at the sound of the voice and turned their faces to the tall, hollow-cheeked man dressed an in ash-gray cassock who strode from the shadows.

Father Garth smiled down at Robin Hood the way a butcher smiles at a well-marbled slab of beef.

"Take him to the Dragon."

The next thing Robin knew a damp cloth was being pressed against the swelling over his right eye. He groaned and lifted his right hand to probe the wound, only to find a woman's fingers laid against his brow.

"Marian—?"

Robin Hood opened his eyes and stared into the face of a dark-haired woman with pale skin and eyes the color of polished night.

"Nay, the name's Morag. Black Morag."

She wore the tunic and hose of a page, dyed the color of a raven's wing. Her dark hair hung over the right side of her face, obscuring most of it from view. Her hands were calloused, the nails chewed to the quick. She licked her lips anxiously and peered at Robin like a two-headed calf in a miracle show.

"You're him, ain't that so?"

"I'm who?" grunted Robin, wincing as he sat up.

"Robin Hood!" Morag snapped, her eyes flashing.

"What if I am?"

Morag's chapped lips pulled into a knowing smile. "Ah, but you are, ain't you? Tam said his brother was Robin Hood. And if you ain't Tam's brother, I'll fuck Dim bowlegged!"

Robin flinched, unaccustomed to hearing such coarse language from a woman. His surroundings were humble, bordering on squalid—a wattle hut with dirt floors, lit by tallow candles and smelling of rancid fat and unwashed men. So this was how Tamlane the Dragon lived.

"This Tam—is he your husband?"

Black Morag laughed and spat at the dirt floor. "A husband? *Me*? Tamlane is my leader, nothing more!

And I only follow him because he's the biggest, mean-
est, blood-thirstiest bastard there is. I respect that in
a man." At that she grinned, displaying stained and
crooked teeth.

Robin decided to say nothing. Allowing his attention to wander from the woman, he noticed for the
first time that he had been stripped of his lincoln green
tunic, hose, and boots, and dressed in a black robe.

Just then the blanket that served as the hut's door
was thrown aside and a man dressed in black entered
the foul-smelling hut. Morag scuttled away like a dog
fearing a boot in its ribs, leaving Robin alone with his
new visitor.

"Greetings, brother," said the man in black, lifting
one of the candles and holding it so its feeble light
fell upon his face. "Welcome to Modred's Wood."

Robin gasped at the sight of his own face exactly
replicated in someone else's flesh and blood. The
resemblance was closer than any captured by a mirror;
yet, there was something different—something *wrong*
with the other man's face. The shape of their features
were identical, but there was a hard edge to the set
of the stranger's mouth, a cruel gleam in his eye that
discerned Thomas Fitzooth from his brother.

"Yes, the likeness is exceedingly close, is it not?"
remarked Tamlane the Dragon. "I'm told not even
our mother, the Lady Joanna, could tell the two of us
apart."

"Do not mention my mother's name again, knave,
or I'll drub you until the blood rises!" snapped Robin.

Tamlane casually kicked his brother in the side with
his booted foot. "Mind your manners, brother dear!
You're no longer in Sherwood." He smirked.

"Stop calling me brother," snapped Robin, struggling to his feet. "And where are my clothes?" Before
he could continue, the cold metal of a dirk was
pressed to his throat.

"My, aren't we used to giving orders?" purred Tamlane. "In that we are very much alike, *brother*."

"Tam!" The bandit turned and glowered at the tall,

gaunt figure dressed in an ash-gray cassock standing in the doorway. "Remember, no edged weapon is to taste his blood!"

"Yet," hissed the Dragon, returning the priest's dark gaze. "And don't *you* forget, Garth," he said, pointing his knife at the older man, "although you may have raised me from a pup, I take no orders from anyone—man or devil!"

"As you wish, milord," responded Father Garth. "Perhaps once you have . . . finished with him, you would bring him by my cell, so I might prepare him." With that the priest turned his back on the brothers and disappeared into the night

"What do you want of me?" demanded Robin.

"Shouldn't I be one asking that question?" sneered Tamlane. "After all, it was *you* who trespassed on my domain."

Robin's face darkened. *"Trespassed*?! How dare you speak of such things to me! It was you who tortured and murdered three helpless people in Sherwood. Even the dimmest of village idiots knows that Robin Hood allows pious clergy, honest women, and innocent children safe passage through Sherwood Forest. And any who dares molest them must answer to me!"

"What a self-righteous prig you are, little brother!" laughed Tamlane, genuinely amused. "Here you dare to call yourself the robber-prince of England, yet are unwilling to dirty your hands with the meat of brigandry. What is the point of being an outlaw if you observe laws?"

"I am a law-abiding Englishman, and always have been so. My rebellion was against unjust laws and corrupt rulers."

This seemed to amuse Tamlane even further. "Ah, I think you and Dim should talk, as it appears you and he are equipped with the same intellect." He grabbed Robin by the forearm and dragged his brother after him. "Come! Why don't I introduce you to the rest of my little band, eh?"

Outside the hut was a large campfire, around which huddled a half-dozen men dressed in filthy rags, worrying greasy gobbets of half-cooked meat like starving dogs. They looked up from their meal as their leader approached, the gleam in their eyes fearful and suspicious. Robin had seen its like in the eyes of the half-wild dogs commanded by his Master of Hounds.

One of the men stood and came forward. Robin had fancied Little John the biggest man he'd ever seen, but this hulking stranger made the notorious John Little look like a tubercular old woman.

The giant stood nearly three ax-handles high, and was at least a handle wide at the shoulders. His arms were covered with coarse red hair, and the seams of his leather jerkin groaned with every flex of his muscled torso. But what Robin noticed most of all was the man's harelip and drooping left eyelid. By the way the simpleton grinned at him, Robin doubted not he was the typical village idiot.

"I caught him good, didn't I, Tam?"

"Yes, Dim. That you did."

The giant moved with surprising speed for someone his size, grabbing Robin's lower jaw in his huge, sausage-sized fingers.

"Can I play with him?"

Tam's voice was firm but smooth, like a master speaking to his favorite hound. "Now, Dim, you remember what Father Garth said, don't you?"

Dim blinked a couple of times and sucked on his lower lip for a moment. "Uhhhh . . . that he's your brother?"

"No, not that, you sluggard!" snapped Tamlane, slapping the giant across the face with the back of his hand.

Dim let go of Robin as if he'd been scalded, rubbing a rough palm over his stricken cheek.

"He said that no harm is to come to our 'guest' here until the moon is full."

"Oh, *that*. I remember now."

Robin turned his attention from Tamlane and his

underling, scanning the faces of the men watching
them. What he saw made his heart sink; there was a
hardness in these men's eyes that reminded him all
too well of the hired jackals who'd done the Sheriff of
Nottingham and Sir Guy of Gisborne's dirty business.
These were men who knew nothing of the nobler emo-
tions; they would as soon kick a dog to death as offer
it a scrap of food. What loyalty they felt for their
leader was that of feral beasts acknowledging the fast-
est and strongest of their number. That Tamlane could
cow such a behemoth as Dim only further proved his
innate superiority in the minds of the rest.

He had indeed fallen amongst dragons.

What impressed Robin the most was that Father
Garth was the reverse of the Merry Men's own good
Friar Tuck. Where Tuck was squat and stout, Garth
was tall and thin. Where Tuck was reminiscent of the
ancient Roman god of revelry, Garth had the look of
an ascetic saint. Where Tuck was plain-spoken and
earthy, Father Garth was a scholar. Most of all, Tuck
was a warrior-monk where Garth was a wizard-priest;
a hybrid to be feared and seldom trusted.

The defrocked monk made his home in a rough hut
of stone and wood with a thatched roof, built across
the mouth of a cave in a low cliff fronting a nearby
river. Compared to the filth the other members of
Tamlane's band lived in, Garth's hermit's quarters
seemed luxurious.

Garth scowled at Robin and motioned for Tamlane
to tie his brother to a chair while he poured over a
collection of yellowed manuscripts. Robin wondered
what this devil-worshipping priest had planned for
him, but he was afraid to ask. After a whispered discussion, Garth rolled the scrolls back up and placed
them in a rosewood box the size of a child's casket.
With that, Tamlane the Dragon left, pausing at the
threshold long enough to sneer a farewell to his
brother.

Garth busied himself with lighting candles and placing them about the interior of the cave, speaking all the while to his captive.

"I'm afraid I can not offer you much in the way of hospitality, Sir Robert. Although I have long since abandoned my vows of poverty, my lifestyle is far from extravagant."

"I thought the Dragon's Teeth were feared far and wide for their banditry."

"Oh, but they are! However, they are not your average band of footpads, my dear Robin Hood—no more than the Merry Men. The Dragon's Teeth are feared because they will attack anyone weaker than themselves: peasants, palmers, widows, children . . . They never attack knights or tax-collectors. There is no 'rob the rich and give to the poor' here. The poor are their livelihood."

"Then they are no more than bullies, cutthroats, and thieves!"

"Indeed," smiled Garth, as he lit the final candle. "That is as it should be." He turned and pointed a finger at Robin. "Have you not wondered why I stole your brother from his crib, those long years ago?"

"Because you are an evil man, dedicated to the service of the Foul One!"

"In part. But there was more to it than that. Much more." The priest drew closer and leaned forward, fixing Robin with his dark, feverish eyes. "I was there when you and your brother were brought to your grandfather's home. You were only a few hours old, but I could already read your destiny. It surrounded you like a tiny halo. I knew then that you would grow up to be a hero.

"There can be no light without darkness. No good without an opposing evil. This is the way of Nature. And so it was with your brother, Thomas. When I looked at *him*, I saw a dark light. It was considerably weaker than your own, but definitely there. You were a bad influence on him. Although you were not yet weaned, I could see Thomas's evil genius begin to fade and flicker, like a candle in danger of being snuffed out by a strong wind.

"I realized that if I did not take action, Thomas would fall under your sway for good. So I decided to steal the child and raise him here in the dark heart of Modred's Wood. I must say, he proved himself an apt pupil. He was torturing animals by the age of five. He raped his first woman at the age of twelve. He committed his first murder before his fourteenth year. He has done me proud!

"Out of the raw material of Thomas Fitzooth I have fashioned Tamlane the Dragon; a villain with a soul blacker than soot, a stranger to conscience, shame, and love."

"You claim my brother loves nothing in this world. What about you? Aren't you his mentor? Surely he feels something for the man who raised him."

Garth laughed without humor. "Oh, yes. Dear Thomas feels something for me! If it was not for certain—connections—I developed over the decades, my foster-son would have had my vittles long before his first whiskers sprouted. Here, allow me to show you."

Garth straightened his back and produced a small brazier, which he lit and began sprinkling with various powders from a selection of stoppered jars scattered about the hut, all the while muttering aloud in Latin. Robin's eyes swam with tears from the overpowering odor of burning myrrh and sulphur. Then Father Garth spoke a name, and the fires under the brazier turned green then blue.

Something in the back of the cave that had not been there before grunted and opened its eyes. Robin felt his scalp tighten and his bladder ache as the solid shadow moved forward, sniffing the rank air.

In many ways it resembled a bear, although it had hands. Its golden eyes gleamed like newly minted coins as it stared at Robin down its long, square snout. Its face was painted like a carnival buffoon's, and it revealed huge, curving incisors whenever it peeled

back its lips. The demon drooled and whined like a
hungry child.

"Not yet, Lucullus," smiled Father Garth, resting
one hand on the demon's matted head while he
scratched it behind the ears. "You must wait until the
signs are right."

"What are you doing, summoning forth that wretched
hell-demon?" Tamlane stood in the door of Father
Garth's hut, staring in undisguised fear and repulsion
at the thing squatting at the priest's feet. Upon espy-
ing the bandit, Lucullus bared its teeth and stood on
its hind legs, exposing a wickedly barbed erect penis
extending wetly from its furred pouch.

"I was merely demonstrating a point, Thomas.
Nothing more." Garth made a complex hand gesture
and the beast disappeared like a mist caught in a high
wind.

"Stop calling me Thomas! My name is Tamlane!"
snapped the Dragon, still visibly shaken by the
demon's appearance.

"But not for long, eh, milord?"

Now that the demon was no longer around to dis-
tract him, Robin noticed that Tamlane had changed
from the black garments he'd worn earlier into a lincoln green tunic, hose, and boots.

"My clothes!"

"No longer, brother."

Robin's guts tied themselves into even tighter knots.
"What evil are you planning, Tamlane? Tell me, damn
you!"

"Can't you figure that out on your own? Surely
you're not *that* dense, little brother."

"You won't succeed. The others will see you for the
pretender you are!"

"Why? Should they suspect otherwise? I have no
doubt you did not bother to divulge the true reason
for your trip north to any of your friends—not even
your lovely wife."

"Please, Robert, don't get so excited. You're apt to

accidentally strangle yourself if you struggle too hard," sighed Father Garth.

"What do you think you'll gain by this unholy charade?"

Tamlane grinned, and for a fleeting second Robin realized how Sir Guy of Gisborne must have felt, time and time again, looking up into his own taunting smile. "My birthright, for one. And perhaps a kingdom or two, to boot."

"You're mad!"

"No, he's not," said Father Garth. "There is a change coming. And when it is finally here, kings will be made—and broken—in the space of a few short weeks. And I mean to see Thomas on the throne. As King Robert the First."

"What?"

"England will be in sore need of a king, brother dear. When that thick-skulled sodomite, Richard, is finally claimed by his Holy Crusade, there will only be Prince John to succeed him. Not a popular choice, don't you think? There will be a brief chance for a usurper to claim the throne, as the Conqueror did a century past. But the usurper must be someone of noble lineage . . . someone of heroic mien . . . someone popular with the Saxon nobles and the peasantry . . . someone who can rally an eager army of knights and hods-carriers, with just a whisper of his name. . . . And that name is Robin Hood."

"No! I would never dream of usurping the throne!"

"We're well-aware of that, little brother. Despite your avowed hatred of the Normans, you are still subservient to the status quo. You would never dare step out of your rightful place in the pecking order—unless it was to right wrongs and see justice done. What a fool you are!"

"You'll fail! Little John and Friar Tuck—they'll be able to tell you're not me. And you haven't got a chance of deceiving Marian."

"Are you so sure, brother?" leered Tamlane. "After all, a change is as good as a rest."

*   *   *

Tamlane reined his horse to a stop, staring up at the distant turrets of Locksley Hall. It was coming true, just as Garth had planned it. He would quietly usurp his younger brother's place as the Earl of Huntingdon, claiming his lands and titles—and wife—as his own. And why not? Except for the wife, they were rightfully his to begin with—

A deer stepped from cover and stood staring at him before bounding away, its tail lifted in warning. Tamlane had spent most of his adult life in the dismal groves of Modred's Wood, a place notorious for its poor game. Sherwood was a virtual paradise in comparison; everywhere there were birds, fat rabbits, and squirrels, and a seemingly endless supply of venison on the hoof.

Tam envied his brother such lush and prosperous land, then laughed. What did he have to envy Robin for? After all, it was all *his* now, wasn't it? He, Tamlane, was the master of Sherwood Forest now, even though he was obliged to hide behind his brother's name.

Still, he could not help but worry. After all, he was riding into an enemy camp alone. It was up to him to make sure that Robin Hood's servants had no cause to suspect that their master had been replaced. He had everything to gain if he could pull off the masquerade—and his soul to lose should he fail.

At the thought of Garth's pet demon, Tamlane shivered uncontrollably. He only allowed himself to do that when he was certain no one else was around. The Dragon's Teeth watched him for signs of weakness like jackals waiting for a lion to abandon its kill.

Garth alone knew how deep and real Tamlane's fear of the demon was. It was the leash he used, in place of familial affection, to control his foster son. Tamlane was still uncertain as to the wizard's personal agenda—but that was nothing new, either. He'd never fully understood his mentor, and was not sure he really wanted to. The one thing he *was* certain of was that the moment he was proclaimed the King of England, he'd have the old man's head stuck on a pike.

"Hail, Robin of Locksley!" bellowed a voice that boomed like good-natured thunder.

Tamlane did his best to keep from grabbing his sword and turned to stare at the short, squat man dressed in a common monk's cassock striding out of the woods. The monk was ruddy-faced and carried a quarterstaff like other men handled a walking stick. Despite his girth, it was obvious the good friar was more muscle than fat.

The monk strode right up to where Tam sat perched on his brother's borrowed stallion and smiled up at him, as would a friend and equal. Tam realized this brash, buffoonish creature was none other than Friar Tuck, one of Robin's boon companions from the days of the Merry Men.

"Good day, Friar Tuck. What brings you this way?"

Tuck boomed out a laugh and gestured at the turrets of Locksley Hall with his quarterstaff. "As if you didn't know! 'Tis time for me to leave my hermitage and hear your lovely lady's confession. And yours too, lest you forget!"

"No! No, of course! Of course I didn't forget. You are welcome as always, good monk."

Friar Tuck's smile waned and his demeanor grew more serious. "I only just heard of your uncle. I'm deeply sorry, my friend. He was a good man."

Tamlane tried to keep his confusion from being too obvious. "My uncle? What of him? I have been on the road for the past few days and only just returned . . ."

The priest blushed. "I'm sorry. I thought you knew. Sir William died at Gamwell Hall, not two days ago. It was quite sudden, or so I'm told. He . . . he was your only living family, was he not?"

Feigning grief, Tamlane lifted a hand to his face in order to hide his smile. "Yes. There is no one else."

*   *   *

For the hundredth time since they'd left him tied to the chair, Robin tested his bonds. And, for the hundredth time, his bonds held. The frustration made the fear for his life seem trivial. Robin Hood was not a man to suffer being held captive lightly.

Cursing mightily, he strained against the rawhide thongs that held him fast. This time, all he succeeded in doing was overturning the chair, with him in it, and cracking the side of his head against the hard dirt floor.

He continued to squirm, his breath growing heavier as rage eclipsed his rationality. This couldn't be happening! He'd escaped from worse death-traps than this dozens of times. The Sheriff of Nottingham and Sir Guy had concocted far more devious ways of ensnaring and disposing him than this, and he'd always managed to free himself.

But back then he'd had the Merry Men at his side; good friends and true who would realize his predicament and do all in their power to help him. Now he was alone, and no one knew where he was—save for his uncle, Sir William. He cursed himself for worse than a fool. He should have at least told Tuck! If he couldn't trust a priest to keep a family secret, who else was there? Now he lay, bruised and bloodied, trussed-up like a Christmas goose waiting the butcher's knife.

He froze at the sound of someone entering the tiny hut. He was afraid it might be that drooling hulk of a half-wit, Dim, again. The moment Tamlane had quitted the bandit's compound, Dim had taken the opportunity to pummel his leader's look-alike into unconsciousness. If Father Garth hadn't intervened, the idiot might have well beaten him to death. The fact that he had Garth to thank for saving what little was left of his life galled Robin.

"Robin? Robin Hood?"

He recognized Morag's voice. While he had his doubts concerning her, so far she'd shown him nothing but kindness—in her way.

"I'm—over here. I've fallen and I can't get up."

Black Morag hurried over to him and righted the
chair with a grunt. She peered anxiously at his swol-
len, bruise-dappled face. "Are you hurt?"

Robin laughed and spat out a loosened tooth. "Now
I know how the wheat feels at thrashing time!"

"Bastards!" she growled, unslinging a wineskin
from her shoulder. "Here, drink this. It'll help with
the pain."

Robin gratefully drank from the proffered skin. He
was too thirsty to wonder about Morag's motivations
for helping him. In any case, it was hard to tell what
thoughts might pass through the girl's head. Her hair
seemed to perpetually hang in her face, making eye
contact difficult. The way she moved reminded Robin
of a dog whipped once too often.

"Why are you doing this?"

She seemed surprised by the suddenness of his question and for a moment he thought she was going to
run away, like a rabbit flushed from cover.

"I'm not like the others."

"Then why are you here? Why do you travel with
these monsters?"

"Because no one else will have me."

"But you must have a family. Someone who loves
you?"

Morag giggled, and Robin felt his bowels turn to
ice. It was not a sane woman's laugh.

"Oh, yes. I had a family, once. My mother died
when I was too little to remember. My father and I,
we lived in the woods. He was a charcoal-maker. He
would go and chop down trees while I stayed home
and made dinner. He took care of me and I took care
of him. We loved each other very much. After a
while, he loved me like he loved my mother.

"Then . . . then there was a boy. From the village.
Matthew. A nice boy. A handsome boy. He would
come to see me when my father was away chopping
down trees. Then one day father came home early.
He found me with the village boy and he hit him with
his axe. After he chopped up the village boy, he

turned on me, calling me names. He said he'd make it so no one would ever want to look at me again. Mark me so everyone would know I was a whore.''

Morag brushed aside the hair hanging in her face and showed Robin her scars. He'd seen worse in his time, but those wounds had been inflicted by the royal torturer, not by a father on the flesh of his flesh. He winced and looked away.

. "You see?" Morag said sadly, letting her hair fall back into place. "After he marked me, he raped me. *Really* raped me. After he was finished, he went into the woods and hanged himself. When the village found out what had happened, they said it was my fault. That I had tempted my father into sin. That I was a fornicator and marked by God. I was chased away and wandered for a long time. I finally ended up in a brothel. That's where I met Tam. He was there with some of his men, selling novice nuns he'd stolen from an anchorage he'd pillaged. He said he liked my looks.''

"And you've been with him ever since?"

Morag nodded, chewing one of her thumbnails. "He said I could be his Maid Marian.''

The thought of this poor, abused mad-girl playing the part of his beloved made Robin ill.

"Is she beautiful?"

"Who?"

"Maid Marian.''

"Yes. She is . . . very beautiful.''

"I thought so." Morag's tone had grown cold. She studied Robin with eyes that had suddenly become remote. "Tam's not coming back, is he?" When Robin said nothing, she revealed her stained, crooked teeth in what seemed more like a rictus than a smile. "You're not fooling me. I know what he's up to. He's going to become you. He doesn't need me anymore, now that he has the *real* Maid Marian." She frowned at the sight of Robin's anger and tickled his beard with her chewed fingers. "Don't look so upset. If I

can't be your Maid Marian, perhaps you can be my
Tamlane the Dragon."

"Robin, my husband ... is there something
wrong?"

Tamlane started at the sound of Marian's voice, sur-
facing from his thoughts. He smiled weakly at his
brother's wife. Yes, something was wrong, but there
was no way he could explain it to the Lady Marian,
much less himself.

Marian knelt beside her husband's chair, placing her
hand atop his. "You seem so ... remote, my love.
Is it your uncle's death?"

"I suppose so," he answered, staring hard at her
fair white hand resting atop his callused one.

"You seem as if there is something you wish to
say," she prompted.

Yes, there is. The ballads did not do you justice,
thought Tamlane the Dragon.

He had never seen such a woman before in his life.
The Lady Marian's beauty was not limited to her face
and form. She radiated a serenity and self-confidence
that transcended that of the uncounted "wives of
Christ" he'd defiled. Her presence was as soothing as
a cool cloth pressed to a feverish brow. No wonder
his brother had gladly faced such overwhelming odds
reclaiming her from Prince John.

But there was more to his ill-ease than his unprece-
dented reaction to this woman. It had been with him
since he'd met the friar on the road the other day. As
they had made their way to Locksley Hall—Tamlane
on horseback, Friar Tuck keeping easy pace alongside
him—he had found himself actually beginning to *like*
the well-fed little monk. The thought made him
shudder.

*Me? Tamlane the Dragon? Feel kinship toward
another?*

Still, Tamlane found it difficult to remain aloof from
the jolly priest's ribald jokes and jests. In all his days
as a robber-lord, Tam had never known such closeness

with a fellow human was possible. The Dragon's Teeth were not his equals; they were a feral band of outcasts used for his own purposes, who followed him solely for the crumbs dropped from his table. He knew they feared and hated him, and that they'd gladly stab him between the shoulder blades the moment his back was turned. He had expected and accepted such treachery because—well, because he'd known no other way.

He'd been brought up to believe the concepts of love and friendship were weaknesses .that the human race deluded itself into thinking were strengths. Along the way, Garth had been careful to crush any incipient signs of affection in his foster son. Tam was only four or five when he'd made the mistake of telling Garth that he loved him. That was back when Tam still thought the heretic priest was his real father.

Garth showed him the error of his ways by summoning forth his familiar, Lucullus, and allowing it to sexually abuse the boy. The lesson had not been lost on the child: love nothing, trust no one.

But now he found himself surrounded by people who truly and honestly loved him. At first he'd looked into their eyes and tried to spot the hidden hate and secret envy Garth had assured him all men harbor in their breasts; he could not. This shook him to his very marrow. It was as if he'd suddenly discovered the world not flat, as everyone knows it to be, but actually round.

Shortly after his arrival at Locksley Hall he'd been approached by a broad-shouldered fellow with a bristling beard. Tam had come close to boxing the bigger man's ears, just as he would have done Dim, before realizing this was no other than Little John, Robin's right-hand man. Before he could react, the taller man swept him into an embrace, all the while professing how sorry he felt about his friend's recent loss. And, to Tam's surprise, he realized Little John honestly *was* sorry.

He'd done his best to respond to the questions put to him by his "friends," while his brain reeled. It was proving too much for him. He felt like a starving man given a chalice of the king's wine. The wealth of emotion surrounding him was threatening to make him lose what little control he possessed. He'd never dreamed impersonating his brother could be so difficult. . . .

Just as he was about ready to scream like a madman and draw his sword, the crowd parted and the sun given human form approached him.

Tam shook himself from his reveries once more and looked at Marian, seated beside him while she busied herself with her embroidery. Even in the most domestic of scenes, she radiated the nobility of one born to the purple. If ever there was a woman deserving of being made England's queen, it was she.

The night before he'd come to her as her husband, and she'd accepted him. At first his lust had been fired by the thought of cuckolding his twin, but as his passion increased, Tam became aware of something different, something alien, in the consummation. Then it occurred to him that in all his adult years, this was the first time he'd lain with a consenting woman he had not paid to do so. He had raped, fucked, swived, and fornicated countless numbers of times, but this was the first time he'd truly been made love to.

As they lay together in each other's arms, Marian had smiled at him and Tamlane felt the ice surrounding his heart weaken. There was so much love there . . . and all of it was his.

No. Not mine. His.

Aye. And there was the rub. None of the love, friendship, and adulation he'd so far enjoyed was rightfully his. While Locksley Hall and the titles and lands that went with it might be rightfully his, the loyalty and support of those around him belonged to his brother.

Father Garth had been fond of telling his ward, *In the Country of the Blind, the One-Eyed Man is King.*

Yes, but what did the One-Eyed King become once he entered the Land of the Sighted?

*   *   *

"You needn't worry that your death will be meaningless," Father Garth assured his captive, tapping a large, unwieldy tome resting on the table between them. The book seemed to be bound in some kind of animal skin, but whether reptile or mammal, or some ungodly hybrid of the two, was impossible to tell. "In fact, your ritual slaughter will ensure that a Saxon king will once more rule these lands." He smiled at the startled look on Robin's face. "Your brother wasn't spouting a madman's delusions of attaining greatness. Given my knowledge of the rituals in this book—the fabled *Aegrisomnia*—I can assure you that Tamlane will succeed in his bid for the throne. All I need is the blood of a hero."

"You intend to sacrifice me to your diabolic master, is that it?"

Garth laughed dryly. "In a way. You Christian dullards seem to think all a warlock needs to do to summon power is dance around naked, sprinkling dog's hair and powdered eye of bat on anything that stands still. It's much more complicated than that." Garth produced what looked to be a small bedroll and laid it on the table next to the book. "Ritual cleansings and purification rites much be observed. The signs must be right; the stars in alignment." He opened the bedroll, showing Robin the assortment of knives and torture implements kept within.

"For instance, the particular ritual I'll be following requires that you die by flaying. And not just your simple tanner's job, either! First must go the outer layer, then the fatty tissue, then the muscle. And different parts of the body must be stripped at certain times, so that you remain alive and conscious as long as possible. I have a special herbal brew to make sure of that. Granted, it's time-consuming, but quite potent magic, or so I'm told."

"You're not scaring me with this talk. I've heard it all before, and from far better men than yourself!"

Father Garth did not seem insulted. "Indeed. But the tricky part about all this are the pre-ritual precautions. The victim's blood can not be let by an edged weapon prior to the ritual itself. Nor can any seed be spilled. The ritual is quite specific about that. But in the end, your hideous, agonizing death will make it possible for your brother to reign as Good King Robin."

"He might be the true Earl of Huntingdon and the rightful master of Locksley Hall, but my name he has no right to!"

Garth's smile grew even nastier. "Oh, but he does! He has *all* the right in the world!" He leaned forward, bringing his face within inches of the captive Robin Hood's. "You see, when I stole him from the nurse's cradle that night, I untied the ribbons on your ankles—the ones that made it possible for even your own mother to tell you apart—to make things even more complicated for your family. It wasn't *Thomas* Fitzooth I took with me, it was *Robert*!" He gave a short, sharp bark of laughter at the look of confusion in the younger man's eyes.

"Yes, that's right. *You* are Thomas, not Robert! You are, indeed, the true Earl of Huntingdon. But you are *not* Robin Hood!"

"It doesn't matter what a man is called. It's his deeds that make him who he is."

"Ah, yes. Just as Tiberius was a honored general, Caligula a darling of the *vox populi*, and Nero a skilled musician and thespian, King Robert will go down in history as an idealistic freedom-fighter who, once he was upon the throne, became a ruthless despot of monumental cruelty and depravity. And I will have attained a favored seat at the left hand of my infernal master's banquet table."

After Garth wearied of taunting his captive with detailed descriptions of the upcoming ritual sacrifice, he returned to his preparations, leaving Robin alone in the foul-smelling gloom.

But not for long.

The rats, like anything else in the camp, seemed to

know he was helpless. He could see their tiny eyes glittering like filthy gems in the dim light provided by the candle guttering on the table.

The biggest of the pack—one-eyed and with a matted black coat—edged forward, sniffing the air hesitantly. The beast stood on its hind legs, fixing Robin with its one good eye as if challenging him to a duel.

"Get away!" Robin was tempted to try and kick at the rodent to scare it off, but was afraid of overturning his chair again. The rats would be all over him in seconds. But, then, might that not be preferable to the death lovingly described to him by kindly Father Garth? Surely the Lord would forgive a suicide, as long as it was committed to keep the victim from dying in a satanic ritual.

Before he could continue along that particular track of theological thought, Black Morag entered the hut. She bared her teeth at the rats and rushed forward, snarling and waving her arms. The big one-eyed rat hissed in return, waiting until the last moment before fleeing with its fellows.

Morag shuddered as she returned her attention to Robin. "Hideous creatures! I hate them! I can't see how the others can bring themselves to eat them."

"Morag, why do you keep visiting me?"

She paused, chewing her ragged thumbnail in contemplation. "I'm not sure. I suppose it's because you're a hero. I've never seen one before. Wanted to know what one was like."

"I'm a man, Morag. Nothing more."

"Maybe."

"Morag—untie me."

Morag clapped her hands over her ears. She shook her head from side to side and made a strange, droning noise, as if trying to drown out something she didn't want to hear.

"Morag, stop that! Listen to me. You don't belong here, not with these murderers. Set me free and I'll take you with me to Sherwood, where you can live free and happy."

"No!" Morag continued to shake her head. "No! No! No!"

"Please, you've got to help me! There is no one else here I can trust. Morag!"

"I belong here! I can't fit in anywhere else! I killed my father! I killed Matthew! I'm unclean! I *deserve* this place! I *deserve* these people! I'm nothing but a whore, who allows murderers and thieves to climb on top of her!"

"Morag! You've got to do *something*!"

Before Robin had time to react, she'd fallen to her knees before him and was busily unlacing the front of his hose. Robin was still in a state of shock as her hands closed on his member.

"Stop that!"

If Morag heard him, she gave no sign. Instead, she lowered her mouth, taking his flaccid penis in her mouth.

Robin was at a genuine loss as to what to do. Tied hand and foot, he really didn't have any say in what was happening to him. Yet he was married to—and honestly loved—the Lady Marian. Never, during their long and difficult courtship, had he indulged in the favors of tavern whores, nor had he ever seduced a peasant's daughter for sport. But what Morag was now inflicting on him—doubtless a sin in the eyes of the Church—was something he'd never experienced before, in or out of marriage.

Whatever her mental and emotional state, Morag was certainly adept in the tricks of her profession. Within minutes Robin felt himself rapidly approaching climax, mortal sin or not.

Just as he was about to empty his seed, there was a noise from behind Morag and Father Garth's gnarled hand dug its bony fingers into her matted hair.

"Bitch!" he shrieked, his voice quaking with rage. "What have you done? What have you *done*?!" With that, he jerked Morag's head free of her work, just in time to send Robin's seed arcing through the air.

"Looks to me like I've fucked you sidesaddle, old man!" snarled Morag.

Father Garth emitted a shrill, almost womanly, scream and producing a curved knife from the folds of his robe. Morag saw the death blow coming but did not offer to escape. Garth opened her throat from ear-to-ear, just like the way a butcher would dispose of a suckling pig. Her lifeblood shot forth, spraying Robin liberally. He gagged as it struck his face.

Morag smiled and tried to lift her hand in farewell, then collapsed onto the floor. Somewhere in the shadows the rats squealed in anticipation of a meal.

Father Garth stood over the dead whore's body, still clutching the murder weapon in a trembling hand. He seemed to be babbling to no one in particular. "Meddling whore! I knew she would cause trouble the moment Tam brought her from that brothel. Stupid cow! Now she's gone and ruined *everything*. The ritual was quite specific about keeping the sacrifice pure."

"So your little magic ritual has been broken, is that it?" Robin sneered. "All your plans for my brother to take over my place and become king have been dashed, eh?"

"It can still work. The ritual would have made it a certainty, that's all. But I can still make it happen." The priest advanced on Robin, his knife still wet with Morag's blood. "Provided that there is only *one* Fitzooth brother left alive!"

"Drop the knife, Garth!"

Both Father Garth and Robin gaped in amazement at the sight of Tamlane the Dragon standing in the doorway, an arrow pointed directly at the heretic priest's heart.

"Tam? Are you mad, boy?"

"Perhaps! Now do as I say!"

Garth frowned and shook his head, as if he couldn't believe what he was hearing. "Don't you understand, Tam? He's *got* to die! That's how it must be if you are to succeed!"

"I've changed my mind, Garth. I don't *want* to be king of England."

"What magic has been worked on you? These are not the words of the Tamlane *I* know."

"You mean they're not the words of the Tamlane *you* created!"

"Damn you, boy! Don't stand there and bandy words with *me*. You know what's at stake here."

"Yes, I do. And I've decided I don't want it. Now stand aside, Garth. I don't want to shoot you, but I will if you give me no choice."

"It was that woman, wasn't it? That bloody Marian! She did this to you, didn't she? I thought I raised you better than that. Women are no more than fields to be plowed—or salted. You're moonstruck, Tam! Now leave off this nonsense and I'll get back to my work at hand." With that, Garth turned his back on his foster son and raised his knife in preparation of burying it deep in Robin's chest.

The bow sang and an arrow blossomed from the middle of Garth's narrow chest. The old priest stared in dumb wonder at it for a moment before dropping the knife. The look on his face was that of a man bitten by a dog he believed cowed into obedience. He staggered backward, knocking over the table, extinguishing the one candle that illuminated the hut. He pointed a long, skeletal finger at Tamlane and murmured something in a strange language, a bubble of blood forming on his trembling lips, then collapsed atop Morag's corpse.

Robin sat and silently waited for a second arrow to take his life as well, but to his surprise, Tamlane freed him instead. Robin's arms and legs tingled as if beset by a tiny army of elves and fairies wielding needles, but the pain soon subsided as his circulation was restored. He stared at his brother's face, half hidden by the shadows, as he massaged the feeling back into his wrists, unsure of what he should say or do.

"It's best you leave as fast as you can," suggested Tam. "He was trying to summon Lucullus, his pet

demon, as he died. I'm not sure, but I think he spoke
enough of the charm for it to work."

"But—why? Why did you come back? You could
have had everything; my name, my property, my chattels, my wife. You could have even become king!"

"Believe me, I was sorely tempted to leave you here
to face whatever fate Garth decided to mete out to
you. But I realized there could only be one Robin
Hood. Not because no one is your equal at swordplay
or archery—but in *here*." He struck his breastbone
with the flat of his hand. "As far back as I can remember, Garth had been twisting me, stunting me like a
freakmaster creates dwarfs, so I would come to manhood thinking his was the true way. The only way. He
told me I was evil, and it never occurred to me to
wonder if that evil was mine by nature—or thrust
upon me.

"But now I've seen how humans live—true humans,
not the twisted, brutalized things I've been raised to
believe were men. I saw how even the simplest peasant was twice my equal. I was shamed—and angered.
Angered that I should have been denied the right to
be able to love and know friendship, and everything
that comes with it. I felt cheated. And I knew who
was responsible."

"Brother, please—I realize your sins have been
many and severe. But the Church assures us there *is*
such a thing as redemption! Come, leave this place
with me . . ."

Tam sniffed the air, grabbed his brother, and
roughly shoved him toward the door. "There's no time
for that! Besides, I'm as much a cripple as poor Dim.
A one-eyed man might miss the sight he once had,
but even with a glass eye he'll never be able to see
through it. Go back to your castle and lands. Go back
to your friends. Return and live out your life as history
sees fit. But whatever you do, never let the Lady Marian slip from your grasp; for without her you'll be lost.
Now *go*!"

Robin opened his mouth, prepared to argue his case

even further, but he stopped at the sight of tears
coursing down his twin brother's face.

"I know I shouldn't weep for him," whispered Tamlane the Dragon. "But—good or bad—he was the only
father I ever knew."

Robin wiped the hot tears from his brother's eyes
and for one brief second he could remember what it
had been like in their mother's womb, pressed belly-
to-belly with his brother, legs and arms intertwined as
they sucked one other's thumbs.

Without further words between them, Robin turned
and left the hut. Within seconds he'd mounted the
horse his brother had left for him, and was on his way
back to Sherwood and his wife.

Tamlane the Dragon seated himself in the chair his
brother had recently vacated, crossed his arms, and
waited. It wouldn't be long. The electrical-storm smell
of the approaching demon was growing stronger by
the second. He glanced down at the bodies sprawled
at his feet and something resembling regret flickered
in his heart as he studied Morag's twisted body. Like
himself, she had been more a victim of her father than
herself. Perhaps that's why he'd fancied her in the first
place.

Tam felt the hair on the back of his neck begin to
prickle, and with a sound of a thousand angry honey-
bees, the air was split and Lucullus appeared.

The demon shambled from the shadows, quickly
scenting the thick odor of spilled blood. The beast
shuffled over to where Garth and Morag's bodies lay
in a tangled heap, snuffling like a bear. When it saw
Garth's pale, blood-smeared face it halted and emitted
a low-pitched whine.

"That's right, familiar! Your master's dead!" hissed
Tamlane.

Lucullus swung his fierce, fang-filled snout in Tam's
direction. Its brow furrowed and lips curled in a snarl.

Tam stood up, kicking the chair aside as he rose.
He pulled a long, sharp dirk from his belt and

motioned with a beckoning twitch of his fingers for the demon to approach him. His grin was almost as wide and sharp as his adversary's.

"Come. Let us dance."

Young Robin

by Matthew Costello

**Or How the Lad Learned How to Shoot
Exceedingly Well—And a Great Lesson
about Women—While Suffering Travail
Among Demons.**

Part the First: Robin after Bed
*Where the famed lad of Nottingham is at once
lured from the haystacks of the countryside
of Sherwood by his good friend Will Scarlett,
who thence imperils him in a most grievous
way.*

As the very veracity of young Robin's incredible
adventures maychance be questioned in times to
come, it behooves the author to set down this account
in as clear and brief a language as possible.

Notwithstanding such adumbrations, I am loathe to
hurry my tale for fear that good readers less familiar
with Robin Fitzooth's early years will look upon my
parole with nothing less than utter disbelief.

For Robin Fitzooth was, in faith, a callow youth.

There was, indeed, a great interval between bonny
King Richard's untimely departure to the most Holy
Crusades, and the famed archery contest that would
launch Robin's justifiably illustrious career.

And during that interval Robin amused himself by
simple acts of thievery and a general good-natured
debauchery, of the randy sort that suits the young, but
would be unseemly in anyone nearing the feared age
of two-score.

Thus, well before his deserved reputation as a brilliant marksman, Robin had found his mark with many an earthly wench who welcomed him in the absence of a husband tending goats or forlornly hunting a lone stag.

Robin's interests in such fleshy matters ran to a roundness and fullness that others may have perceived as too much of a certain thing. But Fitzooth's tastes were undoubtedly shaped by the sad and tragic deprivation of his mother's bountiful love at a tender age.

For indeed, he preferred maids of true heft.

Even Maid Marion was anything but petite. But that account must, by rights, await another day.

Enjoying himself as a cutpurse and in the various hayricks and mud-floor hovels, with the lusty wenches who took his arrival as nothing but good fortune, was the alpha and omega of Robin's severely circumscribed ambition.

The nefarious Prince John, brother to Richard, was already making the peasantry groan under his loathsome yoke. And yes, small bands of peasants had already lashed out at the black and gold lackeys of the sheriff. But Robin was—so far—entirely disinterested.

In truth, young Robin cared not one whit about the fate of the poor, oppressed peasants. He had merely his overriding interest in other matters . . . which is how he came to meet the Lady of the North Wood.

It was, of course, Will Scarlett who brought the news to Robin that so pricked his interest.

Young Will—for he too had only recently attained what could be described as his manhood—was Robin's ever faithful companion in their night and day jaunts. While Will Scarlett's interests didn't run nearly as steady as his good friend's, still he enjoyed the general air of thievery and licentiousness that surrounded any adventure with Robin Fitzooth.

And so it was, he brought Robin the strange tale of the lady.

They sat—at midday—under the shade of an entirely too large beech tree, feasting on the apples of a man named Hubert. Having just finished a visit at Hubert's hut, with his very good woman, Robin and Will were now, in truth, fully sated.

Robin was feeling a languor that would soon yield to a well-deserved nap . . .

When Will Scarlett spoke words that would forever change Robin Fitzooth and—of course—the path of English history.

"Good Robin," Will said.

Robin had his Lincoln green cap pulled down over his eyes, masking what glimmers of sunlight still were able to slice their way through the leafy canopy above.

"Speak on, Will. But hurry. I am feeling most relaxed."

"I was in Nottingham Square last night."

"And I hope that you made good profit of the sheriff's coffers. His foresters walk with bulging pockets."

"Aye, Robin. I did take a moment to replenish my own larder of coins. But as I stood there, I happened to bump into our friend, Allan-a-Dale."

"Good fellow."

"Yes. I say I bumped into the full weight of Allan. In truth, Allan, singing in full voice, bumped into me. For he was in his cups."

"A not uncommon condition for good Allan."

Robin's lids did grow exceedingly heavy at this point. The warmth, the sense of satiety, made it near impossible to listen to Will's story. Young Scarlett let his tales meander like the wind-blown thistle of the daffydowndilly.

And here I risk leading my good readers into a labyrinth worthy of Theseus. As Will did nothing but continue to relate yet another story passed onto him by the wobbling troubadour.

But rest assured that we now enter the last layer of this tale within a tale.

"Allan said—no, he sung—that there is a lady residing in the North Woods, in a small cave. And she is exceedingly beautiful, with—"

Here Will gave Robin a most detailed inventory of parts ascribed to said lady. Suffice it to say that she offered a firm fullness designed to appeal to many a man.

But most definitely to prick the interest of a young coxcomb like Robin.

Presently, Fitzooth sat up, his cap pushed off his face, staring at Will.

Who—having finished the rather lengthy physical description—hurried to matters of even greater interest.

"This lady resides there, alone and scared, Robin. Her father, the Earl of Blackpool, has been possessed by the most terrible demons. She fled to save herself. Now she awaits a champion who will accompany her to Blackpool and kill the demons."

Robin's mind still displayed lush tapestries of the lady in question. But on hearing the word *demons*, he turned and looked at Will.

" 'Tis a difficult problem, demons. Especially when someone old and powerful is sore afflicted. Poor lady." Robin stood up. "Perhaps she is in need of comfort. The North Wood, you say?"

Will stood up, sensing that Robin was taking the wrong measure of his tale.

"No, good friend. This lady seeks a hero. Methinks that this is one of those unpleasant tasks that often befell knights in those years before the Crusades provided a suitably convenient opportunity for adventure, pillaging, and pious good works."

Robin nodded.

As if sensing that movement and direction were truly afoot, Robin's horse—dark brown but dappled with great white spots—snorted eagerly. The horse too still bore the telltale traces of apple peel around its naggish mouth.

"Well said, Will. Your story has revived me. If we were to hurry, we would arrive at the North Wood, at this—"

"Cave, Robin. But sirrah, don't—"

As was his wont, Robin walked away, listening to

whatever sweet whispers his mind conjured. He untied his horse from an elderberry bush.

Robin pulled himself onto his horse.

His knee brushed his quiver, full with arrows.

His longbow and sword were fastened to the other side of his horse.

But whenever real battle was called for, it was Will Scarlett, with a middling to good eye, whom Robin depended on. Though a good swordsman, Robin's prowess with bow and arrow was no more than any other Nottingham lad, and a good deal worse than many.

Worse far still than his aim was his speed.

The same hands and fingers which could move sweetly, with pleasing accuracy, over the humps and hollows of a country maiden became clumsy and cluttered fiddling with the quiver, the arrows, the very size of a longbow.

"Come, Will. You'll not have me make such a long and dangerous journey by myself?"

Will walked over to his gray mare, a horse that looked more lethargic than spirited. It's woeful countenance was equally matched by a glum expression on Scarlett's face.

"Now I regret telling you Allan-a-Dale's story. The North Wood is dangerous. And I don't believe either you or I have any experience dealing with demons."

And Robin laughed. An infectious sound that would prove irresistible when he finally came to form his merry band to fight the evil Prince John and his taxing rule.

But now it held only Will enthralled.

"Come, Will. We'll leave the demons to the good fathers of the Church—though I must wonder what their experience in that province might be. It's merely the lady that interests me. Come or not, I have my cap set on seeing this alluring wench."

Will got onto his gray mare, muttering not so much to himself but for Robin's ears.

"Aye, alluring—if we believe Allan's drunken song.

'Twill be dark by the time we reach the woods. And we'll be hungry again."

Robin laughed again, louder, and a trio of starlings fluttered from adjacent huckleberrys.

A good omen, thought Robin.

Who was often known for misreading augurs and mis-divining messages.

"Come, there's a lady in distress," Robin said, imagining no more than providing said woman with a good ear and tender ministrations that stopped far short of demon fighting in dark castle halls.

But Robin Fitzooth was mistaken in almost every account, as would soon become clear.

Robin journeyed to the North Wood merely to indulge his curiosity and perhaps—if luck smiled upon him—his earthly delights.

Robin, with Will beside him, rode full out, ever north.

To the North Wood.

To where young Robin would learn secrets of marksmanship that would serve him so well when fighting the black and gold foresters of Prince John.

In the years to come . . . after Robin learned the danger of responding to a lady in distress.

Part the Second: Robin Smitten
Where Robin, having made the difficult and
dangerous journey northward, finds the lady
in a odd manner, and falls into a state of
romantic torpor that, for once, removes any
concern about danger.

Now, it might behoove the reader to learn of the sundry adventures which afflicted Robin and Will as they journeyed to the cool and harsh North Wood, a region rarely visited but by the most hearty souls.

There was, for instance, a small but vexsome band of robbers that chased them through the woods—a case of turnabout seeming entirely unfair. But Will, a better than good marksman, quickly dispatched two of the oafs, causing the rest of the band to reconsider their plan of action.

Then, just at dusk, a great black bear—of a size and girth not seen even in London's famed pits—did come charging out at them. Its maw looked open a full foot, wet and hungry, quite prepared to devour Robin and Will, their horses, and any small residue that might perchance be left.

The bear looked mightily hungry.

It was once again Will Scarlett who, with two quick shots from his quiver, planted his arrows, one in the bear's left eye—and oh, the mournful sound the creature did make—and the other shaft in the beast's belly, which seemingly had no effect.

But the bear did stop. Rather abruptly, Robin would later claim, and turn in the other direction.

"Rather like a fishmonger's wife remembering that she had a chowder a-bubbling, eh, Will?"

Will barely enjoyed such jests, still sweating and shaking from his sorely tried marksmanship.

Robin did, in fact, haste to assist Will in both misadventures. But he fumbled too long with his too stocked quiver, and then had trouble getting his longbow into position.

Let it be said that Robin chose his friends wisely.

But by the time they reached the North Wood, a dark and gloomy stretch of oak and pines that reached well into still pagan counties, they were both tired, hungry, and sore-pressed for a drink of something strong and biting.

It was then that Robin asked, "Where did good Allan sing that this cave mayhaps be?"

Will shrugged. " 'Tis not known to me, Robin. Allan's sense of direction was never too keen . . . especially when singing."

It occurred to Robin that he should have, at earlier point, determined just where this lady might be.

"Well, good Will, we're here. We may as well start to search for our prize."

And search they did.

Dusk yielded to a moonless night. Oft, Robin would turn one way while Will Scarlett turned the other, until each was staring into a somber darkness alone.

The reader can imagine the quick screams and halloos that hastily reunited the feckless pair.

It was Will who suggested setting up a camp.

"We can search again in the morning, Robin. My horse begins to act the role of a laggard. And my bum aches from our hours in the saddle."

Robin, his interest more piqued the later it got, finally assented to Will's proposal.

They built a small fire near a stream with water that tasted strong and mossy but provided no ill effects. Will had a small loaf of bread, very dry and hard. And that was all the nourishment that they had.

Robin huddled close to the fire, now wishing, perhaps, that he hadn't strayed from the comfort of his Sherwood Forest, where each bend in the woods brought another friendly peasant cottage with stores of all kinds for their enjoyment.

Will fell to sleep almost immediately.

Robin watched the fire, a strange restlessness hanging over him.

The blanket from his horse, and the neatly built fire, were the only warmth.

He closed his eyes.

He was just at the cusp of what would be an uncomfortable but still most welcome sleep.

When he felt someone touch him.

His cheek. Lingering at his ears, always a source of interest in his amorous adventures.

I dream, he thought.

Perhaps my horse nibbles my ear, stirred to some expression of gratitude for the cessation in the day's quest.

No.

He opened his eyes.

He felt. Yes, he *felt* fingers touching his cheek.

His sword, which he could use with great skill, let it be admitted, was feet away. In sight but not within grasp.

Robin spun around.

And faced a vision of beauty that made his mouth fall open.

He was cold and hungry, and as tired as he ever remembered being in the few years since he left his father Hugh's cramped abode.

But now he had only one thought.

And this woman, this lady, wearing a heavy purple cloak and cowl, smiled and put a finely tapered finger to her lips.

Robin immediately wished that said cloak was off so he could get a good glimpse of the true dimensions of this vision.

She came closer.

An aroma more wonderful than elderberry wafted over him.

Her lips were full and tinged with red—a fashion he had never noted among the women of his own county. Her eyes were dark, nearly black pools, reflecting back the firelight and his own stupid gaze.

"My lady," he said, making no attempt to mask the very deep impression this lady of the north was making on him.

She brought a finger to her lips.

"Quiet, good sir. Do not wake your companion."

As if in response, Will Scarlett snored and snorted.

"My prayers have been answered. I may only have one champion, and, sirrah, I wish it to be you . . ."

Will Scarlett bellowed like a bull calf in his sleep.

While Robin found no reason to dispute the exceedingly fair lady's claim.

The lady pulled Robin away from the warmth of the fire—a deprivation tinged with the promise of greater warmth to come.

Indeed, Robin had felt embarrassed at the very visibility of his interest, for he was a very instinctive lad. Now, in the shadows, surrounded by a stand of brutish pines, he felt that the secret of his interest in the lady was—for the nonce—secure.

The maid held his hand tightly and pulled him so distant as to make Will's rumbling resemble a thunderstorm meandering through a far-off valley.

"I may only bring it one defender, sirrah. Any more and the demon—such a clever foe—will sense our presence and easily defeat us."

Now, in truth, Robin did not believe in demons. He had never, in point of fact, ever seen any demons. Nor had he known anyone who had any direct experience with demons. And even his good father, Hugh, possessed of many a quaint belief, never impressed their existence upon him.

But he did believe in this vision standing before him, turned so that her creamy skin and dark eyes glowed and shimmered from the reflection of the camp fire.

And there was this:

Her words chilled Robin, standing there at the edge of a black universe.

Silly childhood fears were close, as well as an adolescent yearning for this wonderful woman whose smell, touch, her very glance, were so intoxicating.

He gave her hand an encouraging squeeze.

And he forced his face into a mask of utmost concern and seriousness.

Hoping to squelch the telltale grin of concupiscence.

"Pray, tell me your account, fair lady."

And—wonderful maid—she squeezed his hand back.

"My mother died when I was but a young girl," she said.

An opening statement to further increase the bond between them.

Will Scarlett growled at the night air. A noisy sleeper, Scarlett was a vexing sleeping companion.

"And her death propelled my father into the most strange and unpleasant humor. He began to spend long hours in his tower, entrance to which was forbidden."

Here the lady turned away, looking into the night. The poignant pain of her tale was given an added and appropriate emphasis.

Though, truth to tell, had an observer been there, he would have discerned a practiced air to the tale.

"I was left alone to wander the castle, listening to the strange incantations that emanated from the tower."

"My poor mistress," Robin said.

Interested in her tale, but also well practiced himself, knowing that listening and seduction are oft joined at the hip.

"Until one day my father emerged from his tower. And—and—"

Her voice caught. A glimmer of a tear bloomed in the crease of an eye.

Robin wanted to tell her that his heart shared the wrench of her pain.

"My lady. Perhaps this story pains you so. Mayhaps you should recline by the warm fire, and we shall talk of other things."

For indeed, the very darkness and the chill of her tale was starting to make any thoughts of love vanish.

The lady shook her head. "No. We must hasten our departure. My father's castle sits on a hill at the edge of the forest. By dawn the demon will be gone, and my father will be dead."

Robin then understood that this adventure—whatever it would involve—was to take place *now*. Not only that, it was to take place at night.

Now again, his knowledge of demons was—at best—scant. But it did seem that he would have a better chance facing said creatures, or spirits, with the aid of sunlight rather than this dark, moonless night. He hastened to mention said option to the lady.

But she turned to him.

And oh, her countenance offered enough of a moon, glowing a burnished yellow.

"No. By dawn the demon will be loose, sirrah. My father's spirit will have died fighting it." Now, hitting her mark, both eyes became tiny wet pools.

It was just enough to stiffen Robin's resolve.

"We must leave now—"

Robin looked over at Will, snoring peacefully, dreaming of peasant feasts and women who made no pretense of hiding their good-natured randiness.

The maid tugged him.

"We can both ride your steed." She stood close to him. The smell—not elderberry but jasmine and mint—made his eyes cross.

For a moment he though he detected another meaning in her proposal.

No, that would come later.

After the demons were dispelled.

An additional aspect of the matter which he knew nothing about. Again, having no firsthand experience of that sort . . .

She pulled Robin toward his horse.

He got onto it—which snorted in confusion. Then he reached down and pulled the lady up—no easy task.

And they set off into the woods toward the castle.

Part the Third
Where Robin, now in close company with the lady, learns not only her name, but what also will be required of him once he arrives at the castle.

Robin enjoyed having the lady pressing close against him—especially as the movement of his horse produced a not unpleasant rocking motion. Still, his mood turned circumspect as the glimmer of the camp fire vanished and a near total blackness engulfed him.

They had by this time exchanged names. She was

Elaine, daughter of Earl of Blackpool, the aforementioned demon-vexed father.

And Elaine found his surname amusing, saying, "Fit*ztooth*—pray, what kind of name is that?"

A sore point with Robin, who oft suffered teasing from the other village lads. He was brusque in correcting her.

"*Fitzooth,* dear lady. And if my name is a source of such low comedy, perhaps I'd best return to my loyal companion."

His chagrin was quickly mollified when Elaine turned around and kissed his cheek.

"Oh, Robin. Don't be cross with me."

And there was just enough of the coquette in her tone to keep Robin moving straight toward the castle, though the ground turned boggy and the air chilled him even further.

But nothing in his apprehension prepared him for the sight of the castle.

Even his horse backed up a step, as if smelling a foul odor.

While Robin was left gasping at the vision that greeted him on attaining the crest of the hill.

"Faith, my lady. That is the gloomiest sight these eyes have ever set on."

Now, Robin had seen castles before. King Richard's noble estate, now occupied by the loathsome Prince John, was a mighty edifice, majestic and proud.

But this structure was terrible, a nightmare castle formed by a child's fevered dream.

It was surrounded by a moat. Robin could see a dark stream that trailed down to the castle before surrounding it. The moat was vast, impassable, and, of course, the drawbridge was up.

Clearly no welcome here, Robin thought.

Though it was black everywhere, the castle seemed darker still, save for a single light that flickered in a tower.

Perhaps it would be wise to reconsider this venture, Robin thought.

Lady Elaine, as if sensing Robin's shock, said, "*There*. See that light. That is where my father is."

"So I surmised, my lady."

Elaine leaned back into him. "All that you must do, dear Robin, is enter the castle, make your way to my father, and then slay him."

He shook his head at her dramatic proposal. "Slay him? But I though that your father was possessed?"

"Oh, but he is—"

"Then it should follow that I slay the demon—however one does that."

Elaine took a breath.

Her garments seemed to stretch, fighting against the intake of breath.

She breathed in, ending the siege against the fabric.

"Yes. But demons are exceedingly clever. Slaying my father will force the demon to reveal itself. You need not worry. My father will be unharmed, while the demon will be mortally wounded."

Robin was unsure he understood the physics of such a thing. But then, he had no experience of such combat while Elaine seemed to have some.

She pressed her lips against her cheek. "Don't say, sirrah, that you are too scared to champion me?"

Of course not, Robin thought.

He could see the castle over her shoulder. There seemed to be no way in there. Certainly none with the drawbridge up.

"It looks mighty difficult, my lady."

She sobbed against him. A gentle, rhythmic keening that only the most callow heart could resist.

And Robin was, indeed, callow.

But he was also stirred by that appetite that was, at this point in his adventure, all but dominant.

So he said, his voice rising, startling the peepers and bullfrogs pursuing similar courses in nearby mudholes and oily ponds:

"My lady, I am yours as blade to hilt."

The sobbing stopped. His face was the beneficiary of a dozen warm and plangent kisses.

Obviously he had said the right words.

Now, he thought, to make good on such a promise.

He snapped the reins of his horse, and he moved down to the castle.

Robin got off his horse and looked at the moat.

"Perhaps it could be crossed by swimming," he said.

Lady Elaine shook her head.

"No. It is infested with creatures, foul snakes that are wont to attach themselves to warm-blooded animals and drain them of their blood." She shook her head. "No, you can't swim across."

"Is there another drawbridge, perhaps a back entrance to your good father's castle?"

"No. The earl always said that it was best to have one door and no enemies at your back."

"And there are guards inside?"

"I believe so. I myself have not been here in many days. But a few loyal retainers have remained, ignorant of the dark pursuits of my father."

Robin felt that the flow of information was, to this point, largely unhelpful. "Would my lady have an idea how many such retainers there might be?"

Elaine moved away from the edge of the moat. "Perhaps a dozen. Maybe two."

Robin nodded.

He thought then of Scarlett, who would miss all the entertainment to come.

And Robin wondered: Who will Scarlett revel with if I die inside these foul walls?

Lady Elaine turned to him. Her cloak fell from her shoulders. And Robin saw a creamy swatch of shoulder and then, yes, the promising swell of flesh barely contained by the bodice of her gown.

A well-timed movement, he thought, since he was about to consider the relative merits of running to his horse, getting on, and riding away with all speed.

"I know the castle, dear Robin. I know passages, doorways, secret panels. Get us inside, and I will have you avoid all my father's retainers. Besides"—she took a step closer—"they are dotty, elderly men who take all day to unsheathe their blades. Their accuracy with the longbow is laughable."

Robin was about to mention that his own archery skills were not what they should be.

But they heard a noise.

From the tower.

They joined hands, Elaine and Robin, and listened . . .

In his short years of carousing, Robin had never heard such a horrible sound. It was a bellow, a howl, the sort a sow makes when the butcher brings his blade to bear on its throat.

Yet it was an old man's voice.

Robin looked at Elaine.

"My father . . . the poor man."

There was a splash in the moat. Robin looked down only to see tiny ripples in the water.

Methinks that there's something eager there, Robin thought.

He watched and waited for another spray of water, hoping to glance the eels described by Elaine.

But there was nothing.

The lady touched his shoulder.

And faith, he jumped, barely tottering to the edge of the moat.

"We must begin," she said.

Yes, he thought. For in finally beginning, there might lie the end of this matter.

"How do you propose entering the castle?" Elaine asked.

Robin looked at her. He had hoped that she would have a plan, some wondrous way to enter the castle unseen, unheard.

"I do not know," he said. "Do you have any suggestion—"

Elaine shook her head. "No. That—is why I needed you."

Robin nodded.

He turned and looked at the forbidding castle. There's a word to describe this, he thought. Impregnable. Yes, it's impregnable.

He was facing the drawbridge. It was a sheer piece of oak—blackish, splintery—leading up to a low parapet.

He got an idea.

Not a good idea.

There was another splash.

The eels like it, though, he reflected.

He waited, hoping some alternative would suggest itself.

"Yes," Elaine said, sensing his thought processes.

"I—I have only one thought, good lady." Robin raised an arm and pointed to the drawbridge. "I can shoot some arrows into the drawbridge and . . ." He tried to picture the proposed activity, it seeming ever more unlikely. "With ropes tied to them," he added, "I can slide across and—"

Another splash.

He immediately imagined himself tumbling into the moat. A big splash, followed by the hungry excitement of the eels.

He brought his hand down. And shook his head. "No, that won't—"

But Elaine clasped his hand and brought it to her bosom.

"Oh, yes, dear Robin. *Yes.* It will work. You have yards of rope. You can send across as many lines as you need. Then you climb across. And I'll follow—"

Robin chewed his lip, a tasteless morsel but it distracted him from the horrible images his plan conjured.

"That's it!" Elaine said. "That is the way we will enter."

She grasped his hand. And while it certainly felt pleasant for Robin to have it so imprisoned, he noted an odd fact.

There seemed to be no warmth emanating from the fair lady's skin.

He shook his head. The night is indeed cold . . .

Part the Fourth
Where Robin, with great difficulty, enters the castle and discovers the true nature of the demon's defenses.

Presently, Robin got a good opportunity to display his lack of prowess with the longbow.

He needed to shoot his arrows into the drawbridge in such a way as to make them cluster together, tethering the many ropes into a strand strong enough to hold him.

His first shots went well wide of each other.

Lady Elaine cleared her throat. "Perhaps," she said unkindly, "there might be another way we can enter."

Such contumely only hardened the oft-sensitive Robin to pursue his tactic.

And though it took far too long, eventually five arrows were well anchored in the wood, each with a strand of the heavy hemp leading back to the far side of the moat.

"Quick," Elaine said. "Fasten the ropes to this dead beech tree."

Robin moved fast, assured of his knot-tying skill.

He ran back to the moat and—ever aware of the dark, oily water below him—he tugged the ropes.

"They appear strong enough."

"Quickly now. Dawn's light is but hours away."

Robin tested the ropes once again, and then—his bow and quiver over his shoulder, his sheathed sword tied tightly to his right leg—he started climbing, hand over hand.

He grunted. Then cursed, keeping his voice at such a register that his words wouldn't burn the fair lady's ears.

Of course, Robin ordered himself not to look down.

But once, dangling and kicking halfway across the moat, about to climb up to the cluster of arrows, he permitted himself a quick glance downward.

The water, flat and black, reflected back his shadowy kicks.

He thought of what lay in the water, and then his breath caught in his lungs.

"Go on, good Robin. You are nearly there. Go on . . ."

He looked up.

He held the cluster of ropes tightly in his fist.

And Robin thought he felt movement. Was one of the arrows loosening perhaps? Jiggling back and forth, ready to pop out just as he reached the drawbridge?

No, fate wouldn't be that cruel to him.

But that is, in fact, what happened.

A single arrow popped out of the wood. Robin felt a strand of rope go slack in his hands.

Where once five strands held him, now there were but four.

"Oh, dear," Elaine said from the other side.

A response Robin found admirably controlled.

He moved another few feet, grunting now, climbing this up-slope.

Another one of the ropes felt loose.

Yes. There was definitely a looseness in an additional rope.

Another arrow was about to pop out.

If I was a better bowman, he thought, if I worked my bow with a greater pull, driving the arrows deeper in the wood, then I would not be—

There was a popping noise. Then the sickening whistle of a rope cutting the night air.

Only three ropes.

Down to three ropes holding me.

There were eager splashes below him.

Tell me this is a dream, he addressed his mind.

Instead his mind encouraged him to close the remaining distance as quickly as possible.

With no sense of style or poise, Robin clawed his way to the castle wall, cursing aloud, damning his forefathers, while he stared at the arrows wobbling, groaning under his weight.

Until he reached them.

Then, quickly, he grabbed the arrows. They were still loose. But he needed but a second to reach up and touch the blessed stone of the parapet.

Robin pulled himself up.

He threw himself over, not caring whether he'd face one of the earl's guards eager to reward him by slicing his head from his body.

He landed. No one awaited him.

"Well done, Robin Fitzooth," he heard Elaine call to him. "Quickly now, help me to cross."

And Robin stood up, ready to obey.

With remarkable agility uncommon to such a physique, Lady Elaine pulled herself across the moat while Robin fastened the ropes to the parapet. Presently she hugged him close, a token of her appreciation for his services rendered thus far.

Then she took the lad's hand and led him away from the very tower that was their intended destination.

And now it behooves the author of these travails to issue a warning lest some reader proceed without a true knowledge of the type of narrative to follow.

The horrors and shocks about to be recounted may be too strong, especially for those whose experience with the tales of Robin Hood have, in the past, been more lighthearted.

So warned, know this:

What followed would define Robin's personality forever.

And as such, we will follow the pair into the bowels of the gizzard-gray castle . . .

At once Robin asked: "Dear lady, this does not appear the way to the tower."

And Elaine barely turned, saying breathlessly, "We

must avoid as many as my father's men as possible. There is a passage that leads from the stables to the very base of the tower."

Robin nodded. An unseen gesture, so he said, "Oh."

Elaine clambered down stone steps, dragging him quickly. Dawn was but an hour away. She ran across the courtyard.

He heard a voice call out to them.

"Hey there? Who's about?"

Robin made to answer—a response cultivated by his brief time as a schoolboy—when Elaine jerked his arm in warning, but also to pull him into a building.

Robin's sensitive nose was at once rewarded with a rich panoply of smells that could mean only one thing.

"We're in the stables," he said a bit too pointedly, for it was an obvious fact.

But Elaine was on her knees scratching at the scattered hay, searching for something.

It was a dark void in here, colored only by the rich and pungent smells of the animals that Robin could hear shuffling about in nearby stalls.

Robin, ever the good fellow, got down on his knees to help Elaine.

"My lady," he whispered. "What are you searching for?"

"There is a trapdoor, Fitzooth. It could be right here, but—"

Robin began scratching at the wood floor, pushing aside the hay. He also had the misfortune to push at a fresh pile of animal offal that he was sore pressed to remove from his hand.

He was debating how best to remove the offensive substance when Elaine said, "Yes! Here 'tis. The door. Quickly now."

Elaine, already a black figure in the gloom of the stable, disappeared into the hole, and Robin—hearing a voice outside—had no choice but to follow.

He plummeted a good number of feet, right on top of Elaine. "Don't be such an oaf," she scolded him.

He was about to remind her that he wasn't here at his own instigation. Nay, he was in fact performing a dangerous and difficult errand for her.

But she quickly pushed him off her and ran down the tunnel.

There were no torches. No light.

Robin stood there.

He had no choice but to follow the sound of her footsteps.

He ran full out, listening carefully this time, not wanting to drive himself into her.

Then there was a glow.

"There," he heard her say.

"There? What is there?"

The glow was an outline in the ceiling of the tunnel, a thin yellow outline.

"The bottom of the tower!"

But as soon as Robin reached it, he discerned a problem. Neither he nor Elaine could reach this new trapdoor.

"What shall we do now?" he asked.

In the scant light he saw her look past him. And there was scorn in her expression that stung his young heart.

"Lift me up, Robin. 'Twill be an easy thing."

But there the good lady lied. For Robin had a sore difficult time hoisting the maid aloft while she pushed open the door. He felt as if he must let her drop even while she pushed open the trapdoor.

A historic moment that, for this was when Robin Fitzooth first started reconsidering his unnatural penchant for maids of great size.

Lifting them, he thought, is a *difficult* thing.

Perhaps there may be something to maids cut of a more modest stature.

Mark ye well, this was a turning point for Robin.

The lady crawled into the opening.

And—not so much committed but snared in the middle—Robin followed.

*   *   *

As soon as Robin stuck out his head, an arrow breezed by his cheek, its fletching scratching his skin.

"Quickly, Robin. Shoot them!" Elaine said, her excited squeal prompting him to hurry.

Perhaps, he thought, I should have told her of my limitations as a bowman.

This was certainly not the appropriate time.

The room was a great hall lit by long tapers that girded the wall. Two of the earl's doddering retainers, who were both, in fact, strapping young men, took aim at him again.

Robin tried to prepare his own longbow.

Perhaps, he wondered, I am too short and the bow is too long?

For it never fits easily into my hands.

And he never had an easy time removing a shaft from his quiver.

"Robin!" Elaine yelled.

Robin immediately saw one advantage, for Elaine, of his accompanying the beautiful maid. The two guards were taking aim only at him.

He had an arrow out. When a sixth sense suggested that he move his position.

He did so just as two more arrows went flying through the air, cutting into the spot he had just occupied.

"Hurry," he ordered himself. "As Richard is my liege, let me for once . . ."

He fitted an arrow into the bow and, raising the bow, let it fly.

It went so wide of its mark—the chest of one of the guards—that he thought he heard the two retainers laughing.

"Robin!" Elaine said hopelessly.

"Oh, bullocks," Robin said, giving vent to one of his infrequent expressions of coarse language. He tossed his bow to the side and went running up the steps toward the two guards.

They were preparing their next missiles.

But Robin was a wondrous swordsman, as good with a blade as he was a poor bowman.

He had his sword out and ducked first one close-range arrow, then the other. He thought: "These fellows aren't much better than I."

He dispatched one with a quick thrust of his sword, and then whipped the blade out, dripping red onto the stone, swinging at the other guard.

The poor fellow barely had time to fumble with his own sheathed weapon before Robin's blade cut his cuirass bib and deep into the skin.

Not an immediately fatal blow, Robin thought. But enough to cause the fellow to sit and ponder the meaning of his too brief existence.

"Well done," Elaine said. "Truly, I have selected a marvelous champion."

Odd humors and vapors coursed through Robin, filling him with a feeling of exuberance and well-being that would, on more somber reflection, be entirely out of place.

Then a totally unsuspected reward: Elaine came to him, pulled him close, and sealed her mouth over his.

Her tongue snaked into his mouth, an event that had happened to Robin with only some of his more experienced conquests. It was odd, this insertion of the tasting organ, but not without producing a strange ripple of pleasure.

Then . . .

—and I relate this only so that you understand everything Robin was feeling—

. . . the dark-eyed lady reached down and fondled Robin's private matters in a quick and urgent way that, combined with the thrill of bloody combat, brought the lad to a state of instant readiness.

Not that he was often tardy in such things.

He was prepared to throw off his suit of Lincoln green and have it out with the brazen and alluring woman right there.

But ever the mistress of the situation, Elaine pulled away.

"Nay, Robin. 'Twouldn't be safe. Not until we have freed my father from the terrible demon."

Robin, glassy-eyed and shriveling in disappointment, nodded.

Just then he heard the sound again.

The howl, the loathsome bellow, so close now, just up the spiral stone staircase before them.

"Come, Robin . . ."

Robin gathered up his bow and, hungry for the prize and fearless in a way that only the ignorant can be, he followed the object of his heart's desire . . .

Part the Fifth

Where Robin faces the demon, or more properly demons, and learns a number of important lessons very quickly, while a multitude of surprises descend upon him.

Blade at ready. Robin followed Elaine up the steps.

The bleating/howling noises continued unabated. A rich harvest of goose flesh sprouted on Robin's arm. The exhilarated vapors which formerly coursed through his veins had now totally dissipated.

Robin and Elaine came to a heavy oak door.

" 'Tis locked," she said helpfully.

Robin was not surprised, since this followed the pattern of events thus far.

"I am to open it?" he said.

Elaine nodded.

Fortunately, Robin's blade, passed onto him by his father before he had known that his son planned on a wastrel life, was strong.

Robin hacked at the door handle.

"Quickly," Elaine hissed.

"I do my best, my lady," Robin said, not without an air of petulance.

He hacked at the handle and the lock. Splinters flew into the air.

"Hurry," she said.

The voice bellowed inside.

And when Robin saw that the wood was well chipped away around the locked door handle, he stepped back from the door.

And he ran headlong into it, only to bounce back, falling onto the stone floor.

"Nay, Fitzooth. Not so oafish now. Once more!"

Robin nodded. He stood up and hacked at the door while the earl, surely captive of a noisy demon, judging by his wails, answered each of his blows.

This time Robin neatly dissected the door handle.

Again he ran into the door. It popped open and he went staggering into the chamber.

To face the earl, the demon . . .

Now the strange and horrid part of this tale.

For the earl looked nothing like a demon, at least as far as Robin imagined a demon to look.

The earl looked like an old man. True, he had a book on a reading stand, a massive book that he was examining closely. Perhaps 'twas a book of dark magick, to aid his transformation into the demon state . . .

The old man turned and looked at Robin.

"Who are you?" the old man said.

And for the nonce, Robin felt as if he had wandered into a forester's cabin in search of a plump hen.

"Robin Fitzooth," Robin answered, extending his blade so that the man could see it marked with the blood of his loyal, now dead, retainers.

Elaine walked behind him, then beside him.

At seeing his daughter, the old man's face opened into a terrible look of horror. Once again he howled, putting his hand on the terrible and powerful magick book on the podium.

"Kill him," Elaine said rather cold-bloodedly.

Robin took a step.

But the old man was sore old, a white beard and white hair, with a crown of flesh at the top of his head where nature had chosen to do some ignoble pruning of the gray hair.

"Sir, if you kill me, the demon will possess my daughter forever. It will be the curse of the North Wood. And people will curse you with it, Fitztooth."

"Fit*zooth*," Robin corrected the man. The mispronunciation of the name couldn't be overlooked no matter how difficult the circumstances.

"Nay, old man," Robin said, the blade arching closer to the man. "*You* are the demon. And people will cheer the name Robin Fitzooth."

The man shook his head.

Another step closer.

Elaine added a further blunt prompting: "Kill him! Quickly, dear Robin."

Closer . . .

The old man's eyes looked weary with defeat. He didn't seem to be a very effective demon if this was the best display he could present. Perhaps it was some trick, a wile to escape my blade, Robin thought.

Another step.

His longbow slid off his shoulder and Robin quickly pushed it back.

"Now!" Elaine ordered.

Yes, now, Robin thought, before the earl reveals his true dimensions and the shock makes my sword waver.

But then Robin was close enough to see the book.

Good Hugh, his father, had taught the boy to read.

From the selfsame text.

And Robin saw the familiar words of John, Chapter 3.

For everyone who does evil hates the light, and does not come to the light, that his deeds may not be exposed.

The old man closed his eyes, at peace.

Awaiting the blow.

When Robin, never a quick lad when it came to ideas and their particular conjunctions, had this belated thought.

Why, indeed, must this confrontation take place at night?

He looked at the Bible.

The passage he glimpsed, its meaning seemed all too clear to him.

The old man was not a demon. But there was, in truth, a night-loving creature in the room.

'Twas his daughter who became lost to the black arts . . .

Slowly he turned around.

And I will temper my description of what follows lest it precipitate any seizures or faints.

But Robin turned around and faced Lady Elaine. Whose bosom—usually a well of warmth—had felt so *cold*.

She was totally afraid of the coming light, of dawn.

The old man howled, and now Robin could hear—as if 'twere blocked before—the words the man said, the words of the most Holy Bible.

"Kill him," Elaine said.

But already it was too late. Robin's face was no mask. It showed his doubt and then his final certitude that he had been aiding the wrong party.

"K—" Elaine started to say again. But then, as if recognizing the futility of it, she stopped.

She said: "There were wards designed to keep me out of the castle. But you broke their power, and I followed you in. The rest I can do myself."

Robin watched.

While Lady Elaine's very skull did split open like a ripened cantaloupe. And from its top Robin saw two hands that weren't real hands. For real hands don't have three claw-fingers and gray-green scales.

And while this creature crawled out of the split skull, Elaine's mouth—pulled and stretched into a grimace as long as an ear of corn—went on talking:

"My dear father has faith in the forces of light. But it is darkness that is stronger, and sweeter."

And here Elaine, still imagining that Robin could

still be reached in some sensual way, lifted her cloak
and gown and displayed herself.

A not unappealing sight under normal conditions—
fat, rosy hips, the clean swell of an abdomen beckoning one to the joyful thatch below. And as she
turned, the twin dancing globes of flesh in the back,
much more than both hands could easily hold.

Robin shook his head. It was small distraction from
what was going on up top.

But not quite enough distraction.

For the claw-hands pulled out, revealing a stunted
head with a goblin face and a body that came
equipped with a tail equally as long.

The goblin face was a mask of teeth.

Robin backed up, bumping into the book stand.
The old man touched Robin, continuing his mad-
sounding keening.

That, Robin noted, must be a demon. It jumped
from the open skull to the ground, opening its mouth.
Then another followed suit, and another.

Until there were three demons, while Lady Elaine
kept up her obscene posing. The demons' mouths
looked admirably suited for chewing and eating the
most difficult material.

Flesh and bone would prove no problem to them.

"Your bow, son," the old man said. "Use your
bow."

Right, thought Robin.

The demons and Elaine's split skull were still some
distance away. A good bowman would be able to
quickly dispatch them.

Again Robin fumbled.

The Elaine-head—for surely the true woman had
vanished into some mystical haze—jeered at him.

He fit a shaft onto his bowstring and let loose an
arrow. He missed his target, the demon to the extreme
left, by a good three feet.

The demons hopped closer. They moved like frogs
rather than aping a man's upright saunter.

But they are cautious, Robin noted. *As if they don't know I'm a poor marksman.*

He readied another arrow.

When the last surprise occurred . . .

Will Scarlett entered the chamber.

Will, who had been sawing wood like a hearty village of foresters, appeared . . . a vision.

"Will," Robin said gleefully. "What are you—"

"I had my eye on you all the time, good Robin. Didn't want you having any great adventure without your loyal companion in arms."

But Robin's glee quickly faded.

Will was there, sword at the ready, but he was close to the three demons, who turned and faced him.

And jumped on him.

Will screamed.

In seconds their giant mouths would have him chewed and dead.

Robin's back was to the book stand, to the Bible.

The old man said something: "He who does the *truth* comes to the light, that his deeds may be made manifest, for they have been performed in God."

More John 3, Robin recognized.

Its meaning was clear.

Robin fitted an arrow. "Praise God . . . and King Richard."

He let it fly. And the arrow skewered one demon about to chew on Will's handsome, almost royal nose.

Robin quickly fitted another arrow. "Praise God . . . Richard." It flew with a ne'er-before-seen accuracy, this time catching one of the goblin demons in the rump as he was about to remove Will's most treasured physical gift.

Both demons fell to the stone floor, flopping around like speared fish.

The Elaine-head, the two eyes now separated by the distance of the great crack, started rolling around.

One demon bit into Will's leg. Scarlett screamed.

But he said to Robin, "Nay, dear friend. This filthy hell-spawn is mine."

And Will, freed of the attentions of the two dying demons, used his sword to neatly slice this last demon in two. Its head was still affixed to his leg when the body went flying into the air.

At that last death the maid who called herself Elaine, who once was the earl's lovely if well-packed daughter, collapsed onto the ground, into a pile of stinking flesh and purple smoke that had the three men coughing and retching.

But it was over.

And Robin had learned some valuable lessons.

Epilogue
Or what Robin learned.

Despite the loss of his demon-beset daughter, the Earl of Blackpool was beyond gratitude. He fed the two good men, and he pledged his help and support in whatever endeavors were to come.

And Robin had, indeed, a good idea what those might be.

As he and Will rode out of the castle, across the drawbridge, he informed a surprised Will of his plans. "The peasantry need champions, brave Will. Someone to stop the terrible taxing by the lackeys of Prince John."

"Yes," Will laughed. "But who'll stand up to the prince's many foresters?"

Robin laughed. "Robin of Sherwood."

"What?" Will said, for he was stunned. What had happened to effect such a change in his friend?

"I will gather about me men and women of bravery and strength. Marksmen and thieves, horse handlers and tanners. A merry band to fight Prince John until bonny King Richard returns."

Will said nothing, perhaps agape at this change in Robin.

"But, Robin, why? Has your experience so unsettled you that you will now take up a hopeless cause?"

Robin shook his head. "Nay, not hopeless. No cause is lost when it is on the side of truth."

For Robin thought here of his own pathetic archery. In the service of good, his bow skills had improved sufficiently to save his dear and loved friend.

Surely, that was a divine gift.

Or so he thought.

"What say you, Will? Are you the first of that band?"

Will nodded his head and laughed. "Wherever you go, Robin, I follow."

"Good lad. We must, of course, gather others. But they will follow," Robin said with assurance.

Then they were both quiet a moment. Then Will turned to Robin, just as they were about to enter the North Wood.

"Robin, what say you to stopping by the forester Hubert's hut on our way to Sherwood? I believe his wife has been once again left alone, pining for attention."

The woman Will mentioned was of a size and shape that Robin had once found pleasing. And her virtue, well, there was none to speak of.

And Robin looked up at the dark canopy of beech trees. The forest will be my home, Robin thought. Until Richard returns.

And thinking of the woman mentioned by Will brought to mind the accursed Elaine.

Robin knew that thenceforth he would resolve to honor only maids of virtue and comely restraint. And he would honor their virtue by acting the gentleman with them.

"Eh, Robin?"

Robin Fitzooth laughed. It would take Will Scarlett yet awhile to accept this.

"No, Will. We have a merry band to be gathered, an army to fight Prince John, and the Sheriff of Nottingham—"

Will nodded.

And Robin, soon to be dubbed Robin Hood—
friend and fighter for the peasants—started whistling a
jaunty air as they rode south, on to Sherwood Forest.

Muffy Birnbaum Goes Shopynge

by Elizabeth Spiegelman-Fein
(as told to George Alec Effinger)

It had been a couple of years since I'd seen Maureen ("Muffy") Birnbaum, and the time had passed in quiet, domestic bliss, sort of. The old Mufferoo tended to insert herself into my life like a migraine headache, and then leave suddenly, and in-between I forgot how awful it was having her around. And now she had this gigantic broadsword that she threatened you with if you called her by her old nickname. I was her favorite target because we'd been roommates together back at the old Greenberg School. One of the migrainish things about Maureen was that she still looked like a high school junior, while I was now a twenty-six-year-old married woman.

Something else annoying about Maureen was that every single time she showed up, she'd just finished some bizarre adventure on another planet or somewhere, and she had to tell me all about it. It started off with Mars. She'd whooshed off to Mars and killed a bunch of monsters and things, and fell in love with this absolutely def—did I use that right? Part of being twenty-six is losing track of what the kids are doing to the language—prince. She'd been trying ever since to get back to Mars and Prince Van, but her steering component failed her regularly. And she refused to notice that I had a life, too, even if it was just a fern-filled apartment in Queens and a shelf of Richard Simmons aerobics tapes.

Another thing that I just like really hated was that I

*was now a married woman, and my hard-working
Josh, when he wasn't seeing patients, didn't want to
have to hear about Muffy's latest exploit—he didn't
really like her, and could you blame him? Somewhere
in one of these stories I recorded how she'd made her
grand entrance during our honeymoon night. I used to
be called Bitsy, but in the last nine years I'd become
Elizabeth to everybody but certain members of my family whom I couldn't re-educate. And lately Josh and I
had hyphenated our names in honor of the baby that
was due in another four months. We just didn't have
much in common with Miss Birnbaum anymore.*

*So things were going along just fine, with me sweat-
ing to the oldies and sharing the pre-natal experience
with Josh, when one afternoon my husband was out
communicating the golf experience with some profes-
sional men in his building, who should whoosh into
my nice, clean kitchen but Muffy—I mean Maureen—
Birnbaum. It was migraine time, and before I said a
word to her, I went into the bathroom and took some
of the pharmaceutical requisites Josh had left around
for just such an emergency.*

*"Don't I look nice?" asked Muffy. "Tell me I don't
look nice."*

Well, she did *look nice, dressed like a normal grown
person instead of wearing the science-fiction magazine
cover outfits she usually schlepped around in. "You
look terrific, Maureen," I said. "You lost a little
weight, maybe?" This is never true when one woman
says it to another. It was just part of the getting-older
ritual that I'd learned. Maureen had missed all that,
spending her time adventuring God-knows-where.*

*"They wrapped my things for me. Old Betsy—the
broadsword—and the gold brassiere, and the dagger
and everything else. Didn't they make a nice package
out of it?"*

*I was afraid to say "Who made a nice package out
of it?" because that would only lead into the latest
exploit, but before I could say anything, she started in
without a molecule of encouragement from me.*

*   *   *

Imagine my surprise when I whooshed back to Earth
from Lagash* to find myself in Merrie Old England.
I half-expected myself to end up in the New York
Transit System, as I usually do, but not this time. I
knew it was London because there were these big red
buses and everybody talked funny. I'll just leave in
the buses and leave out the funny talking, because it
got to be really boring and tedious and a lot like the
Dave Clark Five after a while, and who wants to
sound like the Dave Clark Five? I usually whoosh
back here, or around here, but there I was in London.
The great thing about London, aside from all the historic things you can see, is that I landed right near a
mall. A mall like we have here, with a food court and
silly things hanging from the ceiling, but strange shops
you've never heard of. Well, I could've gone to the
British Museum, I suppose, or the Tower of London,
but there was this mall right in front of me. And it was
called the Sherwood Forest Mall, because apparently
they'd torn the forest down a long time since, and put
in freeways—which they call motorways—and yogurt
shops and what-all. So I sort of sauntered into the
Sherwood Forest Mall, wearing my metal bikini and
armed to the teeth. Nobody seemed to notice, either,
which was kind of strange.

I walked around the mall for a while, and it was
just a burn, Bitsy, I mean, there were only jeans shops
and record stores and the usual. I was ready to H. T.
P.—hit the pavement, you know? Then I met this nice
couple at a newsstand. We were checking out what
was happening in each other's country; I wanted to
know what was going on in Great Britain, and they
wanted to know what was buzzing in the States. We
got to talking, and the next thing we knew, we decided

*I think I told this thrilling tale as "Maureen Birnbaum After Dark"
in *Foundation's Friends*, edited by Martin Harry Greenberg, published by Tor Books in 1989, and it's at least as wonderful as this
story, so go look it up.

to go upstairs and have some lunch. Lunch in England is really hitting, if you check out the right places. In the Sherwood Forest Mall, there were only two good places, a fish-and-chips place that I wanted to give a miss to, and a cute little teashop like we don't have over here. I voted for the teashop, and since I had the broadsword, I won.

We were just lamping out in front of the teashop, talking, and I introduced myself. "My name is Maureen Birnbaum, intersteller adventuress," I go. The guy, who was totally buff—goes, "And I am Robin Hood, and this babe-o is Maid Marian. Perhaps our reputations have crossed the great water?"

"Robin Hood?" I go. "*The* Robin Hood? The arrow in the center of the target guy, the enemy of the Sheriff of Nottingham and all bad heinies like that?"

He blushed, but the crushin' girl spoke up. "Yup," she goes, "that's us."

Maybe I should have asked to see Robin or Marian's ID before we started out on this venture. They would have been gently amused by my classical living language. "But I thought you lived like entire centuries ago," I go.

"As long as there is a Sherwood Forest and evildoers about, we're sort of immortal," goes Robin Hood.

"But there isn't any Sherwood Forest."

Maid Marian shrugged. "There was a jankin' bunch of trees before you came into the mall, wasn't there?"

You could hear my jaw drop. "*That's* Sherwood Forest?"

"What's left of it," goes Robin Hood.

"What about the Merrie Men?" I spelled "Merry" in my mind the old way, to honor the gang.

"They're down by the Video Arcade," goes Robin Hood. "You should see Little John on the flipper tables."

"Little John!" I go. This *was* Robin Hood. "Like I've always wanted to meet you. See, I'm like this barbarian hero-type, and I've always wondered how

I'd measure up to a real hero like you. Maybe we could have a contest or something."

"Well," goes Robin Hood, stroking his well-trimmed beard, "longbow archery is like out, because that's my big thing."

"Right," I go.

"But we could singlestick across a log; I've been beaten at that before. Or we could try pikes or—"

"No, no, even at your best, I think I'd have the advantage over you," I go. "You don't know the adventures I've had and the victories I've like won."

"Well, if you think so," goes Robin Hood, kind of sourly I thought.

"I know," goes Maid Marian. "How about a shopping duel, right here in the mall!"

"Lady," I go, "I was *born* to shop. You've never seen an American, pride-full-of-country, all together in patriotic merchandising splendor."

"I have no fear of foreign economic imperialism," goes Maid Marian. "I come from a very well-to-do family. The Monceux clan; perhaps you've heard of it?"

"No," I go, "I'm afraid not. Do you have an acquaintance with the Birnbaums? The New York Birnbaums?"

"A shopping duel it is, then," goes Robin Hood. "There shall be three events: a formal outfit; a normal daily outfit; and casual attire. I have no doubt that my Maid Marian will triumph in all three."

"Well," I go, "if there's one thing I know, it's clothesisimo."

"Couldn't tell it from the costume you're wearing now," goes Maid Marian.

"It's not much to look at," I go, "but it's serviceable and just what the contemporary female barbarian is wearing these days."

Maid Marian goes, "It's well past noon. We should meet back here about twoish with the formal outfit? And then fourish with the daily clothes? And then sixish with the casual attire. Then we can have dinner here in this teashop."

"Two hours each?" I go. "To shop for three complete outfits?"

"It's a duel," goes Robin Hood. "Let the time limit be a part of the challenge."

"That's fat, then," I go. "I'll go along with whatever you say."

"And no like sneaking out of the mall to find some better shops," goes Maid Marian.

"Pretty dopey, Marian," I go, and I head off to see what the Sherwood Forest Mall had in the way of clothing stores.

After passing a lot of typical women's wear stores, I found a pretty classy place called Rhodes and Maxwell. You could tell they were exclusive because the mannequins in the windows only had half a head each. I went into the shop, not thinking in the least of how I was mostly undressed. The fashion coordinator—in America she would have been a saleslady—approached me as if I were just another matron coming in looking for a ball gown. She pretended not to notice Old Betsy, my trusty broadsword, or any of the rest of my tough, fierce raiment. "Yes?" she goes. "May I help you?"

I liked her a lot for her spirit, which was a typically British attitude, as I was to find out.

"Well, I wanted a real ass-kicking formal thing. Something to wear to a princess's wedding or something?"

"A Yank are we?" she goes, smiling. "Get invited to a lot of princess's weddings, do we?"

"Never mind about that. Let's see what you've got. The more expensive the better." Fashion coordinators around the world like to hear that.

"Good answer!" she goes, showing that American television gets distributed pretty widely. I could probably have gotten the same response in Sri Lanka. She began pulling things out of drawers, not off the racks. "How's this?" she goes.

The third dress she selected was classic yet glamorous. It was sewn together out of Imperial blue fauxsilk, with a V-neckline that would require a serious, strapless, longline, underwired bra, which I'm sure she'd be able to sell me, too. It had overlapping layers of fringe all the way down to the floor-length faux pearls and matching Imperial blue pumps with a knot of more faux pearls. We found a faux pearl-covered handbag to complete the outfit. I figured I was real costing and definitely "Get up!" It cost me a fortune, but I was playing against a mythical figure, and you got to go with what you know in that kind of semifabricated situation.

"Would you care to wear this now, or shall I wrap it for you?" she goes.

I go, "I'll wear it now. I want to impress all the hanks here in the mall. Is this *really* Sherwood Forest? I'd pictured it as more than three mighty oaks and a few poozley rhododendrons."

She shrugged without replying, and very casually took my golden brassiere and spangled G-string, my dagger and broadsword, and folded them over in nicely patterned paper as if they were everyday items of nine-to-five apparel. I paid her with my father's credit card, which I kept under the G-string. She didn't hesitate for a minute; I gave her full marks for her entire deportment and general zoika. I walked out of Rhodes and Maxwell feeling as if Maid Marian would have to go some to joan me out.

Well, unfortunately, Maid Marian had the secret knowledge of the Sherwood Forest Mall geography, and she *did* joan me out. She showed up at the teashop at two o'clock, wearing, I swear, something you might wear as a visiting monarch among yam-eating natives somewhere. She walked gracefully, on Robin's arm, because someone as formal as she required an escort. "Get up, girl!" he goes. Even Robin Hood had a new outfit—or an old one, the one you picture him in, in Lincoln green.

But Maid Marian! I was ready to toss in the towel,

the washcloth, and the dishrag all at the same time. She showed up in a gown from Whitley's, which apparently is open only by appointment, but celebrities like Robin Hood and Maid Marian have permanent appointments. She was wearing a white chiffon gown lined with white satin, hand-beaded, of course. Gold—possibly *real* gold—and white bugle beads dropped in bunches from the waist to the hem in the shape of what I was given to understand was the emblem of the Monceux family; it had been affixed by hand while Marian shopped for the rest of the items on her list.

She had gold beading draped from the shoulders over antique white leather gloves, and a high mantle of white lace featuring rhinestones and crystals. She had on a rhinestone crown, too, and carried a scepter to go with. For all I knew, the rhinestones could have been vastly more costly and unfaux, but I wouldn't give the bitch the satisfaction. I was surprised not to see big, white plumes stuck into her hair, but it was evident that Maid Marian knew when to stop. I didn't know you could walk into a shop and walk out with such an outfit.

"Well," she goes, "what do you think?" She flounced a little and did this ganky turn on the floor, like I was supposed to be impressed or something.

"It's okay," I go, "but what would you wear that thing to?"

"Oh," she goes, "hospital openings and charity balls. We get invited to quite a lot of that sort of thing. Do they have balls in the States?"

"Do they have *balls?* You just try us sometime. Seems like you did that twice in our history, and we sent you home both times, bitching and moaning about unfair tactics."

Maid Marian got a little ungelled by that statement, and she goes, "Talk about bitch!"

Robin Hood put his hand on her sleeve to cool her down. "Remember where she's from," he goes. "And you've clearly won the first round."

"Yeah," I go, "she did, but talk about unfair tactics!"

"Let's move on to the second challenge," goes Robin. "The normal, daily outfit. That shouldn't be too hard here, and I don't think we have much of an advantage."

"Fine. Back here at four o'clock. And no secret shops hidden behind some totally dis American cheesesteak shop."

"There was no secret about Whitley's," goes Maid Marian. "You could have shopped there, too. I could've gotten you a special guest entrée."

"Oh, thank you very much, your serene highness. You look ridiculous. Go bless some war veterans or something."

We stormed off in opposite directions. Robin Hood looked as if he didn't really want to be a part of this contest anymore, and I couldn't blame him.

I headed back to Rhodes and Maxwell, because my fashion coordinator, whom I'd gotten to know as Miss Haye, had been so cordial. She seemed genuinely glad to see me, particularly now that I was wearing my woofin' blue fringy number and not the barbarian garb. "Yes?" she goes. "Something more?"

"I thought some simple but elegant afternoon wear, in case I meet a fresh young man with designs to take me to tea."

"Ah, yes, we have just the thing." This came off the rack, though, not out of one of the drawers. It was a peach wool cinch waist dress that I could see myself roaring to victory over Maid Marian in. The fashion coordinator threw in a chunky real gold necklace with matching earrings and a fun little floppy beret. She graciously suggested shoes and a handbag that were perfect mates.

I paid again for the costume, and this time she wrapped the extraneous faux-silk number and its accoutrements. I was sure that I looked at the top of my form, and I couldn't wait to see if Maid Marian had found anything better. Maybe there was another private shop somewhere that catered to local mythical types.

We both arrived at the teashop at four o'clock, and this time Robin Hood brought Little John to act as judge.

"Jeez, he's big!" I go.

"Whence the name," goes Robin Hood charmingly. I was definitely hittin', but Robin's girlfriend was a definite goober.

And goober she proved to be. She showed up in a kind of pink and yellow flowered sheath dress with a peplum. Her shoes were simple pink low-heeled walking shoes. Oh, and she had an ice lemon tote that looked as if it had been given to her as a gift from one of the overjoyed war veterans.

"Well," goes Robin Hood disappointedly.

"I award the imaginary golden arrow to Miss Birnbaum, making this contest a tie now," announced Little John. "The winner will be determined by the victor of the casual wear competition. Good luck to you both."

"Terrific!" I go. "Nobody can out-casual me."

"We'll see," goes Maid Marian, whisking off Robin Hood down one of the diagonal aisles.

"And we didn't choose a prize for the winner, did we?" I go. "How about picking up the tab for dinner."

"So damn Yank," goes Maid Marian over her shoulder. "Like the honor isn't enough for her."

I studied the mall's Where-to-Find map for a few minutes, until I saw an entry for a sporty, informal shop called The Box. It looked okay from the outside—no dry-skinned plain girls from Australia, no ethnically-mixed groups with outrageous accessories. I went into The Box and shopped around, and put together a nice assortment of informal clothes. The fashion coordinator was a young woman with pretty red hair and an obligatory green dress. She wore a nametag that said she was Caroline.

"Are you sure you're in the right shop, miss?" she goes. "You're wearing such a nice outfit—"

"Oh, don't worry, Caroline," I go. "I want to get out of this thing and into something more casual. I've picked these right off the racks. I think they'll be okay."

"A Yank, are we? And how are we enjoying our stay?"

"Just total it up," I go. I'd chosen a kind of artsy-radical ensemble that I thought would blow Miss S. Forest out of the water. I could see Paula Abdul wearing the outfit, but not Miss Princess Maid Marian.

"It ought to flatter you nicely," Caroline goes.

"Oh," I go, "I have this one-of-a-kind flair. I don't go overboard into artistic or anything. I just want to be comfortable."

"Oh," laughed Caroline, "anything would be comfortable after that costume. Shall I wrap it for you? Do you wish to wear your purchases out of the shop?"

"You bet I'll wear it," I go. "That was the whole idea." I paid Caroline and wished her a good day, and left wearing a black cotton knit jumpsuit with a baggy jacket and a wild, jungle-print belt. On my feet I had red loafers, and I didn't bother with a handbag—I kept all my little personal items in a bag from The Box. It was a pretty simple shopping expedition, and I knew I had Maid Marian beaten by a kilometer.

I arrived at the teashop about half-past five. Robin and Marian were nowhere in sight, but Little John was inside having some British goodies unknown to us in the colonies. "Hey," he goes, "you look downright delicious! Maybe I shouldn't be the judge, because I'm quantifiably prejudiced toward exotic women."

"*I'm* exotic?" I go, like totally disbelieving, but loving every second of it.

"I like the jacket over the jumpsuit. Very Seventh Avenue. And that intensely sexy Yank accent!"

"You know Seventh Avenue?" I go. It seemed like we had a lot in common. And my New York nasal whine—*sexy*?

Robin Hood and Maid Marian took a lot longer to choose the casual clothing than any of the other outfits. I would've thought their traditional costumes would've been hot enough for show—you know, Robin's Lincoln green and Marian's dynamic retro old-timey gear; but I could tell that Marian wanted to absolutely kill here. So while Little John and I made goo-goo eyes over plates of like this terribly weight-inducing stuff, we waited but we didn't notice the time go by.

"So," I go, "I understand that you're this big superstar in the Video Arcade."

Little John blushed. "Aw," he goes, "has Gentle Robin been bragging on me again? It's just because he has no control over the silver ball. From the time he shoots it, he has maybe three seconds before it drops out one of the exit holes. He only plays those games because he doesn't like the video games where all you do is kill people."

"Except Normans, I suppose."

"Yes, well, killing Norman invaders, it goes without saying."

I stuffed some more pastry into my mouth. "Do you mind me asking a couple of embarrassing questions?"

"No, lady, I fear not," goes Little John.

"Well," I go, "take for instance Robin's name. Surely it's short for Robert, which is of Norman origin."

Little John frowned. "Causes him no end of grief, tackling that one."

"And if I remember right, the date of King Richard's return given in the book is something like 1188."

"Close enough," goes Little John, beginning to look grief-stricken himself.

"And you all escaped together to miss out on like the tyranny of the Normans. But the longbow—your band's chosen weapon—was not the favorite weapon of the Saxons, it was the short bow. The longbow wasn't even known by the Normans. It wasn't introduced until the end of the thirteenth century, at the battle of Falkirk. Am I right so far?"

"Have some more of this cream cake. It's pretty hittin', as far as mall food goes."

"No thank you," I go.

"You seem to have studied up on us right well."

I shrugged. "It was either the Myths and Legends course or a political science thing I never would've gotten through."

"I know the feeling, the first time I saw Robin shoot—and it was a clothyard shaft from a longbow."

"Well," I go, "how do you explain your pardons from King Richard upon his return? In 1188 or thereabouts, the monarch, as far as I recall, was Henry II Plantagenet, not Richard."

A fainter shrug from Little John, "Prettier remembering than I have these days, my lady."

"And then there's your own name. John was introduced by the Normans, and at that time 'Little' meant in Saxon mean or like a lying, skanky son of a bitch."

Little John shrugged. "What can I say about what others thought of me at an early age?"

"Am I making you uncomfortable with all these questions?" I go.

Little John gave me a faint smile. "No," he goes, "I'll give as fair as I get, to the best of my recollection."

"Why do you put up with all this rumormongering?" I go.

"Oh," goes Little John, "it's only among the pedantic academics. Robin's gotten us a new PR firm, though. We'll be hot stuff again soon."

Robin and Marian entered the teashop about six o'clock. They took empty seats at the table with Little John and me.

"Well," goes Maid Marian, "what do you think?" She stood and turned slowly, showing off her outfit. She had bought for herself a pair of Harris tweed pleated trousers, soft grey flecked with yellow, blue, and green. Above the pants she wore a beautiful, pale blue hand-knit sweater decorated with a pattern of colorful May flowers. Under the sweater she had on a leaf green turtleneck. On her feet she had grey woolen socks and sturdy black oxfords. She smiled delightedly at the assemblage and then took her seat. Robin stood up and he goes, "There isn't any more of a casual outfit in England today than right here at this table." He slammed his ale tankard on the table and sat down.

"It will be very difficult," goes Little John, "for me to choose the final winner and award the cherished prize today."

"In that outfit, Marian," I go, "you look like the Queen of the May."

Marian glared at me. "I've been Queen of the May with Robin as King of the May for 700 years. In Nottinghamshire, no one would dare propose any others."

"Well, then, Little John," goes Robin Hood, "don't feel obliged to name us the winners just because we've been winners for over seven centuries. We have a worthy challenger among us. We'll think no less of you for championing Miss Birnbaum over us." Robin was one gracious dude.

"There're both pretty nice outfits," Little John goes. "I think we'll have to look in more detail to break this apparent tie."

Robin stood and finished another tankard of ale. "Never before in seven hundred years," he goes, "has a contest finished as closely as this. Of course, during the majority of those years Sherwood Forest was a forest, not a mall." He sat back down.

Little John got up and walked around to see me and Maid Marian better. First he examined me. I tried not to be ganky, and I kept a straight face, although I knew I was looking good. He made a circuit of our table two or three times, and each time he complimented me on my choices of casual clothes. "I've said it before, but I think you've got crushin' taste in clothes. I'm a sucker for fringe, but I won't let that get in the way of my judgment. Maureen, you're what we've come to call in the last few years a real betty—

that's totally good. I think your figure and your fitness add to your point total because here in Sherwood we expect a woman to be more than just a lovely lady at our service. Your outfit is outstanding. For instance, your belt. What about it?"

"Oh, it's nothing special," I go. "I picked it up for forty pounds. Hand made in Brazil. How much is that in dollars?"

"Very nice. Very nice. Now let's look at Marian's ensemble. Your pants are a lovely Harris tweed. And your sweater?"

"Hand knit of Scottish lambswool."

"And the turtleneck. A perfect spring green background for the flowers in your sweater."

Robin Hood ordered more ale for all of us, the first for Little John and me. Robin took a long draught and, burping, announced, "Can Marian shop or can't she?" At which point, Little John rubbed his well-trimmed beard again and examined Maid Marian's clothes more carefully.

"You know," he said, "I do honestly believe by the king's troth that I've seen that leaf green turtleneck before."

"No!" cried Robin Hood. Maid Marian's expression fell slowly into grief.

"Even after seven hundred years," she goes, "I cannot bear to win under falsehood. I have worn this green turtleneck before. Look, here on my sleeve, this hole. I received this shirt two years ago from my aunt—on the Monceux side. I knew it would look good with these other clothes, and I thought that I might easily dupe Little John who would be the hard judge and Maureen who is not accustomed to our ways. Forgive me! I have forfeited the match! I don't deserve your faith and trust any longer."

Little John's expression was grim. "You've served us in Sherwood Forest all these centuries in every necessary capacity. Surely you've earned our gratitude enough to overcome this one lapse in judgment."

"Thank you," goes Maid Marian simply.

Robin goes "Marian, I love you still, and I always will. Maureen, I'm happy to offer you membership in our Merrie Band. You're right hearty and we'd be pleased to have you as a member of our group."

And just then, with a rich cream pie in my mouth, I whooshed out of Merrie Old England.

"Maureen, listen," I told her, "I'm not as enthusiastic about your adventures as you are. I've got my own life to lead. I'm married now, and pregnant. Although you'll be my best friend for life, probably, and we have our Greenberg School bond between us, I have to tell you that you've become a disruptive force in our family."

"Bitsy," she said, "I don't know how to tell you this, but I've had a really bald time here. I understand from my careful observational studies that Mars is in the sky tonight, and I'll make another attempt to whoosh to the Red Planet and Prince Van. I'm beginning to lose hope that I'll ever find him again, but I have to keep trying. The first time was biscuit easy. Since then, I've been lucky just to make it back to Earth. I wonder if any of the scientists at the Smithsonian Institute or those burly places in England could help me out.

"But if you truly feel this way about me, I wish you all the luck in the world with your husband and your coming child and I suppose I'll leave you alone from now on."

I watched her walk dejectedly out of my house, then slowly she turned on the steps and she said, "We'll always be as good friends as are Robin, Little John, and Marian."

She looked up into the sky and saw that dusk was already falling; it was no problem to pick out the red planet of Mars, and she whooshed off on one last try to corner the terribly unattainable Prince Van.

FLIGHTS OF FANTASY

☐ **SORCERER'S SON by Phyllis Eisenstein.** "Outstanding"—Andre Norton. "Fantasy at its best!"—J.E. Pournelle. As Cray Ormoru, son of enchantress Delivev, grows to be a man in magical Castle Spinweb, he yearns to find his father, who disappeared years ago on a heroic mission. Cray sets out on a journey full of danger and sorrow—a baptism of fire for the sorcerer's son! (156838—$3.95)

☐ **THE CRYSTAL PALACE by Phyllis Eisenstein.** From the acclaimed author of *Sorcerer's Son*—a magical tale of a mortal's quest to find and free the soul of his one true love . . . Cray was intrigued by the image of the young girl in the magical mirror, but who she was remained a mystery until he discovered she was Aliza, a prisoner in her own magnificent crystal palace. (156781—$3.95)

☐ **THE MAGIC BOOKS by Andre Norton.** Three magical excursions into spells cast and enchantments broken, by a wizard of science fiction and fantasy: *Steel Magic*, three children's journey to an Avalon whose dark powers they alone can withstand, *Octagon Magic*, a young girl's voyage into times and places long gone, and *Fur Magic*, where a boy must master the magic of the ancient gods to survive. (166388—$4.95)

☐ **GAMEARTH by Kevin J. Anderson.** It was supposed to be just another Sunday night fantasy game—and that's all it was to David, Tyrone, and Scott. But to Melanie, the game had become so real that all their creations now had existences of their own. And when David demanded they destroy their made-up world in one last battle, Melanie tried every trick she knew to keep the fantasy campaign going, to keep the world of Gamearth alive. (156803—$3.95)

Prices slightly higher in Canada

Buy them at your local

bookstore or use coupon

on next page for ordering.

WORLDS OF WONDER

☐ **BARROW by John Deakins.** In a town hidden on the planes of Elsewhen, where mortals are either reborn or driven mad, no one wants to be a pawn of the Gods. (450043—$3.95)

☐ **WIZARD WAR CHRONICLES: LORDS OF THE SWORD by Hugh Cook.** Drake Douay fled from his insane master, a maker of swords. But in a world torn by endless wars, a land riven in half by a wizard powered trench of fire, an inexperienced youth would be hard-pressed to stay alive.
(450655—$3.99)

☐ **THE HISTORICAL ILLUMINATUS CHRONICLES, Vol. I: THE EARTH WILL SHAKE by Robert Anton Wilson.** The Illuminati were members of an international conspiracy—and their secret war against the dark would transform the future of the world! "The ultimate conspiracy ... the biggest sci-fi cult novel to come along since *Dune*."—The Village Voice
450868—$4.95)

☐ **THE HISTORICAL ILLUMINATUS CHRONICLES, Vol. 2: THE WIDOW'S SON by Robert Anton Wilson.** In 1772, Sigismundo Celline, a young exiled Neapolitan aristocrat, is caught up in the intrigues of England's and France's most dangerous forces, and he is about to find out that his own survival and the future of the world revolve around one question: What is the true identity of the widow's son? (450779—$4.99)

Prices slightly higher in Canada.

Buy them at your local bookstore or use this convenient coupon for ordering.

NEW AMERICAN LIBRARY
P.O. Box 999, Bergenfield, New Jersey 07621

Please send me the books I have checked above. I am enclosing $_____ (please add $1.00 to this order to cover postage and handling). Send check or money order—no cash or C.O.D.'s. Prices and numbers are subject to change without notice.

Name_____

Address_____

City _____ State _____ Zip Code _____
Allow 4-6 weeks for delivery.
This offer, prices and numbers are subject to change without notice.

PERILOUS DOMAINS